THE BLIGHT

Megan Blight

Illustrations by Richard Blight

iUniverse, Inc.
New York   Bloomington

iUniverse books may be ordered through booksellers or by contacting:

iUniverse
1663 Liberty Drive
Bloomington, IN 47403
www.iuniverse.com
1-800-Authors (1-800-288-4677)

Because of the dynamic nature of the Internet, any Web addresses or links contained in this book may have changed since publication and may no longer be valid. The views expressed in this work are solely those of the author and do not necessarily reflect the views of the publisher, and the publisher hereby disclaims any responsibility for them.

ISBN: 978-1-4502-1353-0 (sc)
ISBN: 978-1-4502-1355-4 (dj)
ISBN: 978-1-4502-1354-7 (ebook)

Printed in the United States of America

iUniverse rev. date: 3/23/2010

* Text with an asterisk is quoted from a source listed in the bibliography at the end of the book.

For Richard and Ethan

And for those who suffered and perished,
let us not forget, lest it be repeated.

"For the poverty and distress and misery which exist, the people have themselves to blame."

—Thomas Campbell Foster, the *Times* commissioner, after visiting Ireland during the famine

March 15, 1846

Ireland

Chapter I

The weathered hands of a woman sunk deep into the wet earth, searching for the lifegiving substance her family depended upon. Her hands grasped what they had been searching for, and the earth broke away, presenting to the woman what it had nurtured for the past five months, a single brown oblong potato. Caked mud clung to her soggy skin and filled her chipped fingernails as she tried to brush the dirt from the potato, but it did not matter; the potato was perfect and could be cleaned later in her hut. She placed it amongst the others nestled in a weary rag and gathered the tattered ends of the throw together, flipping it carefully over her shoulder like a knapsack. In the distance, her one-room hut occupied a small area of the village outside Sligo, Ireland. She began the short walk home to prepare the evening meal.

Kathryn softly sang an Irish ballad under her breath and smiled at neighbors she passed along the way. Her strikingly beautiful features were unmatched in all of western Ireland, and she was blessed with the kind of face that people felt fortunate to gaze upon, a gaze profoundly difficult to break. Years of poverty and hard living had creased her brow and toughened her skin somewhat, bringing the subtle struggle of maturity to the forefront for all to see. Her thick brown hair that she inherited from her English father was painted with golden blonde streaks that glimmered now and again with each turn of her head. Long legs supported her tall frame, making her look older than twenty-three, but it was her bright blue eyes that were her most memorable trait. On cold, dark nights, her husband Joseph would whisper into her ear that it seemed God had painted her extraordinary eyes with the same brush he used on the majestic sea. Kathryn walked with a healthy stride, a youthful appearance, and a happy disposition despite years of fluctuating wearisome living. She and Joseph planted potatoes to feed their children, and they had dear friends and a hut in which to live—what more could anyone ask for, she wondered.

Little was she aware that this autumn of 1845 would change the appearance of the country from sea to sea, and not just that of its people, but the topography of the land, the smell in the air, and the blade of each grass. What was forthcoming would alter the face of Ireland so intensely that the deep scars would never fade and the country would be left broken and depressed, sagging idly in time with death strewn about her bosom. The Emerald Isle would never be the same, and she would not ever fully recover.

As she walked toward her hut, Kathryn could hear her children's voices coming from inside as they played about in harmony, and her heart was filled.

"Mam! Mam!" Kathryn heard when she opened the door to her white stone hut.

"Whit is it thin?" she asked her son Brenton.

"Whin's dinner?

"In a few minutes. Run along nar whilst I make it." She shooed him and the others out the door.

She smiled at Joseph as he placed more peat on the fire, warming and lighting the interior and the content face of their seven-month-old daughter. The infant lay swaddled in her wooden cradle with rose-colored cheeks and bright red lips. Kathryn placed her knapsack on the table and brushed off bits of wet earth from the potatoes by submerging each one into an awaiting bucket of water Joseph had brought in. She chopped up each potato as well as a few turnips she had collected earlier that day and placed them all into another bucket of clean water. Joseph carried that bucket to the fire and placed it upon the strong metal frame above the flames that cooked their evening meal like a fiery, hot-tempered demon.

In a short while, Kathryn called the children, and in bounded her nine-year-old son, Brenton, always hungry and always smiling. He was the first-born and the heart of the family with tousled brown hair, gentle hazel eyes, and a compassionate disposition that radiated through his face. He was quiet but intelligent, soaking in any kind of knowledge like a sponge. Following closely behind, his twin six-year-old sisters fought to enter the hut first and plopped themselves down at the table, ready to eat and be off again like two Tasmanian devils. The girls, Brogan and Shay, were identical in all ways, from their blazing, long blonde hair to their lively giggles that echoed throughout the hut.

During the meal, the family laughed and enjoyed one another's company until their door abruptly swung open and there stood a great hefty man with a grand smile. It was Kiernan, their closest friend and neighbor. He strolled in loudly and took a seat at their table, instantly demanding attention and filling the room with his presence.

"A young nun came up to her superior," Kiernan began as all eyes fixated upon him, "and she confessed, 'Mother Superior, I wish to no longer be a nun. I want to leave an' try somethin' else.' 'Whit?!' the Mother Superior asked in great surprise. 'If you no longer wish to be a nun, thin whit do you wish to be?' 'A prostitute,' the young nun answered. The Mother Superior slapped her 'round thinkin' her mighty quare to be sure. An' she kept hittin' her sayin,' 'You shame me so!'"

Kiernan laughed and laughed at the telling of his own joke, until finally regaining his composure to continue.

"'Beg yer pardon, ma'am,' the young nun said between blows, 'but I feel me true callin' to be a prostitute.' The Mother Superior stopped hittin' suddenly an' stood above her asking, 'Did you say

3

'prostitute'?' 'Aye,' she said. An' with that, the Mother Superior sighed deeply, smiled, an' sat back in her chair. 'Me child,' she said, 'you have me blessin' thin, do as you wish—fer I thought you said … Protestant.'"

A moment of silence filled the room as everyone looked at one another. Then an eruption of laughter broke free from their mouths.

"Ha! Ha! Ha!" Kiernan was barely able to contain his laughter. "I knew you'd like that one!"

"Aye! Aye!" the family said in unison as the children jumped up and ran around the table in circles until Kathryn shooed them out the door.

Kathryn instinctively placed a steaming plate of food in front of Kiernan, which he consumed in only a few spoonfuls. Soon his wife Anne came in, and after her, another couple and then another. No one knocked before entering, and each one was greeted with smiles, a plate full of food, and a large cup of water. Jokes spewed from the men's mouths, and bursts of laughter came from the women's. Everyone came happily and enjoyed the company of their neighbors; the next evening, there was sure to be another gathering in another hut. And so was the simple, happy life of the lower-class Irish in Sligo.

The following day in the late afternoon, Kathryn, Joseph, and Brenton carried large buckets brimming with food and began the short walk to the village square. The girls followed behind, skipping and running about.

Kiernan appeared and flung his arm around his wife's neck and kissed her cheek roughly. "Anne! Goin' to a weddin' makes me wanna marry you all over agin!"

Anne brushed him off gently and walked with Kathryn, juggling her bucket and the baby strapped onto her back, leaving the men a short distance behind. They soon met up with hundreds of neighbors and friends, and they all placed their foodstuffs in a designated area. On this September evening, the sun was setting low as the entire town of Sligo gathered in a clearing outside the village. The young and old, the feeble and the robust, all were invited and all were present. They gathered in a circle to witness and celebrate local villagers Marcus and Shannon's wedding. The hard ground was flat and green, there was an abundance of food the children were eyeing, and a mound of peat was off to the side. No other decoration was needed.

As the sixteen- and seventeen-year-old bride and groom gazed lovingly into each other's eyes, the ancient vows were spoken and repeated. Then the priest sealed the union with a prayer and invited them to end the ceremony with a kiss. And with that burst claps and cheers, hugs and tears of joy. The bride and groom each came from a large family, and each person wanted a hug and a moment of their own with the newly married couple. Kathryn and Joseph had their moment and gave their well wishes, although they were not related to the newlyweds.

The food then became the focus, and the crowd invaded the piles that everyone had brought to share. Legs of chickens, pigs' feet, and duck neck were slurped and chewed, munched and gnawed. Soups abounded and bread was flung and wee children tossed apple cores at one another. The villagers ate and ate with gusto as the food was passed and plates were piled high. Toasts of good cheer and laughter caused some drinks to spill as the men began to feel the effects of the potcheen;[1] it entered their bloodstream, making their heads light, their blinks slow, and their smiles wide. Large bits of food and crumbs were strewn about, but it didn't matter; food was aplenty, and twas a grand occasion indeed!

At once, music sprang up and a large, flaming bonfire erupted, spewing sizzling ash high into the sky. The crackle excited the many wee children as they ran around the dancers celebrating the end of the wedding day. Two fiddlers each tapped one foot on the damp grass as they kept time with a penny whistle and a

---

1   Irish Moonshine. Distilled in pots, hence its name. Also reffered to as Poteen, Potheen, Poiti, Poitin.

deep sounding bodhrán.[2] The beautiful music seemed to whirl and dip about the swirling dancers encircling the bonfire. Each note filled the crisp air with sweet, melting particles almost good enough to eat. Two young women stood adjacent to each other and wildly flung their long hair about to the beat of the music. A baby in his mother's lap sat up and clapped his hands together. An elderly man tapped a stick on the ground in front of him, as if he were the drummer. And a young woman sat on the grass with a six-month-old infant in her arms, watching the dancers with straight backs and dipping feet.

Kathryn sat with Joseph as the children played about the moist grass with other kids. The twins came running up to Kathryn and each grabbed an arm, pulling and begging for her to dance with them. She reluctantly agreed, handing the infant to Joseph. Mother and daughters twirled with hands above their heads, circling, smiling, and laughing with enjoyment for three songs.

Then the music ceased, and all the dancers except for the bride and groom went back to their patches of grass. Marcus was giddy with excitement and drink, and with his right hand raised, bellowed out an ancient Irish pledge to his new wife.

Fer yer sweet sake, I'll ignore
Ever girl who takes me eye,
If 'tis possible, I implore
You do the same fer me.

As I've given from me heart
Passion fer which alone I live,
Let me nar receive from you
The love you have to give.

The crowd clapped approvingly, and the two newlyweds kissed. A small elderly man appeared next to the bonfire and hushed the crowd with his hands. It was Lord George Somer-

2 Pronounced bow-rawn. A small drum made of goatskin.

6

haven, the English landowner of the village who was kind and decent to his tenants. He was always happy and jovial, and a gap in his ivory dentures frequently made a well-defined whistle in his speech when he pronounced the letter *s*. Although he was of a highly different class, he always made an appearance at his tenants' weddings to congratulate and bless the newlyweds.

"I am happy that Marcus and Shannon have finally married," he grinned, "and it reminds me of how old I am when just yesterday she was running around with a nappy on! Really, I am honored to send them on their way with a golden guinea to begin their new life together, and hopefully they will return someday to show me their many babies."

A cheer erupted from the crowd as he put his right hand on his chest and bowed his head for a moment until the encouraging cries ceased. Then he looked up at them, smiled, and began his whistle-filled speech.

May you live a long life full of gladness and health,
With a pocket full of gold as the least of your wealth.
May the dreams you hold dearest be those which come
    true,
The kindness you spread keep returning to you.
May the friendships you make be those which endure,
And all of your grey clouds be small ones for sure.
And trusting in Him to Whom we all pray,
May a song fill your heart every step of the way.[3]

With that, Lord Somerhaven kissed the bride's cheek, patted the groom on the back, waved good-bye, and returned to his home.

"Well nar thin, ain't he nice," a woman in the audience said, nodding.

"Ahh, nicer thin a bellyful o' rabbit on a cold winter's day," a man agreed.

A pure dazzling voice suddenly arose with song from amongst the crowd and spread out to the edges of the town. It was Shannon singing a cappella to her new husband. All the partygoers sat quietly and listened to her sing from deep within her soul. It was a ballad of pure love. One of the fiddlers joined her strumming, long, defined notes. Kathryn locked eyes with Joseph, and each loving word that the bride sang, Kathryn echoed to her husband through her gaze.

Joseph's dark brown hair was long to his shoulders with a hint of wave to it. His tall height supported the husky build he developed from having worked regularly since he was a boy. Kathryn loved his tenderhearted soul and the way he carefully wiped the baby's face or brushed the girls' hair when they asked him to. He was her true love, and with him her life was complete. He centered her and elevated her thoughts to create a feeling that anything was possible, and she loved him like no other. Since the day they met, never was there a time she wished for another.

---

3 Written by Grace E. Easley.

Kathryn felt surrounded by love and relished in the good fortune bestowed upon her family. The villagers and family partied with the newlyweds late into the night until the children were huddled in a heap asleep. Joseph gently awoke Brenton and asked him to carry his infant sister as he and Kathryn each carried one of the twins to their small hut a short distance away. They tucked the children between the piles of blankets on their beds and kissed them goodnight. Suddenly Kathryn heard something moving and looked under the bed, where she saw a pink sniffing snout looking up at her. It was the family pig, or rather Brogan's pet; she smiled at the swine and patted its head. It was quite familiar for the Irish commoner to keep a pig in the hut, much to the delight of Brogan. Kathryn walked a few steps to her own bed as Joseph added a few more peat patties to their fire, warming the cold air and making dancing shadows on the wall. He cuddled Kathryn from behind and kissed her head. She closed her eyes in contentment and went to sleep thinking her life could not get any better than this.

Kathryn's father was English, and her mother was Irish. She was born in Ireland, although her parents relocated to England when she was a year old to work for a wealthy landowner. Her father tended the gardens, her mother worked in the house, and for a while she was content visiting her maternal ancestors in Ireland whenever possible. Her father was an orphan and had no information about his own relatives, so she did not feel connected to England in any way. When she turned five, her father died and it was devastating not being able to share her feelings of loss with a brother or sister. The school she attended while growing up was inadequate, and the landowner's daughters, who were six years older, took it upon themselves to teach her more than the scant public educational system when they were home from their private all-girls school. They taught her a bit about history, religion, government, psychology, and anything else they themselves learned. They found playing teacher quite amusing, like a theatrical pastime; they were the knowledgeable ones, and she was so perceptive a pupil.

When her mother also died suddenly, Kathryn was sent back to Ireland to be raised by her aunt and uncle. The ten years of tutoring had given her a keen sense of self and a broad image of the world. The landowner's children sent her back with two books to study from, and she referred to them regularly, not receiving any further education. Growing up amongst the poor, she shared her books with a few friends, although they were not as interested because education was of no use to them. To live a good life, all they needed to know was how to boil potatoes. Kathryn, on the other hand, had seen the other side whilest growing up in England, and the realization of all that she did not know piqued her curiosity all the more. She kept the books by her bedside and looked at the pictures, frequently wondering what her life would have been like had she stayed in England. What other things did she not know about? What were other people like in other parts of the world? What were they learning? There were no answers in the small village of Sligo.

Alas, due to the many years of living amongst the poor, her vocabulary and accent now resembled that of any peasant as she tried almost in vain to hang on to the little knowledge she had once acquired. At the very least, she knew how to read and write somewhat.

Besides the fact that she was more educated than most of her fellow villagers, including Joseph, she was still far below that of any wealthy English child. Every now and then, she would find Joseph leafing through her books, and she loved him all the more for wanting to educate himself instead of scoffing at the idea of a peasant with a knowledgeable brain. Most of the poor children of Ireland had no school to attend, so a parent or another adult taught them how to survive by farming and growing potatoes. No other education was needed, and the government certainly did not provide any schools. They liked the two-tier class system because they were the ones on top. But Kathryn wanted more for her children, so she would gather them—and any other child that wished to learn—by a large hedge next to their village. She wanted to pass on to them as much information as possible. Almost all Irish loved and cherished their land and wanted to live and die nowhere else, but Kathryn had tasted the other side of the fruit, and it was oh so sweet. She was content, although curious about what life would be like if they could perhaps relocate to England and make a better life for themselves, one of a higher quality than she and Joseph lived, one where they could attend school and perhaps rent a large portion of land to grow vegetables of all sorts for selling. It was a dream deep in her mind that surfaced rarely. For now, the hedge school was her focus and enjoyment.

Kathryn wrote on a piece of paper and then held it up to several children sitting before her next to the hedge.

"Nar whit does this say?" she asked.

"I kin read it," an eight-year-old boy said. "It says ... play ... with ... me?"

"Very good," Kathryn said.

"Kin I read the next one?" Brenton asked.

"Alright," she said writing again. Then she held it up for everyone to see.

"It says ... all ... almost ... time ... fer ... tea," Brenton read. "Ah, Mam, do we havta be goin' so soon?"

"Aye, me little angels," Kathryn said, gathering her books, "we mustn't keep yer da waitin', but we kin meet 'ere again in a few days."

As it started to rain, the other children waved good-bye and ran off to their homes, and Kathryn picked up her playful baby and walked with her children back to their hut.

Joseph and his family rented an allotment of land and a hut in Sligo from wealthy Lord Somerhaven. They were very fortunate to have a good landowner to rent from and always felt happy in their home. Lord Somerhaven had one son, John, a few years older than Joseph, although the father/son relationship was strained. From the start, they were opposites and rarely agreed on anything. John believed in discipline and social rank; Lord Somerhaven believed in free will and took an interest in the poor. John was usually serious; Lord Somerhaven was usually smiling and laughing. Their personalities were not complementary, and as John grew and became a man, their conversations were merely cordial at best.

Joseph paid his rent through the years and kept to himself, nodding politely whenever he saw the two men. One October afternoon a few years ago, he met face-to-face with Master John while working in his allotment, and an unlikely friendship arose. Now and again, he would work for either Master John or Lord Somerhaven on their estate, but he never saw them speak to each other.

Early one morning, Joseph was tending to his potatoes when Master John rode up on his horse.

"Good mornin' Yer Lordship," Joseph said.

"Morning, Joseph," he replied as he dismounted. "I have some work for you at the house; come by this afternoon."

"Aye, sir, Master," Joseph answered.

Master John did not leave, but shifted uneasily on the ground. After a few tense minutes, he spoke.

"How many children do you have?"

"Four, sir," Joseph replied.

"Joseph," Master John spoke quietly, shifting his gaze toward the ground where his horse began nibbling some grass.

Joseph did not speak, but waited until John was ready.

Suddenly he blurted out, "You are my only companion. Did you know that?"

"No, Master."

"Gentry believe my manner is gruff and rude, and rightly so. Sarcasm comes easily to me. I never married … never met a woman that would contend with a right grumpy man. My life has not been prosperous, although I don't expect you to understand, having your own wife and family. You do not posses rank or material wealth, but I am thinking that you have more inner wealth than I will ever have."

Joseph said nothing.

Master John continued, "And my father," he laughed uneasily. "He thinks more of you than he does me ... and I don't blame him. We have been fighting one another since my birth. I have seen him worried only once, and it was not because of me." He looked at Joseph.

"I am not a horrible man, Joseph, despite what others may believe."

"Aye, Master, you're very kind to me," Joseph replied.

"I would like to tell you about my father," he said.

"Aye, sir."

Master John began, and as the story progressed, Joseph found himself back in time, standing amid the mental picture that Master John had painted for him.

"One summer day years ago, and well after my mother had died, my father sent for me, and I walked into the drawing room. He paced inside the doorway unlike I have ever seen him. He moved steadfast to and fro, straightening his jacket, streaking back his hair, and unable to stand in the same spot for more than a second. He abruptly jerked after a few moments to begin pacing once again as if there were a fire brewing underneath his feet at each place he stopped. He had called for me, although I was not aware of the reason, nor prepared for the answer.

"'Do I look appropriate?' my father asked for the second time without making eye contact.

"'Yes, Father,' I answered, uneasy because he never asked my opinion for anything. 'You look splendid.' I stood waiting for the reason of my summons.

"'What time is it now?' he asked, moving again.

"I wanted to answer, 'Three minutes more than the last time you asked,' as I usually would, although this day and this moment was different. Strangely, I did not have the saucy swagger that exuded from me since birth, nor the cutting words that burst easily from my mouth. Something in his manner and desperate gait infused me with compassion. I had never seen him in this state, and unbeknownst to me, the answer would appear in a moment.

"'Father—'

"'Shhh!' he stopped me with an outstretched arm, standing still like an animal straining to hear the slightest sound from its prey. 'Did you hear something?' His eyes shot from one side of the room to the other. His mouth hung open, and his limbs remained rigid in their last position.

"'Father, I don't—'

"'Good God, man! Shhh!' he pummeled me once more with his words.

"And then the double doors opened and I was invisible.

"'Sir,' Father's valet bowed, '*she* has arrived.'

"Father did not hear the valet speak. He did not see the doors open. All his senses concentrated on the vision that would appear before him. He relaxed his limbs and stood like a lost child waiting for its mother.

"And I too stood waiting for someone to emerge, flush with nerves and apprehension that crawled through the air and into my veins. I half-expected the queen herself to appear or the ghost of my aunt or my deceased grandmother that my father barely knew. The *she* that filled my father with delirium and that he obviously could not face alone.

"And then *she* arrived indeed.

"In walked a slight young woman with brown hair, an ordinary manner, and a rich maroon dress. She floated across the floor and swooped upon my father, seeing only him and nothing else. Her forehead pressed against his, and her bashful eyes fluttered softly. She spoke in a hushed, soft tone, words meant only for him, although I was not standing far away.

"'Miss you ... cannot bear ... wanted so much ...'

"My father simply smiled with contentedness and tenderly wrapped her small face in both of his hands. As she spoke her loving words, he ever so gently kissed her forehead, her brow, her cheeks, her nose, her chin, blinking slowly each time as if every kiss penetrated his heart.

"I could barely believe my eyes. I had never seen my father in this light and was unaware of this affair. But the most surprising point was her delicate age. My father was nearing sixty, and the woman must have been in her late twenties. He had never shown any interest in other women, and now he chooses a common girl for his devoted admiration.

"Finding myself standing within earshot of their saccharine words, I backed up one step and hit the front of a chair. Clearly the temperature had risen in the room and I felt awkward in the presence of such flagrant affection. Now I was insignificant, obscure and invisible standing right next to them. Since the death of my mother years ago, I had not even thought of another woman for my father. To myself, he was stoic—a pillar of stone and the strong centerpiece in our family. Certainly not the cooing, tenderhearted lover he was revealing to me now.

"The two of them made their way towards an open door and out into the back garden, their heads still touching as they grasped one another as if their lives depended upon their hold—arms, shoulders, and hands melding together. Practically levitating through the air, they stopped and faced one another once more. They gazed into each other's eyes, and the woman reached up and slowly traced my father's lips with one finger. She smiled with elation, and my father leisurely bent down and placed his lips upon hers. They embraced completely with their saturated mouths, their bodies, their consciousness, and their very souls.

"I broke free from the vision of them, my own legs weak with the blatant scene played before me. I grabbed my father's chair behind me and sat down, stunned.

"Thoughts flew into my head. Perhaps this was a dream and I was to awaken to normalcy. No, now was the time to think clearly. Why didn't my father reveal his feelings for this woman to me? And who was she? Was she after money? Status? A father figure? And why was she not married—then again, perhaps she was? I began to feel angry thoughts of betrayal for my mother and I. Never did he touch my mother with such affectionate caresses, nor ever spend much time with me or speak words of love to either of us.

"And then a crystal clear realization removed the negative obstacles from my head like an ocean wave that broke on the shoreline and receded, clearing all debris from the sand. I looked at my father and his mistress once more strolling through the garden and all evil thoughts of wrongdoing departed. My entire life, I tried to win the attention of him and failed. So my thoughts turned sour, and demons squeezed my callous heart. Malice spewed forth from my mouth with bitter hatred, and scornful remarks danced about my head. And now my father was in love. All his life, he trudged through life, upholding his title and family honor. And this commoner, Helen was her name, gave him the one thing he wanted most, the one thing no one else gave him—love.

"It is too late for me, Joseph ... too late," Master John shook his head. "As for me, I only wanted power and status, and now here you are listening to me ramble on when I have been heartless many times to you as well." He closed his eyes and winced as if in physical pain. Joseph said nothing.

"I have never found that kind of love ... never ..."

Master John stopped speaking, grabbed the reins of his horse, and mounted in one swift motion.

"Perhaps someday my father and I can speak freely," he said.

Obviously Master John needed a friend and was reaching out to help him decipher the past, but there was nothing Joseph could say to mend the years of pain, and he simply nodded in agreement. Master John's horse trotted away with its somber, melancholy rider.

Later that evening back at Lord Somerhaven's estate, one of the stable workers saw Master John's saddled horse wandering about the grounds. The worker asked around as to why the animal had not been taken care of after its ride, or if perhaps something had happened to Master John. When no one in the stable had any answers, the question was put to Lord Somerhaven, and in a short period of time, a search party was assembled and sent out. Within ten minutes, the estate dogs found Master John facedown underneath a tree with a huge gash upon his forehead and blood saturating the ground around him. He remained unconscious as several doctors tended to his wound, trying to clean it and stop the bleeding. Lord Somerhaven remained by his bedside day and night, praying. He looked upon his son in a coma, lying peacefully and quietly. By the evening of the second day, Lord Somerhaven began to speak tenderly and aloud about all the regrets he had, about all the missed opportunities and things they should have done together. He expressed his sorrow about their relationship and vowed to God that if he spared his son, he would do anything it took to mend their family tie to each other. Unfortunately, after three days, John died with his father by his side. He never regained conciousness.

When he heard of John's death, Joseph thought about him for days afterwards and only wished that he had died a contented man. He sympathized with him and the agony he kept inside as a son, a man, and as a human being. He felt it was so very tragic that such a wealthy, educated man had lived a life so unfulfilled and died without knowing true happiness.

At his funeral, the usual noble crowd made their appearance, and then there was Joseph with his family by his side. Lord Somerhaven had invited them, and everyone stood with heads bowed, listening quietly to the priest deliver the last rites. No one really knew Master John intimately, and as soon as the priest was finished, the gentry paid their respects to Lord Somerhaven and trotted away in their fine coaches to their stately homes. Kathryn took the children home, and Joseph stood alone with Lord Somerhaven by his side, staring down at the headstone and newly covered casket.

"Children are not supposed to die before their parents," Lord Somerhaven said.

"Aye, sir."

"And fathers are supposed to pass down their titles, wealth, and knowledge to their sons."

"Aye, sir."

"None of that has happened here."

"No, sir."

"It is a sad day indeed. We have all lost ..." He walked slowly toward his manor house without another word.

After tea, the rain subsided and Kathryn and Brenton began digging up the potatoes in their allotment. They worked silently side by side, easily plunging the small trowels into the wet earth. Each shovelful brought up a large brown gourd called a horse potato, which most of the Irish subsisted on. Brogan and Shay ran in circles and played peek-a-boo around their laughing baby sister sitting on the wayside.

For the Irish, the potato came to be the universal source of food for many reasons. The seed is inexpensive, it requires no maintenance while growing, and best of all, many generations have lived relatively healthy lives eating little else. Almost all of the eight million peasants that were living in Ireland at this time were subsiding almost exclusively on the potato. Life was prosperous as long as the potato crop did not fail.

"Mam," Brenton asked, still digging, "whin am I to be married?"

Kathryn sat back startled. "Well nar thin, are you in any hurry?"

"Oh, no, I just need to know whin I should becomin' a man," he said.

"Aye, you'll be a man soon enough, me son. Childhood ends in a blink of an eye me mam tould me, God rest her soul," Kathryn sighed.

Joseph ran up panting and said, "Kathryn! Har do the potatoes look?"

"Fine," she said, "why?"

"I bin talkin' to Kiernan who tould me thar's a blight ruinin' all the potatoes," he said.

"Thar's always a blight ever year," she answered.

"I know, dear one," Joseph kept on, "but this one's mighty quare intirely, not like the others. 'Tis spreadin' all over ould Ireland, and no one knows whar it come from. Kiernan tould me that England an' Europe have lost much of their crops already."

Brenton held a potato in his hand and looked down upon it asking, "Whit does it look like?"

"I don't know, but I'll find out," he said. "Let's git as many as we kin home 'cause it could be in this 'ere dirt or rain." So they worked furiously until the rain came and forced them running home with armfuls and buckets of healthy spuds.

Kathryn loaded the potatoes into their pit in the ground inside their hut. This way of storage was ideal because it kept them cool and fresh for a long time and free from frost or rain. Suddenly the door to their hut swung open, letting in a burst of cold air. Kiernan's wife Anne stood with her face ashen and her brow creased with worry.

"Whit's the matter?" Kathryn asked.

"Have you not heard of that new blight spoilin' ar potatoes?" she asked.

"Aye, Anne," Kathryn said, waving her in the hut and shutting the door.

"We found it in our allotment today. Thar're brown spots all over that ar growin' so fist an' I'm afraid we'll lose our intire crop. Har will the likes of us eat? Ohh … an' the smell already—whit're we gonna do?" Anne cried.

"Don't worry, Anne, I'm sure we kin cut the infected parts off and use the rist. Thar's no time to waste."

Kathryn followed Anne to her hut and they began slicing off the black spots on all her potatoes until they were visually free of the disease. Potato cultivating usually took several weeks, and harvest time had just begun. The women hugged tightly when the work was over and assured each other that all would be all right.

The next morning, Joseph and Brenton placed peat inside the stove to cook the morning meal. After tending to the baby, Kathryn reached inside the potato pit and pulled out a large specimen with several black spots on it. Her mouth fell open, and her mind began racing.

"Jasus, Mary, and Joseph," she mumbled, "look 'ere." She handed the potato to her husband. He said nothing for a moment and then let out a large sigh trying to get his mind around the situation.

"Them all bad?" he asked.

"I don't know," she answered, frantically pulling them one by one out of the pit and onto the floor.

"Mam … Mam …," Brenton pleaded, trying to pick them off the ground. She ignored him and kept digging and throwing, as it was plain to see about every other potato had the blight.

"Mam," Brenton tried again.

"Whit!" she turned around and yelled at him. Joseph put his arms around her, trying to calm her down.

"If only I hadn't gone to Anne's last night, but I felt obleeged. I probly brought it home and nar look," she said angrily.

"'Tis not matter har it got 'ere, we'll jist save whit we kin," Joseph told her. "Don't forgit thar's much out thar to harvest. We'll pick as many as possible today after mass."

Kathryn forced a smile and nodded, trying to stay positive. She turned and kneeled, cleaning up the potatoes on the floor, and noticed a pouting Brenton still standing there.

"I'm sorry, me son," she said, grasping his hand. "I shouldn't have shouted at ye so. Nar I mightn' need a little help 'ere with this mess."

"Aye," he said cheerfully, picking them up.

At this time, Sir Robert Peel was the British prime minister, and during his term, the early stages of the famine tragedy weighed upon his head and fell upon his desk. He consistently tried to search out answers and arrived at a roadblock with each one. Neither he nor anyone else could have possibly imagined what lay ahead for the unfortunate Irish.

Peel lived a life of an upper-crust politician, attending gala ceremonies and political conventions. His main concern was England; Ireland, he thought, was ... well ... Ireland. He leaned toward the extreme Protestant party and enjoyed the political maneuvers of government. He was refined and polished, discreet and shrewd. His family and friends loved him, although others found him to be unlikable and charmless. He was a man of vast experience, especially in Ireland where he had served as chief secretary for six years. Nevertheless, he disliked the Irish way of life and the Irish in general. Although whatever his personal beliefs, he could be trusted to put them aside and administer with the best possible concern and leadership.

Whilst working in Ireland, he became known among his colleagues for one antic in particular. At dinner parties, he would rise and stand on his chair, placing one foot upon the table where he and his distinguished associates ate. Displaying an air of brash demeanor, he would raise his glass in the air, toasting to "the pious, glorious, and immortal memory of William III." This act and others led to his nickname of Orange Peel.*

Peel sat at his desk on the afternoon of September 25, 1845, quietly reading his recently delivered mail. He opened one in particular that made him sit back in his chair as his colleague Dr. Lyon Playfair came in for a meeting.

"Is everything alright, Thomas?" he asked, sitting down.

"I say, it is Playfair," Peel answered without looking up. "I was informed by the Isle of Wight last month that an unusual potato blight had struck and devoured their crop. Now Sir James Graham, the home secretary, tells me that it has spread to Dublin and many of their crops are also destroyed."

"Ah, yes," Dr. Playfair noted, "I have read about it in the *Gardeners' Chronicle and Horticultrual Gazette*. The editor first wrote about this blight, stating it had not been seen before but was not uncommon with all the diseases that have occurred every year. Then he wrote a week later, and the tone of his editorial was different. He wrote that Belgium's fields were completely destroyed, and the disease was spreading throughout Europe and America. He also stated there was not an edible potato in Covent Garden market and that we are sure to experience a great catastrophe."

"I hope that will not be the case, but I have requested weekly updates from Graham to be proactive," Peel answered. "Despite what the press has written, I feel there is no need to worry. We are all aware they consistently exaggerate, and it is best to delay any action due to inaccurate information. But please, let us not concentrate on the unpleasant—come to my country estate in a few weeks where we can relax and discuss politics."

"Splendid!" Dr. Playfair raised both hands in agreement.

As Kathryn and her family were sitting in the pew of their local parish, the last hymn of the mass had just been sung.

"This mass has ended," said the priest standing at the front with his hands folded together. "But I would like to say one more thing." He looked at his congregation, consisting mainly of the poor. "I know thar is much talk about this new disease that has come forth and is spoilin' many potatoes. I know very little at this time, but I will try and get more information as to how to treat this disease. Nar go with God."

Kathryn and Joseph waited for all the parishioners to exit the church before they got up and walked toward the front where a large statue of Jesus adorned the wall behind the pulpit. Kathryn looked at the statue while Joseph and the children continued to walk outside. She looked around the parish for others and saw that she was alone.

"God," she whispered, looking at the statue once more, "please spar ar potatoes from this here blight." She stared at the silent statue, listening for any inner peace that could ease her mind. The statue revealed nothing, so she walked outside into the sunlight and next to Joseph, who was speaking with Father Murphy.

"… and that's all I know at the moment, Joseph." Kathryn caught the tail end of Father Murphy's sentence.

"I'm sure we'll be fine," Joseph smiled. "We O'Malley's have the luck o' the Irish, you know!"

"Father, do you know if the government will help the likes of us?" Kathryn asked.

"I'm sorry, I don't know at this time," he said, "but they won't leave us to starve nar will they?"

They all laughed uneasily.

"Kathryn," Father Murphy placed a hand on her shoulder, "I do know that God has a plan and we must trust in him."

"Aye to be sure, Father," she said. "I'm mighty obleeged and twas good talkin' with you."

Kathryn and her family started the short walk home, and as the children ran ahead, Joseph began to talk about a new sling Kiernan was making. He went on about it being lightweight and how he carved it and how well it swung to and fro even when a large stone was placed inside it.

"Joseph," Kathryn stopped walking and faced him. "Whit we gonna do 'bout the potatoes?"

"Twas tryin' to git yer mind off it," he sighed.

"Well nar thin," she answered, "how kin I whin our food supply is dwindlin' each day?"

"We'll be fine," he smiled at her, "God willin' we'll be fine."

September was harvest time for the potato, and throughout that month, Peel received many letters describing the destruction of crops all over England and Ireland. Ironically, the blight struck like a checkerboard, devouring one crop while leaving the one next to it intact, thus some letters were positive while others cried failure. The government was also concerned for the English laboring class as they relied on the potato almost to the degree of the Irish. Had it not been for this famine, in time the English poor would have surely been as completely reliant on the potato as Ireland was. At this time, 90 percent of Ireland's population was dependent upon the potato either as food or as an export. In spite of all the reports, catastrophic famine was far from the mind of Peel or anyone else. Initially, it was thought by the English government that the blight would destroy some crops, but that it would be a local calamity as previous ruins had been. Nevertheless, the advice from his subordinates was to prepare for famine.

Peel agreed with the Cabinet that to stop Ireland from exporting would be an unwise decision to shield the approaching famine and instead boldly suggested the withdrawal of the Corn Laws. This law was a duty that was placed on foreign grain imported into England, and it was enforced so the English farmer could harvest his grain and sell it for a profitable amount. If the Corn Laws were to be removed, it was believed that anyone connected with the land would be ruined and the entire social structure of Britain would collapse. Passed down from generation to generation, the traditional class system would crumble like a cracker in a child's hands. Short of civil war within the Cabinet among those for and against this withdrawal, the controversy passionately continued day after day. Suffice it to say, no other subject raised such strong sentiments as the Corn Laws as Cabinet members shouted brash opinions to one another across the room. Sadly, this topic was of the utmost concern, leaving the Irish famine issue in the dust. Throughout his term as Prime Minister, Peel firmly believed the repeal was the answer to prevent the famine; it turned out to be his own downfall in the end.

October 1845. Dr. Playfair and Peel were enjoying a brandy snifter at Peel's country home as they had planned a few weeks prior. Like gentlemen, they spoke of the weather and politics in general. As the evening progressed, so did the topics until the potato blight was brought up. Dr. Playfair had been in high regard as a chemist and scientist and had worked under Queen Victoria. He informed Peel that he had currently been studying this particular potato blight to try and find a chemical substance suitable for a counterattack. His theory was that after harvesting the potatoes, those that had small amounts of the disease, or none at all, could be treated with a substance to prevent further rot. Peel thought this possibility over in his head and agreed to let Dr. Playfair lead a team of scientists in the search for such a method. In three days, Dr. Playfair was in Dublin working with other noted professors and talking with other landowners of the area. A few days later, Peel received a letter from Dr. Playfair stating that the destruction of the potato was far worse than he had previously thought. He estimated at least half of Ireland's crops were infected and the disease was spreading rapidly. The necessity of finding a way to protect the remaining potatoes, he wrote, could not be underestimated. Another week of study brought a letter from Dr. Playfair detailing what the scientists recommended. On Peel's approval, he would make thousands of copies and have them distributed in parishes, newspapers, and town centers throughout Ireland. He believed the recipe was easy enough for the peasant to administer himself after he harvested. One pamphlet was for treatment to all potatoes so they would not be affected by the blight; the other was for treating diseased portions to save whatever edible pieces he had left. Peel reclined in his chair, took a sip of tea, and began to read each instruction carefully.

"It says here to dig up all the unblighted potatoes and let 'em dry in the sun," Kathryn read from the pamphlet she had received from her parish. She, Joseph, and Brenton laid out the pile of potatoes they had just unearthed from their plot of land as the two girls ran around and played with the smiling baby. Kathryn looked over the parcel and then surveyed the sky. Grey rain clouds cloaked overhead and refused any ray of sun from pushing through. She raised her eyebrows to Joseph.

"'Tis a pity the person that wrote this probly don't live here," she said. "Next step is to excavate? Whit does excavate mean?" She looked at Joseph.

"I don't know. Whit does the rist say?"

"Ahh … excavate an area six feet wide an' as long as we need. Maybe it means mark out?" She looked at Joseph again who began marking the ground with a stick.

"Thin we make a trench 'round that … ah … two feet wide. We place the potatoes in the middle part, spread 'em out and lay over 'em sods of peat on their margin. On their margin? Go git a bunch of turf, Brenton, an' we'll find the margin."

Brenton returned to the hut and struggled to carry back a large bucket filled with dried peat. He half-carried, half-dragged the bucketful and then brought it up alongside his father.

"'Ere, Da," he said.

"Aye, son."

Kathryn reached into the bucket and held up a piece of peat. She and Joseph squinted, surveying it slowly from all sides.

"Do you see the margin?" she whispered.

"Och no, whit does a margin look like?"

"Maybe 'tis inside," and she broke it in two.

She shook her head, "I don't see it."

"Ahh, I'm jist goin' to lay 'em on top," Joseph decided. "Some'll be on their margin fer sure nar."

Kathryn kept reading the instructions. "'Tis gittin' more complicated and difficult to understand. Nar it says to sift 'packin' stuff' on top. To make it, we need to mix a bucket of smolderin' unslacked lime divided into the size of eyeballs with dirt or sand equalin' two buckets."

She looked up at Joseph who lifted up his eyebrows but said nothing. "Another way to make it is to combine equivalent parts of charred turf and dehydrated sawdust." She looked at Joseph again. "If we had money to git all this stuff we wouldn't be out 'ere in this mist tryin' to—"

"Nar, m'lady," Joseph was face-to-face with her in a flash. "Maybe all these potatoes we jist picked are alright. They haven't ketched the disease yet. 'Tis that pile over thar from the pit that needs help. Let's jist deal with those. Nar, whar do we start?"

Kathryn shuffled her papers until the treatment of diseased potatoes was on the top. "Alright, it says to grate the potatoes into a fine pulp and put it in a bucket, wash it with water, and strain it through a ... si-vee? Whit's a sivee?" She looked at Joseph who said nothing, so she continued, "Do this three times. Thin we're suppose' to drain it one last time and place it on a griddle over a smolderin' fire. The water used fer washin' the pulp kin be mixed with oatmeal or pea-meal. Also, after we cook the pulp, it kin be mixed together with the water to make bread." Then she read verbatim, struggling slowly through the words, "'There will be of course a good deal of trouble in doin' all we have recommended, and perhaps you will not succeed very well at first; but we are confident all true Irishmen will exert themselves, and never let it be said that in Ireland the inhabitants wanted courage to meet difficulties against which other nations are successfully strugglin'.'" Kathryn sat down on the ground and gazed out into the distance, completely frustrated.

Chapter II

In 1801, the Act of Union to bond Ireland and England together had taken place and changed everything. Instead of a cordial partnership between the two countries, it turned out to be a dysfunctional marriage with England as the domineering, ruling husband and Ireland as the meek, passive wife. At times, she would summon all her courage and rebel, trying to escape, but alas, the husband would grin, lasso her around the neck, and yank her back into submission. It was no use; he would always win in the end.

Through the passage of time and a few hundred years, Ireland became a two-tier system with select landlords owning the land and the millions of poor working or renting plots of land from them. This way of life prevented the poor from educating themselves enough to rise to a higher standard of living. They were solely at the mercy of their landlord and completely taken advantage of in many instances.

During this time, the poor Irishman rented his home under harsh conditions. The tenants could not request mending if their hut was in disrepair lest they be cast out into the night. Any improvements the poor made upon their home were not compensated and were the property of the landlord upon dismissal. Some Irish signed leases, although it was the right of the owner to terminate the agreement at any time. The poor were renting because the landlord allowed them to be there, and for any reason whatsoever, they could be dismissed.

The landlords felt no loyalty or compassion toward their tenants, and in many instances there was no landlord at all on the premises. He was given the land and felt no need to visit his property. Instead, he hired a middleman to collect the rent and in some cases visited his property merely once or twice in his lifetime—or perhaps not at all. The absence of the landlord probably added to the indifference between the two parties that was never bridged. The middleman could exploit the poor as he chose because the absentee landlord could not be bothered with the trivial act of collecting the rents. The sole motive was profit, and the middleman was hungry for money. He soon devised a way to make even more collateral by dividing plots of land, some with homes and some without, into smaller and smaller pieces, although the rents remained the same. He became the tyrant of Ireland, squeezing out every drop of money from the poor.

Amid all the thorns on a rosebush stands a beautiful shining rose, and as it were, there too were honest, kind landlords as well. Clean, well-built huts and bits of furniture awaited the lucky few who received such gifts. But overall, more than any other people, the Irish peasant was far worse off than any other European due to this hierarchy system. However, the people were generally happy in disposition, as is their nature, and they not only survived during this time, but actually flourished. They had many babies even though the potato was their main food, and in many instances their only food. The population continually rose as teenagers married, had children, and continued the cycle of the peasant Irish.

Noisy slurping was all that could be heard around Kathryn's table as her family ate their breakfast of oatmeal. All the potatoes had been harvested and stored in their pit. This was their main food for the coming year, just as it had been for their kind for hundreds of years. Each time Kathryn reached into the pit, her heart leapt into her throat, not knowing if she would pull out a few good ones or a sludge of rotting mass. She discarded the inedible and boiled the edible, hoping this way of living would last until the next harvest. As was customary, she saved as many seed potatoes as possible to plant for the next year, although it was hard not to eat them. Brenton ate the small portion in his bowl and looked up at his mother for more. His father pushed his own bowl in front of his son and got up from the table. Joseph harvested a small amount of oats next to his potato plot, but that was for selling and paying his rent. He certainly could not eat his rent.

"I need to talk with Lord Somerhaven today," Joseph announced. "He might have extra work fer me since Master John died." He kissed Kathryn, opened the door, and strolled out into the drizzle of the morning and toward the manor house in the distance.

From the beginning, Lord Somerhaven always tried to help his tenants in any way possible, and they rewarded him with potatoes if they could spare them.

"Yer Lordship?" Joseph yelled out into the back garden.

"Yes?" Up popped the small man with the distinct whistle in his speech. "Oh, Joseph, how are you? How did you know I was back here?"

"You're always in yer garden, sir, and it shows." Joseph bowed his head for a moment, remembering Master John and wanting to say a word of comfort. He looked up saying, "Yer Lordship—"

"I am fine, Joseph," he broke in, "let us speak of other things."

"Well ... me family and I are tryin' to eat whit we kin of the potatoes, but 'tis not goin' well. 'Twas hopin' I could ask if you need any extra work 'round 'ere I could do."

"Ahh, Joseph, don't worry, my good man," he said with a laugh, "I will take care of your family—you have nothing to worry about. Now let me see, if you go into the shed over there and grab a shovel, you can help me out by digging a few holes right here."

Joseph brightened, and with a skip in his step, he got a shovel and began digging with gusto. The drizzle gave way to partial rays of sunshine, and the men worked for about a half hour in silence until Lord Somerhaven finally spoke.

"When I was a small boy," Somerhaven began, "my family and I were wealthy of course, but money was not what I needed. I wanted love and that is what my parents didn't give me. My father was never around, so I focused on my mother. She dolled out a smidgen of love now and then, but I wanted much more. So I would hide something I knew she'd need and sit back and watch the show unfold. She would realize the object was missing—hair brush, towel, scissors—it didn't matter what it was. I'd watch her demeanor turn from anxiety to sheer madness as she ran about searching under blankets, tables, clothes, and everything in her path. I felt victorious, as she was the puppet and I had absolute control of the strings." He paused for a moment. "Some years ago, I had a close friend, Alistair Hewitt, many years my junior. Alistair courted a pretty woman for many months and loved her dearly. She was captivating, radiant, and exquisite—somewhat like this." He quietly gazed at the rose between his fingers, closed his eyes, and sniffed, inhaling its sweet fragrance.

"The problem was I fancied her too, although our affair was almost accidental. We looked at each other one day and … and when Alistair learned that we were to be married, he hung himself on a day I was to visit him. Upon opening the door, I … I tried desperately to cut the rope, but it was a long few minutes before I finally did and he lay on the ground—barely alive. Oh he lived, but his brain was affected so that he could no longer care for himself. His poor mother fed him and wiped his bum like a baby. Alistair looked out with his eyes, but they were completely hollow, never seeing any part of the beautiful world again."

Lord Somerhaven fixated his eyes intently upon Joseph. "When you create misery in people's lives and steal their souls,

God does not forget. He shatters your life in the end as well." He glanced back to his roses and continued working.

"That beautiful rose was my second wife, Helen. We were so in love, nothing else mattered and nothing else even existed. When I gazed out at the world, the only thing that made sense and the only thing in focus ... was her." His lips began to quiver with the memory.

"God let me have her and blessed us tremendously until the night she was to give us our child. After a very hard labor, the baby was finally born and it was ... dead. It took so much out of Helen and she lost so much blood that she too died the day after. I don't believe she fought very hard to live anyway, as she was unable to bear the pain of the loss of our child. So when the light of day shone brightly each morning thereafter, I endured without the warm touch of my wife and the giggles of our child." He stopped and looked at Joseph.

"She scented the air that I breathed," he said solemnly, turning another bud between his fingers. "Now the air is ordinarily stale and without life, and the closest I can get to her is through this rose. She loved roses." He closed his eyes and put his nose to the lavender petals, fully inhaling their scent. He turned toward Joseph once more.

"She asked for nothing," he continued, "giving unconditional love to an old man whose life was meager despite his material wealth. I thank God every day for the time he gave me with her."

"Mighty sorry, Yer Lordship," Joseph swallowed.

"Ahh, you have nothing to be sorry about," he replied. "You are a fortunate man with a wife and four beautiful ones."

"Aye, sir," Joseph gulped and kept digging.

"My first marriage was loveless, but it was not her fault; we were simply wrong for one another. I have done many other horrible things to innocent people, and it took the death of my Helen for me to see the light. Even my son John and I had a chance to be close to one another ... and I messed that up too.

Now I am a lonely old man without any heirs, paying for all my unfortunate deeds that I have bestowed upon others."

He paused for a moment, then continued. "Now this blight has arrived, and I seem to think it is different from all the others. I've lived enough years to know the smell of coming famine in the air. Sell your oats and buy food for your family, no need to pay me rent. I will do my best to provide for you and all the others until you can provide for yourselves again. The rest of my life now will be spent trying to help others in any way that I can."

Joseph stopped digging and leaned forward on his shovel. "Much obleeged, Yer Lordship, I don't know how to intirely repay you, but I know God sees yer kindness nar and will hold a special place for you in heaven ... right next to your Helen."

Lord Somerhaven's eyes began to water as he gently placed his hand upon Joseph's shoulder. "You have already paid me. My son John and I never had a good relationship, and now he is gone. I failed as a father, and there is once again only myself to blame—although if I would have had a son like you, Joseph, then my life would have been worth something. All the noble people right now in government, they will lose in the end as well if they don't help Ireland. Oh it might take hundreds of years, but trust me, they'll get theirs in the end. What is their life worth if they don't help all the hungry Irish? I tell you—it's not worth a damn."

He returned to his roses with pursed lips. The small man looked even smaller this day, and Joseph didn't know what to say. Lord Somerhaven was always reciting and writing poems and blessings, and after a few minutes, he began to speak again:

May flowers always line your path
And sunrise light your day,
May songbirds serenade you,
Every step along the way,

May a rainbow run beside you,
In a sky that's always blue,
And may happiness fill your heart,
Each day your whole life through.

"I had an Uncle Bryn from Wales that used to recite that to me as a boy, and I will try to live such a life, Joseph," he said. "And I am glad for people like you in my life that make it worth living."

Kathryn grabbed her basket and the remaining few coins she had left and told Brenton to mind the other children as she would return shortly. She walked slowly on this clear day, past all the parcels of land strewn with rotting potatoes. Never before had she witnessed such waste and ruin in such a short time and in such quantities. All her neighbors were trying to subsidize their meals with whatever they could, and a few downhearted were near panic.

In the streets, the people's talk was about the blight and only the blight. "Whar do you think it come from?" one old woman asked another on the edge of town. Kathryn walked on and heard everyone in the street discussing the disease.

"It come down from the sky, I say, 'twas in the rain and nar 'tis in the soil!"

"It rose up from the soil ... thin infected ever last potato in Ireland."

"I saw it with me own eyes! A bolt of lightnin' flashed across the sky and struck down on me plot first. From thar it spread to others."

"The water itself is infected."

"The soil itself is infected."

"The ar itself is infected."

"A volcano, I tell you! Deep in the earth it erupted, and the land ketch it that way."

"Me sister laid out her clothes to dry over some of her plot. Her intire field had the disease ... 'cept those potatoes under the clothes. See, 'tis proof it be comin' from the ar."

"This quare blight is made up by the government to git rid of us all!"

Kathryn went into the local market and looked at some of the food she could not afford. Just gazing at the produce made her hungry, and she wondered if maybe someday she could purchase some to make a grand meal for her family. She forced herself to leave the area and make her way across an aisle where some oatmeal was located inside a large barrel. She bought a small portion from the grocer and placed it inside a bowl in her basket.

On her way out, she overheard three women discussing how to treat diseased potatoes and wanted to tell them that she had tried every possible cooking method she knew of and nothing worked. The women exchanged ideas on several recipes as their hands gestured and faces contorted describing the exact way to cook them. She thought about those women on her walk home and it gave her soul peace, knowing she was not alone. Not the only mother trying to find ways to feed her family or the only one laying awake at night wondering how many days were left before all the potatoes were completely rotten. And then what would become of them? What would become of Ireland? She loved her country and had faith that the government would give food to the poor if they truly needed it. When she was a young girl, there were many times the potato crop failed, but her aunt and uncle always pulled through. Except this disease was somehow different, and throughout the counties, stories of complete ruin rushed in like a gust of wind, encircled the villages, and continued on to the next town. But a faint smell of it lingered in the air, and with each hopeless story that was told, the greater the smell of doom became.

Kathryn could see her beloved home in the distance. It was one of six clustered on a small area of the Somerhaven estate. She could see her children playing with other kids and hoped that she could keep that playful spark in their little bodies forever.

She abruptly turned to a spot in the near distance, a small dip in the earth that Mother Nature had made and that Kathryn knew well. She would visit this spot when she needed solace to think of her life, her family, or faraway lands. To ponder anything that she read about in her books and did not fully understand. She knelt now in the subtle incline and surveyed the low hill in front of her. She closed her eyes, raising her chin into the faint breeze, and called on her senses to reach out and grasp the moment. She did not speak but rather let the perfect harmony of nature surround her. She slowly opened her eyes to see tiny blades of grass, heather, and nettles lean slightly with the soft push of each breeze, and nearby, a rodent with a brown fuzzy head poked out from beneath the earth and cared not that he was being watched. The sky was large and blue with stark billowing clouds shifting in unison like giant ships at sea. The warm sun tapped at her skin, and she almost felt embraced by its warmth. A scurrying black ant made its way through the debris of dirt and grass, on a journey with no beginning and no end.

"Thar's no words fer beauty such as yers," a voice from behind intruded on her thoughts.

"Och, Joseph!" she turned around to see him smiling at her.

"Whit ar you doin'?" he questioned.

She paused a moment before responding, trying to find the correct words.

"I believe God lives in places like this," she said. "I know the church is the house of God, but I feel closer to him 'ere."

She looked at her husband who had a puzzled look upon his brow.

"God made the earth, and he's in ever blade of grass and ever white cloud and ever rodent that's walkin' by. I *feel* his presence 'ere. I feel I kin talk to him 'ere. Do you understand?"

"I think so." Joseph suspiciously looked about. Then he opened his hand to reveal several shiny coins.

"Look, m'lady. I bin workin' fer Lord Somerhaven today, and he paid me well." "He said we're not obleeged to pay rent and to use the money to buy food. And if all ar money is gone thin I kin work fer him if all ar potatoes rot this year."

"Thank God fer him." Kathryn reached out and rested her head upon her husband's shoulders.

"Aye," Joseph agreed. "I knew we'd be alright."

Kathryn cooked the evening meal with some portions of edible potato, cabbage, and oatmeal. The family sat around the table for only a short while. It seemed they had only taken a few bites and the meal was gone.

"I'm still hungry," pleaded Brogan.

"Did you know that a little girl once made bould and wished fer more oatmeal, and by the powers that be, her wish came true!" Kathryn looked at all her children's faces. "She walked outside and the stream 'twas not water, but intirely oatmeal! It began rainin' nar little bits of oatmeal all over ould Ireland, and thin whin she came home to sit down and rist, I ask you, what do you think happened?"

Brogan shook her head.

"'Twas mighty quare that nar her chair and bed crumbled altogether beneath her 'cause they too were made ... of ... oatmeal."

Brogan closed her eyes and clutching her teddy bear whispered, "I'm wishin' me chair was made of oatmeal."

Everyone laughed, and Kathryn began to collect and clean the bowls. She then tried to corral the children to bed. They ran around with the small family pig, up and over, jumping and squealing with delight. "Tell us another story!" they yelped.

Kathryn finally got their attention by beginning to tell a scary story. One by one, they stopped running and sat on their beds with eyes wide, mouths agape. The hut was dark except for the fire a short distance away, and the children and pig began to huddle closer to one another as the story continued. Shay sat with the blankets pulled up over half her face so that only her bright eyes were showing, and the pig had the blanket over his head and body so only his eyes and snout were visible. Kathryn kneeled to their level and leaned forward, gesturing with her hands and speaking very slowly to enhance every word.

"Boo!" Kathryn shouted at the end of the story, and the children screamed with laughter as the blankets were flung into the air and came down covering everyone. She kissed each one goodnight and patted the pig's head cuddled between Brogan's arms and then sat down with Joseph at the table.

November 1845. Sir Robert Peel met time and time again with the British Cabinetry as news of the blight grew steadily worse. He summoned an emergency meeting to suggest aid for Ireland's starving.

"I strongly recommend that more employment be created," Peel said, standing before the Cabinet, "a substantial sum of money to be granted to the lord-lieutenant for some food purchases in poverty-stricken districts, and that an Irish Relief Commission is established."

The Cabinet approved all the proposals with ease, so Peel continued his recommendations.

"I suggest that an advance of public money be available for food purchases, and I once again believe that the removal of impediments to import is the only effectual remedy." He was once more asking for the repeal of the Corn Laws.

"Can we vote public money for the sustenance of any considerable portion of the people on account of actual or apprehended scarcity and maintain in full operation the existing restrictions on the free import of grain?" Peel proclaimed, "I am bound to say, my impression is we cannot."

The Cabinet was stunned by such a bold statement, and cornered by Peel, they had to comment. They voted and ended with a split decision with more than half against Peel. A subdued outrage of accusations and finger pointing began to grow within the Cabinet, so the meeting was adjourned for one week. Five more Cabinet meetings took place with an overwhelming majority firmly against Peel. Simply mentioning the repeal of the Corn Laws had brought about such disarray and hostility within the British government with members bickering amongst themselves that one member announced that Peel should not be permitted to die a natural death. Nevertheless, he remained in office and administered his duties as best as possible.

Peel and Dr. Playfair had just finished dinner at his country estate, and they retired to the library to discuss politics and the plans for Irish Relief. Peel settled into his favorite leather chair and placed his feet upon the footstool before him. A servant had just lit the fire and asked if there was anything else he could do.

"No, that will be all," Peel said, lighting his cigar.

Dr. Playfair was a mirror image of Peel, seated in the next chair, and both men stared into the fire for a moment before speaking.

"As you well know, Playfair," Peel puffed, "I am a firm believer of *laissez faire,* that the people should be allowed to act on their own free will and with as little interference from the government as possible. We should assist them somewhat, although the right of private enterprise and property ownership is sacred and I believe in every situation the correct outcome will surface in the end."

"Here, here," Playfair agreed.

"When I first became informed of this peculiar potato blight running rampant through Ireland," Peel continued, "my initial belief was to let nature take care of itself as in previous years. Although, it quickly became evident that this particular disease was ruining more than half the crops in Ireland, and myself as well as the Cabinet knew we must step in, but only in the most non-obtrusive way. I strongly feel that private enterprise must remain strong and lead the way in assistance."

"I agree with you completely," Playfair said. "The government cannot purchase large amounts of food to feed all the destitute without some help on their part. The Irish poor would certainly take advantage, and the economy would be greatly affected."

Peel continued, "Although trade in Ireland is of course different. The poor that live on potatoes grow their own and rarely purchase any other source of food. The Irish are completely dependant on the potato and do not know how to cook or prepare any other type of food. In many remote parts, trade is virtually nonexistent."

"Yes, that is true," Playfair agreed, "I have been to a few of those areas."

Peel suddenly sat upright and faced Playfair. "But I have a plan of my own. I've been thinking about food from other countries that I could purchase so that regular trade in Britain would not be affected, and I believe I've found the answer."

"What is it?" Playfair asked.

"Indian corn from the United States," Peel stated and sat back again in his chair. "I plan to use it to keep food prices from rising too high. Whenever I believe prices are soaring unreasonably, I'll toss in some Indian corn to bring them back down again."

"I never would have thought of that," Playfair mused.

"Precisely why I am prime minister, Playfair," Peel grinned. "You see, the corn is ideal because it is nonexistent in Britain, so the price of it cannot be raised. It is neither imported nor exported and will in no way affect regular commerce. It is also inexpensive to purchase and a person can survive on it."

"I say," Playfair laughed, "what a grand scheme!"

The plan was ideal, but the purchase of the Indian corn was another matter altogether. Peel consulted the Treasury who suggested the government purchase officially, but Peel believed that if the government openly purchased it, the price of the corn would rise. He opted for a private party to purchase the corn on their own behalf and settled on Baring Brothers, a significant international mercantile house. The purchase of this corn was solely by his own official decision, and Mr. Thomas Baring was happy to assist. Mr. Baring consulted his confidential representative in the United States, a Mr. Thomas Ward, whose discretion was impeccable. The plan was for Mr. Ward to purchase orders of Indian corn throughout the United States so that prices would not rise and no one would know who the actual buyers were.

Kathryn was at the stream a few yards from their hut, and on this day, she was washing clothes. She dipped the fabric in the stream and then back and forth, back and forth, she scraped a piece of clothing on a large rock at the edge of the water. She was always thinking about food now and how to stretch out what was available into a meal that would satisfy her family. Brogan sat a few feet from her, playing with her stuffed dog, a present from Lord Somerhaven. She called him Nelson, after Lord Nelson, the one-eyed admiral, as her stuffed dog had only one eye as well, although he was loved unconditionally.

"Time fer supper, Nelson," Brogan said, placing him on the grass before her.

"Are you hungry?" she played. "I bet you are. Nar open wide." She put a small stick to Nelson's mouth and held it for a moment.

"Was that good nar?" she asked. "Mustn't you want more?"

"Okay, ould chap, 'tis not matter, thar's one more *wee bit* jist 'ere." She scraped an imaginary bowl with her hands.

"'Ere's the last wee bit," she said, holding the stick to his mouth again.

"You're *still* hungry? I haven't no more to give you nar, them days are over. No more, I say—nar quit yer cryin', I tell you. I don't have no more, 'tis a sin to be goin' on like that! Will you stop cryin', and don't ask fer no more! Nar go outside an' stop whinin'!"

Kathryn had ceased washing and watched the scene, completely dismayed. Brogan was holding up a mirror of herself, and it was ugly to watch. Didn't her daughter know that she wanted to provide her with more food? That she simply did not have a choice?

"Brogan, come 'ere." Kathryn patted her knee. The child came and sat down.

"I'm sorry we don't have enough food sometimes, but we're tryin' to git more," she explained. "I'm sorry you're hungry."

"I'm always hungry, Mammy," she said honestly.

"I know." Kathryn hugged her and stroked her long hair. "We'll git more food, don't you worry, we'll git more food."

As Peel waited for the shipments of the Indian corn to arrive, he began to set in operation the Relief Commission for Ireland that had been approved by the Cabinet. Peel held a meeting with the leading members of the Irish government to organize the department. The senior member of the commission was Sir Randolph Routh, the head of the Commissariat Department of the British Army, and he was appointed to lead the entire Relief Commission and eventually to distribute the Indian corn. Appointing a man like Routh to command the Relief Scheme was a good choice indeed, because he had vast experience in feeding large quantities of people in times of crisis. Routh had a long resume of great achievements and was known to work well with all types of individuals and to have a well-rounded disposition. He had a medium build, wavy head of hair, and facial hair speckled with dark brown and bits of gray. A slight eye squint glistened with each careful thought or inquiry that entered his head. Most notably, many deep lines appeared around the sides of his mouth whenever he smiled fully, as if it had taken countless years to create.

Routh's first marriage produced six children, two of whom died in childhood, while his current marriage to Marie Louise produced nine children. He adored them all, although he had a special bond with Thomas, his second child with Marie. Thomas was attending Eton, as Routh had, and it was hard to be away from him. The boy regularly sent letters, but Routh missed hearing his voice and looking out the window and watching him play cricket. Routh's own father was stern and distant, and Routh did not wish to mimic that relationship. He listened to all his children and hugged each of them on a regular basis.

Aside from his family, he enjoyed the beauty of the countryside and sought therapy in long walks. And most importantly, he had a genuine loving heart and kind soul. He tried to treat all individuals with the same amount of courtesy and had no ill will toward the Irish.

Routh's position as Commissariat officer, unfortunately, only went so far. All the work his department conducted funneled into the British Treasury in London where each piece of paper was carefully scrutinized. And at the head of this department was the almighty figure of Charles Edward Trevelyan.

"Margaret! Margaret! Where is my hat?" Trevelyan demanded.

A woman came running into his office.

"It's right here, sir." The secretary held out a dapper felt top hat.

"Hmmm," he said, inspecting the rim, "the tailor did a suitable job of mending it."

"Yes, sir," Margaret swallowed, "he did. And the price of two shilling was right too."

"Yes, perhaps I'll let him fix the next item that needs mending," Trevelyan stated. He put on his coat and hat and motioned to Margaret now sitting at her desk.

"Whilst I am meeting with the prime minister, I need you to prepare new files for Irish Relief. I am going to require adequate space as well—perhaps three new cabinets."

"Yes, sir, very well, sir," the docile Margaret said.

Trevelyan walked out from his Treasury office in downtown London to meet with Peel in his offices on Downing Street. The short trek would take the average person only a few minutes, but due to Trevelyan's long legs and ample stride, the distance was a mere minute or two. He walked boldly with his 6'4" frame, a slim build and a valiant presence. Straight dark hair peeked out from underneath his hat and continued down each cheek to make two abundant side whiskers, true to the high fashion of the day. His gleaming white teeth revealed a smug grin and a sly feline smile. He was attractive to most women without muttering a word, although it was his eyes that people remembered to the greatest extent. Deeply set, shadowed, and piercing, they were the kind of eyes that could stare down and transform a charging bear into a whimpering, shaking puppy. At a dinner party, his choice of topics might be morality, political progress, or steam navigation. When the subject matter was of these things, his enthusiasm spilled over the room like a waterfall. Idle small talk was not part of his repertoire.

Indeed, Trevelyan was not your average man. When he was twenty-one years of age and beginning his career, he worked in India for a time. During his stay, he boldly pointed the finger at his direct superior, a well respected man, for accepting bribes, which clearly could have jeopardized his own future. For this he was ridiculed, scorned, and denounced as a traitor by his fellow comrades. Despite this, he did not waver, and although young, his passion for the truth stood strong as he gathered the necessary information for submission to his department. He presented his case, and following an inquiry, his superior was dismissed.

The Treasury was not a popular branch of government, but it ran well with few snags or bumps. Desperately wanting to correct any wrongdoing and constantly making improvements in everything he touched, other government departments complained Trevelyan was interfering in their own work. He found it hard not to meddle in other people's business. Thirty-eight was his age when the blight struck Ireland, and he was brimming with rigor and stamina. His work ethic was unmatched, and at the height of the famine, he kissed his wife and child good-bye and took up residence for a time in an apartment, giving his complete focus and every waking moment to famine relief. He worked round the clock and expected the same devotion from his subordinates.

"Good afternoon, Prime Minister," Trevelyan held out his hand as he was let into the office.

"Good afternoon," Peel shook his hand. "Please have a seat." Both men sat down.

Peel began, "Now, as we discussed in the Cabinet meeting, you and Sir Randolph Routh will head Irish Relief under my direction. I would like to review one more time the itinerary before you begin, in case you have any questions." Peel handed him some papers.

"Fine," Trevelyan answered.

"I would like you first to create the Relief Commission," Peel said, consulting his paperwork. "I have learned from previous famines that the real need for food will not begin until every last edible portion is cut off, every morsel is found, until every last spec of potato is consumed and nothing, nothing is left to eat. Then I would like the plan to begin."

"And what month would this be?" Trevelyan asked.

"I have calculated it should begin in April or May," Peel answered, "and we will need every bit of those five months to prepare. Now let's briefly review my three-part plan. The first and main part is to coordinate on a local level. Landowners need to step up and begin creating and increasing employment on their estates. The Treasury will advance suitable sums to the landowners at three and a half percent interest, to be repaid in ten years. The landowner is responsible for the entire repayment in the district where the work will be done. This single factor, or Labour Rate Act, is the one that will protect and rescue any starving individual in need. It is imperative that landowners look after their own tenants. Jobs need to be created within villages and local committees, and these representatives need to raise money to purchase food for resale to the impoverished or hand it over free of charge to the starving. In addition, fifty thousand pounds will be given free of charge to those districts too poor to bear the cost of the works."

"Personally, I believe free money and food should not be widespread," Trevelyan added. "It makes people unindustrious and indolent."

"That is true, Trevelyan," piped Peel, "although when planning for a famine, we need to review all options and consider them all."

"If that is what you would like," Trevelyan nodded, "we can review them."

Peel went back to his paperwork, not wanting to discuss that topic further. "Now the second part of the plan is to create jobs throughout Ireland on the Irish Board of Works. As you know, during previous famines, the extra work carried out was building new roads, and it should be the same with this famine. I am putting Routh in charge of the works; he will move to Dublin shortly with his family to begin operations. I have advised him to consult with you on any matters of finance."

"That will be fine," Trevelyan agreed.

"The third part," Peel continued, "is preparing for the coming fever which always follows famines. Fever hospitals need to take steps for the sickness and other accommodations such as houses for hire. Each local workhouse needs to prepare for separate housing, as the sick are not allowed in the workhouse itself. And lastly, the sale of the Indian corn will be available to regulate the food prices should they rise unreasonably, and I am happy to inform you that the first shipments will arrive shortly. I am having Routh coordinate the deliveries, and I'm certain he will be contacting you soon. Do you have any questions for me at this point?"

"No," Trevelyan answered, "but our work has just begun. I will review these papers and be in touch with you." He stood up, reached across the desk, and shook hands with Peel. "Good day, sir."

"Good day," Peel replied.

As Trevelyan walked back to his office, he thought about the Irish Relief Plan and how he could amend it. He was a man constantly searching for better ideas and, secretly, he always thought his were the best. Ultimately, he would end up being the main figurehead of Irish Relief due in part to his strong personality. As head of the British Treasury, he became more and more involved until he was *the* person in charge of the entire scheme. Eventually, no one could make a move without his input or approval. Although he was passionate about justice, he unfortunately was not the right person to head famine relief. Cleverness, sharpness, high achievement, and an unmatched devotion oozed from his pores, but he was also cold and callous. The one trait he lacked and needed most to perform this job appropriately was compassion. He was one of many that did not like the Irish in general and looked down upon their poverty and ignorance. Not having time for their complaints and woes, he scoffed at their situation with a wave of his hand and concentrated instead on what he thought was right for Ireland in general. If thousands must die, then so be it, as long as in the end the country ran smoothly and correctly.

"Da!" Brenton came running up with frosted breath. "Mam says bist come home right nar. We need to leave fer mass right away."

"Och, women!" Joseph said, down on his hands and knees, searching for edible portions of potato on his allotment. "There's plenty of time. One thing you need to know 'bout women, Brenton, is they like to nag their husbands. A hundred years from nar, thar will be some poor sod sittin' in his char tryin' to relax and his wife'll come up from behind and start to nag him. And she'll nag him and nag him down to a nub!"

He smiled at his son, who smiled back at him. Joseph stood up with his hands on his hips and announced, "Well, I can't find any more good pieces."

"After mass, we kin come back and I'll help you look," Brenton offered.

Joseph put his arm around his son, and they began to walk back to the hut.

"You're a fine son, ould chap."

The family walked to the local chapel and sat in a pew close to the front. The white-robed priest came out and lifted both palms up for everyone to stand. They sang a hymn and sat down. The priest stood before the pulpit and talked about the terrible blight that had come across the fields. He spoke of prayer and compassion for our brothers who could use some food in this time of need. Kathryn looked about the throng and saw a very respectable family sitting upright in their private pew. They came every Sunday, and their clothes were always impeccable and their demeanor very refined. Their status never changed. She looked about at other people she knew and saw a family that had lost all their food to the disease and their clothes were unclean and torn in several places. Their hands were stained black, obviously from searching their allotment over and over for any edible scrap of potato. The faces of the people were filled with concern and worry, and more than once the mother had to carry her baby outside due to the continuous crying. Kathryn looked back to the priest and the Jesus statue at the front of the parish. *God will help us,* she thought. *He will not forget about the people of Sligo.*

Due to all the Irish Relief planning, the British government believed that Peel had unnecessarily made arrangements that were much too costly. There had never been such preparations, and Peel was once again ridiculed. He explained that every part was indeed necessary and that he imposed an important condition—relief was to be given only to those which were directly affected by the blight. No assistance was to be granted to those individuals who were simply searching for a handout.

Routh moved his family to Dublin to be the eyes and ears of the entire famine, relating accurate and greatly needed information back to Peel and Trevelyan. He had set up his office in downtown Dublin, not far from his rented home, and went back regularly to have lunch with his wife or work from his home. As Routh moved in January, he began to see that to make a distinction between the average destitute and the destitute because of the potato blight was impossible. Many of the Irish were constantly in a state of distress, living merely from day to day. It was estimated that 2,385,000 people were suffering from lack of food on a daily basis, with or without a famine. At once, Routh knew that his job was going to be complicated, and in the end, all reasonable endeavors were a struggle to carry out. His reports and letters began to come in to Peel's office regularly.

The Board of Works does not look promising as the land around the poorest areas is not suitable for building. It consists of fallow swampland, and the only possible roads left to build are those for the landowner himself. Town meetings are called to discuss the road making with rooms packed so tight one can barely move. The shouting and fist slamming is proving to be unproductive and nothing is readily established.

As history has revealed during previous famines, the landowners did not come to the aid of the destitute, and it seems to be the same with this coming crisis. In truth, some are in a bind financially having spent so much on huge mansions, social gatherings, horses, hounds, and borrowing that they do not have the finances to hire their tenants and pay them. This, of course, is not true for the majority. Nevertheless, the landowners have sent a statement stating: "Under their present difficulties and in the apprehension of those which may come on them in the spring, they neither

*can advance funds now, nor can they offer any sufficient
security for the payment by instalments hereafter."*

*Any suggestions on how to respond will be appreciated. For
now, I will stay the course and continue to head Irish Relief
from my position.*

The first ships carrying Indian corn from the United States
arrived in Cork Harbour, and the secret was so well kept that
two weeks passed before the cargo was even discovered. Routh
soon found out that he could not treat the corn like other local
grains. Consulting with grain merchants, he devised an elaborate
plan for the imported corn. The grain was prone to sweating,
so the cargo had to be unloaded as soon as possible. Then, to
prevent overheating, it needed to be dried for eight hours in
kilns. During the drying time, it would have to be turned two
times to defend against parching, then cooled for seventy hours,
dressed, and cooled once more for twenty-four hours. Finally the
corn could be poured into sacks and distributed to the local mills
for grinding. Routh also discovered that the corn was very hard,
sometimes called "flint corn," and local mills were not set up for
grinding such tough grain. He ultimately decided the corn should
be ground twice to develop a suitable consistency for eating.
Trevelyan thought this last measure was quite excessive and he
wrote to Routh:

*"I cannot believe it will be necessary to grind the Indian
corn twice ... dependence on charity is not to be made an
agreeable mode of life."*

Even with these plans in progress, the end result was very
slow due to the grinding process. Ireland hardly had any mills,
and Routh calculated that even though he would have 350,000
bushels by the middle of May, only 30,000 would be ground
and ready for delivery. Trevelyan wrote to Barings to reduce the

amount on the cargoes at this present time and in the future to please send already ground cornmeal if possible. This never happened, and milling the corn was consistently troublesome.

Routh's personal secretary was William O'Riley, and he called him to his desk and asked about the status of setting up the two main depots in Cork and Limerick.

"In the next few weeks, there will be a senior Commissariat officer at each depot," O'Riley answered. "Will the food be arriving shortly?"

"My instructions are to fill them with food, although I cannot purchase any that will interfere with private enterprise. All I have is the Indian corn that will be arriving. Trevelyan has sent a list of food in various government storage facilities." Routh shuffled papers on his desk until he found a letter. "He says here to use bits of biscuit and oatmeal that have been in military facilities since 1843, but personally I found it was not fit for human consumption."

"I'm sorry, sir," O'Riley said.

All at once the two men heard a loud crash in the next room. A skinny white-haired man with bulging eyes stuck his head into their room, smiled sheepishly, and said in a thick cockney accent, "I'm sorry, I reckon some of them things are too heavy for me."

Routh scratched his forehead and said loudly, "Are you alright, Stuffy?"

"Yup I am, sir!" Stuffy yelled from the other room.

Routh went back to his paperwork.

"Now, as to exactly when we should be expecting the Indian corn, I cannot say," Routh said. "Ground corn from Cork is to be shipped to the west coast by sea, although due to the weather, that coastal region is extremely dangerous. We're using admiralty steamers, but Ireland only has two very slow ones. I managed to have two more sent, but as soon as I saw them, I knew they were completely unseaworthy. One of them only moves at four miles an hour."

"Aye, sir," O'Riley said. "Ireland's harbors are very unpredictable, and we haven't had much luck with ships. A perfectly clear day can unpredictably turn into a treacherous one in a matter of hours. I once had an uncle that had a friend who went fishing …" O'Riley stopped when he saw the annoyance on Routh's face at hearing a long drawn-out story. "Is there anything else I may do for you, sir?"

Another bang from the other room was heard, and both men looked in that direction. Miles Stuffy came out with a box of photos and walked up to Routh.

"Should I place these around the office, sir, like in our London office?" he asked.

"Yes, Stuffy, that will be fine," Routh answered.

Stuffy began dusting and placing the photos on desks and cabinets all around the office, all the while whistling a pub song tune.

Routh looked at O'Riley who clearly regarded Stuffy with displeasure.

"I know you dislike him somewhat, but he's a son of a deceased comrade," Routh explained, "and he's been with me for so many years."

"I'm sure you have your reasons for bringing him, sir," O'Riley said through pursed lips. "Now, will that be all?"

"Just these papers here," Routh said, handing him a pile. "File them according to date please."

"Very well, sir." O'Riley collected the letters, walked to the filing cabinet, and began filing. The first letter he picked up was from Trevelyan, and he glanced at the ending. It was about the unseaworthy ports of Ireland and it read in part:

> *"It is annoying that all these harbours are so insignificant. It shows Providence never intended Ireland to be a great nation."* *

"I've seen happier faces at a funeral!" Kiernan yelled from afar as he came upon Joseph in the cold winter air.

"Ahh, Kiernan," Joseph sighed, still digging for any remaining potatoes in his allotment of land. "I thought I might find one we could still eat since Kathryn's gittin' down to the last good ones."

"No worries," Kiernan replied, "me sources tould me the government is sendin' work ar way and we, ould chap, will be first in line. Either way, His Lordship will always keep us fine. Well nar thin, since that's settled har 'bout some celebratin'?"

"Celebratin'!" Joseph wrinkled his brow. "Whatever fer?"

"'Tis me birthday and I happen to have some silver 'ere fer some merrymakin'." He waved the silver coin in front of his face. "Now let's git before the women find us."

Joseph knew what the coin was for and relished the thought of the happy times before the blight when he was not struggling. Kiernan liked being happy and enjoying the little things in life, and his festive personality was addictive. Joseph knew using the coin would be reckless, but he threw his arm around his friend as they marched down the lane.

The two men came upon a tiny white cottage at the top of a small hill. Mud and old rags lined the path to the house and everything looked dirty. Rusted cans and pots were strewn here and there, and a foul smell became stronger and stronger as the men approached the doorway.

Kiernan knocked hard on the door and yelled out, "Gordis! Gordis!"

The door slowly creaked open and there stood a stout woman in her early thirties holding a large jug. Her haggard face looked at least ten years older than her actual years and had dirt embedded in her wrinkles; her mysterious eyes were dark and penetrating, and her scraggly hair had certainly never been washed. Her clothing was ripped and filthy, and she stood shoeless with dried mud and toenails growing every which way about an inch long.

"Eeh?" she said. And when her cracked lips separated and her mouth opened, only seven decaying teeth were visible.

"Ahhh ... Gordis Flynn, you've never looked lovelier." Kiernan bent down to embrace the woman.

"Och, git away from me," the woman sputtered. "I know why you've come—this way." The men followed her across the nearly black room with the putrid smell that was almost unbearable. The floor was drenched with mud, and it squished between the woman's toes as she placed the jug she was carrying on a table. She then hobbled to a small pot sitting atop a peat fire.

"This 'ouse might be a hovel ... fit only fer the reaper, but I only use mountain water, rain, grain, a little potato, and a magic ingredient passed down from me grammy." She poured a bit from the pot into two small glasses, handing one each to the men.

Kiernan and Joseph drank the gulp and smacked their lips. "Poiti!" they yelled with full smiles.

"How much ya got?" Gordis asked.

Kiernan laid his coin onto her open wrinkled hand.

"And this," Joseph broke in, adding his contribution of another coin.

Kiernan smiled at his friend and looked back at the craggy woman. "I love this man," he said.

The woman filled up a small jugful and handed it to Kiernan.

"Mighty obleeged, Gordis," he grinned. The two men left the shack and immediately began to swig from the jug, laughing and joking down the road.

"Ahh," Joseph gulped, "She might be uglier thin a two-headed devil, but she kin make poiti like an angel!"

Kiernan guzzled the drink and said, "Did I ever tell you 'bout the time I was in a tavern and attacked by six men fer walkin' behind one of their women?"

"Aye," Joseph smiled, "'bout a hundred times."

"Well, 'twas late one night," Kiernan continued anyway, "and I had jist begun drinkin' in the pub. Only a lad ... and thar fer the drink, not the women. It didn't take me long to git sauced since I was small, not husky like I am nar." Kiernan puffed out his chest, making them both laugh.

Then he continued, "So I stepped outside and, Lord above, I seen the most beautiful woman walkin' past. She had the face of an angel and the body ... umm ... whew! Her curves were all in the right place is all I kin say, and I was drawn to her like a ... like a ... well ... like a man to the drink!" Both men laughed again.

"Nar I didn't follow her." Kiernan held up both hands. "Me feet was followin' her, but I don't. I tould me feet, 'Don't follow, don't follow,' but they jist don't car. They followed. And thin I ketch a sound of many feet walkin' behind and I knew those shoes are followin' *me*, and all the hars in the back of me neck begin to stand up like a prickly thistle. I jist kep walkin' 'til the noise from thar shoes becomes so loud I can't concentrate on … on … who I was walkin' behind." The men laughed again.

"'Stop, you scoundrel, the woman's ars!' one of 'em shouted to me, so I stopped. I could hear 'em spreadin' out, gettin' ready to pounce, and I seen it all now plain as a pike-start! But I surprised 'em and turned 'round quickly and threw a punch at the first face I seen. Them others were shocked as their mate hit the floor and I stood me ground with me boyish fists in the ar. Another man come at me from the side, and I ducked and swung hard, gittin' him in the jaw. He too fell on the ground, and the others backed away. I had fists of steel, even back thin!" The men laughed again.

"Well, 'twas clear that even six men were no match for ould Kiernan, so them other four picked up thar mates and all of 'um stood arm in arm starin' at me like a bunch a mice trapped by a big cat!" Kiernan clawed the air with a scowling face like a mean feline. He then stopped walking and faced his friend with a serious demeanor and a clearing of his throat.

"'Twas waitin' fer them to come at me agin, but instead they all said together …" he paused to heighten the interest, "'… Leave our mam alone!'" Kiernan and Joseph let the punch line hang in the air, getting the full flavor of the story. After a long, serious moment, the two men burst into uncontrollable laughter.

As the sun began to set, they started to swagger back to their homes in the near distance. Anne and Kathryn heard them singing and laughing and came out of their huts.

Now learned men who use the pen have wrote yer
praises high

That sweet Potcheen from Ireland green, distilled from wheat an rye:
Throw away yer pills, it'll cure all ills of Pagan, Christian, or Jew
Take off yer coat an grease yer throat with the real old mountain dew!

The men sang from the top of their lungs and stopped in front of their wives.

"I know yer mad, Kathryn, but I kin explain everything. 'Twas Kiernan's birthday and I was obleeged. I couldn't let the poor sod down nar, could I?" Joseph swayed.

"'Tis not his birthday," Anne piped.

"No?" Joseph staggered and looked at Kiernan.

"Ugh, no." Kiernan shrugged his shoulders, and the two men burst into laughter again. Anne grabbed a hold of her husband and led him away.

Kathryn began, "Who'd you go see, Gordis Flynn, didn't you?"

"Well ..." Joseph muttered.

"I'm not goin' to lecture you," she continued, "but money can't be wasted on such trivial things nar. We all need food here, not poiti. Whin the children go to bed cryin' with the hunger, you jist remember this day," and she walked inside the hut.

Joseph followed sheepishly and sat down clumsily at the table next to Brenton. The family began to eat in silence until Joseph said, "Hic!"

Brenton began to giggle, but a piercing look from Kathryn halted his amusement.

The following morning, Kathryn walked outside to fetch some water and overheard three women gossiping. They were from the village and she knew them well, so she walked over with a forced smile.

"Kathryn, have you heard?" one of them asked.

"No, what news is thar this mornin'?" she replied.

"On this December day, a child of two years was found dead at the beach. The poor lass, God bless her, had lived fer several days on seaweed alone. This makes three deaths in Sligo alone from this 'ere blight," she explained.

Kathryn was stunned. "I'm very sorry to hear such horrible news." She excused herself and went into her hut and sat down. She looked at the mounds of blankets still sleeping and said a silent prayer under her breath.

February arrived and Routh began to feel the squeeze of his administration. The class system robbed the local Irishman of a proper education, so it was difficult to find adequate help to add to his organization. He needed more assistance with the distribution and setup of the depots and began inquiring at the Irish Poor Law offices. Surprisingly, the officials refused to administer any help whatsoever, explaining that technically, under the Irish Poor Law Act, no relief may be given to any persons outside the workhouse. The term was called Outdoor Relief, and that, the officials said, was illegal. The commissioner determined that no Irish Poor Law official may participate in Routh's Relief Plan because it was administered outside, and that was interpreted as Outdoor Relief.

The temples on Routh's head began to tighten with frustration as he wrote to Trevelyan.

I have found that Irish officials will not help, even when it comes to their own countrymen. I had expected that one organization would work with another, dealing with supplies and supervising accounts, but no participation is available. My Commissariat department is forced to handle the entire Relief Plan, and at the moment it is progressing very slowly. Several raging storms have pounded the harbours, and in February, cargoes were held up for a month.

We are driven into a corner for assistance. March is fast approaching and hardly any of the depots are established. I fear May is going to arrive without much difference. I am continually receiving news of the most horrifying nature, such as Killarty, a small village next to Limerick, that has announced total devastation and that the people are dying. Because of this news, a private charitable fund has sent £15. I have also received distress reports from Baltimore, Crookhaven, Skull, Bantry, and Castletown Berehaven, and estimated that £50,000 in rents has been accumulated during the past year from the landowners in that district. I am going to send an officer to speak with the landowners themselves to settle this matter.

The landowners and even the Irish themselves refused to believe there was such an enormous crisis at hand. This time of year was always lean, they thought, and the landowners refused to hire any needy person or contribute any money. Trevelyan received only one subscription for Irish Relief for the entire County Clare and knew he needed to send a clear message to all the landowners. Forcing them to send in money was the only way to give assistance to the needy. The money would go directly toward Irish Relief and to help Ireland be a self-sufficient country once again. He sent a letter to the local Relief committees stating that they were to report any landlord who refused to subscribe, and that the list would be sent to the lord-lieutenant for evaluation. The Relief committees felt intimidated and were reluctant to reveal any names, so nothing was solved. It was the first sign that the committees were not qualified, and the first meeting was held at Kilkee in County Clare to make sure all members were working appropriately.

At the appointed time of 2:00 in the afternoon, only a few members were in attendance standing about and talking.

"Last night, me an' Ian went to the pub an' stayed thar so late I can't remember har I git home," one member said.

"An' I'll bet you'll do the same tonight," said another.

"Well ..." said the first member, grinning.

"'Tis the first decent day in weeks," said another. "I bist play some two up after this meetin'."

"Kin I join you?"

"Aye."

Another member just entering said, "Wait till you hear whit happen to me yesterday."

"You got caught with Molly McAtee again."

The members laughed.

"Och, no! 'Twas out huntin' an' a rabbit suddenly came into me sights an'—'bang'—I shot it into the ar an' thar was nothin' left. I had me gun filled with buckshot instead o' birdshot!"

The other members laughed again. "Only you would do somethin' like that!"

"Shaun, kin you bring that teapot over 'ere?"

Their dress was slovenly and their manner uncouth. Throughout the meeting, stragglers casually strolled in and some of them fell asleep.

The Relief committee officer was powerless as he banged the table, "Men, this is an atrocity! Do you understand that we are here to do a job? We need to band together and convince the landowners to subscribe here or at least report the ones that refuse."

His attempts to arouse the minds of the members were futile. Unfortunately, they were the only semi-educated people to choose from and they knew it. The government had instructed the officers to hire educated, professional people, but in poverty-stricken and remote areas it was practically impossible. The government was to contribute one-third to one-half of local money that was raised, so with lazy committee members, hardly any money was raised and the government's contribution was thus meager or nonexistent. Landowners were not going to donate funds to the low-class, uneducated Relief member, so some took it upon themselves to help their tenants directly. Other bankrupt landowners avoided subscription due to being laughed at, and absentee landowners denied all responsibility to the land, explaining that the middleman was now liable.

On an early spring morning of 1846, Joseph and Kathryn heard a faraway commotion of galloping horses and yelling. Joseph ran outside the hut and after a few minutes peeked his head back inside.

"Stay here," he said to his family then disappeared.

For a moment, Kathryn looked squarely at Brenton, then out her window in the direction of the noise. When she saw the horse-mounted police, she knew what was about to happen and closed the window.

"Stay here," she said to the children and left the hut.

The minute she left, Brenton grabbed a bucket and propped it upside down on the floor. He stood on it and opened the window, able to see many horses in the distance and his father and mother running toward them.

"What yer doin' is a sin!" Brogan yelled.

"'Tis not," Brenton huffed.

"Thin I wanna see!" Brogan yanked at his pantleg.

"No, you're too young," Brenton told her.

"I wanna see too!" Shay pleaded, looking up at her brother.

"No, girls shouldn't see things like this," he said.

"Mam is goin' to see," Shay whispered to Brogan.

"Aye, but she's also seen yer bum, which is scarier!" Brenton replied.

The girls huffed but had no other choice except to sit back down.

Kathryn snatched her skirts and ran as fast as she could to the neighboring well-kept village of about fifty homes. The huts were the property of Lord Pinkerton, an absentee landowner who had never visited his land. Kathryn knew a few women from this village, and they were no better off than anyone else. Some had lost all their potatoes and some lost only a portion, but none of them felt safe and content in their homes. Kathryn could hear nothing now but the breathing of her own body as she ran toward the village. The cold air iced her breath when she exhaled, and she felt with each step as she got closer, that her heart was actually racing away from it. She really didn't want to view this event but forced herself to see it to remind herself what could happen to her family.

She met up with Joseph and a few others just outside the rural community and watched the scene unfold. Several dozen uniformed infantrymen sat atop huffing horses as they rode into the center of the village accompanied by several sheriff and police. The intimidation of the brash scene sent all the people scurrying about in all directions. The panic of the adults made the children fearful, and most of them began crying, calling for their mothers and not knowing which way to go. The residents scurried in all directions like a bunch of ants as their homes were being invaded.

"Please!" shouted an infantryman. "There is no need for this; there is nothing you can do!"

The scramble of the people persisted until every last resident was safeguarded inside their homes.

"We are the 49th Infantry," the captain shouted out, "and although I am quite aware that you are all current on your rents, I have been instructed to evict all of you, and it is best that you vacate the homes now."

No one appeared.

He shouted again, "Lord Pinkerton has given you prior notice that this was going to occur, so I plead with you again to sagaciously come out with self-respect and honor."

No one appeared.

"His Lordship has instructed that all of his homes be demolished, and if you do not leave, then you will most likely be in harm's way."

Still no one appeared. The captain motioned to two of his infantrymen and suddenly a door flew open.

"Stop! Stop!" a skeleton of an old man shuffled out into the middle of the village, clutching a dented cup. His hands were raised in submission, and he wore only a weathered loincloth for clothing. He had dirt and mud caked on his hands and bare feet, and his hair was standing on end on one side of his head. He was visibly weak, and his mouth hung open revealing no teeth. One of the infantrymen was disturbed by the sight of the old man, so he looked up toward the sky, not wanting to view this embarrassing spectacle. He looked down again and into the eyes of his friend who forced a grin and winked. It must be done.

"One last chance," the captain shouted out, but still no one else appeared. He motioned again to his infantry, and the men began lighting the thatch roofs on fire, chopping down front doors with axes, and demolishing walls. At once there were people everywhere running again, this time with chairs and baskets filled with clothing, grabbing anything they could manage. Frightened children ran about in circles, screaming, not understanding what was happening. One woman slapped an infantryman who apologized and said he was just doing his job. Another woman clung for dear life to a doorpost while being pried off as she wailed. A man was yelling and cursing at the soldiers and had to be forcibly wrenched away so his house could be destroyed. The poor man lost all his strength and let his arms dangle freely at his sides, so the soldiers released their grips and left him sitting on the ground. He watched his house fall before his eyes and onto all his belongings inside his home. He wept openly as he hung his head. Another man was seriously injured when he rushed an infantryman on his horse. The horse reared up and kicked the man in the head, leaving him bleeding on the ground. It was complete chaos and destruction. One by one, the homes were torn down, and the captain on his powerful horse galloped about and told the people to move out, that they were now trespassing on private property.

"Whar do we go nar?" one woman asked.

"That is not my problem," the captain replied and rode off. The homeless people, mentally crippled and grief-stricken, gathered the few belongings they had and pitifully walked down the road in a mournful heap. There was nothing they could do now, and it was plain that they were powerless. They were the pawns that could be cast aside at any moment without so much as an afterthought. They were the disposable piece of trash that was tossed away with unaffected aplomb. They were the offensive belch of the landowner after a scrumptious twelve-course meal that lingered in the air and reluctantly rose upward with the slightest breeze.

But alas, that piece of trash can begin to smell for miles around, and that meal can turn gravely sour in the stomach. Round and round all that rich food can churn, making the stomach incurably nauseated and completely repulsed until the mutiny is put forth and the meal rises up with conviction. Oh, it might not happen for a while, and there may only be a small stain on the landowner's shirt, but the small victories here and there were all the poor would ever have. The landowner himself had put an irreversible mark on his soul and would have to answer to a higher power in the end.

But now these evicted Irish were without any shelter and without rights or authority. And many, many more were to follow in their footsteps down the path of homelessness. Kathryn watched her neighbors slumbering down the road and knew they were leaving with nothing into nowhere. What would become of them no one knew. Sadly, everyone was so concerned with their own plight that there was only enough room to worry about themselves.

The news of the evictions stirred up all kinds of emotions, and it was even brought up in a House of Lords meeting. The sentiments of a Lord Brougham seemed to sum up the feelings of the upper class concerning one eviction, which was quoted at the time:

> "Undoubtedly it was the landlord's right to do as he
> pleased, and if he abstained he conferred a favour and
> was doing an act of kindness. If on the other hand he
> chose to stand on his right, the tenants must be taught
> by the strong arm of the law that they had no power
> to oppose or resist ... property would be valueless
> and capital would no longer be invested in cultivation
> of land if it were not acknowledged that it was the
> landlord's undoubted, indefeasible and most sacred right
> to deal with his property as he list." *

News spread daily of more evictions, but the people began to hear about the establishment of the Relief Commission and that food was being imported into Ireland. The mood settled, and the general feeling was that free food was going to be distributed throughout the country.

Routh wrote a letter to Trevelyan.

> *The workers at government facilities are now eating the Indian cornmeal, but the people hate it. "Never was anything so calumniated as our cornmeal."* * *Trying to wean the people off the potato diet and introducing a new food is almost painful for them. In Limerick, the inmates complained and almost refused to eat, and it caused riots in workhouses. I have learned that part of the problem was that in 1831 a small portion of meal was brought in as an experiment during a famine that year, but it was dampened by the miller for weight increase and grew rancid and unfit for eating. The people who were starving ate it and became very sick, so word spread that cornmeal was harmful. But the people now are consuming the corn, albeit against their will, and most importantly we are accomplishing our goal of keeping people alive.*

As time passed and the poor were forced to eat the corn, it slowly became accepted, and soon Trevelyan became curious and ate some. He even experimented with recipes, preparing the meal in porridge and cakes and produced an inexpensive booklet to be sold.

Meanwhile, Routh kept working and shuffling through all the problems in Cork as more and more reports of destitution came in. He left his apartment one afternoon and ambled through the town, finding enjoyment in taking a long walk. The beauty of the buildings and pleasant atmosphere lifted his spirit and cleared his head. Due to the respectable character of the townspeople strolling about nodding and greeting one another, there was peace and tranquility and no sign that in some remote villages others were dying of starvation at that very moment. On he walked until he came upon an outdoor market where the Relief committee of the Gentlemen of Cork was selling the cornmeal. Routh noticed that a huge crowd was gathering and purchasing as much as possible, and then he saw the sign. It read that the meal was selling at 1*d.* a pound for this day only, and the crowd grew larger and larger, purchasing and purchasing. Hands flailed in the air, waving money, people pushing and shoving to get to the front; it became a frenzied scene, and Routh wondered where all these needy people came from. A moment ago, they were nowhere in sight. Fists flew and a fight broke out between two men, and Routh made his way into the Relief booth. He found the Commissariat officer in charge and asked him why he was selling the meal and at that low price.

"It was just an experiment, sir, to see if they liked it," he choked. "I had no right to do this and I'm truly sorry. We have now depleted our resources." He stared at him.

"You mean there is no meal left?" Routh shouted.

"Aye," the officer answered.

Routh climbed upon the front table and tried to calm the disorderly mob.

"I am sorry to report that all the meal has been purchased for today," he bellowed out.

"Whin kin we 'spect more?" someone yelled.

Routh did not have an answer.

"So we're jist to starve thin nar?" someone else said.

"We demand more, by God, or your lives might not be sparred!" said another.

The mob jeered, "Yaa!" and raised their fists.

"Well I believe another shipment will arrive tomorrow, but the price will not be 1*d*. per pound. I am very sorry, but that is all I can offer," Routh concluded.

"Raisin' prices ain't the answer!" someone yelled.

"Aye! Why you be raisin' the prices? We jist want food to feed ar families."

"You ar most unmerciful!"

"You don't car!"

"Har do you sleep at night, rationin' the food and raisin' the prices!"

"Ar very lives ar at stake 'ere! Do you not understand?"

"Yes," Routh solemnly said, "I understand your situations, and I am trying to help you the best that I can. The price of the meal is not my decision—I am merely the man taking orders from the government. Please know there are thousands of you that we are trying to help."

"Ahhh!" a mobster cried out, but accepted the terms and turned to leave. The crowd stood silent for a few minutes before reluctantly dismantling, and Routh climbed down, taking a deep breath.

"You are never to sell meal at such a low price. Do not ever let this happen again," he told the Commissariat officer.

"Aye, sir," he nodded.

"You were not scheduled to receive any more meal, but I will get you some for tomorrow only," Routh said to him. "The depots will not officially open until May, do you understand? Good day." With that, he left.

On the way home, he stopped by the Commissariat storage facility and made preparations for tomorrow's delivery but none after that. Routh informed Trevelyan that the need and want for the cornmeal exceeded his expectations and described to him the scenes that were taking place. Trevelyan wrote back:

"We must hold out with a little firmness in spite of the wretchedness and bad character of the people." *

The truth was that there was no edible scrap of potato to be eaten, and the cornmeal was the only cheap food available. Some ate turnips and even weeds to stay alive, but it was estimated that four million people needed to be fed on £100,000 worth of cornmeal. The blight of 1845 devoured £3,500,000 of potatoes, and it was obvious the numbers did not add up.

Peel felt that more must be done to ward off catastrophe, and in April, he stood up at a House of Commons meeting and stated, "I have received many notices pleading 'that for God's sake the government should send out to America for more Indian corn.' Although, 'if it were known that we undertook the task of supplying the Irish with food, we should to a great extent lose the support of the Irish gentry, the Irish clergy, and the Irish farmer. It is quite impossible for the government to support eight million people. It is utterly impossible for us to adopt means of preventing cases of individual misery in the wilds of Galway or Donegal or Mayo. In such localities, the people must look to the local proprietors, resident and non-resident.' * From the outset, we did not specify the corn would be sufficient for all of Ireland, but we thought the regulation of the supply would stave off high prices for native produce."

And the words "native produce" hung in the air like a bad smell. It was plain that as the poor were starving, still the most important matter was the price of native produce that was leaving the shores of Ireland daily. It was questioned why a ship sailing into an Irish port with grain passed six other ships sailing out, and why in the name of God a country on the crest of a severe famine would allow oats, wheat, pigs, cattle, butter, and eggs to sail on down the river Shannon and out of Ireland forever. And many times, the foodstuffs were accompanied by military escorts for protection. It seemed incomprehensible to some starving individuals, and it felt as if their very lives were sailing past them to be devoured by some fat, rich, unmerciful politician surrounded by a plethora of food. This one topic angered and bewildered the poor more than any other and would not ever be forgotten.

For his own peace of mind, Routh questioned the necessity of exporting Ireland's own resources and received a straightforward reply by Trevelyan:

> *"There is scarcely a woman of the peasant class in the*
> *West of Ireland whose culinary art exceeds the boiling*
> *of a potato. Bread is scarcely ever seen, and an oven is*
> *unknown. The potato deluge during the past twenty years*
> *has swept away all other food from their cottages and sunk*
> *into oblivion their knowledge of cookery."* *

Sadly, this was true. The small Irish farmer grew wheat, barley, and oats and paid his rent with the sale of his goods. He did not dare eat his rent, lest he be evicted from his own house and allotment of land. Rent payment was his first priority. When the blight devoured his potatoes, the poor farmer had to keep selling his small patch of produce so his family would not be homeless and suffer a worse fate. With this in mind, the women never learned to cook with anything but the potato.

Chapter III

Kathryn and her family were noticeably thin as the portions of their meals were cut in half. Joseph, Kiernan, and the other men from their village were working for Lord Somerhaven, but he began to taper off their hours and send them home early. Kathryn knew the little money she had from the sale of Joseph's oats had to last for quite awhile, and she rationed as much as possible. As she thought of this, she finished scrubbing a few bits of laundry in the creek that almost crumbled in her hands. It really was not laundry anymore, rather torn bits of rags that she managed to piece together as she laid them across some small rocks to dry off in the misty air.

Constant gnawing hunger led her hand to grab a few pots and pans from the hut, cradle her sleeping baby into the hammock-like pouch across her belly, and begin the trek into town. She passed a few hunched-over persons digging in the ground trying to find anything edible, and in town more ragamuffins shuffling aimlessly about, trying anything to stop the pangs of hunger. She was now completely out of potatoes and could not even purchase any in the stores. Walking straight to the pawnbroker, she laid her three pots on the counter. The stoic-faced broker looked them over and replaced the pots with a few coins. Kathryn bid him good day and made her way to the store to purchase some more oatmeal. She had already pawned a chair, some blankets, and one of her beloved books without telling Joseph because she did not want him to feel any worse.

The following afternoon, she was teaching the children at her hedge school, and they all seemed to be tired and lethargic. They were thinner and dirtier, and some of them were lying on the ground instead of sitting up.

"Do you not wish to have school today?" she asked them all.

"Oh no, we like the larnin'," one answered.

"We're jist so tired," sighed another.

"Kin you jist larn us a story while we listen?" asked another.

"Well nar thin, this is a first," Kathryn said, "but alright." She could see that they didn't even want to speak because that took energy. She herself was very tired and wanted to really crawl back into bed and take a nap, but instead she opened up her only book and began to point out places on a map that was inside.

"Ireland's a wee place if you look at other countries," she began. "Thar're many other next to it like England and Scotland and across them patch of water called the English Channel. Thar's France, Germany ... and down 'ere are warmer countries like Italy and Greece." She looked at their faces, and they simply sat motionless. She continued, "The other way from Ireland across this big area of water's called the Atlantic Ocean, thin Canada and Ameriky."

"I've heard 'bout Ameriky," said one boy.

"Have you?" Kathryn asked. "And jist whit do you know 'bout it?"

"I can't 'member," he said sheepishly.

"Well I know a wee bit," Kathryn said. "'Tis very big, this 'ere area's one big country and 'tis warm with lots of land fer growin' food." The children began to sit up. "I've even heard thar government will jist give you free land fer movin' thar whar you kin build yer own house and raise yer own crops."

"Whin kin we go thar?" Brenton asked.

"I wanna go thar too!" echoed Shay.

"You mist pay a far to git on a boat that'll take you cross," Kathryn said, "but don't you love Ireland?"

"I'm so hungry," said Shay, "I jist wanna have some food."

"I knowed this har disease that's ruined our potatoes is quare and very bad," Kathryn said, "but next year'll be better nar. We'll have our crops back and lots of food to eat. We jist have to make it through this year together. I know 'tis hard, but we mist have faith."

One thin little girl who had been lying down sat up slowly and piped in, "Why does havin' faith take so long?"

Trevelyan corralled the Board of Works organization under his jurisdiction, stating that it was a subordinate Board to the Treasury and he would from now on supervise and manage all duties. His first action was to consult the Commissariat department under him to complete his orders from England. Once again, Routh headed this department, and once again it was brimming with problems.

"Margaret!" Trevelyan yelled from his office.

In she came. "Yes, sir."

"I would like the letter from Routh that came in this morning," he demanded.

"Yes, sir ... it's right here, sir," she said, handing him an envelope from her desk.

He opened it and began to read. Routh wrote that he was bothered at all the red tape one Board of Works job was to endure as it passed through at least six departments and countless desks. The letter read in part:

> *I agree that the work performed should not benefit one individual, but the community as a whole, and I do not foresee a problem here. The current difficulties are the quantity of applications that are arriving. Every day, more and more applications pile up with people asking*

for work, and as I write, tens of thousands have besieged this office alone. Since the mere act of approving a site is so excruciatingly slow, more applications keep flooding in, and as it is now April, some people are beginning to panic and become violent. The mayor of Limerick visited my office last week to plead for the employment to begin as soon as possible in his city. A riot had taken place a few days prior with starving people demanding work, and they were only subdued by the temporary employment given to them.

The exodus of approximately 60,000 Irishmen that traditionally leave their homes for the English harvest at this time did not occur because of two reasons. They did not want to leave their families in such a needy state, and the promise of employment in Ireland has kept them home. It seems the country is clamoring for work, any type of work, to save their families from eviction and/or from death. I personally feel the Board of Works department has a tremendous responsibility toward Ireland, and I beseech you to accelerate the acceptance of the Board of Works sites.

Trevelyan did not like being pushed or rushed since it usually meant sloppy work and confusion throughout the departments. He thought for a moment about the panic of the people but then quickly put it out of his mind.

I will not lose focus, he thought. *This is a critical time for the country, and I will proceed as planned. The decisions made at this time could affect Ireland for years to come, and hasty ones may even spill over into England.*

"Here is some tea, sir." Margaret brought in a tray with some steaming tea and scones and placed them on an adjacent table.

"Thank you, Margaret." Trevelyan looked up from his papers. "That is just what I need."

She walked out of his office and sat down at her desk amid piles of paperwork.

When the children were in bed one evening, Joseph told Kathryn that Lord Somerhaven took him aside and told him his funds were depleting too rapidly and he needed to steer them toward the public works that was being organized in Sligo. But he told him that if ever the public works did not keep him employed, he could always come back to his home for work. However, this proposal was only for Joseph because he simply could not afford to employ the others as well.

The next day, Joseph set off with Kiernan to the town hall to sign up for the public works, and they met a gathering with hundreds of other men. They stood in a mob, trying to push their way to the front where a Board of Works employee was signing men on.

"What kinda work do you think we'll git?" Kiernan asked his friend.

"I don't know," Joseph replied.

"Maybe diggin' graves fer all us men that'll be dead 'cause we kin find no work!" shouted a man nearby who laughed sarcastically with frustration.

Joseph and Kiernan looked at the starving man with rags for clothes but did not reply. "We mist find work, ole chap," Kiernan gulped.

"I know ... I know ...," was all Joseph could say. They stood for hours until they were finally in front of the man seated at a small table. Joseph was first.

"Name?" the man asked.

"Joseph O'Malley."

"Address?"

"Four Piper Lane."

"Any work you cannot perform?"

"No."

"Any hours you cannot work?"

"No."

"Able to start immediately?"

"Aye."

"Next!"

"Whin kin we 'spect the work?" Joseph quickly asked.

"Come here tomorrow morning at seven with a spade."

"Mighty obleeged, sir, mighty obleeged!" Joseph backed away and out of the crowd. Kiernan answered the same questions and met up with his friend outside the mob. He and Kiernan hugged one another with happiness and sang all the way to their homes.

"I knowed it'd be alright!" Kiernan patted his friend as they walked into Joseph's hut where their wives were talking.

"You git work, Joseph?" Kathryn asked surprised.

"Aye, both to report at seven tomorrow mornin'," he beamed.

The two families rejoiced in the good fortune and thought their troubles were over. The country was sending work to keep them employed, and it was a peaceful feeling.

The next morning found Joseph and Kiernan standing with the same mob as the day before, many of them carrying spades. The Board of Works employee was yelling names out, and when he came to theirs, they shouted "Aye! Aye!" and raised their hands.

He pointed to a clearing where another Board of Works employee was standing, and when they reached him, he gave them instructions to dig a trench for drainage four feet deep and three feet wide for many miles. The men fell in line with the others, digging and shoveling, and as the days and weeks passed, they felt proud of their work and grateful to be employed. The money was barely enough to keep them alive on oatmeal and turnips, but no one complained.

There were a few men that had stumbled into Sligo looking for work, and they were turned away. They had all the men they needed. One skeleton walked slowly past the digging men and spit on the Board of Works employee that was supervising.

"May God have mercy on yer soul," he growled and kept walking down the road.

Soon the Board of Works employee was called upon to another town and no one was supervising the work being done at their site. Some of the men rested upon their spades and talked amongst one another smoking tobacco. This was fine for them until the time came to collect their pay and no Board of Works employee was available to distribute it. A few days went by as the men looked up now and again from their spades until finally the Works employee showed up one day with payment. Everyone received their money, and no one pointed fingers. They were simply content at being employed, and this is how it went for the time being.

Meanwhile, at the beginning of May, Routh calculated that there was not nearly enough Indian corn to open all the depots, but open anyway they did. He instructed his Commissariat officers to open the depots at different times of the day and with different quantities of meal to be sold. Routh wrote to them in part:

> *"I am instructed not to promise any specific supply; the aim of the depots is to maintain an equilibrium of prices, they are not intended to feed the whole population and are not adequate to do so; meal is not sold as the sole or even the principal resource for the period of want ..."* *

The officers were dismayed with this news as their initial belief was that there would be a regular supply arriving at all times, and a simple order form to receive more was all that was needed.

Kathryn had heard of the opening of the depot in Sligo and she wanted to be one of the first to purchase the strange Indian cornmeal. So on opening day, she sat on the wet grass with her basket in front of the depot and waited. A handful of others joined her as they sat around, gossiping about the taste. At once, the door to the depot flung open and the people rushed to the front with money in hand. At 2*d*. a pound, it was definitely the least expensive food available, and Kathryn pushed her way toward the front.

"Five pounds," she told the Commissariat officer when it was her turn, handing him the money. He took her basket and filled it up, and she squeezed out of the crowd, grasping her basket like it was priceless. She walked home and immediately began preparing the meal.

"Ugh!" Brenton grimaced as he looked inside the cooking pot that Kathryn stirred.

"Och, Brenton." She moved him aside. "Everone sit down nar," she said to her family when it was cooked. They took their seats, and Kathryn poured the meal in each bowl. They all stared at the foreign substance with uncertainty, looking at it from different angles as if trying to find a hidden jewel floating somewhere inside. Brogan sat with Nelson, her stuffed dog, on her lap. She lifted him above the bowl and let his nose touch the top of the warm meal. She turned around the tattered animal and smiled at the light brown spot on his snout.

"He likes it," she announced, and the family laughed. One by one, they ate the funny tasting Indian cornmeal that warmed their withering bodies.

With her spoon in her mouth, Shay looked over at the pile of blankets on the floor where she had covered the sleeping pig. She knew her father would kill the pig for food if their situation got any worse and she would do all she could to prevent that from happening. She would save a little bit from her bowl to give to him later.

Overall, the introduction of the Indian cornmeal was not met with smiles, and the women had to be taught the preparation of such a foreign food.

As it would be, the people rushed to buy all of the meal and asked for more. Routh's desk was piled high with letters from Relief committees pleading for more Indian cornmeal. He responded, writing two or three letters daily, specifying that no more meal was available to give. The want was far greater than anyone had anticipated, and as word spread, the depots were besieged.

Trevelyan sat back in his chair, sipping tea and reading all the letters from Routh about the near panic in some places, and he thought it over. Peel bought the Indian cornmeal to maintain homegrown prices, and the public thought it was cheap food for them that was to keep coming. His intentions were for the meal to be placed in the depots, the depots were to sell the food as subsistence only, and then the depots were to close—for good. He did not wish to hear of the screaming and pleading for more meal. Trevelyan took another sip of tea and kept thinking. Routh had also suggested that the depots remain open until the middle of September at least, because the potato crop planted last year would not be edible until that time. Also, most of the Irish planted the large, coarse "horse" potatoes called "lumpers" which could not be harvested until the beginning of August. No, he thought, this was not the plan. The depots were to close as previously mentioned, and he wrote Routh of his decision.

"Sir, this just came in for you," O'Riley said, handing Routh some letters.

He immediately opened the one from Trevelyan and shook his head.

"Sit down," he said to O'Riley. "I wrote to Trevelyan again asking that the depots remain open, or consequences would surely be disastrous. I felt I needed to make one last attempt, but he won't budge. He's not even moved. This time he's ordered them all closed as soon as each depot's supplies are exhausted."

"Ah ha ..." came a voice from Stuffy shelving books in a nearby room.

"I'm sorry, sir," O'Riley said, ignoring the comment.

"He also feels that we sold the corn at too low a price," Routh continued, "and that the timing was bad. This time of year is always fraught with starving Irish, and as the depots were opened, the entire country swarmed to the food as their salvation. He believes these people were most likely not affected by last year's blight, but were simply searching for an easy handout and we gave it to them."

"Oh, right," Stuffy commented, still shelving books.

"Close the door," Routh said.

O'Riley shut the door to the office and said, "What would you like to do now, sir?"

"Well, we'll juggle supplies of the meal to the depots where the people are most destitute and where the prices were raised to lower the demand," Routh said. "It seems the sale of the Indian corn is finally coming to a close."

Kathryn walked, carrying her sleeping baby through the lush green leaves of her allotment with pride. The new stocks looked very promising, and she felt such a relief that finally the hunger pangs her family had to endure this past year were soon going to be over. They could repurchase some of their old furniture back if it was a really good year, but mostly the fear of starvation could be put to rest. Walking back to the hut, she met up with Anne and a few other women from the village.

"Yer crop looks mighty fine, Kathryn," one woman said.

"Aye it does. Well nar thin, what's the news today?" she asked.

"Same ould sad stories. Breda's husband found no work, the poor thing," Anne said.

"That no good, lazy husband of 'ers spent thar money on the drink an' couldn't git up fer work the next day," another piped in. "An' nar thar really hurtin'. An' did you hear 'bout Mr. O'Toole?"

"No, whit happened?" Kathryn asked.

"Died last night from the hunger. He was so old an' weak that he couldn't git out of his hut to find water nor food neither. Me David found him, poor ole sod." The woman looked down.

"That's terrible," Kathryn agreed.

"An' most of the village Tegan planted no seed last year—they had no food but to ate thar own seed potatoes, so they don't have nothin' to harvest come August."

Another one added, "An' I've heard other villages are in the same situation. I don't know whit thar to do nar, maybe find employment on the public works fer the rest of thar lives I guess."

"If they kin rely on that," another added. "But trust in me, we Irish are niver darn fer long. Everythin'll be workin' out fine, God willin'."

"Aye, I agree," the other said. "An' har's the baby?" she asked Kathryn, pulling back the blanket that covered part of the infant's face. "My, she looks thin."

"She's fine, jist a bit tired. Beg yer pardon nar." Kathryn walked toward the hut where Brenton and the girls were sitting on the grass and leaning on the hut, slouching.

"Why do you not play?" she asked them.

"We're too tired," Brenton sighed. "Kin we have somethin' to eat?"

Kathryn felt the pang of parental responsibility and would have cooked up grass if she was without food. "Aye, me darlings, it'll be ready in a moment." And she went inside to cook some parsnips that Lord Somerhaven had given all his tenants. The children rose slowly and followed their mother. In no time, they were eating and joking with one another.

Joseph entered the hut, whistling, moving his head to and fro and then exaggerating the movements when he saw his children watching him. Although their spirits ran high, it was plain to see that their clothes hung loosely on their thin bodies, and at least half of their belongings had been pawned for food.

"Well nar thin, have you seen har good them crops look?" Kathryn asked him, knowing full well of the answer.

"Aye, m'lady ... I have," was all he said and then went back to whistling.

Kathryn went to the baby and tried to breastfeed her, but she would not wake up. Struggling awhile, she tried to rouse her from a deep sleep to give her some much needed nourishment, but it was obvious the baby was too tired. Kathryn laid her down again, swaddling her in weathered blankets, stroking the baby's smooth forehead, and gazing down upon God's perfect creation.

She whispered a silent prayer in Gaelic and then spoke softly, "August cannot come soon enough, me wee one; everythin' will be fine thin. You jist rist ... a few more weeks and it'll all be over."

Then she began to quietly sing. One by one, the other children gathered around, and Kathryn sang a little louder so they all could hear. It felt like the ending of an era and that soon bountiful times would return.

On July 8, 1846, a boatload of Indian corn was refused and sent back to Mr. Theodore Baring. Trevelyan wrote that the cargo was not wanted and for the crew of the ship to dispose of it as they see fit. Mr. Baring wrote back his sincere congratulations of the success and termination of the Relief Plan. Peel's term as prime minister was over, and his successor was Lord John Russell, a Whig with views similar to Trevelyan's. His stance on Ireland was apathetic and, like Trevelyan, he strongly believed in laissez faire.

With a new prime minister, Trevelyan wanted to be rid of the Indian corn and Relief Scheme, and Russell was more than happy to back him.

Routh wrote to Trevelyan:

Last month was very tough on the poor with the depots still closing one by one, and the Board of Works is still having major difficulties. Of some concern is the news of the early crops. It has been reported that a few incidences of the potato blight has reappeared, and this time a little earlier than last year. Although this is not evidence that the blight will again destroy some or all of the crops in Ireland, and it is much too early for such a dire prognosis. The main crops of the Irish people still look well and promising, and the mood of the poor is very optimistic, as is their nature.

Trevelyan considered the facts given to him by Routh. If there were to be another famine as in the previous year, the Irish people would undoubtedly look to the government for food. He did not believe the government should subsidize in any way and certainly not distribute free food. The Board of Works of last year was a complete disaster, and it was time for Irish Relief to come to an end. Laissez faire was the correct response for any situation that might occur. If the people's crop was abundant, good; if the people's crop was disintegrated by the blight, so be it. He wrote to Routh:

> *"The only way to prevent the people from becoming habitually dependent of government is to bring the operations to a close. The uncertainty about the new crop only makes it more necessary. Whatever may be done hereafter, these things should be stopped now, or you run the risk of paralyzing all private enterprise and having this country on you for an indefinite number of years."* *

Routh did not share the same feelings as Trevelyan. He did not wish to end the Relief Scheme and he looked around his home office for an answer on the wall. He felt confined with a need for some fresh air, so he walked out into his garden where his beloved son (currently visiting during the summer months) and a friend were practicing cricket. Routh was proud of all his children, although there was a unique connection between himself and Thomas. The boy seemed to need him more and ask for more life direction than the others, and as any father, he tried his best to provide the parenting he required. He was a smart, well-mannered boy of nine whose biggest fault was remembering not to look down upon the poor. He excelled in all sports, and his future looked bright with the backing of his father's name.

"Hello, Father," he said when he spotted Routh coming toward him, "would you like to play?"

"No, not today," he replied. "I've just come out for a bit of air. You two go ahead." He motioned a finger toward them.

Thomas readied the bat and focused on his friend with the ball in his hand. His friend clumsily threw the ball, and Thomas didn't even swing.

"No, no, boy," Routh said to the friend, "you have to concentrate." He knelt down on one knee and called the two boys over to him. "Whenever you do something in life, you need to clear your head of any distractions and focus. Center your mind and body so they are strong and will work together to accomplish the feat. Now … are we ready?" The boys nodded their heads. "Now let's play."

They walked over to their spots. Thomas creased his wavy dark brown hair with his hand and steadied his feet. He positioned the bat, turned his head, and waited.

"Lift your head high," Routh yelled to the friend as he reached his spot. "Now imagine where you want the ball to go … take a deep breath … and bowl it when you're ready."

The friend waited a moment, concentrating on the spot he had in mind, and then bowled the ball. Although it was a little off, Thomas swung—"clack"—and the ball went rolling past his friend.

Routh clapped, "Ahh! Good! Good! Now just keep practicing, and you boys will be on a winning team in no time."

"Thank you, Father," Thomas beamed.

"Yes, thank you, Mr. Routh." The friend raised his ball in appreciation.

The boys continued their practicing, and Routh walked into the house for a cup of tea. He watched the boys from the huge window in the parlor overlooking the garden and was thankful that they would never go hungry. Thomas would be returning to Eton soon, and he would miss him dearly. In fact, he missed England and his own home and was looking forward to returning when Ireland was in order again.

"Here is your tea, sir." One of the servants held out a tray. "Shall I take it into your study?"

"Please, thank you," Routh said, and he went into his home office and sat down upon his worn leather chair. His many years of military training and respect for Trevelyan overrode any personal feelings he had about the mission. He made himself believe that what he was doing was the correct thing for Ireland and its poor. He dipped his pen in the inkwell and began to write out his orders to his senior officers to close all the depots.

> *"The apprehensions for the new crop make it all the more*
> *necessary that we should close our present labours on*
> *August 15 so as to allow the government time to make*
> *up their opinion as to the future. If we were to remain*
> *at our stations and depots until the end of September*
> *when the fate of the late crop will be determined, it might*
> *be difficult to relieve us, and the authorities might be*
> *forced to continue with the same measures without a fair*
> *opportunity of consideration."* *

Trevelyan was also writing to close all the Public Works on the same date, and he received a letter back from the offices explaining that three weeks' notice was clearly not enough time to wrap up loose ends. Numerous roads were indeed dangerous to the people and simply could not be left unfinished. Trevelyan gave his consent to continue on the unsafe roads and began to prepare for the blight to attack the potato again. He received daily news on the new crops, and it did not look promising. He quickly submitted his plans to officials in Ireland concerning the Relief Scheme for the coming year, and it was read with utter disheartenment. He wanted absolutely no interference by government assistance except for some Public Works on a small scale. Private enterprise would lead the way with positively no food being imported and sold at the depots.

Alas, before the officials could respond, a heavy blow struck Ireland unlike any other. Hard rain and thunderstorms ravaged the country at the end of July and completely wiped out all the crops from the same blight as the previous year. It had struck this time with such a vengeance that it seemed Ireland's entire harvest was lost. In a rare instance, Routh wrote a candid, somber letter to Trevelyan.

Last week whilst visiting Meath, I traveled at least thirty-two miles, and looking out of the coach as far as the eyes could see, I gazed upon acres and acres of magnificent lush crops at every turn. My heart raced with pleasure and exultation as a feeling of well-being settled my soul. The Irish poor have had a dreadful year filled with intolerable and ghastly sufferings, and now they had worked hard and their fields looked very promising. It looked as if God had smiled upon their crops as the little potato stocks waved to me in the gentle breeze. But alas, the very next morning, I looked out into my garden at the brutal pounding that would change everything. God's smile had indeed turned into a frown and then an angry snarl as the clouds rushed to cover Ireland in its black blanket and plummet it with enormous rain. It came down as if God himself was tossing a bucket of harsh water over the side of heaven, and it has remained as such even as I write this letter with lightning and flooding in many areas.

I wanted to see what the rain had done to the crops, so one week after the rains began, I took a coach to view all the fields, and it was exactly as I had feared. The unrelenting storm swirled in the sky and with terrible fists beat all the green stocks into merciful submission. They were left black and covered with the blight, rotting with an unmistakable, terrible stench. It has been confirmed that from Galway to Dublin and from Causeway to Cape Clear, all of Ireland's crops have been devoured by the blight. It seems to have happened overnight and has changed the face of the entire country. I am saddened and dismayed at all that has been lost and the work that will now be before us. My heart is weeping that I must inform you the report of this year's potato crop is total annihilation.

"Kathryn! Kathryn!" Joseph screamed over the bursts of lightning in the sky from the storm. In the low evening light, he spotted her in their crops, kneeling and stooping in the filthy mud as terrific rain fell hard, drenching her completely. She was digging up their potatoes with her bare hands, trying to find one that was not rotting with the blight. Joseph was still trying to make his way over to her, attempting to walk in the sucking mud that grabbed his foot with each step.

"Kathryn!" He finally reached his hysterical wife and tried to reason with her, saying into her mud-spattered face, "Won't you come home, thar's nothin' more to do 'ere!"

"Thar mist be one potato that's good …" She pulled away, ignoring him, and kept digging and searching. "I mist find at least one in this quare horrible mess!" She flipped a rotting spud over her shoulder and splattered Joseph with mud.

"Listen to me, Kathryn! Listen to me!" he persisted grabbing her shoulders. "I don't know har we're gonna make it this yer, but I kin still work, and we'll not starve!"

She stopped digging and glared at him, yelling, "Har? Har we gonna make it, Joseph? The depot is closed and the Board of Works will too by next week. We can't rely on His Lordship forever." She paused with a defeated whimper. "The baby's not well and is losin' her fight. I've no more milk to give her, and I can't and won't stand by and watch each of us die one after the other!"

He lifted his hands, cupping her cheeks hard, and screamed over the crackling thunderstorm, "We'll make it, Kathryn, by God we'll make it! I don't have the answer, but if I mist work all day and night beggin' and stealin' to find a scrap of food, I will! Ar children won't die if we stick together and don't give up hope nar!"

She slowly pushed his hands away and fell into a heap, weeping, shrouded with mud and exhaustion.

"'Tis not far," she wailed. "Why has God not spared us one wee potato to last us one more miserable day? I can't believe that all's lost ... all's lost ..."

Joseph lifted up her limp, drenched body and stumbled back to the hut. The children huddled for warmth next to the fire, covered in torn blankets, and merely looked up when Joseph came in carrying their mother. Shay had her arm around the pig and rested her head on its head.

"Everythin's alright," he said to them and stood Kathryn up, shivering, next to their bed. He peeled off her few layers of clothing and almost gasped at her sunken, meager body, clearly deprived for months of any nutrition. He placed her on their bed, one of the few pieces of furniture still left in their home, and covered her with a few raggedy blankets. She closed her eyes in submission. Joseph dipped another rag in their water bucket and ever so softly wiped the mud from her face as if she were made of glass. He watched a tear slide down her forlorn face and kissed it. Listlessly, she opened her eyes and smiled at her loving husband.

"*Tá cion agam ort,*" she whispered to him.

"I love you too, m'lady," he grinned. "And I'll return shortly." He left the hut, walking at a fast pace in the pouring rain and thunder to Lord Somerhaven's estate.

He banged on the door with his fist. "Yer Lordship!" he shouted over the lightning. "Yer Lordship!"

The door opened, and the small man stood sprite and gallant in his tweed vest and jacket. "Joseph, my man, come in out of the rain. What brings you out on an evening such as this? Are Kathryn and the children alright?"

"Och, you have no idea, sir. Ar intire crops lost to the blight and we've no money nor food left. I'm here to make bould and plead fer some food fer me family," he panted.

Lord Somerhaven turned to his valet standing a few feet away. "Edgar, tell cook to prepare a basket and fill it with as much food as possible. Be sure to include some of that soup we had this evening—and hurry." He turned to Joseph. "Come over here by the fire and warm up."

"I'm sorry to be botherin' you again, Yer Lordship," Joseph shivered, "I'm much obleeged and will repay you any way I kin—"

"Nonsense!" Lord Somerhaven broke in, "I should really do more for you people. Do all the crops have the blight again this year?"

"Aye, I don't know whit to do anymore."

"Well, it is obvious I need to do something, and I've been thinking about how I can help." Lord Somerhaven sat down. "Tomorrow I will set up a soup kitchen in the back where all the tenants can come and get meals. How does that sound, Joseph?"

"Very good, Yer Lordship." He still stood shivering.

"Now where are my manners, you poor lad." Lord Somerhaven got up and retrieved a thick blanket and put it around Joseph's shoulders. "I will be here for you, my good man; not to worry."

Edgar arrived with a huge basket filled to the brim, and Joseph's eyes widened with the thought of all the food.

"I'm so grateful to you, Yer Lordship," he said, salivating as the basket was handed to him.

They walked to the door, and Lord Somerhaven motioned to Edgar for another blanket, which he put over the basket. "You will need a blanket for the children too."

"Aye," was all Joseph heard himself say.

Lord Somerhaven grabbed his arm before he left. "I wish I could do more for your family specifically, but then the others will want the same treatment, and more and more will come and then my home will be filled, you see. You will not starve, but food is all I can offer. Please understand."

"I understand," Joseph said. "Much obleeged fer yer kindness and all you've done already. God bless."

Joseph walked as fast as he could as the rain still poured down. He reached the hut and found his family asleep. He covered the children with one blanket and ripped his drenched clothes off, covering himself and Kathryn with the other blanket. Then he gently woke them to eat. The children nearly cried with the sight of all the delicious food, most of which they had never tasted before. Their pallets had never known such divine provisions, and they savored each bite, being carful not to eat too fast. They all dipped the pieces of bread in the jar of jam and slurped down the warm soup that gave strength to their dwindling bodies. At one point, the girls became so elated that they rubbed each piece of food over their faces before eating it, as if they were getting nourishment through their skin. Kathryn tried to feed the frail baby as best she could, and was happy that at least she ate a bit. Joseph was feeling lightheaded and very weak himself and put a few more pieces of peat on the fire before drifting off to sleep.

The next morning, Kathryn was a new woman as she rationed the food and tended to the baby. She hid the basket under her bed and told the children not to speak of it.

"I'm feelin' sorry 'bout last night," she said to Joseph. "I need to be strong for the children."

"We'll keep each other strong," he grinned at her.

Joseph and Kiernan worked a few more days on the Board of Works until the officer told them their services were no longer needed. He handed them their last payment, and Joseph walked home with a mountain of responsibility weighing on his back. Each day, the family received two soup meals at Lord Somerhaven's estate, but this clearly could not last forever. The remainder of the day, they went hungry or ate the last bit of morsels from the large basket. Kathryn gave the basket to Lord Somerhaven while in line for soup one afternoon and thanked him. He smiled and gave it to a servant standing beside him. The next night at about 3:00 in the morning, there was a knock at the door and that same servant stood at the threshold carrying the same basket once again filled with delicious foodstuffs unlike they had ever seen. He told Kathryn not to hand it to them directly but rather to leave it in the garden brush by the kitchen when she was finished. They ate lavishly and found a note between the crackers and cheese. It read:

> *A blessing upon your home*
> *A blessing upon your hearth*
> *A blessing upon your dwelling*
> *And upon your warming fire*
> *A blessing upon your animals and land*
> *A blessing upon your kith and kin*

A blessing upon you in dark or light
Each day and night of your living.

And Kathryn and her family did feel truly blessed. So for a few weeks, this secret basket was passed to and fro until it was evident that all the other tenants were getting pale and thinner while Kathryn and her family maintained their weight. The baby began to eat nonstop, and the rosy color returned to her checks. Even the pig grunted happily about the house. With each basket, a lovely blessing was inserted between two pieces of food. Kathryn used the blessings to further teach the children how to read and write since her hedge school was no longer. The other village children were too tired or were busy taking care of other family members. Soon Anne and the other women began to gossip about them, but no one would ask outright how they were getting their food.

"Maybe we need to be sharin' with the others," Kathryn suggested one night.

"Och, no," Joseph nearly choked on a mouthful of bread. "His Lordship wouldn't approve, and it'd jist stir bad feelin's 'bout. I know har you feel, Kathryn, but we mustn't tell or we mightn' be starvin' too. Next yar will be different to be sure."

Suddenly there was a knock at the door, and Joseph quickly gathered the food in the basket and hid it under the bed. All neighbors knocked now in the hard times of the famine. Kathryn creased her hair and opened the door; one of their neighbors stood, holding an unconcious child in her arms.

"What's the matter with her?" Kathryn asked.

"She be needin' food, ain't she. We all know you're gittin' food from somewhere. Lord above, I ask you, kin you help her?" she begged.

Kathryn did not hesitate. "Of course, set her on the bed." She gave a quick glance to Joseph, knowing that if she retrieved the basket it would alter their lives forever. They could no longer secretly receive food from Lord Somerhaven, which meant they could possibly starve themselves.

Joseph broke in quickly as one last resort. "Why didn't you not take her to His Lordship? He'd surely help."

"Ahh, that whistlin' ould man's only good fer a bit o' soup a day," she moaned. "He don't car if we be starvin' nor not."

Kathryn gave a deep breath and looked at the child lying on her bed with her eyes closed. She was probably seven years old but looked about five. The woman lay down beside her mumbling and groaning daughter.

"They have food, wee child," the woman said, stroking her forehead. "You won't be starvin' much longer."

Kathryn shot another glance to Joseph. She went to the table and retrieved a turnip from a bowl.

"'Ere," she offered the woman.

"Come nar, Kathryn," she scoffed. "The lot of you can't be livin' off one turnip, can you?" She turned again to the moaning child. "We Irish stick together, me lass, food be comin' nar."

The girl let out a loud wail as if in severe pain, and the noise shot through Kathryn's heart. A child's life was at stake, and there was no more time to waste. She reached under the bed and brought out the large basket about half full of food.

"Well nar thin!" the woman screamed. "Har's it that you be havin' all this food and we be starvin' in ar homes a few feet away?"

Kathryn could not speak; she looked at Joseph. He didn't know how to respond either and simply muttered, "'Tis …'tis … hard to explain."

"Git up nar, Maggie." The woman nudged the girl lying on the bed who sprang to a sitting position at once and gazed upon the basket of life before her. Without asking, she began ripping into all the edibles and shoving it down her throat.

"Och, so she's not dyin' nar, is she?" Kathryn now felt cheated and placed her hands on her hips in defiance. "'Tis all a plan? I see har you people work—"

"Har *we* work?" The woman also placed her hands upon her hips. "I demand to know whar you git this food!"

"I don't think 'tis any of yer business nar!" Kathryn shot back.

"Well I'm makin' it me business, I don't car," and at that moment Maggie pushed a piece of paper from the basket, and the woman looked down and recognized the logo on the stationery. She picked it up and replied, "Nar I see. His Lordship bin treatin' you people well whilst the rist of us wither away! I should've known, that moneygrubber … that old skinflint!" She roughly grabbed Maggie's arm and practically dragged her across the floor and out the door as the child still stuffed food into her mouth.

Kathryn sat down on the bed amid all the crumbs and half-eaten food. "Har 'twas I to know, Joseph, I'm sorry."

"'Tis not matter, 'tis not yer fault," he sighed. "I would've done the same thing. I mist go and tell His Lordship what's happened 'ere." Joseph informed Lord Somerhaven, who could only offer Joseph food now and again that he could stuff into his shirt.

"Maybe this is the just thing to do," he told Joseph one day. "If I cannot afford to feed everyone, it is not rightly fair. I simply give what I can without going bankrupt myself. I know someone like you must think me a hypocrite since I have all this and you have nothing, but it would do me no good to give it all away. There are too many poor people in Ireland for it to make the smallest difference. The government needs to change the way the system works, Joseph, or your future generations will not have a chance."

"Aye," Joseph agreed. He knew Lord Somerhaven was right, but it still hurt him every time he heard his children ask for something to eat and he could not provide it. He was unemployed and without any food. The only thing keeping his family alive was the food Lord Somerhaven gave him and the soup that was provided.

"What're we to do?" Kathryn asked Joseph when he returned. She tried to think rationally and needed hope for the future.

"Are we barely to survive on watery soup and scraps ferever? The children're weak and thin, and we only have a few more pieces lift o' furniture to pawn. We don't have seeds to plant them crops fer the comin' year, so what're we to do nar? We can't go on livin' like this."

"I know," was all Joseph could say. He did not have any answers either, and the future looked as bleak as ever.

Kathryn knew he felt responsible for the well-being of the family, but she almost wanted to scream at their circumstances. She was the type to evaluate the situation and take action, not simply shake her head and let the circumstances dictate the course of her survival. When she lived in the big manor house in England and saw firsthand how the wealthy conducted themselves and how they made things happen, she realized she could make things happen in her own life as well. Kathryn obviously would never achieve their status because of her peasant lineage, but she at least wanted some control of her life. Starting the hedge school had been a way to provide some sort of education for her children so they could possibly make a better life for themselves when they reached adulthood.

Food is the first and basic necessity of existence, and that need must be met before a person can move on to other essentials. Kathryn's every thought was of food—she was literally at the bottom of the barrel. She found herself searching, scrambling, and ultimately elated to find one morsel to drop into the ravenous mouth of one child, while the others merely licked their lips in anticipation of their turn. Each day, the struggle continued, worsening as each hour passed. She felt helpless and insecure, angry and annoyed. She became befuddled each day when she awoke and looked at her children getting weaker and thinner, then felt her own stomach turning inside out with shrieks of hunger. The first thought on her mind when she awoke each day was about food, and it was the last thought exhausting her mind as she was absorbed by tormented sleep at the day's end.

On August 1, 1846, Trevelyan presented his plans for Irish Relief to the new prime minister, Lord John Russell. The government was well aware that all of Ireland's potatoes were ruined and without question something had to be done for the coming year. Armed with Trevelyan's memorandum, Lord John Russell addressed the House of Commons, explaining the dire situation of the people and Trevelyan's new ideas. What transpired was the new Labour Rate Act, once again intending to force the Irish landlords to pay for the relief of their direct tenants.

This new Relief Plan had two different parts. The first part was to resurrect the Public Works, but on a larger scale than before. Trevelyan felt that it was the responsibility of the landowner to take care of his tenants, and this was forcing them to do just that. He thought the landowners would be practical and employ the majority of them, while sending only the most distressed to the works.

Even though there was no free grant from the government this time and the landlords had to pay for the entire cost of the works, again ten years was granted for the repayment although this time the liability was spread over all the taxpayers in a district. The landlord himself was not solely responsible and to the landlords, this was a lenient loophole that was to be taken full advantage of. Every landlord assumed that the other landlords in his district would pay if he could not, so the green light was given to spend any money he had and indulge in parties and goods. And splurge they all did in parties, horses and furniture. At presentment sessions, ridiculous sums were being accepted without much thought to the repayment, and soon these sessions became complete chaos.

The second part of the plan was not even a plan at all. It simply stated that the government would not assist the people in any way with food, imported or supplied from Ireland. They were not going to purchase Indian corn and sell it in the depots as last year. In fact, the depots were not to be opened at all. Ireland was turned loose without any assistance from England or its own government. Laissez faire was the rationale behind this new plan, and Trevelyan explained the reasoning in his memo. He believed that trade in Ireland was deeply affected by the purchase of the Indian cornmeal from America, if not simply by the fact that the government had it in storage. The traders could not be free to purchase large quantities because they knew that as soon as their prices rose, the government would throw their stored food out there at a low cost and the traders could not profit. This time, the government would not interfere with private trading under any circumstances. Trevelyan believed that with these two plans in place, the coming year would prove to be tough, but overall fair. He thought that the poor could maintain a steady income through their landlord or on the Public Works and that private trade would provide them with the food they needed. He was now in full control of Irish Relief and delegated responsibilities as he saw fit. But no amount of hard work could counteract the horrific catastrophe that lay ahead for the people of Ireland.

"Nobody listens to the hired help, oh no," Stuffy whispered under his breath, but loud enough for O'Riley to hear. He swept around the tables and chairs as O'Riley worked at his desk. No other person was around. "I know everything that's going on here, and don't think I don't."

He whistled as he swept, clearly goading O'Riley into conversation and unmistakably getting on his nerves. Stuffy would hit something with his broom and cough or blow his nose loudly. All the while, O'Riley sat at his desk trying his best to ignore him. He faced his paperwork, but his mind was being harassed by his fellow employee.

"Ireland is going to fall, and it will have the stamp of approval from all the people that work here," Stuffy said, sweeping fast. "Got your stamp ready, O'Riley?"

"How dare you suggest such a thing!" O'Riley turned around and addressed his tormentor. "And you have no idea what's going on!"

Stuffy leaned into O'Riley's personal space and said, "I file lots of paperwork here and my hearing is very good."

"You shouldn't be reading—"

"Ohh ... and don't tell me you don't read some of the memos, O'Riley," Stuffy grinned. "I'm not daft!" He looked around to see if anyone was about, then added, "I know the plans for Irish Relief this year are really to safeguard England more than to help Ireland. Mr. Trevelyan is well aware of the Public Works catastrophe of last year when only some crops failed; this year that blight has ruined all the crops around here. It's going to be total anarchy!"

"You can't predict such a thing," O'Riley said. "The Public Works is here to assist the people, and it will be available for as long as it takes—"

"Ah ha! Another lie," Stuffy broke in. "Or perhaps you're just not properly informed. If you had read last week's memos, you would know that Trevelyan has placed a cap on the Public Works so they will be in force for one year only."

O'Riley sat with his lips pursed, despising every word that slithered from Stuffy's mouth.

"He even chose a date on their closing," Stuffy added. "Now let me see, how did he word it, 'Absolutely no works will continue to carry on after 15th August, 1847.' It went something like that."

"Trevelyan is working day and night, seven days a week, trying to help these poor Irish people," O'Riley said.

"Yes, that is true, I must give him that," Stuffy agreed. "I heard that he practically lives at the Treasury, combing over each application as they pour in. And he also expects all his subordinates to do the same. Did you know that he wrote and sent books to Commissariat officers to study and is working his employees so hard they're completely exhausted? One wife of a Commissariat officer even wrote to Trevelyan complaining of the hours her husband is required to do, saying that it was affecting his overall health. And did you know what Trevelyan smartly wrote back?" Stuffy leaned in a little closer. "That he had never heard of anyone damaged by working too hard."

"Do you get pleasure from being an idiotic meddler?" O'Riley asked. "I don't know how you of all people landed your position, but there are others that would do the same job without snooping around. In fact, I have a good mind to inform Sir Routh—"

"Ah ha!" Stuffy broke in. "That proves you are just as bad as I am. As children, we are told not to be the snoop nor the tattle-tale, isn't that right?"

"You're a disgusting human being. Now I have work to do." O'Riley swung back around in his chair. Stuffy went about his business sweeping, but he planned to continue pestering his workmate. There would be plenty of time to tease and heckle this straight-laced follower, he thought, plenty of time.

Kathryn and Joseph awoke one morning and stiffly rose out from beneath the blankets. All the rations from the basket were long gone, and Lord Somerhaven was keeping his tenants alive on his soup. He told all his tenants not to pay any rent until this famine was over, and that lifted their spirits. But the family got thinner and thinner as the days passed and their clothes hung loosely on their bodies.

Joseph sat at the table and eyed the pig sleeping next to Shay, then looked at Kathryn.

"It'll break her wee heart," Kathryn said, and Joseph sighed loudly. "But," Kathryn continued, "thar seems to be no other way. We niver should've lit her git so attached."

Joseph picked up the runt of a pig from his warm place under the blankets and grabbed a large knife with the other. He went outside and placed the now awake pig on the ground and tried to steady it with his left knee and hand.

He raised his right hand over the back of his head when suddenly he felt a small hand. He turned around to see tiny Shay holding his hand with two of hers. She said nothing as she let go and calmly walked over to her pig lying quietly on the ground. She bent down and kissed his head like a princess kissing her prince. Then she stood up and looked Joseph in the eye with a tranquil look upon her face. Peacefully, she turned and walked back into the hut as Joseph continued his dreadful task. He tried to hide the dead body from the children as he brought it into the hut and laid it on the ground. He placed a few large pieces on the table for Kathryn to prepare a meal and washed up outside with a bucket of water. Neither he, Shay, nor the other children ever spoke of the swine again. The skinny pig was only good for a few meals, and after boiling the bones and head with turnips for some nourishment, all the food was once again gone. Kathryn looked around her kitchen.

"I'm goin' to take a few spoons and this 'ere pot to the pawn shop," Kathryn told Joseph one day as he sat listlessly at the table. Also cradled in her arm was her last beloved book. Joseph knew it was hard for his wife to part with such belongings, knowing full well that they would never own such things again.

"We mustn't jist sit 'ere and do nothin'," she justified her actions.

"Aye," was all he said.

Kathryn knew that her husband was becoming depressed and guilty about their condition, but rational answers did not exist. She left the children huddled beneath the blankets, as they sometimes did to keep warm, and began walking into the town. Once again, she passed the fields once lush with greenery, now barren and foul smelling with rotting potatoes. As always, in a putrid field, there scavenged a starving person or two, hunched over and trying to find one last morsel. Kathryn knew that if it were not for Lord Somerhaven, they would most definitely be in their own fields searching for that spec of rotting food to sustain them one more day. As it were, the soup was barely enough to keep them from starvation, and once again the baby was not doing well.

As she walked through the town, human skeletons roamed aimlessly about, knowing not where to go. She spied a group of angry protesters yelling at a Commissariat officer to open his depot. She did not see the officer, but suspected he remained inside trying to hide from the mob. The depot had been closed for some time, but the officer was seen about, which teased the people into believing it might reopen. The entire population was getting desperate as the wrath of gnawing hunger was beginning to push them over the edge.

Kathryn reached the pawnbroker and walked inside the store.

"Ayeee?" a woman droned, looking straight at her.

"I ... I ... git somethin' to sell," she said.

"Fine, lay it on the counter." The woman tapped it with her long yellowish fingernails.

Kathryn put the well-used pot on the counter and placed the utensils inside with a clang. She looked at the woman who made a face at the condition of the goods.

"Hmmm ..." she said looking them over, "two pence's all I kin offer."

"Har 'bout fer? Or maybe three?" Kathryn bargained.

"Two," she stated boldly.

"Aye, that'll be fine." Kathryn did not have a choice. She took the meager coins and walked across the street to the vendors selling produce. She wanted to grab all the available food and run, but it was just a wild thought. Instead, she bought one turnip and a handful of oatmeal. On the way home, she noticed the young woman whose wedding they had attended the previous summer.

"Well nar thin, Shannon," she came up to the famished young woman, "har're thee?"

"Oh, Kathryn, the hunger's 'bout us all," she said, "but 'tis mighty fine to see you."

"Har's yer new husband?" Before she could even get the words out, the woman broke out sobbing.

"Whit's the matter, child?" Kathryn put her arms around her bony frame and tried to comfort her.

"He left me!" Shannon blurted out.

"Lord above, he left you? That's mighty quare intirely. Har you livin' thin?"

"I'm stayin' with me mam at the moment," she said, wiping away tears.

"Such a pity, Shannon. If God Almighty spar's us, we'll make it through alright." Both women crossed themselves.

"Och, I know," she sniffled into her frock. "Did you har Mr. Callaghan and his intire family died last week, bless 'um all. And yesterday Ronan and Breda were found dead in their hut also, bless 'um too. All from the hunger, you know." Then she began to sob uncontrollably. "I lost me baby 'cause of no food and losin' so much weight … me body couldn't hold her and she came out fully formed and so beautiful, but without a wee soul!"

"Jasus, Mary, and Joseph, Shannon, I'd no idea!" exclaimed Kathryn, cradling her head.

"And me husband blamed *me*! This should've bin the bist yer of me life and 'tis the worst!" she cried. "I've no family of me own, and thar's nothin' nar but death starin' at me right in the face. Ever day, someone I know dies and it'll only be a matter o' time before it be findin' me too."

"Don't speak so!" Kathryn said, brushing her hair. "You're stronger thin that, I know you are."

"Maybe," she said, lifting her head. "The Board of Works is comin' back, and me da is sure to find a job."

"The works are returnin'? I didn't know." Kathryn felt better. "You'll see, everythin'll be alright nar. Yer da will git on and soon you'll have some food."

"Aye." The poor girl brushed the tears from her cheeks, gave a weary smile, and said, "Much obleeged, you've made me feel better."

"I'm glad, me dear," Kathryn replied. "I mist git back to me own family nar."

She walked fast all the way home and straight to her husband who was collecting more peat for the fire.

"Joseph!" she panted, trying to catch her breath. "I jist spoke with Shannon—"

"Who?"

"Shannon, the lass whose weddin' 'twas last summer," she still panted.

"Weddin'? What weddin'?" he looked puzzled.

"Och, never mind! She tould me the Public Works are returnin'."

"Really? I'll find out more from Father Murphy." And off he went to find Kiernan.

Kathryn went into the house and began cooking the porridge and turnips. The children smelled food and came walking into the house. They never ran now as their small bodies were so thin and sustained little energy. The baby was not progressing normally and refused to walk, preferring to store as much energy as possible by simply lying down and sleeping. She did not talk much either, and Kathryn tried not to dwell on her difficulties. Her main concern was feeding her family, and with the Works returning, perhaps they would make it through the year and even buy some seed for the next year's potato crop.

Joseph came home that afternoon and said he and Kiernan were going to a meeting the next day to sign up for the Public Works. It was called a Presentment Session and anyone could attend to present their recommendations for a particular site. The only condition to a proposal was that it should be large enough so each district could possibly employ all the people. If your proposal was not chosen, employment on the Works was not a certainty; the men were only assured a job if their proposal was selected. Joseph asked Kathryn to write his proposal on a piece of paper he got from the parish since her writing was much better than his. He carefully weighed each idea he had and relayed them to Kathryn to jot down. He placed the paper carefully down on the table and instructed the children not to touch it.

Joseph and Kiernan headed out early the following morning to get in line but found a mob of about one hundred already ahead of them. Interestingly, there were several police pacing outside the Town Hall where the meeting was to be held in case they were needed. The men barely squeezed into the back rows, trying to see the front. The place was packed, and it was hard to breathe or see anything. The men waited for a while and then a fight broke out amongst two men, which forced some of the pack out the door as the others backed away from the flying fists. More and more men were forced out as the fight was literally carried out the door. Suddenly there was a large gap in the mob, and Joseph nudged Kiernan with his elbow and they made their way toward the front. Now Joseph could see that there was a small table in the front that everyone was trying to get to. The mob pushed forward when two clean, well-dressed men entered from the back. One of them stood up on a platform and tried to quiet the crowd with his hands. The other sat down at the table. Three more gentlemen entered from the back and sat down together, away from the table.

"I thank you all for attending this Presentment Session and hope that this will lead to beneficial work and pleasant and suitable employment for you all," the Board of Works employee began addressing the crowd.

"Yah! Here's me proposal, let's git on with it!" one man said, holding his paper above his head, and the crowd cheered waving their papers.

"Right." The man was startled with the crowd's reaction. "My name is Eddie Belbin, and this is Trevor Stubbs. The other men are landowners in your district you might very well know. Please form one line on the right of this table and present your proposal to Mr. Stubbs. He will collect all the papers, and they will be reviewed. Then the appropriate ones will be submitted to the Board of Works. The Board will then select—"

"Enough talk!" shouted a man next to the table. He handed his paper to Stubbs and said to him, "Me family not aten in two days an' I expict this 'ere pro-po-sal …" he looked him straight in the eye, "to be selected." He smiled and turned to leave. More men began to shove their papers onto the table, and Belbin quickly made his way over to help Stubbs who was almost engulfed.

"Whoa!" Belbin pleaded, sticking his arms out so no other papers could be placed on the table. "Let's not get uncivilized here."

"Uncivilized?" Another rough-looking man slammed the table with his fist and creased his brow. "I kin git *real* uncivilized, 'specially whin I've five children, a wafe, an' her mam starvin' an' waitin' fer me to bring home some *feckin' food*!" he screamed.

"Now ... now ..." Belbin sat down next to Stubbs. "I just want to maintain some order here, that's all."

"I'd like to maintain order too," the man calmly said. He lifted his rolled up scrap of paper and held it an inch from Belbin's nose. "Nar I expict that this har'll be selected an' I'll be workin' right soon, mustn't I?"

"Yes, I think you will be." Belbin carefully slid the scrap out of the man's dirty grip and placed it on the table in front of him. The sinewy, gruff man disappeared into the crowd, only to be replaced by hundreds of more men like him, also thin and desperate. The three landowners got up and left out the back without a word, leaving Belbin and Stubbs to battle the mob. Joseph and Kiernan pushed and shoved their way to the table after half an hour, and by this time Belbin and Stubbs were accepting all proposals and refusing none.

"Mine'll be selected too?" Joseph placed his paper on the table.

"Yes, sir, whatever you say!" Belbin assured him without even looking up.

"I need to be sure," Joseph implored.

"Aye, me too." Kiernan placed his on the table.

"They will *all* be selected." Belbin forced a grin.

Joseph and Kiernan squeezed their way out of the mob and made their way toward the entrance. The thick crowd was even denser on the outside as about two hundred more waited to get their papers into Belbin's clean hands. The policemen were still standing quietly outside next to a black coach. It was a bright afternoon, so Joseph and Kiernan decided to sit down on the grass outside the crowd and rest before heading home.

"Do you think we have a chance?" Joseph asked his friend.

"Aye, 'specially since we were before all these men," Kiernan said, stretching his hand out before the mob.

"We'll know soon enough." Joseph lied down and closed his eyes, exhausted.

"'Tis a pity His Lordship's almost bankrupt," Kiernan said. "He can't even give us any more work. Where'd all his money go?"

"Don't know," Joseph sighed, enjoying the rest.

The two friends talked for about twenty minutes until they were startled by a commotion outside the Town Hall. The swarm of men began to sway this way and that until Belbin came running out the door, hands flailing hysterically in the air. The policemen rushed to help him as he fell to the ground and the mob began to throw things at him.

"He's the one, I tell you!" a mobster shouted. "He's the one that didn't want the Board of Works comin' 'ere in the first place."

"That's not true!" Belbin pleaded.

"Aye, 'tis!" the man shouted. "He tried to skip this village— 'twas goin' to let us starve!"

The mob descended on him in a wrath of anger as the police tried to drag him away. Unmercifully, the crowd continuously pelted him with their shoes, jackets, stones, and anything they could throw. The police threw Belbin into the coach and shouted for the horse to run while the people ran alongside still throwing objects. The last thing Joseph and Kiernan saw was the coach sprinting down the lane with a gang of angry mobsters shouting and throwing articles until they were out of eyesight.

"I wonder whit happen' to the other one?" Joseph smiled at Kiernan.

"I don't know," Kiernan laughed.

The men returned home and waited to hear about their proposals. They checked with the clergy, the Town Hall, and anywhere they could to hear of news of the Works. The days passed like years as panic gripped the country. The people saw the Public Works as their only means of survival, and each day they grew increasingly worried. The Irish are generally an optimistic people and content with what little they have, but optimism was nowhere in sight. Presentment Sessions all over the country were packed with hostile, desperate people fighting for their lives, and the thousands of proposals that were collected were going into a black hole. The government sent a form stating that each household was required to write down the number of people in the house and the number of people who needed to be employed on the Public Works. But after this form was collected, the government did nothing with it, due to lack of organization, inadequate employees, and the simple fact that there were just too many forms to siphon through.

A Commissariat officer from Skibbereen wrote to Routh,

> *"The utter inadequacy of the Government measures was
> impossible to describe." There were "hundreds, thousands,
> nay millions of starving people … I defy anyone to
> exaggerate the misery of the people … it is impossible …
> Whatever is done by Government or Public Works will be
> too late, after people have been driven to desperation by
> hunger. The whole country is nothing but a slumbering
> volcano. It will soon burst."* *

"Sir, it is two o'clock," Margaret said, standing in the doorway.

"Yes, I am well aware of the time, thank you, Margaret," Trevelyan said.

"Yes, sir," Margaret turned and humbly tiptoed back to her desk.

Trevelyan shuffled a few papers together and made his way down the hall and into a large boardroom where a massive oblong table made of dark walnut adorned only the middle but seemed to fill up the entire room. About twenty gentlemen sitting in high back chairs surrounded it, and when Trevelyan entered, all talk ceased as each man faced his superior. Trevelyan took his rightful place at the head of the table and remained standing as he spoke.

"Gentlemen of the Treasury, I know we are all performing at our very best and taking great care with each new dilemma that comes our way from Ireland. I believe the choices we make now could affect Britain as a whole for centuries to come and perhaps forever. But today I would like to share with you a situation that transpired in western Ireland that clearly cannot reoccur." He looked around at his department and at the faces of the men that sat upright, listening attentively.

He continued, "Last Monday, the inspector-general of the Coastguard Service, Sir James Dombrain, wrote to Sir Randolph Routh informing him that some of his officers had given away free meal to some of the starving people. They had come upon dying people in remote districts in the west and acted upon their own free will. Dombrain justified the act by saying surely they were not allowed to visit these areas and simply walk away when they had meal to save them—if not for a while. He described the misery of the people and was taken aback by their conditions. Gentlemen, this type of action is unquestionably inefficient and indisputably reprehensible!" he shouted loudly and banged the table with his fist. The Treasury officers sat stiffly and said nothing.

Trevelyan continued, "I wrote to Dombrain explaining that his detrimental actions were disloyal to the government and that he was not authorized to give away any more food. The proper action should have been to gather the respectable people in each district and have them form their own Relief committees through private donations, and in the future, this is what I expect him or anyone in his situation to do. And if the people still require *more* assistance, a government donation might be granted in the future." Trevelyan stopped lecturing for a moment and let silence fill the air.

Then he said quietly, "Sir Dombrain somberly responded by explaining that there were no respectable people about. They were in a remote area with miles and miles between them and the next district. The people were dying, he wrote, and the people were seized by hunger, and he could not walk away and leave them to die. I understand it would be extremely difficult to leave, but even the nearest district would have been more helpful in the long run than to simply hand out free food. I urge you men to really discern what has happened here and comprehend what a negative impact acts such as these relay to the Irish people. We must all concentrate on the larger goal here to correct Ireland for generations and generations to come, regardless of the lives that might be sacrificed."

Chapter IV

Routh sat in his Dublin office and peered out his window as people passed by. He opened his lunch that his wife had given him and laid out all the food on his desk. He was hungry and began eating, thinking it was such a simple thing to do. When you're hungry, you eat. But it was not so simple for thousands of poor Irish peasants. He knew that most of them that strolled by on this clear day were not the poor destitute that were in need. These were the ladies and gentlemen that had businesses and opportunities in town. Most of them did not feel the sting of the famine. But every once in a while, he saw a starving individual stumble by, and as the famine grew worse, more of these people filtered in. They probably came to Dublin in search of some type of food. He personally believed that the government should send food to the starving, but since he was not in command, he followed orders instead. A part of him wanted to feel optimistic about Trevelyan's plans, and he worked very hard to make them happen, but in the back of his mind, he knew many people were going to perish.

He spotted a little girl and boy walking up the lane with a few rags on for clothes, and he stopped in mid-chew. Their faces, hands, and feet were caked with dirt and mud, probably from searching in the dirt for something to eat. They walked so close together that not a spec of light shone between them, as if they were one, and they came steadily and carefully up the walkway. With facial similarities surely making them siblings, both looked to be about five years old with long hair packed with sludge and debris. The lad had his head down and looked physically worse than his sister. The lass searched about for people, and as they passed by, she looked up shyly and stretched out her dirty, boney hand. Most people just walked past, sometimes without even noticing them. They came right in front of Routh's window, and Routh and the little girl locked eyes. He saw the anguish and pain in her eyes and the days and weeks of famine she endured. Normally, he would have kept on eating and returned to his work, but something in her eyes made him stop and speculate, ponder and survey, contemplate and behold. Perhaps it was her filthy garments or her sallow, sunken face, or the fact that she was obviously taking care of her brother when she could barely sustain life within herself. Or maybe it was the fact that only a thin pane of glass separated an educated, wealthy, robust man from a destitute, starving little girl with absolutely no future except to die in the streets with no one to take notice and no one to care.

The sting of guilt pierced Routh's heart like a fine-edged knife, and he could take it not one moment longer. He stood up and stuffed all his food back into his bag while choking down the mouthful he was already chewing. He flung open the door to his office, and in front of him stood the children. He handed the little girl his bag, and she took it from his hand ever so gently. *"Go raibh maith agat,"* she said, and Routh knew that meant "thank you" in Gaelic. She didn't even know what was in the bag, but she thanked him for giving her something, anything. When she did look inside, her eyes and mouth fell open as if she were viewing the most precious thing in the world—and it was to her.

Like the angel she was, she reached inside and pulled out a large red apple and held it in front of her brother. His eyes widened too, and he began devouring it without pulling his face from it. He wanted to smell it, hold it, look at it, and savor it, relishing each and every bite. His sister stood on the other side of the apple and took glorious bites of her own. As the brother sucked on the remaining bits of the core, the sister pulled out most of a sandwich, and once again the two shared the food.

Routh stood there watching them, unable to pull himself away from this pitiful sight. He wondered if they had ever eaten such food and knew that he had never been that hungry. In fact, suddenly he was not hungry at all as he watched the two kids inhale his lunch faster than he ever could. Routh ducked inside his office one more time and grabbed his coat from the cloak room. By now they were finished, and the little girl turned the bag over and opened her mouth for any morsels that might be hiding at the bottom as the boy searched on the ground for small crumbs that he put readily into his mouth. Routh handed them the coat, and the little girl grabbed his hand and kissed it, saying, *"Go raibh maith agat"* again. The little boy went to hug him, but suddenly realized he was dirty and stopped. Routh said, "It's okay," and smiled at them both. The girl opened the coat and draped it over their shoulders and continued walking down the lane.

Routh went back into his office and sat down at his desk. He looked out the window again, saw respectable people walking about, and wondered if he was going mad or did he just encounter two starving children. He tried to focus on the work that lay before him and began reading some memos but could not concentrate. He went to the door again, opened it, and looked down the lane where he last saw the children walking. They were nowhere in sight, and he wondered if he would ever see them again.

A soft knock at the door one rainy afternoon startled Kathryn. She opened it, and there stood one of the village girls soaking wet.

"Darragh, whit's the matter?" Kathryn brought her out of the rain.

"Why don't we have any more larnin'?" the six-year-old asked.

"Well nar thin, is that the problem?" Kathryn said, relieved. "We kin have it nar. The girls are next door, but Brenton's 'ere. Brenton!"

"Aye," he said sitting up. "'Twas jist restin'."

The girl sat next to him, and Kathryn got a blanket and tried to dry her hair as best she could. She placed the blanket around her bony, shivering shoulders and tried to think of something to discuss without any books. Her mind was blank, and she put her hand to her forehead.

"Please tell me 'bout whin I was born," Brenton suggested.

"Aye," Darragh said.

"Alright," Kathryn began. "'Twas early mornin' and clear whin I felt you wanted to be born. I woke your da and told him 'tis time and to fetch Mrs. McGavock. He git out of bed, and as fast as a rabbit, Mrs. McGavock 'twas here with towels and water. She stayed with me the intire day as I tried to give birth, talkin' to me as if she were me own mam. Thin quite suddenly, I looked out the window and the darkest clouds you'd ever seen come in from the wist and it begin rainin' and rainin' like you've niver seen rain before. Thunder and lightnin' bolted from the sky and was touchin' down on roads, fences, and fields, and thin you begin to be born. Mrs. McGavock helped you into the world, and yer da held me hand and was so strong. I hard a wee whimper, and yer da said, 'Lord above, 'tis a boy.' 'Twas the first thin he said 'bout you. Thin he helped Mrs. McGavock, and whin he spoke to you firstly, you turned yer head and looked straight at 'em. 'Twas like you knew yer da ... like you knew his voice and that he was different from ever one else. Thin he brought you to me all bundled up, and thin we marveled at God's perfect gift. I put me finger on your wee hand, and you grabbed it, and at that very moment a shot of sunlight came through the window and upon ar family. 'Twas like we were bein' blessed by God Almighty himself. Thin the clouds went, and the blue sky came sparklin' through, shining down on us all. 'Twas a magical day, and I'll treasure it forever."

Brenton and Darragh sat motionless through the story and didn't want it to end.

"Do you knowed 'bout whin I was bein' born?" Darragh broke the silence.

"No, child, but I'd love to hear 'bout it," Kathryn said.

"I'd git me mam, but she's dead," Darragh said matter-of-factly.

"I'm very sorry," Kathryn said, "I didn't know."

"She died a fortnight ago and she niver tould me 'bout whin I was bein' born. But I was thar, so I should 'member." The little girl sat for a moment thinking, then said, "I know, I 'member nar."

"We're listenin'," Brenton said.

"'Twas a bright sunny day!" she smiled. "Me da was probly workin' in England like he is all the time, but me grandmam was thar. She was helpin' me into the world and she said somethin' to me and I knowed her too. 'Twas a sunny day and God smiled and blessed us too."

Kathryn reached over and hugged the child, saying, "I know he did, I know he did."

At the end of August, Routh sat down at his desk once more and got out the memos addressed to him. They were reports from officers explaining difficult situations in other districts, and not one of them had a positive statement. In Roscommon, another person died almost daily. In Longford, some of the poor had a coin or two and searched the town for food, but not a slice of bread or an ounce of meal could be found. A letter was found from a small farmer who wrote to his landlord that he would only be able to pay his rent if he sold his oats, which meant starvation for his entire family. The dead bodies were found next to this note. A horrific eviction of three hundred people occurred in Ballinglass, County Galway, with the assistance of armed troops—the landlord was a wealthy woman who intended to convert the land into a grazing farm.

Routh monitored the private trade industry and saw that it was functioning with vigor, although the Irish merchants were not of the same respectable class as merchants in England. Here the private traders were the sneaky, greedy, vicious scoundrels that bought as much as they could and sold the meal and other foodstuffs at exorbitant prices. The consumers were the wealthy class, certainly not the poor person who was in need the most. Routh felt that he needed to meet with Trevelyan personally to persuade him to purchase some food and to possibly reevaluate the current Irish Relief Plan for the coming year. The letters he wrote of the destitution had no effect, so he made the trip to London to plead his case.

"Sir Randolph Routh is here to see you, sir," Margaret said, standing in front of the doorway to Trevelyan's office.

"Show him in," Trevelyan answered.

A moment later, Routh entered and greeted his comrade, shaking hands and smiling.

"Good to see you after this past year, Randolph," Trevelyan said.

"It was a tough one, wasn't it?" Routh commented.

The two men discussed several topics before Routh paused a moment and then began his plea.

"The Irish will not make it another year unless drastic measures are taken. I cannot urge you enough to buy more corn and reopen the depots that have already closed. Additionally, we need to provide more work. So many people will surely die if we do not."

Trevelyan sat back in his fine leather chair, knowing full well that Routh's entire purpose was to come and plead for Ireland. He grinned and shook his head, holding the lives of thousands in the palm of his hand.

"Let me first remind you that the Irish are not the only ones troubled by the blight; Europeans, Americans, and Britains are also greatly affected, although they are not as needy," Trevelyan stated. "With this in mind, I have already purchased a minimal amount of corn, but only from Britain. As I have said many times, I refuse to purchase overseas again, as it will interfere with private enterprise. We will have only a few depots open in the most needy areas."

"I understand," Routh nodded.

"I initially ordered 2,000 tons of Indian corn," Trevelyan explained, "although the trader quickly made it clear that this request was out of the question. The supplies in Britain were depleting rapidly, so he was only able to purchase 900–1,000 quarters, which he was very lucky to buy at this late date. The trader explained that due to the famine in Europe, all of the meal was gone."

"There must be some other way. I must ask you again—" Routh began.

"Need I remind you that I am head of the Treasury here and in charge of the entire Relief Plan. I know what is best for Ireland, even more than the people themselves," Trevelyan shot back without moving.

Routh wanted to say more, but he respected Trevelyan's authority. Instead, he held back and said nothing and just shook his head at what this meant for Ireland.

"Nevertheless, I do not believe that the lack of corn is such a negative occurrence," Trevelyan said, grinning. "In fact, the high prices in Britain are actually a great blessing."

Routh looked at him and waited, knowing an explanation would follow.

"Now due to the corn shortage," Trevelyan rationalized, "the prices will rise and regulate themselves, which is necessary to attract from abroad the supplies needed to fill up the void from the destruction of the potato crops. Nothing is more calculated to attract supplies, especially from America, than the rise in prices. Alas, then the supplies of Indian corn will trickle down from Cincinnati and Ohio, which was previously used to feed their pigs. It's as simple as that."

Routh could see that Trevelyan was getting excited and passionate, truly believing he had found a way to help Ireland without disturbing private enterprise. He went on to explain in detail exactly what would happen, and Routh wanted to believe him. He wanted to believe this fellow human being was doing all he could for other humans in need and in the very best interest of them. Routh agreed with his theory, knowing so many lives were at stake and realizing his attempts to persuade Trevelyan to simply hand out food to the starving was useless. However, Trevelyan did not witness the famished little girl taking care of her brother or pass by the skeleton beggars in the streets every day. He was removed from the torture of looking into their deep-set eyes and instead dealt with numbers and quantities, plans on paper, and stoic reports of the dying in faraway places. It was much easier to divorce oneself from horrific circumstances and make decisions based on what was written on paper. Routh returned to Dublin, trusting in Trevelyan and his ideas, believing that assistance was forthcoming.

During the next few weeks, Trevelyan's letters to Routh were positive as he reported his order to the United States for all the corn he expected to flood out of that country. But his plan did not materialize. He failed to understand the precise time of exporting the corn, which had already been purchased and shipped. Europe had acted quickly and bought as much as possible, paying high prices. Also, no ship was going to sail after September due to the dangerous conditions of storms and ice. The only corn left to buy was for 1847, which would reach Ireland in the spring. As he began to realize this, the tone of Trevelyan's letters was anything but cheerful. He wrote to Routh that there was no food available at this time. There was some leftover biscuit in a few military stores that had been in storage since 1843, and he may do with it as he wished. Trevelyan also wrote that Routh's desire for more food for the Irish was simply not realistic. Need he remind him again of the food shortages in Europe and also Britain herself. No, the Irish must depend on themselves for relief.

During this month, the *Times* newspaper wrote:

> *"The Irishman is destitute, so is the Scotchman, and so is
> the Englishman ... It appears to us to be of the very first
> importance to all classes of Irish society to impress on them
> that there is nothing so peculiar, so exceptional, in the
> condition which they look on as the pit of utter despair ...
> Why is that so terrible in Ireland which in England does
> not create perplexity and hardly moves compassion?"* *

Joseph came excitedly into the hut one afternoon in search of his
family.

"I've bin selected!" he shouted. "I've bin selected for the
Works!"

He ran to his wife and children, and they all hugged as one
large mass. It was the glimmer of hope they had been waiting for,
and they prayed, "Thank you God for this great blessin' upon ar
family in time of need." Joseph explained that this time he would
be gone for a period of time; how long, he did not know. The
site was at least two days' walk, so the government required the
men to sleep on the grounds. Kiernan had gotten his notice for
the same site yesterday, so he left the day before and was waiting
for him. The family gathered outside the hut to bid farewell to
Joseph.

"I love you so," Kathryn said, hugging her husband.

"Och! I'll be back soon enough," Joseph grinned.

"Do you have everythin'?" she asked.

"Aye," Joseph replied, throwing a bundle tied in a blanket
over his back.

The children hugged his legs, and Brenton held up the baby
to be kissed. Joseph knelt down, hugged and kissed each child,
and stopped when he came to his son.

"One day soon, you'll be seein' me walkin' down that road with money in me pocket an' a skip in me step. You jist wait for that day." Joseph winked.

He backed away and headed down the road, waving. Kathryn and the children waved back and wondered when they would see him again. They waited patiently each day for any sight of Joseph, but the days turned into weeks, and the weeks turned into months. Kathryn sold their table and chairs, their clothes, and their kitchen utensils. Their beds and blankets remained as their only comfort from the cold hard ground. They continued to live on a few scraps they found and Lord Somerhaven's soup, and all through Ireland, the people searched for food and starved. No type of food was distributed to the needy, but in the event of any disturbance, the troops were at the scene in the flash of an eye. Often times, when the government could smell the uneasiness of the people and sensed they were going to riot, the troops were called upon to casually gallop through the streets, trying to dispel any notion of upheaval. At this time, the feeling in the air was not so much anger anymore, it was rather despair.

Through the whisperings of the town, Kathryn heard there was to be a respectable movement downtown, and she left the children at home to meet up with the other townspeople. She walked with Anne through the crowd of what seemed like hundreds. The two women simply followed the mob, flowing in and out of every crevice, to what occurrence they knew not. For the first time, they saw for themselves how widespread the blight had become and how many families it had devoured. They looked upon the faces of horrific starvation and the thin sallow cheeks and wrecked skeleton bodies that stiffly moved about. This movement differed from others because respectable citizens also took to the streets and filtered throughout the crowd. Then suddenly, something mysterious happened, and they grouped together into four rows, picking up the pace as the mob grew larger. Those too feeble or sick to walk stood by the wayside and waved to the marching people, giving them inner strength. The event had turned into almost a parade with shoulders straight and heads held high. The fragile marching crowd of fours finally reached the destination of Lord Sligo's estate, a grand manor house on the edge of town.

The people quietly assembled around the front of the estate, and Kathryn and Anne filed in toward the right front side. Patiently they stood shoulder to shoulder as more trickled in. Kathryn bumped into someone on her left, and as she turned around, she saw it was no ordinary woman.

"I beg your pardon, ma'am," she gasped. The woman was very respectable, dressed in highly fashionable clothes, and looked as if she should be living in that house herself.

"No need to apologize," the elegant woman said. "We are all here for the same diplomatic reason, and I too will do what I can to contribute to the ideal belief of equality." The rich luxurious accent delicately cradled Kathryn's ears and sent her memory back to the manor house of her childhood. The statement flowed from the woman's moist lips like verbal velvet, and Kathryn was in complete awe of such grace. The woman was divine perfection, like a sleeping newborn embellishing and enriching even the air that is graciously breathed. Kathryn secretly hoped that someday, somehow she could be as affluent and stunning as this kind woman. And then the lowly gravelled sound of her people scratched her ears, bringing her back into unjust reality.

"Whit's goin' to happen?" Anne whispered to Kathryn.

Kathryn caught her breath and the ugly sound of her own voice, "I don't know; someone mist have a plan."

The gathering was suddenly quieted by the two huge doors of the estate that were slowly opened by two men. A moment later, Lord Sligo emerged and stepped out from his grand home. He stood waiting for a response, and suddenly someone from the crowd yelled, "Kneel! Kneel!" Like dominoes, the gathering of about four hundred fell to their knees in humble mercy. Lord Sligo stood dumbfounded, consumed with understanding and compassion. He bowed his head and raised the palm of his right hand to the crowd.

One of Lord Sligo's men ran to the front and yelled, "Lord Sligo doesn't have any money and now no food 'cause he gave it all away—don't you understand?"

Someone else from within the gathering began to sing, and little by little, more and more people joined in the chorus as they remained kneeling. Soon the entire mob was singing, and it sounded breathtaking. Anne, Kathryn, and the elegant woman sang with gusto as the words echoed through the streets and floated into the clouds. Kathryn felt connected, the bond between rich and poor melding and intertwining with each word.

> Be Thou my vision, O Lord of my heart;
> Naught be all else to me, save that Thou art.
> Thou my best thought, by day or by night,
> Waking or sleeping, Thy presence my light.
>
> Be Thou my Wisdom, Thou my true Word;
> I ever with Thee, Thou with me, Lord;
> Thou my great Father, I thy true son;
> Thou in me dwelling, and I with Thee one.
>
> Be Thou my battle-shield, sword for my fight,
> Be Thou my dignity, Thou my delight.
> Thou my soul's shelter, Thou my high tower.
> Raise Thou me heavenward, O Power of my power.
>
> Riches I heed not, nor man's empty praise,
> Thou mine inheritance, now and always:
> Thou and Thou only, first in my heart,
> High King of heaven, my Treasure Thou art.

High King of heaven, my victory won,
May I reach heaven's joys, O bright heav'ns Son!
Heart of my own heart, whatever befall,
Still be my vision, O ruler of all.[4]

Lord Sligo joined in the latter part of the song until he could stand no more and retreated inside his estate, weeping. When it ended, ever so slowly the people began to rise one at a time and once again filter into the town.

Routh had heard that the southern seaside town of Skibbereen, County Cork, was fast becoming one of the most destitute in Ireland. Rumors swarmed through other villages about the horrific conditions, and by this time, not a single spec of food could be found in that town. A few people had money but no food to purchase. The Commissariat officer in Skibbereen was asked by the Relief committee for some of his meal, but he explained that he could not give out any food because his orders prohibited it. Some people gathered in the town and began to throw stones and yell about the government's refusal to help the people. A few days later, the committee returned with a large crowd of skeletons behind them. When the Commissariat officer opened the door, the scene was too much for him to bear, and he handed over two and a half tons of meal. He later explained to Routh that he felt he had no choice. The neighboring town of Trellagh heard of the gratuitous food and asked for two tons, which he again handed over freely. Then another neighboring town of Leap asked for ten tons, and this time the Commissariat officer refused, knowing that the asking would not cease until all the meal was gone.

The Relief committee of Leap condemned the officer and told him that any breach of peace from the people would be his fault.

---

4   Ancient Irish Hymn from 6th Century, Be Thou My Vision by Dallan Forgaill.

"What was I to do?" the officer wrote. Routh replied to stand by his orders and not to distribute any further meal unless directed to do so. Many more letters from his Commissariat officers poured into Routh's office, describing in Rathcormack, County Cork, that the people were living on cabbage leaves. In Clashmore, County Waterford, the people were living on blackberries. In Mayborough, the last morsel of food was seen three weeks ago. In Leitrim, there was no food in the town and literally hundreds were dying.

All the while, Irish exports packed with food sailed on down the rivers and away from its starving population. Every boat was carefully monitored by armed guards, and at this point, the people could not stand much more and riots began to occur at many docks. This time, the riots were fierce compared to the previous years, probably since the poor had nothing to lose. Death by a gunshot was probably better than death by starvation anyway.

At the urging of one of his Commissariat officers, Routh decided to take a trip to Dungarvan, County Waterford, to assist in the local Irish Relief. The officer wrote that the village seemed to be self-destructing. It did not matter that a local depot was available because most people did not have any money to purchase food. So they turned their attention to the numerous exports leaving their shores.

When his black shiny coach arrived on the evening of September 28th, Routh was very aware of the uneasy feeling throughout the coastal village. Day after day, boatloads of cargo filled with foodstuffs shipped out of the docks as the starving inhabitants could do nothing but watch from afar. The Commissariat officer that wrote to him thought that some disturbance was about to occur as more and more destitute people lined the docks and watched the food that could save them and their families from certain death pull away toward England. It was like a serrated knife was piercing their very souls, and the officer could feel the anger and bewilderment from the people toward every single person involved in the exporting. The skeletons dressed in filthy rags stood and watched each piece of food being carefully lowered into the cargoes, and if it were not for the armed guards keeping close surveillance of all the boatloads, that food would be in their mouths for certain.

The following morning, Routh walked with the Commissariat officer through the center of the village discussing the situation when suddenly a few hundred country men and women formed an angry mass and walked toward them, entering merchants' shops and coming out again. They stormed the village streets, shouting, cursing, and banging the walls and counters for intimidation. They entered each shop and demanded that all the merchants stop exporting grain at once. Routh and the officer stepped aside into an alleyway and watched the master plan unfold. Certainly this had been thought out and contrived for many days as each starving individual did his best to gain some control over his life.

"Why don't you get a job on the Works?" one merchant bravely asked.

"Thar ain't no jobs left, stupid, or we would," one man sarcastically said. "Do you think we wanna do this? Jist look at me! We're forced to do this or we'll all die! I've bin kicked out of me home and haven't no place to go; I've buried three children an' I have two more in a ditch somewhar that're sick and starvin'! I want to work but thar's *no work* ... I'd like to know ... what would you do if you were me, huh?"

The merchant shook his head and said nothing, not wanting to aggravate the man any further. In the street, Routh noticed three men in particular leading and goading the pack as the yelling mob that followed formed into a company of raging, uncontrollable derelicts. The armed guards that were protecting the cargoes immediately left their posts and ran into the streets to break up the disturbances. Now the only thing in the way of the food and the destitute were the workers loading the boats, and they were certainly no match for starving people. The workers observed the hungry crowd and scampered out of the way when they saw the people running toward them. They were not about to be beaten or trampled for a few boatloads of food. When the mob reached the cargoes, they pried open the crates with any tool nearby, and when each box broke open, there was a mad scramble to shove as much as possible down their throats. They could not get the food into their mouths quickly enough, and most of them choked and coughed trying to swallow before chewing it thoroughly. They were like filthy, wretched animals pushing and shoving their way to gorge as much as attainable. Their mouths were left wide open most of the time, ready for their hands to grab anything and shove it in to be devoured. One man thrust so much food into his mouth that he could not close it enough to chew. It was a horrible, somber sight to watch as bits of food flew everywhere. And every morsel—crushed, broken, smashed, or stepped on … either on their bodies, in their hair, or on the floor—was eaten.

Other mob members continued to drift in and out of local businesses as the guards contained only a few. The mad crowd was like a fluid liquid, encompassing the village streets and flowing down into every nook and cranny, gaining momentum as the stream of people cascaded into a gushing plethora of effervescence. Routh and the officer remained stunned as they watched the frenzied crowd gain control of the village as the adrenaline seeped through their weak veins.

"My God, sir," the officer said, stunned. "My God."

"Yes," Routh echoed. "I hoped it never would have come to this, but I don't blame them." He shook his head, feeling responsible. "I'm certain the authorities will be arriving shortly."

The two men remained in the alleyway and witnessed the ringleaders being hunted down and seized by the police. On horseback and on foot, the police rounded them up and bound their hands together tightly with one rope. One grand policeman on a beautiful sleek black horse was handed the end of the large rope, and he marched the stumbling ringleaders through the middle of the village. The peasant followers booed and vowed revenge as the three men were taken away and thrown into jail.

"On the orders of the captain, I demand all of you to disperse!" a policeman on horseback yelled.

The people responded by gathering at one end of the street and forming one large mob that would not budge. The police repeatedly kept ordering them to disband, but the people remained.

"We'll not be layvin' till our layders are set free!" one man shouted, raising his fist in the air.

"Yaaa!" the crowd shouted in unison. They knew they were strong as a pack, and it felt good. The standoff persisted for about twenty minutes more until Routh and the officer heard the sound of many horses coming around the bend; they were startled to see that the 1st Royal Dragoons were summoned in full gear. Ironically, this infuriated the mob further and they began yelling and pelting the infantry with stones. With each passing minute, the crowd became more and more enraged until the Riot Act was read, but still the fury in the people did not wane. All of a sudden, the Dragoon captain ordered his men to fire and twenty-six shots rang into the air and into the thin bodies of the rioters. The vivacious mobsters instantly stopped yelling, with gasps and screams now filling the air.

Routh instinctively ran out into the street to try and quell the situation, but one officer grabbed his arm and pulled him back pleading, "Please, sir, I don't think it's wise."

"Now step back all of you!" the Dragoon captain roared. This time the crowd obeyed and receded, except for several men who were injured and two others who lay dead on the ground with blood oozing out of their wounds. One half-naked woman was flailing above one of the bodies crying, "You've killed me husband! You've killed me husband, you bastards!"

"Back up, ma'am!" the Dragoon captain commanded. The woman stood up, weeping and shaking, and walked backwards away from her husband's body.

"Now I order all of you to disperse and depart out of the village!" the captain said, pointing toward the countryside.

The peasants had no choice. With slumped, beaten shoulders, they made their way through the streets and into the countryside, looking around to find a dry hole in the ground or perhaps a quiet place to simply lie down and wither away. Death was the only solution now.

Routh spoke with the Dragoon captain and several police, but nothing more was to be learned. The riot was over and it was time for Routh to return to Dublin. He boarded the next coach and passed the time by making notes on the occurrence and what could possibly have been done in case another catastrophe should arise. Trevelyan was informed of the scene, which further soured his attitude toward the Irish.

Soon after the riot, four military companies were sent to Dungarvan to maintain the peace, but the revolt had a lasting effect on the merchants and exporters. The laborers hired to load the vessels with grain for export were too afraid to continue working. Trevelyan now ordered all vessels to have a naval escort as they traveled the River Fergus loaded with grain and meal, and a vessel of war loaded with marines lay in waiting off the coast of Bantry and Berehaven, ready for any disturbance. The few government depots in the area were guarded by troops, and even the corn in the fields was protected. The police were sent out daily to guard the fields because the people were cutting the harnesses off the horses so the carts of corn would not be carried off.

Joseph was digging a large trench alongside a group of men he did not know. He was physically beat up from sleeping on the ground and constantly being cold. He kept thinking of Kathryn and the children, and that was what kept him alive in such a dreary atmosphere. He knew the Public Works was the only way to stay alive, but once again problems with inadequate or not enough employees lead to chaos. It seemed the right hand did not know what the left hand was doing, and confusion was leading the way. He overheard some men next to him discussing how many of their friends had sent in their applications, but only a few ever got a response.

"Only some of the districts providin' work," a man said, "but most ain't."

"We kin stand together and demand more work," said another.

"Why bother," piped in an older man. "If we riot, thin they only call out the troops."

"I don't know why we even bother workin'," said another. "Thar's no one 'ere to see all the work we bin doin' anyway. We bist be standin' 'ere and doin' nothin' and git paid the far they give us. 'Tis not even enough to live on with the prices bein' raised ever day. They expict jist that one man over thar walkin' 'round to keep track of all of us? Lord above, what a job, how hard kin that be intirely."

The men suddenly noticed the Works employee approaching and abruptly ceased all talk. The supervisor walked straight up to the last man that spoke and stared him in the face.

"Do you know I have very good hearing?" the supervisor said. "I don't blame you men for being unhappy, but do not think for one minute that my position here is easy. At presentment sessions, we're scorned and ridiculed, and once we're out supervising, the hours are long and the work draining. I'm usually up at 7:00 AM and work every day until 2:00 or 3:00 in the morning; then I'm up again at 7:00 AM the next day. I need to supervise several sights, so I'm thrown here and there, traveling long distances in all kinds of weather where I'm sometimes pelted with rain and various storms. You men of course are starving and I'm sorry about that. But you take it out on us, yelling insults about the required work and the low pay. I don't make the rules here, I just follow them. And then because of the conditions of this job, many men cannot take it and quit in the middle of their shifts and never return.

This leaves the rest of us to take up the slack. So don't think that because I'm not digging that I have it any better than you."

The man he had been speaking to said, "Sorry, sir, I guess the famine is affectin' us all."

"Aye, it is," the supervisor said and walked away.

Joseph and the other men worked steadily all day and never spoke of the incident again.

As winter approached, Kathryn and the children were very weak and sat in and around their hut most of each day. The children had no strength to play, and the baby slept constantly. Their bodies actually hurt from lack of food and inactivity. The daily ration of soup at Lord Somerhaven's was now distributed to their village due to the weak condition of the tenants. The landowner was almost bankrupt, but he said nothing to the people. He knew they would surely die if his soup was not available. Almost daily, a person knew of a person or two who died of starvation, and the talk surged through each village and on to the next.

The days passed one after another as Kathryn rationed her food and tried to keep a positive outlook for the future. Then one late afternoon, the family was in their hut placing more peat on the fire and trying to stay warm. A shuffle was heard outside, and the door swung open. Joseph stood at the threshold carrying his bundle and a bag. Kathryn and the children sprang up as best they could and engulfed him in hugs and kisses telling him how much they missed him.

"Ohhhh, let me sit down," he said. He was visibly worse than they were as he stiffly sat on the edge of the bed.

"Da, don't ever leave us again," Shay swooned, sitting down beside him and holding onto his arm. She gazed up at him like he was a prince, and Joseph got a lump in his throat.

"Don't worry, me princess, I'm here nar,'" he smiled at her, taking in the precious beauty of a child. "Nar let me git some things 'ere in me bag." He shuffled around unnecessarily as the children gathered round and tried to peer in. He brought out three large apples, and the children gasped. Joseph handed them out and then retrieved two more for Kathryn and himself. He went over to the baby and bit a portion of his apple.

"Wake up, baby," he coaxed. He placed the piece of apple to her lips, thinking she might awaken with the taste of food. She opened her eyes and licked her lips. Joseph helped her sit up and fed her small portions as if she were an infant. She was clearly underdeveloped physically and rarely spoke a word or sound at twenty months old. She did not crawl or walk and needed help sitting up. No one asked where Joseph got the apples, but instead relished each bite. After feeding the baby somewhat, he laid her down softly on the children's bed and went over to his bag again. He shuffled around and pulled out some money, which he gave to Kathryn. She hugged him, counting it out, and he grinned sheepishly.

"It should've bin much more," he said. "The Works employees kept layvin' and reappearin', quittin' and losin' paperwork. 'Twas hard, but we built a big road fer miles that should last a lifetime. They let most of us go since it's almost done. Kiernan and a few others should be layvin' by tomorrow. Ohhh ... it's so good to be home." He lay down on his bed again and in no time was fast asleep.

On a daily basis, Trevelyan received report after report informing him of the destitution of Ireland and the insufficient way the Works was being handled. He read each one and put them aside, focusing instead on his job of running the Relief Scheme. He still had faith it would work in the end even though he knew many would die. In October, he received an envelope from America informing him that the current crop of Indian corn to be exported in the spring was being sold at ten times the normal price, mainly due to the French who were purchasing the most. It's either the Irish or the French, Trevelyan thought.

"Margaret!" he yelled out.

She instantly appeared. "Yes, sir."

"What is the conclusion on your research of other food for the Irish?"

"There is none, sir. Most of it has already been bought," she replied. "But the suggestion of yams—"

"Ohh ... yes ... yes," he said, waving her out the door. Routh had suggested yams as a possible import, and Trevelyan considered it every now and then, but never took the step to purchase any. More and more letters were piling up on his desk describing the destitution of the people—about how they were living on weeds, nettles, and seaweed even after local Relief committees were formed and money was raised. There were just too many people without any food. A Relief committee wrote that it seemed as if private enterprise had not succeeded, and they pleaded with the government to send food. Trevelyan responded by sending more troops to the most destitute districts where anarchy was becoming the norm. He had reached a point of irritation with the constant cry of distress and had become immensely annoyed. Through all the days and nights of work, his plan should have succeeded; all that he could offer had been applied. The Treasury was also in charge of England and Scotland, and he could not take any more away from those countries. Trevelyan wrote to Routh.

> It would be unjust "to transfer famine from one country to another. You cannot expect the English and Scotch labourers to support Ireland and pay famine prices as well. My purchases are carried to the utmost point short of transferring the famine from Ireland to England."[*]

Routh remained calm, but he felt the pinch of uneasiness. He dared not think of the consequences if the spring supply of Indian corn did not arrive. He could feel the tension in the air and feared a revolution could occur at any moment.

"Yaaa!" Joseph heard someone yell outside at the top of their lungs early the next morning. The family began to stir in their beds as Joseph went outside to find a group of men gathering outside the village. Some were from neighboring villages, but most of them he had not seen before. A thin, young man jumped up on a box, and with an animated face and gestures, he began to speak to the crowd.

"I'm tellin' all o' you that thar the reason we all are starvin'!" he began as his pitch grew with each word. "They have enough food and money to feed all o' Ireland, but don't. They sit thar big fat bodies in front o' the fire whilst we shiver from the cold and die in our beds! I curse ever one of 'em that's responsible fer our misery, and them days are over if we all git together. Thar the ones that'll lose in the end!"

"But he does give us soup," a woman offered.

"Soup! Soup!" the man shouted. "I could put a pot outside to ketch rain and throw in a turnip or two! Don't be fooled by the wee bone he be throwin' yer way. Weren't you still hungry? He only wants to keep you barely alive so that you kin pay yer rents. Don't you see the differ'? Don't you see it all nar?"

"Aye, he's right!" a villager yelled. "He bin givin' Joseph 'ere baskets of food whilst the rist of us ate seaweed!"

"You're with me nar!" the man said, gaining momentum. "And I know a way of gittin' all the food and money you want. Jist come with me and I'll show you har we kin git it. Lit the women mind the children, and we'll bring back enough food fer a feast! Doesn't that sound good—we'll have music and food for everyone tonight! Come on all of those who want to live!"

The man marched toward Lord Somerhaven's estate while all the men followed. Joseph looked at Kathryn who was now standing beside him.

"I won't be long." He kissed her forehead and followed the men.

The mob walked straight up to the front of the grand estate and banged on the door.

"We demand you open this 'ere door!" the mobster shouted.

"Aye!" the crowd agreed.

The great wooden doors opened, and the butler was shoved to the ground and trampled as the men went running in. They stopped to look around at the huge pillars, polished stone floors with drapery, and fine furniture everywhere.

"Lord above, look at all this," the mobster continued. "An' you were lift in rags to dig fer worms to survive on! Do you call this justice? Come on, lit's find 'im!"

They shouted and howled in unison up the stairs, around every corner and in every room of the mansion. Several men found the kitchen and began gorging themselves as the cooks ran screaming out the door. The mob infiltrated every nook and cranny like ants upon a food basket. Joseph walked in the front door and knew he could not stop this riot. The lavish rugs on the floor were much grander than the rags that hung on their bodies, and the men ran about yelling for justice. They were skinny, weathered, and weak, but he could hear the power in their voices. For once, they were not begging and cowering. They were taking charge of this situation and there was no turning back.

"I got him!" screamed a mobster upstairs.

Joseph stood in the entryway and watched a crowd of men carry small Lord Somerhaven above their heads and to the top of the stairway. They dropped him onto the stone floor, and Joseph could see the fear and sadness in his eyes. It was clear he had been beaten somewhat already; it was hard to see him in this state. He sat at the foot of the leader with his head bowed as the man took this opportunity to rally his troops.

"Well nar lads, 'tis whit I've said true? Look at the riches kept fer himself and lift all of you starvin' nor givin' us none. He card more 'bout his rents and whit you doin' fer him, thin whit he could do fer you. All the time the likes of us scrounged 'round fer food, he sat in this grand estate eatin' all he wanted. Nar whit we come at here is he don't car 'bout you and he niver will."

"Stop!" Joseph heard himself shout. "That's a lie! His Lordship don't have riches as you might be thinkin'. All he has is this house—"

"This *house?*" the leader asked. "This not a house, mate, this is a palace. And you have bin mislead."

"I've not!" Joseph lurched forward as several men grabbed him and held him down. They beat him about until he was bleeding and weak and then left him slumped on the floor.

"It is alright, Joseph," he heard Lord Somerhaven say. "If this is the way it must be, then so be it. I will finally be with Helen."

"Oh, the grand man dares to speak," the leader mimicked. He grabbed him by the shirt collar and lifted the old man to his feet. "Whit we do with him nar'?"

"Hang 'em!" someone shouted.

"I think sooo!" the leader sang. Several men grabbed some drapery cords and tied them together as the rest of the men raised their fists and shouted for justice. Joseph could not believe his fellow men could do such a thing, but they were in such a physical and mental state that he understood they were taking all their anger out on Lord Somerhaven. He shouted, trying to reason with them to stop, but his voice was drowned out by chants of rage. All at once, Lord Somerhaven's hands were tied behind his back and a noose was tied around his neck. The cord was wrapped around several banister rails and thrown down to the men below and the gory scene was set. Several men hoisted him on their shoulders and were ready to throw him over the railing at the leader's command.

Joseph screamed, "Yer Lordship!" The old man looked down on Joseph and forced a grin to let him believe he was all right in his heart. The crowd hushed, and Lord Somerhaven looked up and began to speak.

Give us, Lord, a bit of sun,
A bit of work and a bit of fun,
Give us in all the struggle and sputter,

Our daily bread and a bit of butter.
Give us health our keep to make
And a bit to spare for other's sake.
Give us, too, a bit of song
And a tale and a book to help us along.
Give us, Lord, a chance to be
Our goodly best, brave, wise, and free,
Our goodly best for ourselves and others
Till all men learn to live as brothers.

Then the leader shouted, "Nar!" and the mobsters threw him over the railing. Lord Somerhaven's body swung from side to side; no one spoke a word. They watched him for a moment and then dispersed quietly into the kitchen and throughout the estate. Joseph lay on the stone floor and wiped the blood dripping from his head. He knew these men were not in their right minds, as they never would have beaten him so badly. He rested a moment and then tried to get to his feet, but collapsed. The mobsters gained more momentum and now ran about in all directions, grabbing chairs, pots, and blankets while Lord Somerhaven's body dangled above. Suddenly Joseph was lifted and he felt himself being carried out the door. He could barely see through the blood that it was another man and Edgar the valet and he tried to thank them. Then his eyes rolled to the back of his head and he became unconscious. The men carried him all the way home to a startled Kathryn. Edgar told her what had happened and that the men were just acting out of starvation. The estate and land would now probably be handed over to Lord Somerhaven's nephew, Lord Augustus Sebag Montefiore, who was well known in London for his tough, abrasive manner. The two men vanished out the door with Edgar mentioning that he was not staying to find out or to meet this nephew.

Kathryn mopped the dripping blood from Joseph's head as he drifted in and out of consciousness. The children helped care for him and brought him water that they dripped into his mouth.

They spoke to him softly, and after three days, he awoke in the middle of the night.

"Kathryn?" he whispered, "Kathryn?"

"Aye, I'm here." Kathryn went to his bedside and grasped his hand.

"I can't see, whar am I, whit happened?" he mumbled.

"You're home, Joseph. You were beaten at His Lordship's house."

"Ohh ... I remember ... I remember ..." he trailed off. She placed more peat on the fire, which lit up the room a little. Then he looked at her sideways through swollen eye sockets. "Thar, m'lady, I kin see you nar."

"Rist to be better soon," she said.

"Har could men do such things," he said. "Har could this happen?"

"'Tis not matter, 'ere's some food," she soothed.

"Aye ..." he said, drifting off to sleep.

He awoke in the morning, drank a little water, and ate some cabbage. For the next few days, he was either sleeping or eating, trying to build up his strength once again.

Brenton walked to Lord Somerhaven's estate and tried to see if anyone was about. He saw a butler he knew walking outside and went over to him.

"Mr. Cleary, Mr. Cleary!"

"Brenton! What are you doing here?"

"Beg yer pardon, I heard 'bout His Lordship. Whit will happen nar?"

"Most everyone has gone back to their own homes or to London. There's only myself and a few maids left. And how's your father, is he alright?"

"He's gittin' better."

"Fine. I'm glad you're here, boy. I need a strong hand. Do you think you can help me bury His Lordship?"

"Ahh ... aye," Brenton gulped. "Won't his family come to git him?"

"His Lordship only has his nephew, and he wrote for us to bury him ourselves, the uncaring scoundrel. Come with me."

Brenton followed the butler to a grand room in the estate where two maids were cleaning up Lord Somerhaven's body and dressing him in fine clothes. Brenton looked at him quietly lying on the table as if he were sleeping and would wake up at any moment. In fact, his face looked rather peaceful and demure, like he hadn't suffered at all.

"Is he really dead?" Brenton whispered.

"Quite," Mr. Cleary answered. "Let's get the spades to dig a deep hole. The coffin should be arriving shortly."

Mr. Cleary grabbed a few pieces of bread and slathered them with preserves. He handed it to Brenton who hungrily stuffed it down his throat. Then they picked up some spades and walked up a small hill where a large, old oak tree stood overlooking the great estate.

"I think His Lordship would like it here, don't you think?" Mr. Cleary asked.

"Aye," Brenton said.

And the two of them dug a large hole that took them all afternoon. Brenton was weak from malnourishment and had to rest on his spade every now and then. One of the maids came up the hill carrying a large basket filled with food, and Brenton could barely concentrate on anything else once she put it down and walked back to the estate.

"Maybe we should stop for tea now?" Mr. Cleary eyed the boy.

"Aye!" Brenton smiled, sitting on the edge of the hole.

Brenton only ate what was offered him, and it seemed the butler's arm kept dipping into the basket and handing over food faster than a ... well ... than a starving boy being handed food.

Why did they hang him?" Brenton asked between chews.

"My boy, these times are hard for all of Ireland and especially for the likes of your kind. The men that killed His Lordship were only hungry. They were searching for justice, and wealthy men are the first target. If those men had jobs or food, they would not have killed. Starvation is a terrible thing as you well know, huh?"

"Auph," Brenton answered with a mouth stuffed with food.

"His Lordship was a kind man and didn't deserve to die so," Mr. Cleary said. "When I was about your age, I had done something my mother didn't like. I can't remember what it was now, but she was dragging me through the village and beating me as she always did, and His Lordship saw her. He walked over to her and said, 'Ma'am, if you do not like the boy and wish to be rid of him, I'll take him and give him a job.' And she answered, 'Take this foul boy and do with him as you see fit.' She threw me to the ground and walked off, but His Lordship extended his hand to help me up. I saw that clean, kind hand and knew that this man was unlike any other. He brought me to this estate and raised me as a human being, teaching me the ways of the world. I have lived my whole life here and now I will go into the world and be as kind to others as His Lordship was to me." The butler looked down and noticed that Brenton stopped eating.

"There's more in the basket, boy," he said.

"Please kin I take it home to me family?" Brenton asked.

"Of course," he answered. "I can finish this myself later on today since the official burial with Father Murphy is not until tomorrow morning. Let's go back to the house now and get more food, especially to help your father."

Brenton walked as fast as he could back home and shared the basket with his family. They savored each glorious bite and went to bed feeling quite satisfied.

Chapter V

Joseph sat on the edge of his bed, frail and thin as a crispy cracker. He felt he must get up and do something to help his family. Lying there useless only made him feel worse.

"Da!" Brenton came into the hut. "Are you alright?"

"Aye, I need to git up and walk 'round. His Lordship bein' buried today—is he not?"

"Aye, he is, lit me help you nar," Brenton said, taking his father's arm and assisting him as he hobbled about the hut. He sat down again on the bed, out of breath and exhausted. Kathryn came in carrying a cabbage and a few turnips.

"Da's walkin' 'round," Brenton announced.

"Is he nar?" Kathryn smiled, looking at her husband sitting upright. "Har do you feel?"

"Better ... I should be goin' to the burial."

"Don't be quare," Kathryn stated. "You need rist, and do you really think we're invited?"

"But His Lordship would like us to be thar," Joseph said.

"Aye. 'Ere, have some water." Kathryn handed him a cup.

Kathryn, Joseph and the children attended the buriel alongside Mr. Cleary, the maids and a few other tenants. It was a very quiet buriel and afterwards Kathryn and her family walked slowly back to their hut without speaking to one another.

Once inside Joseph broke the silence saying, "I've bin thinkin' of a plan."

"Weren't you?" Kathryn said. "And what might that be?"

"We mist pawn our bed tomorrow, and with some of the money, I'll go to Ameriky and find me cousin Miles Burnett in Richmond, Virginia, who'll surely help us. I know you'll not be agreein' intirely, but somethin' mist be done. I've lost me job on the Works, and chances of me findin' another are slim nar. Even if I beg to have it back, it kin be taken away any time. I don't wanna leave ould Ireland, but thar's no future fer us 'ere. If we don't do nothin' we'll ... we can't stay 'ere, 'specially with the new lord arrivin' soon, and we'll mightn' have no soup with His Lordship gone nar. Trust me on this, Kathryn, I'll be sendin' fer you and the children whin I git enough money. I've heard many men are immigratin' to Canada and Ameriky and findin' good, stable jobs right away."

Kathryn stopped and turned to her husband. "The last thing I wanna do is separate this family. Why can't we go with you?"

Joseph pulled her close. "I know, I don't wanna leave you neither, but 'tis better if I go first—git a job and a place to stay. Thin you and the children kin come right over and won't have to worry 'bout nothin'. Besides, the baby be needin' rist."

Joseph held his wife tightly, assuring her that all would be well once they got to the new world. For the next few days, they scraped together bits of food, and Joseph walked around the hut inside and out, trying to build up his strength for the long journey ahead.

"Tomorrow's the day," he announced to Kathryn one afternoon. "The far'll be better if I make me way to Dublin first, thin cross to England instead of lavin' from 'ere. But for nar, Brenton and I'll pawn ar bed and git some food."

At this announcement, Brenton began taking off the blankets. Joseph carried one end on his head and Brenton the other, and down the road, father and son carried a valuable belonging that would surely be missed. They returned with some food and a bit of money. Joseph took only enough for the ships fare, explaining to Kathryn that she needed it more for the children. Late that evening, Kathryn kissed her sleeping children piled on top of each other on the one small remaining bed and felt somewhat thankful that they were alive and still fairly healthy. She covered arms and legs sticking out here and there as the bed sagged almost to the floor. She lay down on the ground next to Joseph in front of the fire. The hard floor was uncomfortable, but she was happy to have her family about her as they began talking of the future. They dreamed of a new life in the new world and of a bright future for their children. A home they could call their own and an abundance of potatoes in the garden. They held onto this dream as if they could grasp it with their own two hands if they wanted it badly enough, although the rope of hope was unfortunately tied to a bucking bronco that kicked in every direction trying to throw them off at every turn. And they knew if they held on together the rope would not fray, nor would they lose their grasp. And alas, the bronco would eventually have to submit to the regime of its captor, and they would for once in their lives be sovereign of their own destination. They fell asleep with mixed emotions and hearts bursting with love and hope.

The following morning Joseph got up and placed a few bits of food in his pocket for his long journey. He gathered a few belongings and wrapped them in one blanket.

"You bist take another one," Kathryn pleaded. "You'll ketch cold."

"Me heart will keep me warm knowin' you and the children will be atin' lots of food soon," he smiled.

He kneeled on one knee and called to the girls, "Come 'ere, me wee ones."

They went to their father and stood side by side. "I'm goin' on a long journey out of Ireland and to a new world. I'll write and send money so you kin come over too whin I find our new home."

"Har we find you?" Brogan asked.

"I'll write har to git thar and send it to you, and Mam will lead you back to me," he explained.

"Har long will that be?" Shay asked.

"I don't know, lass," he said. "Maybe a long time."

"Lots of food thar?" Brogan asked.

"Lots of food, sweet one, and whin you come over, we'll fill them bellies till thar nice and plump!" he smiled, patting their sunken stomachs. "You jist be waitin' fer that day. It'll come soon enough. Give me a hug nar." He embraced them and walked over to Brenton.

"Me son, you're mighty smart and brave. I know you'll take good car of the girls and your mam."

"I will, Da, I will." The boy tried to swallow the lump in his throat.

Joseph hugged him and then reached over to the baby sleeping. He kissed her forehead and then turned all his attention toward Kathryn. He said nothing as he brushed the side of his wife's head softly and pulled her close. The wind blew slightly outside and straight through her body, grabbing her heart and weighing it down, down, down until it shattered upon the floor into tiny pieces. How would she ever live if he did not? She gripped his body and closed her eyes, willing herself to remember this moment and store it for future lonely evenings. She cupped the back of his head, neck, back, then shoulders, secretly wanting to feel, smell, and taste the moment until it completely filled her empty inner core. She brought all her senses to the forefront, pleading with them to grasp whatever they could and then to retreat back into her body and lie dormant until called upon. And then on frigid, bitter forlorn nights, she could lie in the black of the hut and replay the film, scene by scene, recalling all her senses to perform. She could once again brush against the stubble of his cheek and take in the scent of his neck, feel his arms around the small of her waist and the warmhearted kisses upon her lips. With this thought, the veil of self-perseverance slowly lowered over her head and throughout her wistful muse.

Joseph looked into her eyes and searched his mind for reassuring words.

"If you not har from me ..." he said.

"I'll har from you, I will," Kathryn almost demanded, feeling numb. She did not want to believe she was losing her husband.

"Shh, okay," Joseph calmed her. "I'll send a letter and money whin I kin so we'll be a family again—"

"We are a family; we'll always be a family," Kathryn broke in.

"I ... I know ..." Joseph continued. "I jist mean I know it'll be hard waitin' fer letters and takin' care o' the wee ones. We have no choice har, but this goin' to turn out, I know it will."

"Aye, 'twill," her voice broke.

"This is intirely to be a good thing," he said.

"And 'tis, Joseph." She held his hands, forcing a smile and making light of the moment. "We'll jist miss you so."

"Aye," he replied, kissing her lips and right hand.

Then he leaned in close and whispered into her ear, "I tried me best as a man and husband. I'll love you ferever and mightn' the blessin's of God be with you ever an' always."

He exited the hut quickly with all of them crying. His weeping family followed him outside and stood in their rags draping over their thin bodies. Joseph began walking down the road and turned to see his family waving good-bye. No one knew if they were going to see each other again, and the agony of that thought was almost too much to bear. They were a desperate family being torn apart by hunger, and the odds were stacked against them that all would turn out favorably.

"Bye, Da!" Shay yelled through her tears.

"Write soon!" Brogan wept.

The family stood crying until Joseph became a spec in the distance and Brenton could take it no longer. He bolted, running as fast as his skinny legs would take him, shouting, "Da! Da!" Joseph heard him and stopped. He ran a little toward the boy until he dropped to his knees and they embraced with all their strength. The boy was sobbing, and Joseph fought to hold back his own tears.

"Don't go, Da," Brenton wept.

Joseph stood his son at arm's length and looked him in the eyes.

"I mist so we kin have a good life fer you and food to eat," he explained. "I mist … I've no choice."

"Thin take me with you," Brenton pleaded.

"Someone has to take car of Mam. You're a mighty smart boy, Brenton. You git your larnin' from your mam, and in Ameriky, maybe you kin even git to a national school. But right nar you mist fill me shoes till we're all in the new world. I'll find us a hut with lots of room whar you and I kin grow all sorts of food and niver be hungry again. Be strong thin and take car of yer mam and sisters."

"Aye," the boy sniffed.

Then Joseph had to pull himself away and continue walking down the road, away from the only life he knew and the only things important to him. As he kept walking, he could hear Brenton sobbing in the distance, and the innermost feeling became so emotionally painful that it actually became physical. The sadness shot straight to his feet where they almost collapsed beneath him as he forced himself to keep walking. A million stab wounds would not have been as piercing. He looked back once and waved, and the boy slowly waved back, secretly thinking he might never see his father again.

"Bye, Da … bye, Da …"

Joseph kept waving, and walking backwards, he shouted out to Brenton:

May you see God's light on the path ahead
Whin the road you walk is dark.
May you always har, in time of sorrow,
The singin' of the lark.
Whin times are hard, may hardness

Not be turnin' yer heart to stone,
Fer whin shadows fall, remember,
You do not walk alone.

After a few days, a soft tap at the door awoke Kathryn from her daydream inside the hut.

"'Tis me, Anne," a voice said softly, "I know 'tis only bin a few days, but kin I come in?"

"Aye," Kathryn replied.

Anne creaked the wooden door open and peeked inside, not wanting to overly disturb her. She and the children were huddled around the small fire burning with a few peat embers. They all stared into the small flames, dispirited, numb, and mesmerized. Anne knew they felt melancholy and needed to grieve their absent husband and father.

"Kiernan's away on another job, and I'm goin' to see me mam. You like to come?" She thought a walk would help her at least get out of the hut.

"No, Anne." Kathryn looked up at her still standing outside the door. "We'll be alright."

The constant gnaw of hunger never left their thin bodies; it was a feeling so familiar to them that they forgot what it actually felt like to be satisfied. They were like animals in the wild, constantly on the search for food either with their bodies or with their minds.

Without a word, Anne came into Kathryn's hut carrying a bucket of water and a small mass of rotting potatoes. She exited the hut and returned in a moment with a tiny portion of cabbage and a cup. She placed more peat on the fire and placed the bucket of water on the makeshift stove. With a loud *plop*, she poured the rotting potato mass into the water and added the few bits of cabbage. The stench was horrible, but the sound of *anything* being cooked piqued Kathryn and the children's interest and they sluggishly made their way around the fire. Anne lifted the grungy cup above the bucket.

"What's in the cup?" Kathryn asked.

"Blood."

"Blood?" Brenton made a face. "From whar ... and from ... whit?"

Anne placed the cup down.

"Well nar thin," she said, looking around at the faces peering about. "Is this bein'a grand hotel or we in the middle of a famine?"

"Sorry," Brenton said sheepishly.

"The blood is from Mr. O'Toole's cow," Anne explained. "The beast will probly be eaten in the next day or two, but I git a bit from him last night and no one is the wiser."

"Hmmm," Kathryn muttered as Anne poured the blood into the pot.

After it boiled into a right sordid mess, they ate the disgusting soup and nearly vomited on the spot. They thanked Anne for the meal and she left. For the next hour, they all laid about the hut trying to digest the foul meal and wondering if vomiting might actually make them feel better. They stayed in the same spot for a while longer until Kathryn looked over at Brenton.

"We mist be pawnin' yer bed nar," she said to him.

"Aye," he replied. The two rose and began removing the few blankets. Kathryn carried one end and Brenton the other as they made the trek into town. They all slept on the cold, hard ground that night, but the blankets and fire at least kept them warm.

One afternoon, the valet of Lord Somerhaven's estate came by to inform all the tenants that the estate was officially being turned over to Lord Somerhaven's nephew and that he should be arriving shortly from London to sort out the specifics. When he arrived at the estate, he drove up to the tenant homes in his black carriage and stepped out. The healthy young man stood straight and tall with his fine jacket and boots and his glorious black hat. He remained erect and poised upon his black cane. All the tenants heard the coach and sheepishly stepped out from their huts. They looked the exact opposite of the splendid man standing before them with their filthy bodies and torn rags, their hair in knots and skeleton-like bodies. The man pursed his lips when he saw the people and cleared his throat to speak.

"I am Lord Augustus Sebag Montefiore," he stated. "And I have heard about all of you people." He waved his cane at them. "I understand my late uncle recently ceased the monthly requirement of payment, but this is my property now and I will require the rents, you see. I understand these are hard times; they are tough for us all. But the Board of Works is employing, and I know you can all get jobs if you simply apply yourselves. I expect the rents on time payable to my middleman, Mr. Jones, since I reside in London. Good day to you all."

He stepped back into the coach, sat down, and slightly leaned forward. Then with his right index finger pointing into the air, he said, "I say ... I almost forgot, there will be ... no soup for you. Really, do you people have any pride?"

The coach drove away as the tenants stood for a moment in silence and then retreated back into their huts. Kathryn added a few more peat patties to the fire and with each piece she fed her own fire brewing in her soul.

"Who does he think he is?" she said, looking at Brenton. "Your da was jist as fine as he in his day and I tell you that he not be gittin' the bist of us. I'll show him that we kin be jist as smart as he."

She thought for a moment and then said, "We mist pawn the pots we have lift; help me, Brenton." They carried two battered utensils and two pots and bought some food to last a few more days. It was their last hope of purchasing any food, and when they returned, they sat inside the barren hut and tried not to think of the dire situation that lay ahead. Two tattered blankets were all they had left in the world. After these were gone, there would be no way of buying food.

"Mam?" Kathryn awoke to Shay tugging at her blanket one morning.

"Umm … aye … what is it?" She suddenly sprang to attention.

"The baby—"

"The baby?" Kathryn sat up and searched the blankets for the little mound underneath. She found the small body and picked her up.

"Me poor wee lass," Kathryn cooed, "you weigh nothin' at all." Her painfully thin arms hung limp at her side, and it seemed you could almost see through her. Her eyes were closed and her tiny mouth hung open as if the swallowing of air would bring some substance and relief. "I *mist* be gittin' you some food," she said, placing her down on the blanket. "Let me think nar."

The other three children stood on the other blanket and knew there was nothing left to pawn but their very souls. Kathryn tried to clear her head and think as she looked around. The extreme despair of the moment broke the children, and they began to whimper.

"Me wee darlin's, don't cry." Kathryn knelt before them. "I'll find a way out."

"We all gonna die?" Shay asked.

"No … no we're not," she replied, trying not to panic. "I'll not lit you. Mam will find a way, I will."

She opened the windows to let in as much light as possible and began searching on her hands and knees for something, anything to pawn. The children sniveled in the background, and Kathryn turned to them.

"Help Mam find somethin' to pawn, nar. Look fer anythin' … anythin'."

The children dispersed, crawling on the floor with their hands outstretched, feeling nothing but the cold hard ground beneath their fingers. Kathryn wanted to scream in desperation, but knew she must remain calm for them. A few minutes went by, and suddenly Brenton yelled out, "I got somethin'!"

They all huddled around Brenton who was trying to uncover something wedged in the dirt.

"What is it?" Brogan asked.

"I don't know." Brenton kept digging with his hands. Finally it popped out and he picked it up in his hands.

"Bring it over to the fire so we kin see," Kathryn said excitedly.

Brenton hung on to the object and tried to dust it off with his hands, but years of dirt and soot would not give way. Kathryn handed him a rag, and he was finally able to break off enough caked earth to see something shiny.

"'Tis an angel!" Brenton beamed. He kept cleaning and cleaning until a form appeared and he held it up for all to see. It was made out of metal, with slender lines and deep etched carvings. Kathryn sat back on the dirt not believing her eyes. She kept shaking her head and mumbling, "He's still givin'."

"What is it?" Shay asked.

Kathryn looked up and said, "'Tis a har clip, a fancy one yer da gave me a long, long time ago."

"Why was it in the dirt?" Brenton asked.

"Don't know. Yer father probly buried it, savin' it fer that grand ball we're goin' to someday," she smiled and huffed.

"Did you not war it, Mam?" Brogan asked, running her fingers over the rim.

"I did once. Yer father gave it to me the day we married. He didn't have any money or anythin' to buy such things, so I treasured it all the more 'cause 'twas his mam's and probly her mam's fer all I know. 'Twas the most precious gift he gave to me besides you wee ones ... and 'tis the last thing I have from him nar." She got up from the floor, took the object from Brogan, and held it up in the air.

"And yer father would definitely want me to sell this fer food. I think he'd smile mighty at the thought, don't you?"

"Aye!" the children yelled in unison.

"Thin off to pawn I go!" She went over to the baby, lowering her head and voice. "Hang on, me baby, I'll be back with some food, jist hang on." She kissed her forehead and left out the door.

At a fast walk, she could see the pawnshop in the distance as a thick fog began to roll in. She saw a dark figure enter the shop and hurried a little faster. As she opened the door, a big gust of wind blew past and it was hard to close it behind her. The usual woman that helped her was not behind the counter; rather, it was a large, bearded man. The small dark figure covered in a cloak was in front, and Kathryn formed a line in back of her. The figure was so small that Kathryn could see above her head and that she placed a bank note and two coins on the counter. The merchant eyed the small figure and grabbed the note and coins.

"I kin give you £2 fer the note and 3*d*. fer the coins," he said. Kathryn knew the figure was being cheated because the note plainly said it was worth £5 and the coins added up to 8*d*. She wondered where this person received such a huge amount of money. No one she knew had that much money.

"I'll take it," came a deep, gruff voice from within the black cloak. The figure grabbed the money that the man placed on the counter and dashed off through the door. Kathryn wanted to explain she was being swindled outright and ran out the door and stood in front of the figure.

"Ma'am! Please! Did you know you were misled in thar?" she said to the cloak. "He cheated you intirely."

The cloak lifted her head and revealed a ghastly, severely wrinkled, old woman with no teeth. "I don't read none," she growled. "And I don't car." She dodged past Kathryn and was off into the wind.

Kathryn walked back and opened the door to the pawnshop again. The bearded man rested on one elbow and sneered as she walked in. She was suddenly conscious of her looks and tried to crease her hair back and straighten her clothes with her hands. Her pitiful appearance was all the information the broker needed;

she walked up like a meek lamb ready to be slaughtered. She placed her beautiful hair clip on the counter, and it shined like a star in the night. The man lifted his eyebrows at the object and looked down upon her, probably wondering where she acquired such a grand piece.

He cleared his throat and stated, "I kin offer 11*d*."

Kathryn almost gasped at the low offer, knowing a fair price must be about 20*d*. or even £1.

"Beg yer pardon," she bartered. "Kin you please consider 20*d*.?"

"Eleven pence," he stated again, motionless.

"Me husband's not 'ere and I have four hungry children at home, sir. Kin you please consider 14*d*.?"

"Eleven pence," he said, slowly leaning forward and creasing his brow.

"But I need at least—"

"Ten pence!" he blurted.

Kathryn's heart sank as if she had been beaten down. She nodded her head and the man placed 10*d*. on the table. She took the money and left, walking straight to the grocers where she bought as much food as she could carry. She felt somewhat uplifted knowing she was bringing home nourishment to her children and she still had a few pence left in her pocket. She walked through the thick fog as fast as she could. Upon seeing her hut, she noticed the children standing outside and she half ran, holding the food close to her chest.

"I'm comin'!" she shouted, "I'm comin'!" She hurried into the hut and dumped the food on the blankets, scrambling for an apple and biting off a piece, which she held in one hand. She saw the baby lying there motionless and rubbed the food across her lips to awaken her.

"Come on, baby, come on," she panted, but the infant would not stir. "Please … please … wake up," she pleaded. She put her ear to the infant's bony chest and closed her eyes, realizing the unbelieveable had occurred.

"Me baby! Oh me baby!" she cried, picking up the limp, lifeless body. "Me wee baby! How could this be happenin'?"

She sobbed and wailed into the infant's chest, crying for her baby, for her husband, for her other children's pain, and for her own personal loss. She had given life to this child and now she had inadvertently taken it away. And she had no one to blame but herself. After a few minutes, she reached out and held one of the infant's hands in the palm of her own as if it were glass. She did not want to accept that there was no life left in this small body despite the fact that it was a complete skeleton. She wanted desperately to believe that somehow a finger would move slightly or an audible noise would come from the baby's mouth to ease some of the pain that she was feeling. How could God entrust her with such a perfect gift? She was obviously not worthy because she just let her die. This precious life was just thrown away, and it was her fault.

"I'm so sorry," Kathryn cried, cradling the little form, rocking back and forth. "I'm so, so sorry."

Kathryn stayed in the same position for a long while, stuck in a span of time as the moments turned into hours. Brenton finally came up behind his mother and put his hand on her shoulder.

"Okay," Kathryn solemnly whispered, and she and the children borrowed a spade and buried the baby without a coffin and wrapped only in a blanket. The burial spot she chose was the area where she would go to talk to God. It was the place with the slight incline and the low hill in the distance. *God will look after me baby here,* she thought. The family prayed and prayed in the dark until Father Murphy came and administered the last rites. They prayed some more until it became too cold, and then they went inside. They ate some food and went right to sleep. Kathryn stayed up a little longer, clutching the blanket for comfort and wishing Joseph were there. He was probably on the boat to America, but she longed for a letter or some reassurance that everything was going to work out.

Winter 1847. Kathryn slammed a large hammer down on a big stone with a grunt. She swung back and forth with all her might, letting all her aggression and frustration out on the stone. She had found out that the Works were meant to close this month but remained open due to the desperation of the people. She also learned at the parish that the only requirement for employment on the Board of Works was destitution and she definitely qualified. She submitted her application and was surprisingly chosen within a matter of days. The work was long and hard, but she felt no pain. Brenton held on to the large stones that needed to be broken into smaller pieces, and she smacked the hammer down hard to complete the task. There was one other widow working down the line, but mainly she worked alongside men. Children came and went as they were needed, but the very old had the hardest time with this type of work. The stamina simply left their bodies as they tried in vain to break one stone. Two old men on the line had to be carried off, and they both died in a matter of hours.

One day, several men built somewhat of a large shack that became a drinking house for the men as they took breaks or after their workday ended. Every so often, bursts of laughter and shouts came from the shack and Brenton would look up. They would stagger past Kathryn and Brenton and all the others working, reeking of liquor and tobacco.

"Why do they waste thar money on the drink?" Brenton asked, watching a man stumble his way down the road.

"'Tis not whit we do, son, 'cause we need food," Kathryn explained, "But maybe 'tis thar last plashur in life. Maybe the family died, and it takes away the pain. We don't know thar life, so we don't pretend to know. Do you understand, Brenton?"

"Aye, I think so," he replied.

"'Cause we didn't plant seed last year," she said, changing the subject, "we won't be harvestin' any potatoes. We jist didn't have the money. As 'tis, we'll barly make the rent and have a few pence lift over fer some food."

Kathryn could see the circumstances weighed heavily on his head, and she added, "But 'tis not your place to worry; I kin take mighty good car of you and the girls, God willin'."

"I'm the man nar, Mam," he said matter-of-factly. "I'm not a wee boy anymore. I kin handle what needs to be done too."

"Alright, me son." Kathryn loved his strength, "We'll do it together."

Brenton reached for another stone, and Kathryn chipped away at it piece by piece.

The reports on Routh's desk continued to be one disturbing letter after another, begging him to open the depots so the poor could purchase some food. The truth was the depots were almost empty, but he dared not inform his Commissariat officers. Thousands died here and there, and thousands more wandered the streets searching for the life they once had. Routh worried that the Irish would become completely dependent on the Works and use it as their total means of income from now on. The plan was for the Works to provide jobs until the poor could get back into the fields as before, not for the Works to remain as a permanent fixture of employment. Many suggestions were made on how this should be done, although none were acted upon.

Routh took a coach to visit some of his officers and passed fields and fields of barren land being choked by weeds. He wrote to Trevelyan that the poor did not plant seeds last year and thus there were no potatoes to harvest this August. That meant that the people were totally dependent on the Works and would be for the entire next year. Trevelyan creased his brow at this realization and thought to himself of how lazy the Irish were and what an irresponsible, foolhardy people. They should have thought of this state of affairs themselves. Did he have to think of everything? *Trying to help these people who do nothing to help themselves is deplorable,* he thought. Petitions for the government to buy seed was gathered and forwarded to Trevelyan—although it was of no use. He stood firm in his belief that it was not the responsibility of the government to feed and clothe the people; they must help themselves.

The winter of 1846–1847 became commonly known as the "black winter of 1847" due to the length and unrelenting brutality. In better times, the poor did not need to tend to their crops because potatoes do not require cultivation during the cold months. The Irish winter is usually cool with an occasional bit of snow some years, so the Irishman can remain indoors next to his peat fire without too much discomfort. But the winter of 1847 was a heathen just waiting to pounce on the Irish landscape. The snow began to fall early in November and continued until the early part of spring. Gale force winds raced through from the northeast that had swept across Russia, and it was so dreadful that it hit the skin like piercing bits of ice. Hail and sleet added to the recipe of snow as it whipped around in small hurricanes. It was treacherous to even walk around outside, but the penniless Irish on the Works were required to continue working if they wanted to get paid. It was not enough that the poor were starving; Mother Nature added a bit more and stirred the pot as if she were a heinous witch, laughing and sneering at the misery she was administering. She kept adding more ingredients of cold and wind that tested the poor's will to live from day to day. Some Board of Works employees felt sympathy for the workers as they staggered to just remain standing against the wind and snow. Many froze to death and died or were taken away from sheer exhaustion, and one officer wrote to Routh:

> *"… as an engineer I am ashamed of allotting so little task-work for a day's wages, while as a man I am ashamed of requiring so much."* *

The Board of Works continued to be a disaster with thousands of applications left piled on the floor in the offices. In the end, most of them were a logical way of defining the whereabouts and names of the thousands who were to die without any answers. Some emaciated men walked about with their spades searching for work, and the ill-advised fool spread the word that they were arming themselves. True, many mutinies had occurred on the Works and also to other Relief committees, so fear was universal to all. The distrust and hatred usually felt for the landlord was redirected to the officers on the Board of Works and the finger was pointed for all to see that, "This is the man who is starvin' you."* The officers were intimidated, except for one man in particular. Captain Wynne, an Inspecting Officer, could stand no more of the fraudulent Relief lists and acts of brutality against the employees. One of the most chaotic and disorderly areas was west Clare, and Captain Wynne exemplified nerves of steel as he stood in front of a large, angry crowd and called out the names that were on the Relief lists and coolly crossed those off that he felt were not destitute. The people yelled rude remarks and threats, but Captain Wynne continued. When finished, he wrote to Trevelyan.

> *"I have displaced upwards of 9,400 persons, chosen and placed upon the works by several committees in my seven baronies, and I have placed upon the lists the poor starving labourers who had been neglected because nobody had a direct interest in their welfare, and I have not refused employment in any instance to real destitution."**

Stuffy whistled as he dusted around the office with a massive feather duster. He passed by Routh's office and peeked in.

"Cupa tea, sir?" Stuffy asked.

Routh looked up from behind his large desk.

"No thank you, Stuffy," Routh said and went back to his paperwork.

Stuffy immediately looked over at O'Riley across the room and gave him a smug sneer. O'Riley was sitting at his desk and quickly looked down at his own paperwork. Stuffy took his time dancing about and tiptoeing to the harassed assistant, whistling and dusting everything in his path. He slowly made his way, stretching out the annoyance factor as much as possible. O'Riley was seriously trying to ignore him, but Stuffy knew all the attention was on him. He got out of view in back of O'Riley and abruptly stopped dusting and whistling. O'Riley sat with his ears straining and his nerves pushed to the limit. A few moments passed, and O'Riley could not take the suspense. He looked up from his paperwork and quite casually picked up a metal letter opener that sat upon his desk. He turned it this way and that, trying to see from its reflection where Stuffy was behind him and what he was doing.

"Aha!" Stuffy suddenly whispered into O'Riley's ear. "You are paying attention."

O'Riley swung around and began speaking in a loud voice, "You are the most ..."

"Shhh," Stuffy said, "we needn't alarm Sir Routh, now, should we?"

"What do you want, Stuffy?" O'Riley demanded.

"Did you hear about what happened in west Clare?"

"No," O'Riley said. "It is not imperative that I am informed of every single incident that occurs in Ireland."

"Ohh ... but it is," Stuffy grinned. "I think everyone should be aware of every single incident that occurs in Ireland. There is history being made here and you would be stupid not to be enlightened of all the facts. After all, this is *your* country, not mine."

O'Riley turned around in his chair, saying, "I have a lot of work to do."

"And so do I, and so does Routh, and so does every single Irishman as they carefully plan their murders one by one," Stuffy said.

"What are you talking about?" O'Riley turned around in his chair again.

"Ohh … now we're interested," Stuffy smiled. "Well, I'll not keep you in suspense. Remember Captain Wynne? Well, on December 5th, his main officer was going home at 5:30 one evening in a place called Clare Abbey. The officer, Mr. Hennessy, was accompanied by his clerk, Mr. McMahon, and a small boy. The three of them were walking along a road with three soldiers of the 73rd Regiment ahead of them and two others a short distance behind. The three were suddenly confronted by a man who sprung out of the roadside bushes wielding a blunderbuss firearm, and without speaking or warning, he fired two rounds into Hennessy point-blank. Hennessy fell on a nearby fence, and the gaunt man in rags calmly stated that he was not going to hurt anyone but Hennessy. Then he peacefully walked away. McMahon looked at Hennessy writhing in agony and turned to the infantrymen, asking, 'Boys, what have we done? Mr. Hennessy is dead.' Neither the soldiers nor McMahon attempted to help the dying man or apprehend the shooter. Instead, Hennessy managed to swagger and crawl to his home approximately three-quarters of a mile down the road and collapsed inside. One hundred and twenty shots pierced Hennessy's coat, but only 85 proceeded into his body and some on his thigh. His thick black coat saved his life, but a small gathering of local villagers came around to see what had happened. They stood outside his home laughing and joking, giving no sympathy or aid to him whatsoever."

Stuffy stopped talking for a moment and moved closer to O'Riley.

"Now you tell me, O'Riley, that the Irish poor are truly being helped by what we are doing here."

O'Riley said nothing. He turned around one last time and began working through a pile of paperwork.

Routh sat at his desk and opened a letter from Captain Wynne and began reading.

I myself have made a trip to Clare Abbey on December 24th to see if I could help in finding Hennessy's attacker. Since he was almost killed, the government has since stopped all works at Clare Abbey until the assailant is brought forward. Since my arrival, the bitter cold and snow has persisted each day and the village people are starving. "I ventured through the parish this day to ascertain the condition of the inhabitants, and, altho' a man not easily moved, I confess myself unmanned by the intensity and extent of the suffering I witnessed more especially among the women and little children, crowds of whom were to be seen scattered over the turnip fields like a flock of famishing crows, devouring the raw turnips, mothers half naked, shivering in the snow and sleet, uttering exclamations of despair while their children were screaming with hunger. I am a match for anything else I may meet with here, but this I cannot stand. When may we expect to resume the Works? Nothing but dire necessity would make me advocate this step, feeling as I do that I thereby throw away the only armour we possess against the bullet of the assassin, but it cannot be helped."*

On December 28th, the Works were reopened and Hennessy's attacker was never found.

The middleman from Lord Augustus Sebag Montefiore's estate rode up on his horse one afternoon outside the hut and called for Kathryn. The only thing on her mind was eviction as she tried to compose herself, creasing her hair before exiting the hut. The children stopped playing and looked at one another as they could hear their mother conversing with the middleman outside. They heard the heavy gallops of the horse riding away, and then Kathryn came back inside. They searched her face for any sign of distress but found none.

"A letter from your Da!" She smiled and held up a small piece of paper.

The children gathered round their mother, full of excitement, wanting to see the paper, touch it, and smell it. It was the first piece of mail they had ever personally received and they relished the moment. All thoughts of the constant gnawing hunger within their bodies were forgotten while Kathryn began to open the letter and read.

Me Der Kathryn, Brenton, Shay, Brogan, and baby,

After manee days of kind peple givin me rides I mad it to Dublin and thin used sum muney fer a fery to Liverpool. Thar ar peple everwar in and out of bildings and in the strets movin bout. So manee peple lik I hav niver sen befor. Manee Irishmen ar headin fer Ameriky as me and I hav mad frends with to bruthers that I wil travel with. The ships ar big and grand and with me tiket I am leevin today. I think bout al of you ever day and wil send muney as soon I kin. I hop lord seebag montafuree wil kep givin you soop. Me love to al.

Joseph

Kathryn and the children cried and hugged one another as if they had won a prize. Their father was alive and well and the plan was progressing. Soon he would be arriving in America and sending money for food and a ticket for their fare. All they had to do was wait and survive until that time came. The children begged Kathryn to read the letter over and over until they could recite it from memory. They each held it as if it were a part of their father himself and then they asked Kathryn to read it some more.

"Brenton will read it fer you girls, won't you, me son?" she said. Her mind was thinking now about how she was going to tell Joseph about the baby. Her poor, innocent infant that lived so little, dying as a mere flower bud without fully blooming into a radiant pink rose.

"Aye, Mam," Brenton answered, and the three of them cuddled in the blanket, reading and listening. They talked about all the things Joseph might be seeing on his journey and all the food that would be awaiting him in America.

"I heard in Ameriky they have choclite," Brenton announced.

"Whit's that?" Shay asked.

"'Tis a dark sweet that tastes like heaven," Brenton sighed.

"But I don't wanna eat heaven. Thin whar will God live?" Shay asked.

"Oh, Shay, don't be quare an' ruin the dream!" Brenton snapped. "You don't *eat* heaven; choclite jist tastes like the bist thing in the world."

"Har'd you know?" Brogan asked.

"Before you two bin born, His Lordship gave me some at Easter," Brenton explained. "'Twas a mighty piece the shape of an egg, and I ate the whole thing intirely!"

"Have you ever had the choclite, Mam?" Brogan asked.

"Aye, I drank it once in England whin I was young," she answered. "And I had some of the hard type from Brenton's egg."

"I'm goin' to have some whin we git to Ameriky," Shay said.

"Me too!" Brogan smiled.

"Me too!" Brenton added.

In the early part of December, the Works were employing approximately 300,000 people with more than twice that amount waiting for employment. The works had reached a crisis mode as letters of correspondence soared rapidly from one place to another, each employee asking questions, making comments, or passing on information. On November 30th, two thousand letters had flowed into the Board of Works offices, and on the 12th of December, 2,500 more gushed in. Men scrambled about, trying to administer four or five jobs at once, and one man later wrote:

> *"... looking back on it ... appears to me not a succession of weeks and days, but one long continuous day, with occasional intervals of nightmare sleep. Rest one could never have, night nor day, when one felt that every minute lost a score of men might die."* *

The only one not dismayed was Trevelyan. The numbers employed on the Works continued to rise, and at the end of December, it was estimated 450,000–500,000 people were working in the freezing weather, some getting paid, some not. Trevelyan wanted the numbers on the Works to diminish, not rise. He wanted the needy to be employed on the Works for a short period of time, then for them to proceed to live as before, without government assistance. The people wanted the same, but they were so impoverished that the only thing on their minds was getting food to survive one more day. He shook his head at the numbers and wrote to Routh.

> *"The great evil with which we have to contend is not the physical evil of the famine, but the moral evil of the selfish, perverse, and turbulent character of the people."* *

Routh was walking with his wife, Marie Louise, one crisp afternoon on their way to the local bakery shop for high tea. They strolled the cold streets arm in arm, passing by the respectable as well as the poor. They entered the shop with the glorious aroma of oven-baked goods and ordered two cream teas. This delicacy is made up of several freshly baked scones that are sliced in half and slathered first with clotted cream, then topped with strawberry jam. The meal is also accompanied with a pot of piping hot tea. Routh loved this sweet cuisine that originated from his country; each bite was like tasting a bit of his beloved England. They sat down on two ornate chairs next to a large window that faced the street and began discussing their two eldest sons' studies. Their server came to the table, laid their meal down before them, and left. Marie Louise began to carefully prepare each scone as she talked about their sons, and Routh looked out the window at all the passersby, feeling fortunate for his family and sympathy for those that were simply trying to survive one more day. Unexpectedly, he stood up with a jolt, still looking out the window.

"What on earth is the matter, dear?" Marie Louise asked in alarm.

Routh looked down at the prepared scones, grabbed the entire plate, and said to his wife, "I'll be right back."

He quickly maneuvered past various tables, flung open the door to the bakery shop, and hurried down the street making sure he did not drop any food. He went down one street, then the next, turning his head this way and that, searching and searching. He abruptly stopped and spotted the same two children he had given his lunch to so many months before. The coat he had given them was wrapped around their bodies as they sat huddled on the ground with solemn faces and downcast eyes void of any spark. As if gazing at the ground revealed their future ... there was nothing to see but dirt. Routh walked over to them and, kneeling down, displayed his plate of beautiful scones before them with cream and strawberry jam dripping down the sides. The children's mouths hung open, and it was plain to see they had never before seen such a glorious dish. Routh smiled and moved the plate forward a little more. The children wasted no time and both grabbed a scone and shoved it down their throats, then another, then another. A bit of jam oozed out the sides of their mouths and a bit more got onto their hands as they tried to get it into their stomachs as quickly as possible. None of the delicious treat was to be wasted as they licked their lips and hands thoroughly, like a cat washing its face. He knew that he would not have appreciated those scones half as much as those children did, and he relished their absolute enjoyment. Left on the plate were small crumbs and tiny clumps of jam; the children looked at Routh but said nothing. He offered the plate and they licked it clean, smiling at him and saying, *"Go raibh maith agat,"* and handing him back the plate.

"You are most welcome." Routh stood up. "And I hope we meet again soon." He turned, walked a few paces, and stopped. He abruptly turned around and went back to the children.

"I wish I could help you more," he said vehemently as he looked into their sunken eyes. "If I give you money, someone could steal it and you probably would not even know the value of it ... I cannot bring you home with me; there are so many just like you walking around ... and there is no orphanage to help you ... I can give you food now and again ... that is all I can do for now. Please understand I am striving to help you and all the people of Ireland, trying to find relief for this famine and to straighten out this situation." He looked at their blank faces. "If you are at the end of your rope, if you need help or you will die, you remember where my office is?" He pointed down the street, but the children just looked at him stoically. "If you need me, go to my office and I can help. Do you understand?"

Still they just looked at him, and he had no idea if they understood. He smiled one more time, then left. He went back to the bakery shop, placed the plate on the counter, and walked over to his wife still sitting at their table.

"Where have you been, Randolph?" she asked.

Routh sat down and said, "There are children without families or homes, and I have befriended two siblings that need help. I'm sorry about my abrupt departure, but I was afraid I would lose sight of them."

He reached out and touched her hand, and she smiled her acceptance. Their server approached their table and offered, "Would you like another cream tea, sir?"

"Yes," Routh said. Then he looked out the window and saw more destitute people wandering the streets and saw his wife's eyes look down with uneasiness on her face.

"And may we change tables," he added to the server. "Perhaps to one over there," he said, pointing to one in the corner without a view of the street.

"Absolutely, sir," the server said and showed them to their new table.

Kathryn kneeled alone in her parish church pew, praying to God for Joseph to make it safely across the sea to America. Her clothes were so ragged and dirty that they ripped here and there from being worn day and night, from sleep to work and back to sleep again. Her hands and fingers were encrusted with dirt and small cuts of blood. Her entire body ached from just being in it and the sheer energy it took to simply move it about. She knew she reeked but did not have the strength or the soap to wash herself. All the money she made from the Works was for the rent, and a tiny bit was left over for a few morsels of food. It was just enough for her and the children to meagerly subsist and not be blown away by the next gust of wind—just enough to remain barely alive and in a constant state of starvation. She was teetering on the edge of survival and knew just one little push like losing her job or a cut in pay would send her family into the swirling black tunnel of oblivion where a person can no longer lift his own head. There he lays in the dank pit of worthless dejection and can only pray to God to rid him of this wretched body and take his soul to the afterlife.

"God will take care of us, missy," a scratchy voice suddenly said, breaking her concentration. She looked beside her to see a face that weathered many famines and was knowledgeable in the struggle of survival.

"Gordis Flynn, well nar thin, how are thee?" Kathryn asked.

"No one wants to buy me poiti," she said, kneeling beside her. "No money 'bout."

"Aye, I know. I'm on the Works nar so we kin eat."

"Whar's yer husband?"

"He left for Ameriky and will send money soon so we kin join him."

Gordis let out a big scoff of disapproval, munching on her gums and mumbling something under her breath.

"Whit was that?" Kathryn was not going to let her get away with a snide remark no matter how physically weak she felt.

Gordis turned around, and with a scowl on her face, she said, "I jist said I'll bet he'll send the money!"

"You don't know me Joseph." Kathryn turned away.

"He's an Irishman, ain't he?" Gordis continued. "I've met him before and thar all the same. In thar hearts they wanna be doin' the right thing with women and cryin' babies lift behind. But 'tis mighty quare intirely whin he be lookin' down at the money in his hand; he'll forget everythin' and everbody and Lord above he's as helpless as a newborn baby. By the powers that be, his feet will take him to the tavern without bein' asked, and the drink will slide down his throat without him tastin' it. And before you knowed it, all the money will be gone."

Kathryn could take no more and stood up in the pew, saying loudly, "I've had enough of this talk. Me Joseph will send the money!"

"Shhh!" Gordis said, waving her hand for Kathryn to kneel back down. "Alright, alright, he'll send the money.

Kathryn kneeled down again. "Don't you put a hex on me Joseph; he'll do the right thing. Soon we'll all be in the new world and plantin' good crops."

"'Twas thinkin' 'bout goin' to Ameriky meself," Gordis said. "Lots of buyers fer me poiti, God willin'."

"Jist don't sell any to men who have wives and wee ones waitin' back home," Kathryn remarked.

"Don't worry, child, Gordis Flynn be knowin' the scoundrels from the gentlemen."

"How are you ladies?" Father Murphy appeared in the pew in front of them.

"Och, times be gittin' hard, Father," Gordis scoffed.

Kathryn's head was bowed and she tried to search for words to describe how she was doing.

"Your baby's no longer in pain, Kathryn," Father Murphy said, patting her dirty hand. "She's with the Lord." Kathryn looked up. "Aye, I know Father. I'm jist tryin' to survive."

"And survive you will," he smiled at her. "God is testin' our strength, but we'll trust in him and let him lead the way. We'll all get through these tough times." He got up and disappeared into the back of the chapel.

Gordis leaned over to Kathryn and whispered, "What tough times is *he* goin' through? You seen that clean white girly hand? He hasn't lost a bit of weight, he hasn't. His rents paid fer, and all the food he kin stuff in his mouth is paid fer by the government. I could stand up in this 'ere chapel and talk on and on 'bout the Lord all day too if they'd be feedin' me. Hmmm ... maybe I should—"

"Please let me finish me prayers," Kathryn broke in as she closed her eyes and folded her hands together in prayer.

News of the distress in Ireland spread all over England, and some people wanted to see for themselves if what they heard was true. Mr. William Forster was one such man. Upon his return to England, he wrote to Trevelyan after learning that he was the man in charge of Irish Relief.

Dear Mr. Trevelyan,

I have just returned from a visit to Ireland and felt compelled to write my own perspective on the famine. My findings on the people of Ireland "disclosed a state of destitution and suffering far exceeding that which had been at first supposed." The children were "like skeletons, their features sharpened with hunger and their limbs wasted, so that there was little left but bones, their hands and arms, in particular, being much emaciated, and the happy expression of infancy gone from their faces, leaving the anxious look of premature old age." In many remote places, the Works still had not begun, but it didn't matter because the people were "scarcely able to crawl." The weather was horrible with "constant storms of snow and hail," and upon visiting one village, the storms were so bad that the local fishing boats were full of snow. The people were so weak, but even if they had been stronger, fishing was not an option. The boats capsized at once and they were left with no aid from the government. I offered to start up a soup kitchen at almost every destitute village, and all but one accepted.

When we entered a village, our first question was, how many deaths? "The hunger is upon us' was everywhere the cry, and involuntarily, we found ourselves regarding this hunger as we should an epidemic, looking upon starvation as a disease." When we came to Mayo, there was "a strange and fearful sight, like what we read of in beleaguered cities, the street crowded with gaunt wanderers." The people "were like walking skeletons, the men stamped with the livid mark of hunger, the children crying with pain, the women, in some of the cabins, too weak to stand ... all the sheep were gone, all the cows, all the poultry killed; only one pig left, the very dogs ... had disappeared." We were "quickly surrounded by a mob of men and women, more like famished dogs than fellow creatures, whose figures, looks and cries all showed they were suffering the ravening agony of hunger." I have seen this with my own eyes and "no colouring can deepen the blackness of truth." Can Ireland be saved? Is there anything more we can possibly do?*

Signed your most trusted servant,
William Forster

More requests for food and aid filed into the offices in London. And again Routh wrote an urgent letter to Trevelyan.

"The distress of the wretched people is heart-rending ... there is absolutely nothing in the place for food ... A panic

appears to have come over the people's minds; they are
apprehensive there is not enough food in the country …
Pray do something for them. Let me beg of you to attend
to this. I cannot express their condition. I assure you that
unless something is immediately done the people must die."

As expected, Trevelyan's response was annoyance, and he
wrote back to Routh:

"Our purchases, as I have more than once informed you,
have been carried to the utmost limit short of seriously
raising the price in the London market. I deeply regret
the primary and appalling evil of the insufficiency of the
supplies of food in this country, but the stores we are able to
procure for the western division of Ireland are insufficient
even for that purpose, and how can we undertake more? If
we were to purchase for Irish use faster than we are now
doing, we should commit a crying injustice to the rest of the
country."

And *"with reference to what is now going on in*
Skibbereen" … there are *"principles to be kept in view."*
You must "act with firmness and be prepared to incur
much obloquy, but it will be as nothing compared with the
just reprehension you would rightly incur from government
and public if you were to allow your depots to become
exhausted." [*]

And what was "going on in Skibbereen" was the worst the
famine had to offer. The locale did not have a Relief committee;
therefore, it was not qualified for government relief. However,
even if Routh had given all his supplies to the starving, it would
have made as much difference as a grain of sand on a long stretch
of beach. Mr. Townsend, a clergyman from Skibbereen, made
a trip to London to speak and appeal to Trevelyan himself on

behalf of his townspeople. They informed him that no respectable people were willing to form a Relief committee and subscriptions could not be gathered. No one wanted to help the starving people. Although some were employed on the Works, only 8*d.* per day was the payment, which was hardly enough to feed a man and his family. Mr. Townsend stated his plea, returned to Skibbereen, and waited. He waited and hoped that food would arrive, but it never did.

Meanwhile, new plans were being made on how to assist the poor, and the idea of soup kitchens was brought up and accepted. The government agreed that the Board of Works was a complete disaster and should be closed. While this was gradually taking place, the government would supply soup to the needy without requiring payment in return. The people were notified and the lines began to form. They walked for miles and waited in line day after day for one bowl of soup, and when February arrived, the scenes grew worse. It was the coldest month of the winter, and with so much snow and such forcible winds, the roads became impossible to ride on. The horses and people could not walk through the deep snow, and many people just gave up and died in their huts.

Now with the Soup Kitchen Act set in motion, Trevelyan decided that the districts where soup was provided should close down their Public Works immediately. Unfortunately, before some kitchens were running smoothly, the Works in many districts began to shut down and once again the people began to panic. Many letters of appeals were sent to Trevelyan, asking for more time to set up the soup kitchens, but all were turned away. He wrote back specifying that the counties had better use their time setting up the kitchens fast before the Works closed indefinitely.

But Mother Nature was not yet through with Ireland. The black winter of 1847 was to turn even blacker as the last attempt to torture the people was now coming upon them. As in previous years, after every famine, disease raises its ugly head, and in Ireland, it emerged and ran rampant throughout the country. It was easy for the disease to spread with thousands of people pressed together in huts to keep warm and thousands more flocking to the cities to find work. There were several diseases that entered the villages and huts, causing havoc and death and almost bringing the country into collapse. They were flowing through Ireland as fast as the wind and infecting the poor and respectable alike. It did not distinguish between the two. The Irish are generally hospitable toward one another and are a tight-knit race, trying to help each other through the bad times and celebrating the good times when it comes their way. But news of the fever and horrible diseases left the sick abandoned and even family members too frightened to attend to their own.

Chapter VI

On the floor, Kathryn and the children shivered around the fire in their hut. The days were long and hard on the Works, but the nights were even longer. It was getting tougher and tougher to find peat to burn, and it was their only means of warmth. The girls stayed in the hut day and night and were constantly cold. Kathryn counted the coins she made from working and had enough to pay the rent and buy food for about two weeks. They would have to stretch out the food; there was no other way. No furniture graced the hut, only one pot, a few bowls, and a few utensils that they inherited from deceased neighbors. The clothes on their backs stayed day after day and night after night because it was the only clothing they had. Washing themselves was out of the question in the freezing weather, and even fetching water or emptying the bucket was a chore as their bodies were so weak.

Anne came running in the hut saying that Mr. McGavock next door had come down with the fever and he had no money to pay his rent. He and his family would be evicted for sure.

"Calm down, Anne," Kathryn tried to soothe her.

"It's mighty scary to be havin' the fever right next door to us," Anne cried. "Kiernan's always away tryin' to find work and I don't wanna go near that house."

"Nor do I," Kathryn swallowed. "The last thing we need is sickness in this house. Lord above, that would do us in fer sure."

The women heard a commotion outside and peered out from the window. There was frost and snow on the ground and the air was icy cold. They witnessed Lord Sebag Montefiore's middleman banging on the door to the McGavock hut.

"Come on out nar, you mist leave at once! Thar's no freeloaders here. If you don't pay yer rents, out you go!" he shouted for all to hear.

The door opened, and Mrs. McGavock had a hold of her husband as she came into view. She placed one of his arms around her neck and one of her arms around his waist as she pulled him from the only home they ever knew. His head and his other arm hung limp, and his feet tried to walk but were mainly dragged. It was only possible to do this because he was so thin it was as if he were invisible. What she was dragging was his bones and the rags that covered them. The man was definitely near death, and instead of helping, the middleman put a handkerchief to his nose.

"Out with you," he waved. "Out with all of you!" He went into the hut and came out again. "Thar is still someone in there."

Mrs. McGavock turned her head around and said dryly, "She's dead."

Kathryn and Anne looked at one another, knowing the only other person in the hut could be their twelve-year-old granddaughter.

"What a tragedy," Kathryn said. She walked away from the window and sat on the floor. "How could this be happenin'?"

"I think there'll be a lot more of these evictions 'ere," Anne said, sitting down beside her. "How kin anyone be payin' the rents whin thar's no food to eat? God has abandoned us intirely, Kathryn. He's abandoned us all."

Kathryn looked up. "No he hasn't. He wants us to fight, and I'll fight till my hands bleed and the only thing I'm eatin' is the grass on the ground. But I'm not givin' up 'cause I've three children to look after, and even if we all die, God will not abandon us.

He'll be beside me whin I take me last breath and I kin tell him that I did whatever I could to stay alive. And you should too."

Anne nodded her head.

Kathryn got up and looked out the window again as the evicted couple wobbled in the cold. "The McGavocks have nowhere to go, Anne. I can't lit them die in the snow."

"Lord above, don't bring 'em in 'ere!" Anne got up aghast. "The fever will be in yer house thin, and you'll all git it fer sure."

"Maybe," Kathryn said, still facing the window, "but I can't lit them die like that. Mrs. McGavock brought ever one of me babies into the world and didn't abandon me whin I was needin' her the most; I'm obleeged. I'll not lit her walk to her death. What if that 'twas me, Anne, would you be abandonin' me?"

"Well … no …" Anne stuttered. "That would be different."

"I see," Kathryn said. "You mightn' well go nar 'cause I'm bringin' 'em back 'ere." Both women exited the hut, and Kathryn quickly made her way to the couple staggering down the road.

"Mrs. McGavock!" Kathryn reached her. "Do you have nowar to go?"

"Och, no," she answered with panic in her voice. "Please help us, Kathryn."

"Don't worry, come with me." She got a hold of the other side of her husband and they carried him back to Kathryn's hut. They laid him down next to the fire, and Kathryn could see that he was barely breathing. Brenton appeared at her side with a cup of water that one of the neighbors gave him.

"Much obleeged, darlin'," she said. She took the cup and tried to lift the man's head to help him drink. When she did, his head fell limp. She slowly put the cup down and got out of the way to let Mrs. McGavock cry and grieve over his body. After about an hour, Mrs. McGavock got up and went to Kathryn across the room.

"I have no money fer a coffin," she cried.

Kathryn held her hands. "'Tis no matter, we kin place him next to me baby. They will comfort one another."

"Aye." She wiped away tears.

Kathryn held her as Brenton left the hut with a spade he borrowed from another neighbor. It seemed he was a man already as he took over the man's jobs. He tried to dig through the frozen ground and barely scraped off bits of an inch or two. The women placed Mr. McGavock's body on the frosty earth and covered him with snow. A proper burial in the spring was to await him. It was the only thing they could do; they had to return to the hut quickly to keep warm, lest they themselves freeze to death.

That night, Shay coughed uncontrollably as sweat trickled down her face and Kathryn knew she was sick with the fever. The next morning, Shay was worse, but Kathryn had to leave for work.

"Don't worry," Mrs. McGavock consoled, "I'll look after this child as if she were me own."

Kathryn knew she had no choice and was grateful for Mrs. McGavock once again. When she and Brenton returned that evening, Mrs. McGavock and Brogan were also trembling with fever and Kathryn felt the world crumbling upon her hut. For many days, she and Brenton tended to them day and night, and about twice a day, Anne would visit and help. Kathryn knew she would be out of a job and completely without money within a week. She tried her best to hide her growing anxiety from Brenton and prayed that they would not be inflicted with the horrific disease themselves. The little girls cried with fright, and Kathryn dabbed their swollen faces with her skirt and sang sweet songs to them.

Mrs. McGavock and the little girls lost recognizable features as they became swollen and their skin turned a dark color. Their temperatures soared intermittently, which lead to violent convulsions, and at times they became delirious and were completely unmanageable. Little did Kathryn know this was just the beginning. The disease was very painful as their bodies vomited violently and sores began to arise everywhere on their skin. It was horrific to watch their limbs rot with gangrene, which lead to a repulsive stench that was almost impossible to stand. The girls shrieked at an earpiercing volume, complaining that their toes, legs, hands, and fingers ached with terrible pain, and Kathryn felt dreadful knowing she could do nothing to help them. She knew the deadly disease was winning as their bodies struggled to stay alive.

With little strength, Kathryn half ran and half fell, making her way to the one person she felt could help. Once inside the parish, she screamed, "Father Murphy! Father Murphy!"

Wistfully seeing there was no one in the church, she went outside and searched for anyone. In the distance, she spotted a young man digging a grave and she stumbled over to him.

"Whar's ... Father Murphy?" she gasped, panting.

"He's gone to bless the dead, miss," the young man said.

"Ya know ... if he's ... any medicine?" she said, wheezing as she attempted to get the words out.

"No miss, he ain't."

"Whin's ... he returnin'?"

"Don't know."

"Ask him ... come to me home ... right away. I'm ... Kathryn O'Malley."

Dizzy and weak, she made her way back to the hut. She spotted Brenton in the distance fetching more water, and out of the corner of her eye saw a black silhouette enter her hut and instinctively knew something was wrong. She hurried back inside the hut and saw the figure grab Brogan's bowl by her side with a bit of oatmeal still left in it. The figure looked up when Kathryn entered and pushed past her almost knocking her to the ground.

"Har dar you steal from me sick child!" she screamed after him as he ran. "You are death himself and you will not take me child! May the Lord have mercy on yer wretched soul!" She passed out, completely exhausted, and slept for almost twelve hours.

When she awoke, Brenton was asleep next to her and Anne and was sitting silently by the fire. She sat up and looked over at Mrs. McGavock and the girls. None of them stirred, and she knew they were dead. She crawled over to the girls, clutching their bodies and weeping from the depth of her being as only a mother can. She stroked their still warm faces and covered their wrecked bodies with their filthy blankets. She wept and wept until Anne came over and gently put her arms around her shoulders, guiding her back to the fire.

"Whit happened, Anne?" Kathryn cried.

"God Almighty ... first Mrs. McGavock gave way to the sickness and passed on. Thin Shay be followin' shortly after. And whin Brogan looked beside her and seen her sister ... ohhh ... mighty quare intirely ... she jist lost her will to live thin died a few ars layter."

Kathryn went to the girls' bodies again and stroked their hair and touched their cheeks.

"They look so peaceful," Anne said.

Kathryn stayed with them until Brenton awoke from the sound of her weeping and sat down beside her.

"I'll miss them very much," Brenton said, his voice cracking with emotion.

Kathryn folded her hands in her lap and only moved them periodically to wipe away tears or nose run from her face. After a moment, she spoke.

"People die ever day," she said specifically to Brenton. "But these girls ... are mine—me flesh and me blood, me spirit and me spark, jist like you are." She stared into the air for a moment, then continued.

"These are me girls that danced 'round our fire so free and happy ... nar 'tis so quiet. Why's it so quiet? Har kin I manage nar without me very soul to keep me livin'?" She thought again a moment until her face grew flush and she angrily wiped away a tear.

"This famine has taken ever thing I have ... and still it wants more. I tell you 'tis not gitten any more." She looked squarely into Brenton's eyes. "Me and you is goin' to make it, you hear me? God Almighty, we're not goin' to die layin' in this pit!"

Anne softly touched Kathryn's shoulders and led her away from the bodies. She brought over some meal, and it sickened Kathryn that the severe hunger made her pounce on the food and gulp it down within a few mouthfuls.

Anne left saying she was going to fetch Father Murphy who had still not arrived.

After Brenton ate some food, mother and son went outside to breathe some clear air and regain their composure. Brenton did not speak much that morning; instead, he sat around outside, throwing stones and drawing in the dirt. He found several sticks somewhere, broke them in twos, and tied them together with some long strands of grass to make three separate crosses. He came inside every once in a while and sat down next to his sisters with the crosses in his hands. He did not speak, but just stared at them. In the afternoon, he finally took a borrowed spade and dragged it to a clearing where some dried nettles were swaying in the cold breeze. Kathryn knew the area well as they had just laid the baby and Mr. McGavock there. He began digging the hard ground once again, and Kathryn watched him for a while. One of the village men approached him, and they spoke for a moment. Then the man walked away, only to return with several other men, each carrying a spade; without speaking, they all began to dig alongside Brenton.

Awhile later, there was a knock on the door and Kathryn opened it to find three men standing next to three plain pine coffins. They introduced themselves and said they had been paid to deliver them. They said Lord Somerhaven's valet Edgar heard about the girls and Mrs. McGavock in town, apologized that he could not come himself, but wanted to send his sympathy. They also handed her a rag with a few pence in it. Kathryn thanked the men and asked for a few moments to say good-bye. She closed the door, went over to the girls, and stayed beside them until Brenton and the other men walked through the door and stood about the room, bringing the coffins with them. They all lingered, and Kathryn knew why they were waiting. She wished they would all just go away … but it was time. She patted Mrs. McGavock's lifeless hand and thanked her for all she had done. Then she went to Shay and Brogan's side and held each little girl's hand one last time, kissed them on each cheek, and turned to the other side of the room. With all her strength, she kept from turning around. She wanted to scream and hold the girls in her arms, to yell at the men taking her babies; instead, she stood heartbroken and wept from her very soul. This was an unbearable nightmare that she would never awaken from.

The men gently placed each body into its coffin, and when they were fastening the top to Brogan's, Kathryn peeked from the corner of her eye and suddenly yelled, "Stop!" The men stopped and watched as Kathryn went to a dirty pile of blankets and retrieved Nelson the stuffed dog. She placed him under Brogan's arm and turned to face the wall once more. The men carried each coffin on their shoulders outside to the large pits they had dug. Kathryn followed slowly behind them to the burial site and watched the men throw dirt upon the coffins. Other women and children from the village began to gather round also to pay their own respects. Brenton placed his crosses at the head of each burial spot, and everyone stood with their heads bowed. A woman stepped forward, and with one hand outstretched, she said:

The blessin' o' Mary an' the blessin' o' God,
the blessin' o' the sun and the moon on thar road,
of the man in the east and the man in the wist,
and me blessin' with thee and be thou blest.

Kathryn felt cheated that Father Murphy had still not arrived to administer the last rites, but tried to concentrate on the love from the few people around her. She had not heard from Joseph in quite a while and could not even bring herself to think of how to tell him of this grievous day in a letter.

As it was, they buried the girls amongst prayers and little else. With mourners standing and a heavy awkwardness absorbing the moments immediately following the burial, a village woman began to sing an Irish ballad. All present joined in the somber song and then ever so slowly, one by one, the people began to walk away, back into their huts where starvation and misery awaited, greeting them with maniacle smirks.

Each and every day thereafter and at all hours, Kathryn could be seen at the burial spot, motionless, speechless, and virtually spiritless. She sat on the wet ground feeling absolutely nothing—numb with the continuing, unrelenting tragedies. She felt not cold, or lonely, and sometimes not even hungry. She didn't cry, wail, or even pray. She simply sat as if waiting for something to occur or someone to appear like a mirage upon a sea of wet winter grass. Since the beginning of the blight, the steady stream of the loss of life had surrounded her village, although it was completely different when the angel of death swooped down upon her private hut and took her own heart and soul, leaving a tormented mind and a wisp of a body behind. Every day was so devastating, she could not seem to break herself from simply sitting idle by the gravesites. The occasional blink or frosted air that exited her faint physique was work enough for her as she grieved her losses. The suffering was indeed physical with every fiber in her body weeping, although the agony did not ooze out as tears. Instead, it swarmed inside her being and manifested itself into an anguishing mottled knot of sorrow. Just one more hug, one more laugh, one more smile upon their wee faces. What she would give for just *one more* moment with them.

I'll never have such pain, she thought. *Never again will any pain be worse thin this.* She thought of Joseph, completely unaware, and wondered if it was better not knowing the truth.

"Mam," a voice suddenly broke her thoughts.

It was a familiar sound that made her heart leap. She turned to gaze upon the only person left in the world to her. Brenton stood, unaware of what to say or do for his mother, how to comfort her in some insignificant way. Immediately Kathryn opened her arms wide as the accumulation of tears finally stampeded freely down her seasoned face. Mother and son embraced tightly, wholly, and without reservation.

"I'm alright, me darlin'," she whispered. "I'm alright 'cause God has lift you. Ever mornin' I wake up and I can't believe this is happenin' to ar family. Why has this happened to Ireland? And har kin the masters and government jist sit and watch us die? One by one we crumble, and those people do nothin'? I don't know why ... I rightly don't know ..."

She wiped away her tears, trying to wipe away the sorrow that gripped her heart.

"But we have each other nar, me precious boy, and we'll be mighty fine. Don't you worry nar, we'll be mighty fine."

With the loving arms of his mother wrapped around him, together they faced the mounds of dirt and crosses of the girls. Kathryn began to sing a well-known Irish tune, trying desperately to focus on the precious child God had left behind. When she sang, she thought of her beautiful, healthy little girls running and laughing and that lifted her spirits.

All things bright and beautiful,
All creatures great and small,
All things wise and wonderful:
The Lord God made them all.
Each little flow'r that opens,
Each little bird that sings,
He made their glowing colors,
He made their tiny wings.
The purple-headed mountains,
The river running by,
The sunset and the morning
That brightens up the sky.
The cold wind in the winter,
The pleasant summer sun,

The ripe fruits in the garden,
He made them every one.
The tall trees in the greenwood,
The meadows where we play,
The rushes by the water,
To gather every day.
He gave us eyes to see them,
And lips that we might tell
How great is God Almighty,
Who has made all things well.[5]

And then she spoke, "And till we meet again, mightn' God hold you all in the palm of his hand."

A few days passed, and Kathryn realized she had not seen Anne in almost two days. She made some meal and, with Brenton following, stepped inside her hut to see if anything was amiss. It was very dark and cold, and she found Anne huddled in a corner barely breathing. Brenton quickly made a fire and brought some water as Kathryn fed her and tried to clean the filthy mess around her friend.

"Lit me die, Kathryn, lit me die," Anne begged.

Kathryn ignored her requests and tried to comfort her with talk of Kiernan and where he might be.

"I've not heard from him in so long. He mist be dead by nar, and I wanna be with him," Anne whispered. "I don't have a child to keep me 'ere."

Kathryn begrudged her bid until she sat with her shivering and gasping comrade, clearly in severe pain.

"You've bin me good friend, Anne, and I'll miss you," Kathryn said, holding her hand. "Don't lit me keep you from Kiernan and yer place in heaven. Thin you'll be free intirely from pain and hunger. Go and be with God if you wish."

A few hours later, Kathryn and Brenton dug another hole and buried their friend Anne, then mother and son walked back

---

5   All Things Bright and Beautiful by Cecil F. Alexander.

into their hut and laid more peat on the fire. She prepared some oatmeal, and they cuddled next to the fire under the blankets. She thought about the fact that they just ate the last bit of food in the hut, they were certainly out of a job, and she had no money to pay the rent next month. The more she thought, the more fired up she became. She vowed to God that whatever happened she would not let Brenton die. Whatever had to be done, she would do it. God had spared them from illness and death for a reason.

The following morning, Kathryn awoke and fed the fire. When Brenton got up, she told him, "Lit's go," and walked out of the hut.

He did not know their destination and did not ask until they got to the work site where they were previously employed.

"Do we still have jobs?" Brenton asked.

"Aye," she answered, making her way to the Board of Works officer.

"Beg yer pardon, sir," Kathryn began, "I've bin takin' care of sick people, but I'm 'ere and prepared to work nar."

The officer looked down upon her and Brenton and the state of them.

"What is your name?" he asked.

She told him, and he shuffled through his paperwork.

"I don't see your name ..."

Before he finished, Kathryn dropped to her knees and looked meekly up at the officer. Brenton immediately dropped to his knees also. The officer didn't know what to say.

"Please, sir," Kathryn begged, "please give me job back."

The officer looked to his paperwork again, this time saying, "Oh, here you are ... you've been away awhile. What makes you think you still have a job?"

"'Cause I, or we, are hard workers and we'll be 'ere ever day nar." She paused a moment. "Please, sir."

He looked at them again, soiled with dried sick and filth, and motioned to an area where a few other women were working. "I think they could use some help."

"Much obleeged, sir, much obleeged … God bless you."

"Alright … alright," he said, walking away.

They rose and walked over to the work area, breathing a sigh of relief. From that day on, they worked as much as possible and felt glad that they could support themselves.

One evening in the beginning of March, Routh informed his family that he thought it was necessary to visit other parts of the country so he could better understand the plight of the people. It was one thing reading about it in letters from his officers, and another thing to witness it firsthand. His itinerary was to take him to the most destitute places, starting in northern Sligo and ending in southern Skibbereen.

"I need to see the worst," he told his wife, "to be completely informed so I may administer the best leadership to my administration."

He made arrangements, took a coach to Sligo, and checked in at the local accommodation. After lunch, he decided to take a walk since he had never before visited this town. The clear day was cold yet welcoming and bright at 4:00, and it made him happy to gaze upon the lush green land of Ireland. He secretly wanted to forget the catastrophe that was killing her people and devastating the minds of those that lived, but knew he could not. The decay of the entire country was beyond any imagination, and Routh walked solemnly toward the outskirts of town to find the locals. The heavy load of responsibility weighed on his shoulders as he walked, thinking and pondering how to save Ireland from its doomed fate. He came to a clearing where seven men were working in a field of about three acres. He felt good that at least these men had income on the Board of Works and decided to watch them.

He sat out of sight behind a hedge with a good view from a small gap. The seven wore filthy rags as clothes and moved as if in slow motion. The field had recently been sewn with oats, and they were clearing the trenches for water by breaking the dirt clods with spades and shovels. One feeble, old man rested upon his shovel and almost seemed to doze off until someone said something to him. The men were so fatigued that rest was a necessity after swinging a spade only one time. They crawled and staggered about the field, swaying with the slightest breeze, and it seemed to Routh they barely accomplished the work of one man. He continued to watch for some time until one old worker broke away and stumbled to the border of the field. He bent down and crawled through a space in the hedge, coming out the other side on his hands and knees, leaving his shovel behind. He dragged his sinewy body to the road and little by little began to try and stand, stiffly moving each limb as if it were frozen. He lurched to and fro like he'd been drinking and after some time finally tilted upright. Wobbling down the road, his feet shuffled one after the other, and Routh watched until he noticed the old man's shovel sticking out of the hedge. He retrieved it and made his way up to the man.

"Excuse me, you forgot your shovel," Routh said, walking beside him. The man turned around, and Routh was shocked at his appearance that the distance had not revealed before. He was not an old man, rather about forty years of age, but his skin was completely sallow as if death were already upon him. His protruding bones stuck out in various places, stretching loosely and drooping like the crust over an apple pie.

"Ahhh, thank you kindly, yer honor," his voice strained as he grasped the end and leaned on it for support.

"Pardon me, but are you going home?" Routh asked.

"Aye, master, I bin workin' in the fields fer as long as possible and I mist go home to rist nar. You see, I'm so weak with the hunger I kin stand no longer," he explained.

"But since you are employed on the Board of Works, you are getting money to eat, is that correct?"

"You would be thinkin' that, but I've a wife and six children and I'm only paid 8*d.* per day. We buy meal but it don't last none," he sniffled.

Routh figured that since the price of meal was 2*d.* per pound, for eight people it bought four pounds, or eight ounces of meal for one person for one entire day.

"We try an' eat wee bits of meal so it mightn' last, yer honor, 'cept we're so hungry we end up eatin' the intire lot in two days an' be starvin' the rist," he said, swaying.

"Let me assist you home." Routh grabbed his arm, and they stepped with a slow, definite gait down the road until they came to a lowly shack he declared his home. He collapsed on the damp floor and introduced his wife and children huddled in a heap for warmth in the middle of the room. The woman lacked any emotion or vigor and simply looked at Routh with hollow eyes. Two of the children looked near death as they could not sit up, and none of them spoke, probably for lack of strength. Sadly, the faces of starvation and the empty homes did not appall him as they once did or as he thought it should. He had seen so many destitute individuals that it no longer became shocking. He bid the family good-bye and walked on.

He came to another field where many people were breaking stones and rocks. Here there were half-naked women and children working, and he tried to find the Board of Works officer, although to no avail. He went over to where a young woman was trying to break a large stone. She swung with little strength as a young boy tried to hold it steady.

Routh walked up to the woman and said, "Excuse me."

"Aye?" she looked up and swung crooked, missing the stone and hitting part of the boy's hand. The boy yelped in pain, and Routh quickly went to his side.

"I'm so sorry," he said, looking over the gash. "The wound is pretty deep."

"I'll jist pour water on it, master," the woman gulped. "It'll be alright I'm sure."

"It is my fault this happened. Please will you come with me into town so we can properly cleanse it?" he offered.

"'Tis mighty kind of you, master," she said.

Routh retrieved a white handkerchief from his pocket and wrapped the hand to stop the oozing blood. He held the boy's hand up and walked with them the short distance to town and into Routh's accommodation. The woman and boy walked in awe through the clean room and into the bath area. They were completely out of their element and amazed that a gentleman of such status would be tending to them. Routh unwrapped the bloody bandage and washed the wound in soap and water. Magically, the boy did not feel the pain as his concentration was spent gazing about the rooms. The bleeding stopped, and as Routh dried it, he thought it looked odd that the boy was covered in filth and mud, but his one hand sparkled clean and bright. Routh wrapped it in clean bandages and sat back satisfied.

"Now that's better," he sighed.

"Much obleeged, master," the boy said.

"No need to thank me," Routh said. "I caused the accident in the first place. Now what is your name?"

"Brenton," he said.

"And what a fine name that is. How old are you?"

"Nine."

"Is that so? I have a son that same age; isn't that extraordinary!"

Brenton smiled, showing his bad teeth, and Routh cleared his throat.

"My son likes to fish. Do you like to fish too?" Routh asked.

"I've niver bin fishin', yer honor. We don't have the rod or nothin'," he explained.

"I see," Routh said.

"Are you from Dublin?" Brenton asked as his mother shot him a glance. He should know better than to ask such a bold question to someone of such class.

"Oh, no, my home is in London, but I am here to assist in the famine." Routh suddenly felt uneasy. There was a knock at the door, and a woman informed Routh that his dinner was almost ready and she could bring it up if he preferred. Routh stepped outside, leaving the door ajar, and spoke with the woman in a quite tone. Then he came back inside and sat in front of Brenton again.

"You're a fine boy," Routh said, putting his hands on the boy's shoulders. Brenton grimaced because his arms were sore from working, and Routh could clearly feel the shoulder bones with no muscle around them. He turned to the woman.

"Please forgive my manners, I am Randolph Routh."

"I'm honored, master. Me name's Kathryn O'Malley. I'm sorry we've taken so much of yer time already."

"No need to apologize. Now I would like to ask if you would accept a gift from me for the accident I've caused you and your boy. There is a basket downstairs with food for you. Please accept it on my behalf."

"Much obleeged, master." Kathryn's eyes lit up with excitement. "We're very grateful to you—much obleeged fer bein' so kind, I don't know whit else to say—"

"It's quite alright." Routh felt guilty for her shower of gratitude. "I will show you to the door."

Routh noticed how oddly they stiffly sat up and walked, as if each step was painful, and with each movement a sharp pain shot through their limbs here and there. He knew he should not offer assistance to every needy person, but he looked at the boy with his dirty hair and torn clothes and thought of his own son.

"Kathryn," Routh called after her as she walked away. "If you need help, please do not forget I may be able to give assistance."

"Aye, much obleeged, master, much obleeged," Kathryn said, in shock of the offer. Then mother and son walked away. They retrieved the basket at the front desk and hurried outside to see the glorious contents. They walked around the corner, sat on the ground, and feasted. Their taste buds celebrated with each mouthful, and Kathryn reminded him that they should eat only to be comfortable, being careful to ration some of it. After a short rest, they got up and began the dreaded walk back to the fields to work. They hid the basket under some brush and approached the Works employee to inform him what had happened. The employee noted it in his booklet and then called for all the workers to gather around.

"The government has ordered us to close down the works within the next month," he shouted amid a few gasps. "Now just a minute. The reason for this is because the government wants you to go back to tending your fields. And in the meantime, soup kitchens will be provided as soon as possible so you can have something to eat."

"But we don't have no seed to plant!" someone yelled.

"Then go ask your landlord," he said. "He should provide you with some."

The crowd shouted that the blight was still in the soil and the Works was the only means of staying alive. The Works employee stated that he was not the one that made this decision; the matter was out of his hands. The crowd responded with questions and comments until the Works employee ordered everyone back to work until further notice. Kathryn and Brenton retreated back to their station, and they worked hard the rest of the day, looking every so often in the direction of their food basket.

"I wish Da was 'ere," Brenton said.

"Me too, son," Kathryn replied.

Routh continued on his journey and entered the town of Roscommon with little knowledge of its inhabitants. He made arrangements to stay the night and made his way to the local chapel, passing walking skeletons everywhere. He wanted to hear how the priests were holding up with all the death around them. He spotted a priest sitting down in his dormitory to have dinner, introduced himself, and asked about his position during the famine.

"And good afternoon to you too, sir," the priest replied. "I am John Madden. Would you like to join me?" he offered, pointing to his food.

"Oh, no thank you, I have eaten already," Routh said. "But go right ahead, please don't mind me."

"Thank you." The priest began to eat and tell his tale. "The life of a priest durin' times like these is very troubling indeed. There are too many people dyin' and not enough priests to administer the last rites."

All of a sudden, there was a slight knock on the door and someone pleading outside, "I need food, please help me! Jist a little food to keep me alive is all I be askin'."

Both men looked toward the door, and Madden sighed, "I hear that all day and all night long."

"Has the Public Works closed down yet?" Routh asked.

"Aye," Madden said, "and we have set up a soup kitchen, but it's so inefficient compared to the thousands that need food. There is just no way that we can feed them all. Is there any way that you can help us?"

"I will see what I can do," Routh promised. "I can submit for more food, but the outcome is not for me to decide."

"Ohhh ... please give us some type of work so we kin eat," another voice from outside moaned.

"Me children are slippin' away from me. Please kin I have jist a wee bit of food to stay alive?" another voice wailed.

The men tried to concentrate on their conversation as Madden finished his meal and pushed it aside.

"Sometimes I feel sick when I eat somethin', knowin' that that food could save some child's life," he gulped. "I have lain in bed listenin' to the groans and pleadin' voices outside and wished that I could be sent to another country. Let me tell you what a day is like for us priests. We rise at four o'clock ... when not obliged to attend a night call, and proceed on horseback a distance of from four to seven miles to hold stations of confession for the convenience of the poor country people, who ... flock in thousands ... to prepare themselves for the death they look to as inevitable. At these stations, we have to remain up to five o'clock PM, administerin' both consolation and instruction to the famishin' thousands. The confessions are often interrupted by calls to the dying, and generally, on our way home, we have to ... administer the last rites ... to one or more fever patients. Arrivin' at home, we have scarcely seated ourselves to a little dinner when we are interrupted by groans and sobs of several persons at the door, cryin' out, 'I'm starvin', 'If you don't help

193

me, I mist die,' and 'I wish I was dead.' In truth, the priest must either harden his heart against the cry of misery or deprive himself of his usual nourishment to keep victims from fallin' at his own door. After dinner—or perhaps before it is half over—the priest is again surrounded by several persons, callin' on him to come in haste—that their parents, or brothers, or wives, or children are 'just departin'.' The priest is again obliged to mount his jaded pony and endeavor to keep pace with the peasant who trots before him as a guide, through glen and ravine, and over precipice, to the infected hut. This gives but a faint idea of the life of a priest here, leavin' scarcely any time for prayer or meditation."

"Ahhh ... a little food fer us poor souls, dyin' in the night," a voice from outside howled.

Madden continued, "The other day, a woman begged me to enter a hut to look in on her brother who, rumor had it, had died. I went to the hut ... provided with a coffin ... and had to creep in on my hands through an aperture. The lifeless and putrid corpse was reclining against the wall. The poor wife and one of the children endeavored to get to their knees (they could not stand) to help me to coffin his remains, but I had to beg of my curate to help us. The poorhouse is packed with people, and thousands more beg to be let in. The people don't like the poorhouse because of the shame, and it sometimes separates families, but they flock to it because it's better than dyin' in the fields and having their bodies being consumed by animals."

"Ohhh ... I've no place to die, God have mercy on me soul," came another wail from outside.

Routh stood up, unable to witness or hear any more. "I thank you for your time, Mr. Madden, and I will try my best to help you with food or other means. And I hope to meet you again under better circumstances."

"Aye," Madden said and showed him to the door. He opened it, and standing there was an emaciated old woman's face unlike Routh had ever seen. She lifted her hand of bones and pleaded, "Jist a wee bit of food an' a blessin' fer me dyin' child."

"I will take care of this." Madden nodded to Routh and turned to the woman. "Take me to your child." And they disappeared into the night.

Routh practically ran to his accommodation and shut the door behind him to block out the scenes that played in his head. "God," he prayed, "please show me how to help these people."

The following morning, he boarded a black coach to take him through Galway and then Clare. The journey would take many hours, and each time the coach stopped, he found the same wandering poor and destitute. He decided to spend a day in Clare and went to the parish to find the clergyman. Routh was told he would find him in the workhouse hospital tending to the sick. Routh went in the direction he was told, found the hospital, and walked inside. The immediate stench was putrid, and Routh put his handkerchief to his nose. He saw sick, dying people laying everywhere, sometimes two and three to a bed. In the aisles, on every spot on the floor, lay people in various stages of illness. Some were sweating, some were shaking, some were vomiting, and some were at the moment of death. He saw a man darting about the room with bits of vomit and feces on his white apron. Routh clumsily made his way to the man, lowered his handkerchief, and introduced himself.

"Glad to meet you, sir," the man panted. "I am Mr. Cooper."

"What can you tell me about Clare?" Routh asked.

"Well, I don't know where to begin," he said, wiping his brow. "The last two months, the people have been pourin' into this workhouse so very sick from typhus and the fever. More and more people keep comin', and we have no place to put them. My staff can't handle so many people … I thought the famine was terrible, but this is beyond words, affecting everyone rich and poor. Last week, the deputy governor, the deputy matron, the turnkey, and a Catholic chaplain died. At the moment, we have about 250 ill people here, and we can't keep accepting more because there's nobody to help and we're so much in debt already.

Can the government send us doctors and money to help these people?"

Routh hesitated. "Well ... I ... I think perhaps ... there might be ..."

"I see," Mr. Cooper said coldly.

"Bear in mind, Mr. Cooper," Routh interjected, "that after seeing all this, I will try my best to get you the proper assistance available."

"All this?" Mr. Cooper said. "This is nothing; let me take you to the back."

He led him down a hall, mentioning that seven hundred people sleep and sometimes eat where they are every day. They came to a room, and Mr. Cooper stopped at the threshold.

"One hundred and twenty people are here on forty-five beds and we're lucky if we tend to them every other day. We desperately need more assistance."

Routh followed him to another room where children were crammed together.

"This is where the orphans are, Mr. Routh. Please take a good look," he said. "Last night, 102 boys slept here. This room is forty-five by thirty feet with twenty-four beds. Some beds hold six tragically ill children."

Routh looked directly into the face of horror as the poor, sick children lay on top of one another, simply waiting to die.

"I cannot stress enough to you, Mr. Routh, how much we need the government's help. Please send us some assistance," he begged.

Routh looked him straight in the eye.

"I will do everything in my power to get you the help you need, Mr. Cooper. I will not forget what I have seen here."

"Thank you, sir." Mr. Cooper reached out to shake his hand and pulled back, knowing that was not wise. "By the way, you might want to check in on the fever hospital down the lane. I haven't been there in over a week—God only knows how they're faring. Excuse me, now I must attend to my patients."

"Thank you for your time." Routh nodded and maneuvered his way toward the door. He reached it and was almost run down by a very ill man stumbling onto the threshold.

"My word!" Routh exclaimed. "Let me get some help for you." He looked for an available bed but of course found none. Instead, he found a spot on the floor and helped the man lay down.

"Mr. Cooper! There is a man here that needs help!" Routh yelled across the room. Mr. Cooper waved his hand in acknowledgment and went back to assisting another person. Routh looked down on the sick man and wondered if he would ever get the help he needed. Then he walked out the door and down the lane until he came to a sign that read Fever Hospital with a large building behind it.

He saw that the structure looked in disrepair and proceeded to walk through the front doors. He was slapped across the face with such a terrible stench that it literally threw him back a few steps and he instinctively covered his nose with his handkerchief. There was no attendant at the front, so he proceeded down the hall that branched off to many rooms where people were once again lying in any space accessible. He peeked into one room and saw so many people crammed into every inch available that the floor was not visible. Some were on cots, some were on straw, and some lay on the bare floor, grumbling and wailing. Most of them were covered in sweat, dirt, vomit, or excrement, and one woman opened her eyes and asked, "Doctor?"

Routh looked at her and said, "I am not the doctor. Please can you tell me where he is?"

She only replied, "Doctor?"

Routh hurried down another hall to another room and another hall to another room. Some people were clothed, some were partially clothed, and some were not clothed at all. Moans and groans were all he heard, and filthy disgusting conditions were all he saw—adults with children, the sick and the recovering, and the dead intertwined with the living. All rooms were the same, with no doctors or nurses in sight. In one room, a person with severely cracked lips pleaded to him, "Water ... water ..."

In another room, "Help me ... please help me ..."

He was running now almost in a panic when he saw from a window a small person outside by a well. He sprinted toward the person and instinctively screamed, "What in God's name is going on here?"

A young girl looked up, and Routh could see that she was no more than fifteen years old. Obviously a pauper with dirty rags for clothes and a few teeth missing, she tried to smile and said, "I'm jist gittin' some water, master."

"Ah ... yes ... I see ... please accept my apologies for the outburst." Routh was trying to catch his breath. "I am looking for the doctor. Could you please tell me where he and all the nurses are?"

"Dead, master," she answered. "Most of 'em anyway. 'Cept one doctor an' one nurse are lift—both sick."

"You are the only one here?" Routh asked in astonishment.

"Aye, master."

"For all these ill people, you are the only one attending to them?" Routh asked again, unable to believe his ears.

"Aye, master," she said. "The others ketch the faver an' git sick one by one, an' I bin takin' car of 'em. Nobody nor none come 'round."

"I understand now." Routh looked around, irritated at the complete chaos. "I will try and get you some help, alright?"

"Aye, master," she said.

Routh's head suddenly went in one direction and then another, seeing but not believing yet another atrocity. "Are these ... graves?"

"Aye, master."

Surrounding the well in all directions were newly dug graves. "Why did someone bury the dead around the well where you draw water?"

"I don't know," she said. "Pardon me, master, I mist be gittin' this to the doctor."

Routh carried the girl's water bucket to the doctor and nurse—two deathly ill people surrounded by hundreds. The doctor was incoherent, so Routh excused himself and began heading straight for the exit to recruit anyone that could help. Amongst the cries and sobs, he kept his eyes fixated on the door and had almost reached it when a throaty cough startled him. He unwillingly gazed down upon a man who resembled eighty years of age although he was probably forty. He locked eyes with the creature whose head was too heavy to lift and whose lips barely moved without any sound. Something about this man's eyes made Routh bend down and put his ear close to hear the words.

"Beg pardon ... me ... me ... me wife," the man uttered. "Take me out ... to the tree."

Routh felt he had to do something and carefully lifted the bones of the man, as there was no muscle left in them. Once outside, he spotted a tree and laid the man down in the shade of its branches. The creature did not gaze at the tree, the hills, or the nearby river; he fixed his eyes on a freshly dug mound not far from him.

"Your wife is here?" Routh asked.

He nodded ever so slightly.

"I'm sorry," Routh offered.

The man asked Routh to find a bag under his cot in the hospital. Routh found the cot and retrieved the bag from beneath a woman who had already taken the man's place. He returned to the tree and opened it. The contents were a dented cup and a small booklet.

"Master ..." the man whispered in Routh's ear. "Please bury me ... next to me ... wife. Booklet ... take it ... lit ... all the unborn Irish know ... har we suffered 'ere."

"Alright," Routh answered. "I will lay you next to your wife myself. And many years from now in Ireland and lands far away, millions will know of this famine and the agony and torment you sustained. I will let them know."

The man managed a faint smile and a slow blink.

"Good-bye ... master," the man whispered.

"Good-bye." Routh stood up. "God bless you ... God bless you."

He clutched the booklet and walked away with watery eyes, heading straight for the town center. He tried to speak to anyone in charge, asking for help for the Fever Hospital. No doctors or nurses were available, but four boys headed out with spades to take care of the dead. No one else was available until he met with several women from the Ladies Association.

"Don't worry, sir," the woman in charge told Routh. "The Ladies Association will go and help the young girl. War not afraid. We'll be thar at sunrise."

"Thank you so much, ladies." Routh breathed a sigh of relief.

He borrowed a spade from the women and headed back to the hospital and the tree in front. As the sun descended, he buried the man next to his wife as he had promised and recited a few prayers for their souls. That night, he read the deceased man's diary and felt some relief that he was no longer in pain.

The following morning, Routh left on the first coach to travel through Limerick, Munster, Cork, and finally his destination ... Skibbereen. He boarded and tried to think of topics to ask the clergyman he had arranged to meet. What he witnessed in Clare was what he expected in Skibbereen, although he had heard that no town had the destitution and utter misery of Skibbereen. It was the town that everyone talked about as being the worst the famine had expelled. At Limerick, the coach stopped and picked up another passenger. Now seated across from him was a Roman Catholic priest who bid him good day as the horses began to trot down the road.

"I've been to Skibbereen once before," the priest said, "although it was under much different circumstances. The streets were bustlin' with activity, and respectable people were walkin' about purchasin' goods and services. I'm afraid 'tis no longer as such throughout our Ireland."

From what the priest learned from other priests, he did not think the town population would survive the next three months unless drastic measures were taken. More rebellions occurred there than in other places mainly because the citizens were far more desperate.

"I will review for myself if what you hear is true," Routh said, "and I am in a good position to hopefully lend assistance to the town. The Public Works you see here," he pointed out the window, "should be enough to help Skibbereen until the soup kitchens are situated."

The priest thought him to be boastful and replied, "If England had different views of Ireland and loved her as deeply as the people, she would see to it that every family was nurtured in the lovin' arm of her bosom."

"Let me assure you that whatever views England had prior to the famine, her thoughts are now compassionate and merciful toward Ireland's people," Routh replied.

The priest had no more to say. He took his gaze out the window, as did Routh. He did not mean to offend the priest—he simply believed strongly in his work and perceived the Relief Scheme he and Trevelyan were administering as the only way to save the people. He was compelled to believe his involovement in Irish Relief could work, lest he lose his mind. As the coach swayed from side to side, the mood of the pictures passing by the window began to change. Every so often, the road was interrupted by people working on the Public Works, and Routh noticed that even the horses looked thinner with each village they passed. Fields lay wild and untouched. Dark clouds seemed to appear out of nowhere, and upon passing one small village, a plain pine coffin stood on its end, leaning against a house. The road wound through barren, dismal mountains with no sign of cultivation or life. And every so often, foul, stagnant swampland appeared at the window. Finally the coach pulled into the town of Skibbereen, and as both men disembarked, a flutter of half-naked skeleton children engulfed them with tiny, boney hands outstretched and begging, "The kind gentleman fer one ha'penny to buy food."

Routh checked in at the only accommodation available in town and set out to find Mr. Townsend, the local clergyman he had arranged to meet through Trevelyan. As he walked through the center of the village, he noticed that all the stores except three were boarded up, making it resemble a ghost town. Two store merchants stood propped at their entrance waiting for somebody, anybody to buy something, and the only merchant busy was the carpenter making coffins. He had plenty of them standing on end outside the bustle of his store, and sawing and banging could be heard inside. One man waited while holding his dead wife in his hands, his head buried in her chest. With each thrust of the hammer heard inside, the man groaned and moaned as if he himself were being punctured. The thought of each nail piecing together his wife's coffin made the reality of her death absolute and placing her in an oppressive wooden coffin intolerable. He sobbed over and over his agonizing emotions amid stoic onlookers who had deep troubles of their own.

Routh continued walking with unease, knowing he was perhaps the only healthy person around. Human skeletons were everywhere, slowly shuffling aimlessly about, with nowhere to go and nothing to do, simply waiting to be stuffed inside one of the coffins they passed by. He witnessed one woman singing a lullaby, perhaps as a means to bear the gnawing pains of unmistakable hunger. Some people were propped against stores, rocking and mumbling, clearly in their own mad world of delirium.

Routh made his way to the parish and found Mr. Townsend trying to comfort a woman who had just buried her fourth child. He waited in the back until the numb, filthy peasant limped past him. He introduced himself to Mr. Townsend and explained his intention of the visit. Mr. Townsend first offered information concerning the town and how it had once been a bustle of activity from morning till night, how God smiled upon the beautiful, flourishing village where good will and prosperity swam through the streets. Alas, he now believed the entire population would be destroyed, especially since typhus fever was prevalent. One of the worst things to report was that due to the frequency and multitude of deaths, it was impossible to grant the dying or dead proper church rites. He invited Routh to his home for tea to further discuss Skibbereen, and the two walked across the garden to a front door. Upon entering, he met Mrs. Townsend in the drawing room, sitting at a round table with large bundles of plain, brown linen strewed about. She smiled pleasantly, explaining she was sewing shrouds for the dead.

Properly seated and sipping tea, Mr. Townsend went into further detail about the village. He estimated the population was about 20,000 and that since the blight a few hundred had perished. Hundreds more were ill inside the town hospital, which was bursting at the seams with three or four per bed. A person recovering might be sandwiched between two others raging with fever or dying. And they were the fortunate ones. Hundreds of others whom space would not allow had to endure the hardship of typhus in the dark confines of their own cottage. They lay on the damp floor, clinging to their only hope—that someone would die and a space might soon be available in the hospital for them. He further explained that now is the time for planting potatoes and the coming August is the time for harvesting, but as one can see for himself, no one has been planting. The small farmer must resort to the Public Works and spend all his earnings on immediate sustenance since he has no food; therefore, there is none left over to purchase seed. On the other hand, the larger farmer exports all he can and hordes away the money, saving to purchase a ticket out of Ireland to the fertile lands of America.

After a while, Routh was tired and had heard enough for the day. He excused himself and headed back to his accommodation for the remainder of the evening.

The next morning, Mr. Townsend came round to show Routh what he had come to see—the people themselves. They walked to one end of town where a cluster of homes stood. They tried to determine which home might be better than the other, since they were probably all ravaged with typhus. After much discussion, they decided on one and walked up to the threshold and peered inside. Routh was immediately struck with the absolute dark interior and foul, offensive stench that escaped from the entrance. They stood still, trying to make out objects as their eyes adjusted to the darkness. Then they slowly crept inside. The walls were bare and the home completely empty except for a few rags in one corner. The inhabitants had sold every piece of furniture and belonging in order to purchase food. It was as if every memory of the people had been erased. The floor was damp and there were remnants of a fire from long ago.

They continued on to the house next door, and as Routh entered, his ears were filled with the sound of mud gushing out from underneath his shoes with every step he took. He immediately covered his nose from the putrid odor that hit him like a fist, lest he be sick. A woman with only a small rag covering her bony shoulders was hovered over some smoldering remains of peat, her only source of comfort as she clearly suffered from diarrhea. Mr. Townsend went to her and asked what was wrong in an attempt to determine her sanity, and she replied, *"Tha shein ukrosh,"* meaning "Indeed the hunger." Routh would hear that reply again and again throughout his travels.

"Everone be dyin'," she repeated in a weak, shaky voice. "The world 'tis no longer ... everone be dyin'."

Routh could hear moans and movement from each of the black corners, but could not see any people. This home had no furniture either except for one small bowl.

Upon entering the next hut, Routh found an elderly woman partially clothed, lying on filthy straw, moaning piteously. She had barely enough strength to lift one shaking hand and implored the men to give her something to eat. She herself looked at her arm in aversion and swayed it from side to side, showing the men how her skin hung loosely from her bones.

The next hut was deathly quiet except for Routh's breathing that filled his ears. Each time they entered a home, he braced himself for whatever was inside, man or beast. He walked around thinking the hut was vacant until he spotted a mound of filthy rags in one corner. Upon closer observation, he saw that three little children were huddled together on a bit of foul, soiled straw. They did not stir, moan, or complain, evidently in the last stages before death. He could see their perfectly emaciated bodies and a limb or two outside the rags that was scarcely human. Their sunken eyes were closed, but between the torn rags he could plainly see a complete rib move as one of them breathed. It was like looking at skeletons already dead. They were so pitiful Routh could not pull himself away. When it came to children's lives, he was overcome with despair. They were the innocent ones that did not have a chance. They did absolutely nothing wrong, but it did not matter; they would be silenced, exterminated, and erased from all memory nevertheless.

"Mr. Routh," Mr. Townsend said, touching his shoulder, "please."

Routh turned and exited the hut, feeling sorrow and outrage. Upon entering the next hut, Routh could immediately hear several people moaning in each of the corners. Four children, a woman, and what had once been a man were lying almost naked on some filthy straw, shivering and raging with fever. A few feet from the door, Routh was stopped cold by the sight of a young woman who had obviously just given birth. She stood looking at him with the bloody, limp infant in her arms and covered only in a filthy piece of rag tied across her loins. Her eyes were hollow and completely lifeless, and Routh was transfixed until the moment was abruptly interrupted by several hands that grasped his arms and legs. Two wailing skeletons crawling on the floor were pulling and tugging at his clothes. Mr. Townsend yanked him in the other direction and out of the hut. He had escaped from being pulled down into their own personal hell, but their demonic cries would forever ring in his ears, and their unspeakable images would eternally be stamped upon his brain.

The men did not speak to each other as they entered another hut, and then another, then another. All the homes were filled with the same misery except one in particular a few yards away from the others. They entered and were met with the familiar foul air, damp floor, and dark interior. The home was larger than the others, and Routh made out an object in one corner. It was a sick woman, huddled with a wet rag and obviously near death. Routh knelt down, and she looked at him with piercing eyes of pain and anguish. Her lips trembled as if trying to speak. He could clearly see her bony frame with gray skin pulled loosely over it, and he stood up feeling helpless and worthless. He saw Mr. Townsend exit the front and began to follow, but suddenly another mound in a near corner caught his attention. He walked toward it and again knelt down to get a better look. He saw two small corpses huddled together in a heap and three large rats gnawing at every part of their decaying bodies. Routh shrieked at the sight and ran out of the house white with fright. He relayed the scene to Mr. Townsend who was not shocked.

"Aye, there are many corpses everywhere and we try to dispose of them before the smell gets too bad," he said. "'Tis a pity when we cannot get to them in time. Please do not think of me as callous, 'tis just that I have seen so much misery in so little time."

The next hut they entered was so dark they could barely see as they looked around. Routh could hear something, and once he located the direction of the audible noise, he crept closer and closer, wanting at the same time to flee to the safety of the outside. Suddenly he was face-to-face with a wretched, filthy, wild woman with frenzied hair and barbaric eyes, completely demented and frantically chewing like a savage on her child's arm that was still connected to its lifeless body. Routh jumped back with a howl and scrambled for the door, yelling, "Let me out of here!" Outside, Routh thought he was going to vomit, and Mr. Townsend came up behind him asking what had happened. Understandably, Mr. Townsend apologized that he had to witness such a scene. He did not see the woman but had witnessed plenty of cats chewing on the deceased.

Routh tried to calm down as they walked and said he did not wish to enter any more homes. Mr. Townsend agreed and led him to another part of the town. As they walked down the lane, Mr. Townsend spoke about how even the terrain had changed since the famine, but Routh only heard the beginning of his tale, for his mind once again wandered back to the cannibal and the one poor wretched woman dying a slow agonizing death. Her house was dreary enough during the day, he could only imagine how very cold and miserable she must be, lying there in the pitch black as each moment ticked by—tick ... tock ... tick ... tock ... with no one to comfort her, shivering in the night and listening to her children being devoured by the savage rats! And the other woman, so insane with hunger, she was eating her own child!

"Mr. Townsend," Routh stopped walking and rudely interrupted him, "those were *people* back in those homes. Not animals, not some creature from the deep, but people. Just like you and I."

"Aye," Mr. Townsend replied, knowing he could say no more.

Routh shuffled his feet in frustration, taking deep breaths and looking upward for any answers hidden in the foggy midst. He wished God would write a message across the sky that he could read and put to use immediately—something that would put an end to this famine.

After a moment, he asked, "When are the bodies of all those children going to be picked up?"

"Well ... uh ... this afternoon, I imagine," he answered. "Aye, the funeral cart makes the rounds every afternoon 'round this area."

"Alright," Routh said, forcing himself into reality, "alright." He then turned to see one of the most horrific scenes he could ever imagine. He was standing in a churchyard next to a large pit in the ground where about two hundred skeleton bodies lay one atop the other. Two men on one side of the pit flung two more bodies on top and then began covering it all with dirt. An emaciated man came around one side of the pit and began calling, "Sally! Sally!" He lifted a leg here and an arm there, and the workers apologized to the grieving man when the description he gave them did not bring any answers. He shuffled off mumbling, "Sally ... Sally ..." under his breath.

Mr. Townsend mumbled a few religious words to the heap with his right hand held up and finished by making the sign of the cross. He then turned and said, "'Tis obvious we don't have enough coffins to keep up with the dead."

The two workers covered the heap with only about three inches of dirt, leaving tops of heads and toes protruding, and began hurrying off with their cart for more.

"Excuse me!" Mr. Townsend shouted. "You must cover them more than that."

"Aye, sir," one of them replied, "but we've six more to git nar, and as the weeks pass, they be dyin' faster thin we kin bury 'em."

Mr. Townsend nodded and bowed his head, and the men scurried off with their cart. As they continued to look around the churchyard grounds, there were several mounds of dirt that clearly indicated mass graves were plentiful.

"Pardon me," Mr. Townsend said to two more workers digging next to the mounds, "why do you not dig over there where there's plenty of room?" He pointed to a large green patch that was untouched.

"I dar not, sir," said one worker, shaking his head. "I dar not."

"'Tis nothing to be afraid of," Mr. Townsend said, grabbing one of the spades and digging himself. He had only uncovered a few inches when a portion of a brown shroud appeared. The worker retrieved his shovel, and Routh and Mr. Townsend left the churchyard and began walking back toward the town. They came to a fork in the road where a small cottage came into view on one side. It was the usual type made of mud and loose stones. It seemed deserted with the front door closed and the one window half boarded up. The funeral cart with the two workers appeared and stopped in front. This time, the cart carried a large coffin and the workers explained that in the home lay an entire family stricken with the fever and so sick and weak they could not remove the body of the mother who lay dead next to them. One of the men motioned to his fellow worker to assist him in carrying out the body, and the other man suddenly became weary and shook his head in refusal. Impatient, the man cursed and yelled at the other, demanding his help. At last he agreed, and they both covered their mouths and noses with rags and were gone inside the doorway. When they returned, they carried a bony skeleton, naked except for a dirty yellow rag placed atop her genitals. Her thin arms void of flesh hung down, and her hands dragged on the ground with each step the men took. They flung the body into the awaiting coffin and were off down the road for more.

As they proceeded into the town, Mr. Townsend pointed out people he knew that had become destitute.

"See that man over there?" he asked, pointing to a hunched over person in rags cowering in a corner.

"Yes," Routh said.

"'Twas only last week that the poor creature dragged the dead body of his father into town through mud and sludge so as to beg for a coffin in which to bury him. He went all over town draggin' the body like it was a dog on a leash. Just pitiful."

Routh could not answer.

"And that woman," he said, pointing to a wretch with a bandaged arm, "I tended to her last week, poor woman. It seems when she returned home one day without any food, one of her children was so out of his mind with hunger that he bit a chunk out of her arm."

Routh could not speak.

"Oh and look, over there is the beggerman. No one knows his name, and he cannot walk or speak much, but he mumbles constantly, poor ole chap." They made their way to a man sitting on something like a half-stretcher that was made of wood and able to support the cripple.

"If no one has any food to give him, they can at least grab hold of the stretcher and drop him off wherever they're goin'," Mr. Townsend said almost in a whisper.

Routh neared the man whose face was covered in wrinkles and looked so old it was almost inhuman. A few dirty straggles of hair protruded from underneath the rag tied around his head. He was sitting up with his legs stretched out in front and clasping his hands together in begging fashion. The man's face was extremely sallow and gaunt; his cheeks and teeth were completely gone, replaced by sunken in holes that almost seemed to touch each other. His eye sockets sunk into his head so far that it was plain to see the complete shape of his skull as his tired, loose skin draped around it. His entire head was like a picnic table with the tablecloth skin sliding this way and that as if it needed to be tied down better. Long thin hands were held together by sheer hope, resembling sticks rather than human limbs. They appeared almost completely void of color and skin.

Routh bent down and looked into the pitiful face. "I'm sorry I do not have any food with me, but would you like me to move you to another location?"

The face did not move, but the tiny eyes gazed up and blinked. The toothless beggerman kept mumbling, and Routh took it to mean yes. Mr. Townsend nodded as Routh lifted up the front end and moved him as the back wooden stakes dug into the grass. Routh felt like he was carrying the entire world on his back as they continued to walk until the chapel came into view; then they stopped and he set the beggerman down.

The men solemnly made plans for the next day, and Routh bid farewell to Mr. Townsend as the priest walked back toward his home. With Mr. Townsend out of earshot, he said to the beggerman, "I will leave you here, but I am going to return with a plate full of food and a warm blanket for you."

The man simply kept muttering.

"Are you praying?" Routh asked, but again the man did not respond.

Routh went to his accommodation and retrieved a warm plate of food and another bag of goods under a blanket so no one could see. He went to the beggerman and placed everything onto his lap, explaining that he might wish to keep the food underneath so he would not be robbed. Routh once again looked into those faraway eyes, and without a trace of the man's face changing, he saw several tears streaming out of one eye. Routh tried to speak but could say no more and began walking toward his accommodation once again as the mumbling behind him continued. After a few steps, he heard, "God bless," as plain and clear as anyone speaking and he stopped but did not look back. After a moment, he continued and knew that he would never see the beggerman again.

Early the next morning, Routh sat with Mr. Townsend, both men looking mentally beaten and weighed down. Routh felt for the man who stayed and tried to help while his countrymen died all around him. He tried to shy away from the dismal topic of the famine, but inevitably the conversation always went back to the dying people of Skibbereen. Each bite they took of food was not satisfying, as they felt ashamed and sick at eating it.

"We must stay strong to help them," Routh said to a now downcast Mr. Townsend.

"Aye, I know," he replied, "'tis just that I heard a friend of mine had to bury his wife last night. I don't know how he did it because he is so weak with the fever. Would you come with me to visit him?"

"Of course," Routh said, and they rose and began the short trek to the small cottage just outside of town. During the walk, Mr. Townsend explained that his friend used to own a thriving business until he was forced into bankruptcy when no one bought his goods. The merchant and his wife buried two children and then both caught the typhus themselves. Fortunately, they still had one child left who was not sick to help care for them. The poor lass was only six, but carried out the work of a grown woman.

"Michael! Michael!" Mr. Townsend yelled as he entered the dank cottage.

"Aye ... over 'ere," came a scraggly voice from one corner.

"Michael! I'm so sorry, me friend." Mr. Townsend embraced him. "Are you alright?"

"Och, no," he said.

"Tell me where you buried Aileen, and I'll bless the spot."

Michael did not answer.

Mr. Townsend gently prodded, "Michael, I want to help, please tell me—"

Routh put his hand on Mr. Townsend's shoulder and said he would look for loose dirt outside. He turned and faced a small girl with glorious blonde hair. Without a word, she sat down beside Michael.

Routh easily found the burial spot not far from the front door. The dirt was spread loosely about the hole merely a few inches above ground. He could not find any remains and went back into the cottage. He found Mr. Townsend tending to Michael and was going to explain when another voice was heard outside.

"Michael!" said the voice, and in walked a tall thin man. "Ahh, beg pardon," he said to everyone. "Me dogs ran amuk last night an' brung home this." He held up what was clearly the head of a woman by the hair and had the face loosely covered by a dirty cloth.

"Aghhh!" Michael screamed as Mr. Townsend threw the neighbor outside, cursing and yelling at him to get out. He dropped the head, running, and Mr. Townsend came back and tried to comfort his distraught friend.

"I'm so sorry, Michael. Come back with me, and I will take care of you."

"No ... lit me die ... wanna be with Aileen ... leave me alone nar ... I'm in hell already." He turned his face into his blankets and sobbed.

Routh bent down slowly to the little girl who now stood stiff and was obviously in shock. She did not scream or cry, but stared stoically at nothing. It was hard to imagine she had witnessed so much at such a young age.

"It's okay to cry, little one," he said to her.

She looked directly into his eyes and blinked a few times.

"Them dogs came 'round," she whispered, "an' Da tould me to shoo 'em away, but they bit at me an' I was scared."

"Do not worry, little one," Routh tried to sooth her. "We will take care of everything."

"I'm alright, master," she whispered again. "I mist be 'ere fer me da."

"You need help, child," Mr. Townsend said to her.

"Why?" Nothin' to do nar."

Mr. Townsend hugged the little girl and reluctantly agreed to leave her and Michael, making her promise to come to the chapel for any reason. He would also return later that evening with food. Then the two men buried the head, and Mr. Townsend blessed the spot with his right hand outstretched.

Routh had seen and heard all he could bear and told Mr. Townsend as they walked back to town that he was leaving on the next coach. Routh thanked Mr. Townsend for his gracious hospitality and vowed to keep him abreast of any relief.

At the inn, Routh learned the next available coach was due in three hours, so he inquired about a large batch of bread loaves to be delivered to his room. The word quickly spread of his obvious intention, and a mob of starving townspeople soon gathered outside his window. Routh had initially planned to distribute a loaf or two to the passersby during his coach ride home, although he now knew that plan was impossible. He asked the innkeeper if he had any ideas about distributing it fairly, but the young man simply shook his head. Instead, he offered his assistance, and the men soon decided to carry it out the front door. When the crowd saw the bread in the lobby, there was such a rush from outside that the door was nearly taken off its hinges. Routh decided the only safe way was to throw it out his window even if it felt wrong in his heart. He broke each loaf into several pieces and flung them out the window to the screams, gasps, and waning faces below. As the bread flew through the air, the mob swayed in its direction and it landed on a hundred hands, each one fighting and clawing to grab a piece. Time itself seemed to slow down when each piece of bread was airborne, soaring and swaying with the slightest breeze, landing on a pair of chosen hands that could survive another day. To see the hundreds of flailing arms and to hear the crowd of mostly women beg and plead for a scrap or morsel clearly resembled animals rather than humans.

And what Routh had thought was a heartfelt act had instead deviated into an absolute nightmare. His good deed had twisted into a rancid, sour task, and he felt anguish and despair instead of goodness in his heart. When he shouted out his window that all was gone, the exhausted crowd rested and calmed themselves, but still did not move.

He now wanted to leave Skibbereen as fast as possible, and he practically sprinted down to the lobby when he saw his coach pull up. He walked out the front door to the noisy mob, and it was with some difficulty that he boarded. The crowd tried to engulf the coach, but backed away as the horses moved to and fro and began to trot away. The most resilient and strongest women ran alongside, thrusting their faces in the window, still begging for bread. A young mother clung to an emaciated infant as she ran, and Routh wanted to yell at her to stop as she might endanger the baby who was obviously barely alive, if at all. Instead, he took off his jacket and thrust it into her hands, hoping it would at least give the infant some warmth. The gaunt faces were now gone, and he did not look back. In fact, he did not look out the window once until he reached Cork.

Upon arriving home, he hugged and kissed his wife with all his might and went to each child and held them, thankful for all their lives. The babies especially, he buried his head into their blankets and wept. He did not mention what he had seen, rather taking great pleasure in hearing insignificant stories of ladies meetings or about letters the older boys had written. It was like he had been awakened from a horrific nightmare and he needed some kind of normalcy lest he himself go mad. Grateful to be home, he needed to clear his head before taking pen in hand and writing to Trevelyan. Later that evening, when his wife was in bed, Routh sat down at his desk and began to write.

Dear Charles,

I write to you with a heavy heart and grief upon my soul. My trip to some of the destitute areas of Ireland is complete and I now wholly understand the dire straits this country is enduring. I am aware not all of Ireland is destitute, but I believe if we do not grant more assistance now, the entire country of Ireland will be equivalent. I was wrong initially presuming the Public Works was adequate; something more must be done. I cannot describe to you what I have seen, as it is unfit for anyone to witness and impossible to fully and accurately recount. So many people have died this past winter that entire towns will surely be vacant. The only thriving business is the coffin maker who cannot keep up with the need, although there are many who bury their loved ones in the cruel soil of Ireland because they cannot afford a simple pine coffin.

The priests are doing what they can to assist the dying during their last moments on earth, and the abbeys are feeding as many children as possible. It seems everyone is helping in good faith, but more and more keep dying. I visited the abbot of the Cistercian Abbey of Mount Melleray and he said to me, "Even in this isolated place, on a most ungrateful and profitless mountain, we relieve from eighty to a hundred wandering poor daily, besides thirty three families around us, who are our regular weekly pensioners and whom we have, under God, saved from hopeless starvation. To have been enabled to do even this little for the sons and daughters of God, is a luxury beyond the banquet of kings." There is a genuine goodness in souls such as these, and I honestly wish the world could witness the tragedy the Irish are enduring. The hideous torment and wretchedness some people are weathering is beyond any savage imagination. I find myself bewildered at the thought of all the depots closing permanently and I beseech you to reconsider until August when the new crops will be available.

It is in the evening I write to you with images swimming in my head that cannot be expelled. Let me privately confide to you that in the dark here I sometimes feel I cannot go on like this any longer.

Your humble servant,
Sir Randolph Routh

Chapter VII

"I'm sorry but you must vacate the premises," the middleman explained.

"I'll git you the money," Kathryn pleaded, "please don't throw us out into the cold, we've no whar to go."

"That is no concern of mine," he said. "The rule is payment on the first of every month or out you go! Now leave at once! If you persist, I will call the authorities!"

Kathryn knew it was no use arguing. She would find a way to make it. She forced herself to think that in the end it would all be okay. She gathered the two blankets, one cup, and the spade they inherited when the rightful owner died, as everything else had been pawned. Deep down she knew it would come to this and was almost numb with all she had already endured. Brenton said nothing, and she hated that he had to be a part of this eviction.

"Kin I come back to see if me husband sent a letter?" Kathryn asked.

"Absolutely not!" the middleman shouted. "I don't ever want to see you on this property again!"

Kathryn and Brenton began walking down the road in the direction of town. She blew a kiss toward the graves of her children, knowing full well she could not stop.

"And good riddance to you!" the middleman shouted out to them before entering their hut.

The Works had closed, so no money was coming in and the soup kitchen was being established in town. The kitchen was their only hope of surviving as it was to serve one meal a day. Kathryn found a spot on the ground just outside of town where they each took turns digging to form a hole in which to lie down that was free from any wind. From this spot, Kathryn could see the soup kitchen; she wanted to be the first in line when it opened. As the two of them dug, they did not speak because there was nothing left to say. This was the end of the road with a split family and no income, home, or food. They lay down huddled together in the hole in the ground and covered themselves with the blankets. Thankfully it was the end of April and the harsh winter was over, but the cold wind still blew fiercely threw their emaciated bodies. They stayed there for three days and nights, eating the tiny portions they had left. Now Joseph had no way to reach them and they had no way to reach him.

On the third day, Kathryn noticed a small gathering next to the soup kitchen and she very stiffly rose and slowly made her way to the entrance.

"Pardon me, sir, whin will you open?" Kathryn peeked her head in and asked a man organizing inside.

"Tomorrow mornin' as the sign says outside," he said, pointing.

"Och, didn't see it," Kathryn grinned. "We jist have one wee cup; kin you spar two bowls?"

"Sorry." The man departed from view.

Kathryn blinked slowly and swallowed the harsh words from the worker. She did not really expect him to pity her alone while thousands of others just like her waited, probably without bowls themselves. She turned to leave and was suddenly face-to-face with a sickly man.

"I've git two extra bowls," the man practically whispered. "Me wife an' daughter are dead."

Kathryn retrieved the bowls and gently held one of his hands in hers—two filthy, starving individuals looking into each other's eyes. She gave him all she could in return, a smile. She turned and now noticed that people were sitting down and forming a line, so she went back to get Brenton.

"Come, Brenton, we mist git in line nar."

"I don't wanna git up," he moaned.

"Please, son, we'll git warm soup tomorrow mornin'. I've two bowls fer us, please git up," she said, helping him to his feet.

They shuffled to the end of the line and sat down, covering themselves as best they could. Night quickly came, followed by morning and the bustle of crowds gathering about them.

"Wake up, Brenton, we mist keep our place in this mob." She held on tight to her son. Kathryn looked back and could see hundreds of people coming from nowhere. The soup kitchen finally opened, and a rush to the front had people pushing and shoving, all sticking out their bowls. Kathryn got hit in the head a few times from waving bowls until they ultimately made it to the front. Kathryn shoved her two bowls on the counter, and a worker on the other side splashed in a large ladleful of liquid with bits of vegetables into each one. She and Brenton struggled to get out of the mob, both walking and frantically slurping down the warm soup. A man from behind ran up to Brenton, grabbed his bowl, and ran.

"Hey! Hey!" Brenton shouted, but no one cared or even made an attempt to stop the thief.

"Lit's go to ar spot," Kathryn said. "We kin shar mine."

One bowl of soup was not nearly enough for two starving people to last the entire day, but they survived by saving their energy and lying in their hole and sleeping. When night arrived, they positioned themselves in line with a hundred others to be certain and receive some nourishment the following day when hundreds more showed up. They survived like this for about two weeks.

"I know this intirely looks bad, Brenton," Kathryn said one late afternoon as they lay huddled and shivering in the hole, "but it'll not be like this ferever. I've faith in God that we'll make it somehar. It seems we're all alone in this world, but yer father's thankin' of us and I know he'll be sendin' fer us soon."

"I know, Mam," Brenton mumbled. He paused for a moment and then said, "Do you ever think 'bout the girls and the day Da left?"

"Aye, all the time. I'm so prid the way you were helpin' whin the girls were so sick and for bein' so strong fer yer da."

"Do you think the angels came and got the girls?"

"Aye, to be sure." Kathryn thought back. "The angels came to lead thar souls to heaven. Thar not sick any more; thar with God."

Mother and son clung to that thought for hours as they huddled in their ditch.

The following morning, as they left the soup kitchen, a familiar voice rang through the air.

"Kathryn! Kathryn!"

She turned around to see Edgar Cleary, Lord Sommerhaven's valet, his hand waving in the air.

"I'm so glad I found you," he said as he reached them. "Are you alright? Well, of course not, what a stupid question. Well, I have been searching all the soup kitchens in the area hoping that I may find you."

"Oh." Kathryn didn't know what to say.

"The reason is I have something for you." Edgar reached into his inside jacket pocket and brought out an envelope, holding it out for mother and son to see. On the outside were the written words, "For Joseph O'Malley upon my death."

"I found it while cleaning out His Lordship's papers. I know Joseph has left for the new world, but I thought you should have it," Edgar explained, handing it to her. "Now good day to you,

221

ma'am," he said, tipping his hat and exiting as quickly as he came.

Kathryn opened the envelope to reveal beautiful handwriting upon a letter. It read:

Joseph,

My time has finally come to be united with my beloved Helen. I take with me the complete knowledge of the past—all the pain, the sorrow, and the happiness. I know I am happy now in the beloved arms of my love, and perhaps there is even a way to contact my son John to ask for his forgiveness. Maybe this is a place to start over.

I realize upon my passing Lord Sebag Montefiore will take possession of my estate and will most likely not treat you well. I am sorry in advance for this. There is although one possession I would like to give you in return for your years of friendship. In my back garden grows a beautiful lavender rose that reminds me of my Helen. Under the earth that binds its roots you will find something that is treasured most by me, as it was my gift to her. I would like you and your family to have it.

My good man, I want you to know that I loved you like a son even though we were miles apart socially and economically. My time spent with you indeed held no boundaries. Thank you from my heart for your friendship—it meant a great deal to this old man.

Lord George Somerhaven

Kathryn and Brenton hugged and smiled, clinging to the thought of the prize underneath the rose tree.

"Whit will it be?" Brenton asked.

"Don't know."

"Har we gonna git it?" he asked again.

"I don't know that either," she smiled, "but we'll find a way."

Kathryn knew that Lord Sebag Montefiore was an absentee landowner and most likely in London, but the middleman that evicted them lived there with the gardeners and maids. Somehow she would unearth the bottom of that rose tree and claim the gift beneath it.

"Let's eat nar and talk 'bout har to find that tree."

Much of that day and night was spent whispering about the safest way to approach the mansion, what to tell the gardener if he spotted them, and what could happen to them if they were caught. And they also let their minds wander to the juicy thought of the treasure that could be awaiting them when the tree was lifted.

As they ate their soup the following morning in their hole, Kathryn's mind was racing and she informed Brenton of the plan. Night was the only possible time to dig up the rose, but they needed to find out which one it was in the daytime. They gulped down the last drops of soup and gathered their few belongings to make the trek to the estate.

They were so used to destitute people and death that they didn't even take much notice of the half-naked woman holding a limp infant in the distance. The woman stumbled up to a man walking alongside the road and said something to him. He shook his head. She frantically looked around, spotting Kathryn and Brenton, and hobbled up to them.

"Beg yer pardon!" the woman pleaded. "Kin you spare a penny so I kin bury me baby in a right coffin?"

"Sorry, miss," Kathryn shook her head. "We've no money. I buried me other children in the soil of ould Ireland knowin' that she'll be taken' good care of 'em, God willin'."

"But I jist can't be throwin' dirt on her wee face and har," the woman appealed.

"Put a cloth over her head or wrap her in a blanket—"

"I've no cloth nor blanket!" she cried.

Kathryn looked at Brenton, and he knew what she wanted him to do. He held out one of their blankets without reluctance, as if he had a dozen of them.

"Take this blanket, miss," Kathryn said, "and bury this poor wee child."

"Much obleeged, God bless." The woman took it and continued walking down the road.

"Come on, Brenton," Kathryn nudged him, "we've no time to waste."

They continued walking until they could see the estate in the distance. Their pace grew faster and faster until they reached the stone wall encircling the grand home. They waited and looked over the fence for people or dogs, but saw no one. They noticed some greenery in the front, but most of the plants were in the back garden.

"I'll go and see whit plant it is," she said to Brenton. "You stay 'ere, and I'll be back shortly."

She kissed his head and climbed over the wall, instinctively crouching as she crept like a veteran spy. She got as close as she could and hid behind some hedges to take a peek at the bushes and flowers in the front. She spotted a few rose trees with small buds on them and gasped. What if the lavender rose was not blooming? She had not considered that, and her heart sank. On she crept behind pots and plants to the back garden and an array of roses. Unfortunately, they seemed to be scattered everywhere as she dotted in and out of every crevice. There was a plant with small buds, but she could see that they were yellow; one large white bloom; three peach blooms; a few roses with white on the inside and a pinkish color on the outer petals; and many red buds and blooms that resembled rich velvet. No lavender. Anxiety overwhelmed her, and she sat up against a hedge to calm down.

"What do you think you're doin'?" a man's voice demanded.

Kathryn looked up and stared right in the face of a man she had not seen before with shears in his hands. She had practiced this scenario in her mind if it should happen and she calmly stood up and regained her composure.

"Beg yer pardon, sir, I hope it's no offense to have walked on this property," she began. "I had no right intirely to do so, but 'twas only wantin' to pick a few roses to sell 'em in town fer a few pence."

"Well, I'm only a gardener here," the man grumbled, "but I don't think—

Suddenly Kathryn spotted a beautiful lavender budding bloom behind the man and her heart pounded in her throat. The exquisite teardrop shape was perfect. It was screaming out at her with the pristine, silver, intertwining petals, and she wanted to inhale its glorious sweet scent. Quickly she mentally mapped out its position behind this hedge, to the right of this pot, etc. and her mind faded back into the stern lecture the gardener was giving.

"—so if you think for one minute that you kin come into someone else's garden ..."

"You're intirely right, sir. I'll be layvin' nar." Kathryn didn't wait for a reply and was gone in an instant.

"Did ya find it?" Brenton excitedly asked, helping her over the wall.

Kathryn gasped for breath and said, "Aye, I found it ... I found it ..."

She began to feel lightheaded and dizzy, so she lay down on the ground.

"I saw that dazzlin' lavender bloom singin' its sweet song in the breeze," she mused and then thought for a moment. "Somehar the bloom shape 'twas quare—like the plant had sprouted a tear of sorrow that His Lordship felt for his wife. 'Tis a beautiful rose tree, and Lady Somerhaven 'twas a lucky woman." Kathryn sat up slowly. "A gardener saw me, but all's well. Whin the sun is set, we dig fer ar treasure."

They huddled together to keep warm and passed the time talking about what the treasure could be and all the food they would buy with it. Their mouths would relish all the wonderful things they would eat. All the glorious food would be rich and flavorful, and they would roll over with full bellies and smiles on their faces as they closed their eyes in complete satisfaction, knowing they could eat not one morsel more. The thought of that moment made Brenton's mouth water, and he became restless waiting for the sun to settle. The light of day ever so slowly faded to be replaced by darkness everywhere, except for the billions of glistening stars above. On this night, even the moon was slim and narrow, providing no light for sneaky villains.

"Well nar thin," Kathryn grinned, "I think it's time."

Brenton grabbed the spade and was beginning to climb over the wall when Kathryn grabbed his arm.

"Wait a minute! I don't know har God would feel 'bout us stealin' the treasure."

"Och, Mam!"

"Okay, okay." She let go of him. "'Tis rightfully Joseph's and he'd want us to have it. 'Tis not like we're stealin'. Har kin you steal somethin' that's rightfully yours?"

"That's right," Brenton agreed. "Kin we go nar?"

"Aye, lit's go take what's intirely ars," she smirked.

They climbed over the stone wall and could see in front of them just enough to maneuver through the damp terrain. The night-cloaked mother and son crept and moved like nocturnal animals, scouting the area for any movement that could reveal their whereabouts. Kathryn looked over at the grand estate and could see light from many candles in two rooms, but no people inside. They continued until they came to an area with lots of roses and then searched about to find the precise rose. Kathryn stood in front of it, motioning to Brenton where to dig. They took turns scooping and placing the dirt aside with their spade until the main part of the rose was uprooted and they placed it on the ground. Kathryn stood up and took one more look at the estate, making sure no one was watching, and then dropped to her knees and dug with her hands in the loose soil. Brenton searched too, and when nothing turned up, she motioned for him to dig deeper.

She sprang up again like a periscope and looked at the estate again, noticing that one of the room's candles had been blown out. Scanning the land for any people, her senses were keen and sharp like a lion in the wild about to pounce on its prey. She was so focused on hearing or seeing anyone that she did not feel the sudden drop in temperature or the wind that began to blow.

Brenton stopped digging when the spade hit something hard, and down they both went again to uncover with their hands a block of dirt before them. Kathryn broke away enough dirt to uncover something small wrapped in a cloth. She set it on the ground and motioned for Brenton to help her put the dirt back and replant the rose. They replaced everything as before, and Kathryn picked up the treasure and held it tightly to her chest. One last time, she eyed the estate and saw that one room was still lit. Cupping the lavender budding bloom in front of her with one hand, she inhaled, closing her eyes at the marvelous fragrance of the rose. When she opened her eyes, the lights in the one room had been blown out and a cold chill swept through her body. She grabbed Brenton by the hand and they crouched and dashed, running for their lives and their entire future. They didn't stop until they climbed over the wall and collapsed, panting and wheezing on the ground.

"We ... we made it ... we made it ..." Brenton gasped. "Whit's the treasure nar?"

Kathryn sat up and could now feel the cold air engulf her body.

"Help me light some peat, Brenton, quickly so we kin see it better," she said. Brenton took out the flint stones and made a spark, lighting some dried brush first and then some peat, shielding the area from the wind with his body. He was trying to hurry so fast that at first it would not light.

"I've got it. I've got it nar," he said at last. Kathryn held up the bundle next to the mound of glowing peat and could now see that it was wrapped in a thick wool cloth. She began to unravel it as quickly as possible. Her dirty hands shook, and her mind raced at what treasure she would unwrap. Underneath all the wrapping was a small red cloth sack or pouch, with a gold pull tie at the top. She unfastened the tie, opened the pouch, and pulled out several wads of colored paper that were folded one over another. She took one of the papers and held it up to the glow from the fire. Now she could plainly see that it was British currency and gasped.

"'Tis money, Brenton. Lit's see ... one ... two ... three ... umm ... it adds up to be £100!"

Brenton carefully examined each piece, turning it over and over. Kathryn looked into the pouch again, and at the bottom laid a white handkerchief. She lifted it out and felt something inside. Unraveling it, there appeared something she had seen only on highly respectable women. Glimmering before her was a pristine broach covered with several radiant stones. It was the most beautiful object she had ever seen, and she held it up, transfixed with its exquisite beauty. Seven delicately cut sapphires surrounded one prestigious diamond, and although Kathryn did not fully understand its value, she understood its precious, heartfelt significance. A piece of paper lay at the very bottom of the pouch, and she retrieved it, holding it close to the swaying flames, and read:

May God give you …
For every storm, a rainbow,
For every tear, a smile,
For every care, a promise,
And a blessing in each trial.
For every problem life sends,
A faithful friend to share,
For every sigh, a sweet song,
And an answer for each prayer.

May God bless you and yours, Joseph.
Lord George Somerhaven

Kathryn sat back and took it all in. She looked at her weathered son examining the broach and knew this was a pivotal moment.

"These gifts are goin' to change ar lives," she said to Brenton. "His Lordship, bless his soul, believed in yer da as we always have, despite whit others might have thought."

"Is this fer the har?" Brenton innocently asked, holding up the broach.

"No, son, 'tis to be worn on yer clothes."

"Why don't you wear it?" he said, returning it to Kathryn.

"Ohh," she said, waving him on. "Whit use is this to me? 'Tis fer respectable ladies of class like Her Ladyship." She looked at it lying in the palm of her hand. "We've enough far to git us to Ameriky, and after we find yer da, this brooch 'ere will git us some land. I'll pawn this beautiful thing fer quite a bit of money to be sure."

"Jist put it on fer a moment," Brenton persisted.

"Very well thin," she said, opening the front of her outer garment to reveal a still filthy but somewhat cleaner garment. After fastening the gleaming brooch at her neckline, she looked back at her smiling son.

"'Tis beautiful, Mam," he said. "I wish Da could see you nar."

"Aye, me son." She cupped the side of his head and noticed her shaking hand, looking so old and weathered. "Perhaps I'll wear it fer a bit. Lit's lay 'ere and sleep a wee moment before the sun comes up."

She added more peat to the fire and lay down on the ground. Brenton snuggled close to his mother for warmth and closed his eyes.

"In a few ars, we'll have some food," she said, drifting off to sleep with the pouch, the paper, and its treasure tucked securely under her arm.

Each day since his travels, Routh woke and walked around his home in a daze, unable to sit for very long or find comfort in the company of others. His wife would often see him staring into space and ask if she could help, but he just shook his head. He would not burden his loved ones with the reality of what he saw. Neither could he concentrate on his work at his office. He would sit and stare at the wall until a sudden noise would snap him back into reality. On one of those days, in the late afternoon, he was staring out of his window and felt the walls of his office closing in on him. Even Stuffy could not shake him out of his deep depression. His letter to Trevelyan made no impact, so he wrote to the media, the governor, the prime minister, and every government official he could think of ... but only letters of inquiry, explanation, or finger pointing were sent back. No action was taken.

"I'm going for a walk," he announced to O'Riley as he grabbed his coat and hat. The keen, cold air felt refreshing in his lungs, and he let his feet take him wherever they wanted. People were dying and suffering at that very moment and there was nothing he could do about it. He felt guilty for living and ashamed that he was not motivated to help the starving like he thought he would. The entire trip was taken so that he would have the ammunition he needed to do his job better, but instead he was useless. He tried to shake off the depression and looked around at his surroundings. He was at a local pond that used to be full of fish at one time. In the distance, he saw a mound on the embankment and squinted to get a better look. Routh proceeded toward it, and as he got closer, he walked faster and faster, and at the end, he practically ran to the mound. He stopped, dropped to his knees, and hovered over the mound. Unbelievably, he looked straight into the eyes of the starving little girl he had seen so many months before. Lying on her back, she was covered with the same coat he had given her and her brother. She looked so emaciated and weak that Routh forced a smile so that she would not be afraid of him.

"Where is your brother?" Routh whispered.

The girl's eyes shot to her right, and Routh lifted a portion of the coat to see the brother's face. He was mere bones, and Routh could see that he was already dead, so he covered him up again. The girl suddenly gasped for air, and he knew that she was near death as well. Even if he gave her some food now, it might kill her since her body was so very weak and thin.

"Why didn't you come to me?" Routh asked.

"Not find you," the girl whispered, and he knew then that she had understood his offer to help.

"I will stay with you if you would like," Routh offered, sitting down.

He was shocked that she had survived the freezing winter at all and was dismayed at the suffering she and her brother had obviously endured. Her body had become completely emaciated, like she was a different person altogether. The little girl managed a smile and lifted her hand to find his. Routh wanted to jump back at the skeleton arm, but instead he held her hand softly and smiled at her. Holding it was like clasping an inhuman object with no color, feeling, muscle, blood flow, or warmth.

He felt completely helpless and worthless as a human being, watching this little girl die. And where were her parents? Obviously dead, or perhaps they abandoned her long ago. Right now, she should be playing in the grass with rosy cheeks and skinned knees. Perhaps one day she could have been in a great ballroom with a glorious dress and sparkling chandeliers above as dapper gentlemen took turns dancing with her. At the very least, she deserved to live a long healthy life with a good husband and a few children of her own. How could this have happened? How could he be here holding this cadaverous hand on such a bright, crisp day? This child was innocent, and society had killed her and her brother.

"Can I do anything for you, little one?" Routh asked

She slowly shook her head and then stopped. "Aye," she managed. "A prayer fer me?"

Routh wanted to recite one that she would possibly know, so he began:

> Our Father, who art in heaven,
> Hallowed be thy name.
> Thy kingdom come, thy will be done
> On earth at it is in heaven.
> Give us this day our daily … bread
> And forgive us our trespasses
> As we forgive those who trespass against us.
> Lead us not into temptation
> But deliver us from evil.

The little girl looked one more time at Routh and then she closed her eyes and died. Routh still fixated on her face as tears began to stream down his cheeks.

"We have trespassed against you … we have. All of us as a society … and I am so sorry … I am so sorry," he wept.

He stayed with her and cried until there were no tears left in his body. Then he wiped his eyes and covered her head with the coat. His body felt extremely heavy as he got up and walked to the coffin maker's shop and ordered two small coffins. He paid for them and for two young men to assist him in the burial at the cemetery. The parish priest was not available, so the two young men dug the graves and helped Routh put the bodies in the coffins. They carefully placed the coffins in the ground and covered them with moist soil. One of the boys stuck a rudimentary cross at the head of each grave and took out a small can of paint and a brush.

"What's the name of the girl, Yer Honor?" he asked.

"Name?" Routh answered. "I am uncertain. Just write 'A brave little girl.'"

"And fer the boy?" he asked.

"I do not know his name either. 'A brave little boy' sounds fine to me," he said.

The young man painted the letters and left with the other fellow. Routh stood over the graves not knowing quite what to say.

"You small children have been very valiant and heroic," he said, "as courageous as any man fighting for his life and his country. I would like you both to know that as a young man I was well educated. I performed duties during the Peninsular campaign and held the office of senior Commissariat officer at Waterloo. I served in Canada and rose through the ranks until I was instituted into the executive council and ultimately knighted for my performance in the Canadian rebellion. I am now senior Commissariat officer in charge of Irish Relief and I … have personally failed you. You only found relief in death, and that is not a just mode of life. I have vast experience in war and death, and I have seen things that would … let's just say the best and worst characteristics of the human being. However, on this day, your little faces and your little hand have changed me forever. It is truly a dreadful outrage what has happened to you and others like you. Now it is not within my authority to administer food to all the starving, but I vow this day to work hard and try my best to save as many lives as possible. I want you to know that you did not die in vain. I saw you, I heard you, and now I will go and do my duty to the best of my ability. May God be with you both."

He returned to his office and quite unexpectedly had a fire in his belly. His mind was clear; he knew there were many dying people that still needed his help. He felt that with all he had seen on his travels, he needed to visit and speak with Trevelyan personally.

"O'Riley!" he shouted.

O'Riley came into his office. "Yes, sir."

"Sit down," he instructed. "I realize that I have not been myself lately, but I have seen unbelievable things that are simply indescribable. Naturally, I needed to break from this sorrowful place inside my head and plainly discern the noteworthy job that shall not further be delayed. I resolve to leave tomorrow for London, speak with Trevelyan to review what I have seen, and implore him once again to give more relief to this dying country."

"Very well, sir," O'Riley said.

Routh leaned back in his chair, took a deep breath, and added, "This famine was more than I had ever expected."

"Yes, sir," O'Riley said. "And I hope we can still accomplish what needs to be done here."

"I'm certain we will; we just need the kind of stamina young men have," Routh noted. "In fact, when I was twenty-one, I woke up every morning and thought that I could personally change the world for the better." Routh thought back. "I had that much confidence. But the older I get, I feel sometimes that it is just not achievable."

"When I was twenty-one, I woke up every morning and thought that I needed to make as much money as possible to be happy," O'Riley added.

"When I was twenty-one, I woke up every morning and asked, 'Whose round is it?'" Stuffy abruptly stuck his head inside the office and grinned.

The wet, misty air sprinkled Kathryn's cheek and woke her up. She blinked, remembering the previous day, and looked at the pouch still tied around one hand. Her shoulder and entire body ached, and it took a few minutes to sit up. Brenton stirred also and slowly made his way to a sitting position as well. His hair was tousled, but he grinned and said, "Kin we git some food nar?"

"Aye!" Kathryn beamed.

They both creaked their bodies to a standing position and walked rather slowly into town. Kathryn felt the brooch with her fingers and fastened the outer garment to conceal her treasure from others. They reached the town and entered the market, grabbing any edible food they could find.

"That'll keep us fer a while," she said. The merchant gave Kathryn a sideways glance as she handed over the one-pound note, not used to her kind having anything of the sort. Once outside, the two feasted.

"I know jist har we're goin' to git to Ameriky," Kathryn said, chewing.

"Hmm?" Brenton swallowed.

"Whin we're done 'ere, we'll go to the docks and barter fer ar far," she sighed, wondering if this could really be happening.

When they finished the meal, they saved any remaining bits in a rag, and with the clothes on their backs and the pouch, they walked to the docks where hordes of destitute Irish gathered for emigration. Everyone was talking about leaving Ireland and how many people had died in their family. A few children picked at the bits of dried fish guts stuck between the planks, and every so often a horn could be heard in the distance from a faraway ship. The entire dock area was wet from the sea air and thick with mist and portions of fog. Peeking out here and there were three tall ships as grand and colossal as mountains. As the sea currents lapped the docks, they sent the wooden ships swaying and creaking as if they were calling out to all passengers, "Come aboard if you wish to live!" The wooden chariots of God had come, and all those that climbed aboard would be safe from the perils of hell. But woe to those that stayed behind; their only certainty was to cascade starving and suffering over the edge, and to spiral down ... down ... into the fires of eternal damnation.

Kathryn and Brenton walked around to each ship and learned that all were deporting for Canada since fares were much cheaper than fares to the United States. There were so many people about, Kathryn felt as if Ireland were losing all her countrymen and that not one person would remain. Some of the poor received free passage on board from their landlords simply because the landowner wanted to be rid of them. Others obtained money from families abroad or stole, swindled, and bribed to get out of their dying country. The country they all dearly loved ... but alas who did not love them back.

One man told Kathryn that there were lots of ships departing for America from the Liverpool docks, and she thanked him for the information.

"Thar's only one thing to do. Lord above, we'll be needin' a coach to Dublin and—"

"A coach!" Brenton exclaimed.

"Aye, we'll not walk since we've the money," she said. "Thin we'll cross to Liverpool, and thin git on a boat to Ameriky to find yer da."

Brenton smiled like he had not smiled in years, genuinely beaming from ear to ear with a belly full of food and a real future ahead. They bought their tickets for the next available coach, which was to depart that afternoon, and upon looking at themselves, Kathryn felt they needed a good cleaning. She bought a bar of soap, some scissors, and a brush, and they washed in the creek. The water was freezing, but it felt good to finally have hope and happiness in their lives. They cut each other's mangled knots and brushed through their hair. One hand or eye was always monitoring the tied rag, and every so often Kathryn felt near her throat to make certain the brooch was still there. When they finished washing, she held her son at arm's length, marveling at his sparkling face and slick back hair until her eyes began to well up.

"Maaam ..." Brenton cast his eyes down.

"Jist can't believe 'tis you in thar, 'tis bin so long," she said.

"I know." He put his arms around her neck. They embraced, letting go of the past and all its suffering. All the sickness, death, starvation, and burials they had to endure. All the misery, uncertainty, and sheer wretched hardship they fought through each and every day. They held on to each other knowing they had made it; they had survived.

"We'll git new clothes layter—don't have time nar," Kathryn said as they hurried to catch their ride.

They boarded the beautiful coach and sat back on one side. Two respectable ladies seated adjacent from them forced a smile, blinked rapidly, and proceeded to gaze out the window. It didn't matter; Kathryn and Brenton were excited to be on the coach and grateful for a full stomach and the bit of strength that was finally beginning to pump through their veins. Brenton felt the fine leather seats with his hands and looked around at the walls of the coach covered with fine fabric. It was a marvel to behold.

The coach jerked forward and began moving down the road in the late afternoon. Brenton stared out the window, surveying the land and the only life he ever knew as it passed by. He looked at his mother and asked, "Will we ever come back?"

"I don't know, son," she answered. "Maybe someday."

He turned back toward the window again and saw his world racing past him. He waved at nobody and muttered, "Good-bye, Brogan ... good-bye, Shay ... good-bye, Baby."

Many hours later, the coach jolted to a stop. The small door opened, and the two respectable ladies departed with the driver's assistance. Voices could be heard here and there, and the driver began taking down bags and luggage from the top, peeking his head in the window and announcing, "We've arrived in Dublin, miss."

"Waa?" Kathryn awoke, looking about. Upon realizing her surroundings and feeling her brooch, she softly brushed the hair away from her son's forehead as he lay across her lap.

"Wake up, Brenton, we're 'ere."

The boy sat up, announcing, "I'm hungry."

"Well nar thin, let's git somethin' to eat." Kathryn was happy to say what had become such an extravagant sentence. They departed and met the early afternoon bustle of the large city. Mother and son stood, watching people dart about, hurrying to get from place to place.

"Come, Brenton," Kathryn said, clutching her pouch. They walked into the first restaurant she saw with a sign outside that read: Now Serving Lunch. Pulling from her memory, she ordered and followed the people in front of her, imitating every move they made. It had been nearly a lifetime since she had been in any type of restaurant and did not want to embarrass herself. They sat down in a booth with Brenton eyeing everything. He had never been inside any type of establishment before.

"Whit do we do nar?" he whispered as the people in the next booth were served their piping hot food. His mouth fell open at the sight of the glorious display of fresh food, the exquisite aroma, and the divine quantity all served upon a clean white plate! He watched the man bite into his crunchy sandwich and had to close his mouth lest he salivate all over the table. In the next moment, a hand placed two large bowls of steaming vegetable soup, two crispy sandwiches, and a piping hot pot of tea directly in front of him and Kathryn. His mouth hung open again, not believing this was actually real. Imitating the man, he grabbed the sandwich with both hands and bit into it, tasting its full flavor of fresh cuisine. Kathryn mimicked him, and they both began to cry softly with full mouths of food.

Upon swallowing his last bite, Brenton wiped away his tears and asked, "What was that called?"

"A sandwich, me son."

"A sandwich," he repeated. "Whit a fine thing, the sandwich."

Kathryn was overcome with emotion watching her son discover things she never thought he would and longing for her three girls in their graves, wishing they too could be a part of these wonderful moments. She wondered how her son would react to England and what mysteries awaited them both in America. In fact, she had no solid idea of how she was even going to find Joseph. She just knew their future was not in Ireland anymore, and if it took years to find him, then so be it, she would search until the day she died. After finishing every last morsel and drop of tea, they strolled the busy town looking for the town docks. They could see the lean spikes of the ships from a distance and went in that direction until stretched before them was a bustling dock complete with fisheries and numerous ships large and small. Some were making their way into the port and some were pulling out into the sea.

"All aboard that's goin' aboard!" yelled a seaman on a large schooner.

Kathryn grabbed Brenton's hand and hurried to the man.

"Is this ship goin' to Liverpool?" she asked.

"Aye," he said. "'Tis the last ship departin' today."

"What's the far, sir, so we kin git on?"

"Three shilling," he said holding out his hand.

Kathryn paid and the man stepped aside to let them through. They boarded the ship with the two large masts swaying to and fro. Brenton marveled at the mastery of the vessel, feeling the shiny wooden edge and watching the men working below to release the ropes from the dock. He oberved other men hanging on the masts untie more ropes with yells and commands, and with a sudden *poof*, the white sails filled and captured the wind. The ship pulled away from the dock and forward, closer to the mother country and closer to his father. Mother and son stood at the side, watching Ireland shrink smaller and smaller until a voice broke their silence.

"Well hello, Kathryn."

Kathryn turned around to see a familiar, smiling, dapper gentleman.

"Well nar thin," she too smiled, "fancy seein' you 'ere, master." She was astonished that a man of his class would remember her and acknowledge her once again.

"I'm surprised to see you here also. And how is that hand, young man?"

"Fine, Your Honor." Brenton held it out.

"And what a clean hand that is!" Routh laughed.

"Aye, Your Honor!"

Routh turned to Kathryn, not quite knowing how to ask, "Are you leaving Ireland permanently?"

"Aye, ar future lies elsewhere. Me husband left for Ameriky months ago an' we're goin' to find 'im."

"Find him? You do not know where he is?"

"Well, no." She paused a moment. "We were evicted from ar home and he had no way of reachin' us, but Richmond, Virginia, is whar he'll be. I'm sure we'll be findin' him jist fine."

"I'm sorry about your eviction, but since you know his whereabouts, I'm certain it will be no trouble at all." Routh turned toward some empty seats near the bow. "I don't know anyone on this ship; would you like to have a seat?"

Kathryn knew this man was not being fresh, just kind. Nevertheless, she was astonished that he wanted to sit with them in public and converse as if they were of the same class when nothing could be further from the truth. She hesitated, wondering what to do.

"I would like to discuss with you the perils of the Irish famine if you would be so kind."

"If you don't mind the likes of us, master," she smiled.

"Not at all." He motioned to a seating area.

They sat together, with Brenton in the middle, exchanging stories and events good and bad in their lives. She learned the importance of Routh's position and how he tried to help the Irish people, about what he witnessed in Skibbereen and about the meeting he was going to have with Trevelyan when he reached London.

"We are well aware that the Irish people are being suffocated by the wealthy gentile," he explained. "If they were only granted a proper education, they could provide for themselves and this famine would have been nonexistent. As it now stands, I will try my best to supply more relief to the Irish so that the country can begin to rebuild." He shook his head. "It is simply inhumane that people must suffer in such horrific conditions."

Kathryn had never met a man so educated that truly cared so much about her people—except for Lord Somerhaven. She told him about the kind man and his terrible fate.

"Many are not in their right mind," Routh said. "It seems this lengthy famine has brought about the worst in people."

"Aye, but also the bist." She told him about the basket of food His Lordship gave her family and mentioned "a bit of money and a gift," which is how they were now able to travel to America. She thought it best not to report that they had to trespass to get the money and did not mention what the gift was. He asked about her life, and she informed him about her three girls and burying Anne and Mr. and Mrs. McGavock. She told him about Joseph and his departure for America to make a better life for his family and how one day she hoped to have a home of her own.

"I've even had a dream 'bout it," she said. "Ar house is small and warm, sittin' proper in a wide open area. The stream is nearby, and we're growin' lots of food in ar garden, and ever night we git in bed with full satisfied stomachs. Ar village is jist bonny and the people are very friendly, and in the distance, wee rollin' hills lead to the ocean … and I know that I'm so happy 'ere and that this is ar home."

Routh sat quietly, listening to this poor woman dream simple, practical dreams. To her, these things would be success and she could live content the rest of her days and die happy. She did not desire wealth, status, or power—rather, the most important elements to all humans … food, family, and shelter. He admired her spirit and courage to obtain these dreams, venturing into the far-reaching unknown with a young son to achieve them.

"I wish you and your family great success in finding your dreams," he said. "I have heard there is lots of opportunity in Virginia." Then he asked Brenton what he thought America would be like.

"I've not intirely thought 'bout it," he said. "Maybe it'll be like Mam said. I jist want us to be together again with me da."

"Is there anything else besides your father you are looking forward to?"

"Chocolate!" Brenton smiled.

Routh laughed out loud. "You're a fine brave boy, Brenton, and I'm quite certain you will find both in the new country."

The conversation continued until the ship pulled into its slip and the dockhands jumped out to tether the ropes. The three of them rose and walked over the plank and into Liverpool amid thousands of poor Irish waiting to immigrate. Immediately, Routh smiled wide and spread out his arms, embracing a boy waiting for him.

He turned to Kathryn and Brenton. "This is my second eldest son, Thomas. He attends Eton and took a few days' leave to spend with me." He stopped, not knowing if they had even heard of Eton. "Thomas is the same age as you, Brenton. Please will you join us for a cup of tea before we say good-bye."

Thomas looked up and said, "The coach is waiting, Father."

"Ohh … let him wait," he said. "If he leaves, we can get another."

Kathryn pulled at her weathered dress. "Beg yer pardon, master, I don't think we're right fer tea. We'd be an offense to be sure."

"Nonsense," Routh said.

Kathryn grinned sheepishly. "We're goin' to git some new clothes 'ere before layvin', 'cept right nar we need to purchase ar tickets to Ameriky."

"Oh I can assist you with that. Right this way," Routh offered.

They made their way through the crowd, and Routh gestured toward a huge docked boat and a fast-talking man waving his hands about.

"He should be the passage broker." Routh motioned in his direction.

Kathryn and Brenton walked up to the man while Routh and his son waited a distance away.

"Father!" Thomas whispered. "Who *are* these people?"

"Be a gentleman, son, they are just poor Irish. If I speak with them, it helps me to better understand their plight so I am more useful in my position," he explained.

"Is this ship goin' to Ameriky?" Kathryn asked the man.

The broker eyed her for a moment before answering.

"Har much ya got?" he asked.

"Well ... I ... I've enough fer two tickets, no problem," she answered.

"Thin this 'ere boat's goin' to America, New York city to be exact," he stated with a grin. "Lit's see, fer the two of you, it'll be £10."

Kathryn opened the pouch and handed the clerk the money.

The passage broker held out her tickets, saying, "Right, an allotment of food is given daily, but 'tis not enough to live on. Bring yer own an' you kin cook it up on deck. It ships out tomorrow mornin' at 6:30—be on board or we're layvin' without you!"

"Much obleeged," Kathryn said, stepping aside.

She untied her outer layer of clothing at her neck and unfastened her brooch.

"I don't want to lose this whin we git the new clothes, so I'll put it in the pouch," she told Brenton. "I'll put the tickets in this pocket 'ere ... Hold the pouch a moment," she said, fumbling with the tie at the top.

"Is everything alright?" Routh suddenly walked up.

"Jist fine, jist fine," she smiled. "The ship's layvin' at 6:30 tomorrow mornin'."

"Splendid. Now how about that cup of tea? Just one cup before you buy your new clothes," Routh persisted. "Over here, there is an eatery where your attire will not be a problem."

"Very good thin," Kathryn agreed.

Instinctively, Routh and Thomas walked ahead with Kathryn and Brenton following. Brenton looked Thomas over with his crisp white shirt, pressed black suit, and colorful tie. His black shoes were immaculate, and his hair, face, and hands were cleaner and more perfect than he had ever seen on a boy. Walking straight and tall with his shoulders back and an air of absolute superiority, he would probably follow his wealthy, important father in the area of politics or the military. Brenton thought about what his life must be like every day, carving out his future with unrestricted certainty, and he knew that this boy was never mad with the hunger and never would be. He petted the pouch in his hand, knowing that his future was now a possibility.

"Here is a good table," Routh said, putting his arm out for everyone to be seated in their own chair.

Routh ordered some tea and scones and crossed his hands on the table, looking around to start the conversation. Kathryn and Brenton sat, looking a bit uneasy at the opulent surroundings.

"Do you play any games, Brenton? Cricket perhaps?" Routh asked, not realizing how absurd the question was.

"Not really, master. A boy in the next village had a ball once an' I ketched it one time," Brenton answered.

Routh understood how truly insensitive the question had been, as the boy's feeble answer dangled submissively like a half-dead rodent in a cat's mouth.

Routh realized comparing the two boys was cruel and unjust as they were worlds apart. They would never join hands to conquer a task, or help each other out if times were tough. He thought it best to find out more information from Kathryn, so he turned his attention toward her.

"How did you fare on the Public Works?" he asked, sipping his tea as it had just been served. "Was it …" And the dialogue between the two adults progressed and advanced until they were only aware of their conversation.

Brenton happily drank his tea and ate his crumpet while watching Routh, but he could feel piercing eyes staring at him from across the table. He tried to ignore them, but the obvious stare was no match for him as crumbs fell onto his shirt that mimicked the inner wall crumbling right before the sterling, cold-blooded warrior. Cautiously, he moved his eyes bit by bit until he faced the prominent eyes in front of him. Thomas was a distinct figure that added up to smart sophistication, a dapper scholar who was the same age but couldn't be more different.

"What do you think you're doing here?" Thomas whispered.

"Nothin'," Brenton quickly answered, gulping his last morsel and wiping his mouth with his arm.

"Just because my father invited you here does not elevate your position or social superiority," he quietly slithered. "You poor Irish are a dimwitted, perverse bunch that cannot survive on your own. England must step in every time to rescue and preserve your country."

The harsh words struck Brenton like a slap across the face. He had never been spoken to in such a manner, and he glanced to his mother to see if she had heard. The parents were deep in conversation themselves and did not hear the remarks.

"Mummy can't save you *neither*," Thomas rudely impersonated softly so as not to be heard.

All the words fueled Brenton's anger, and he shot back, "Ireland's people are pure and gracious to one another. We mightn' ask yer help this time, but we'll make it through this famine. Ar country is intirely great as yers."

"You are quite unsuitable to make such a statement," Thomas counter-attacked. "And where is *your* father, or are you a bastard as well?"

"Me father's in Ameriky, an' we're goin' to find him …"

"Find him? You mean you don't even know where he is? Indeed! And if Ireland is so great, then why are you leaving? I presume your father is a drunken idiot like all Irish men."

Brenton grabbed a knife from the table and struck it down on Thomas's sleeve, holding it there and recounting softly, "Me father's not a drunk, but I kin see that you're nothin' like yer own father. You're a stupid, uncarin' fool."

"Let go of me, you degrading loafer!" Thomas whispered through clenched teeth while beneath the table he thrust his foot on the edge of Brenton's chair, giving a hard push, knocking him and the chair over.

"Lord above!" Kathryn stood up and yelled at seeing Brenton sprawled out on the floor.

Routh went quickly, helping the boy up and asking, "Are you alright?"

"Aye, master." He shot a glance to his perpetrator. "Mighty quare intirely, I must've lost me balance."

"Well nar thin, I think we've taken enough of your time, Mr. Routh," Kathryn said.

"Very well, let me see you out," Routh offered.

The four gathered at the opening of the pub, and Routh grinned, "It was a pleasure meeting and speaking with you both, and I wish you much success in America." He handed Kathryn a piece of paper that had his address written on it.

"Please write to me someday when you find your husband and you purchase that farm of your dreams," he said.

"I will." Kathryn took the paper and placed it in her dress pocket. "I can't tell you har nice you've bin, Mr. Routh. You're mighty kind, and I'm obleeged and honored to meet such a wonderful man that cares a great deal fer ould Ireland and its people."

"It is my job, Kathryn," Routh said.

"Aye, but you have a good heart that's probly not intirely required in yer job," Kathryn said. "And that, Yer Honor, makes all the difference. The Irish are most lucky to have a man like you, and if anyone kin git help fer 'em, I'm sure you'll be the one. We won't forgit you."

"Much obleeged fer everthin', master," Brenton said honestly.

Thomas did not say anything, so Routh nudged him on the back.

"Ahh ... yes ... have a safe trip abroad," Thomas said nonchalantly.

They walked their separate ways, and after a few paces, Routh said to his son, "You could have been a little more polite."

"But, Father, they are just peasants."

Routh stopped and looked Thomas deep in the eyes.

"I don't ever want to hear you speak of the impoverished in such an inconsiderate manner. They are simply poor without the lineage, knowledge, or opportunities we have. There is no need to be discourteous."

"Yes, Father."

Kathryn and Brenton walked the streets, making their way through the crowds to find a clothing shop. They stepped inside a store and were met by a kind saleswoman. She showed them around and had them try on several pieces until they found ones that were satisfactory. Kathryn and Brenton were speechless as they gazed into the mirror at the person staring back. They were flush with gratitude as the new clothes elevated them to a status they had never known. The fabrics were crisp and clean without any tears or frays. The shades were rich and vibrant, like a colorful circus encircling their bodies. It was a wonderful event and Kathryn was beaming. Their lives had suddenly changed, and finally she felt like they were living instead of merely surviving. The saleswoman offered to throw their old rags away and Kathryn agreed. They made their way to the cash register and Kathryn looked for her pouch to pay.

She turned to her son. "Och, Brenton, I gave you the pouch, didn't I?"

He looked shocked for a moment. "I have it?" he asked.

"Aye, I gave it to you whin we bought the tickets. You don't have it?" she said with concern filling her voice.

"Umm ... I don't know ..."

"What do you mean you don't know! Maybe it's with yer ould clothes."

The kind saleswoman retrieved the old clothes and dumped out the rags on the counter as they frantically searched through them.

"I forgit, maybe I left it at the pub," Brenton said, thinking back.

Kathryn turned to the saleswoman. "We'll be right back, we must've left our money whin we have ar cup o' tea."

"That is fine, ma'am, but I cannot let you leave with the new clothes; you'll have to put your old ones back on."

They changed once again into the well-worn garments that reminded them of their social class. Any degree of distinction was stripped away as they looked into the mirror once more at the person without prestige or importance. Racing out the door and down the walkways, they entered the pub and spoke with the woman at the front counter. She walked them back to the table, and they looked all about, under and over the table and chairs. Kathryn was beside herself and on the verge of tears. Brenton clutched her hand and walked her outside.

"'Tis all me fault, Mam, an' I'm so sorry. We've lost everythin' nar, and we're back to whar we started. Ar intire future is no more without the brooch and money. Har kin you ever forgive me?" He bowed his head.

The unexpected blow shocked Kathryn, but she knew being angry at her son would not help the situation. He had not meant to lose the pouch, and his life was affected as much as hers.

"'Tis not matter, we've not lost everythin', me son," she soothed.

She opened her dress pocket and held between her fingers the two tickets to America. "I'm sure thar're jobs in Ameriky, and we're still alive thanks be to God. Don't hang yer head, son; we'll still prosper if we keep larnin' an' workin' hard. Ar ship is awaitin' thin and so is yer da. Tonight we'll find a place fer sleep, and tomorrow we'll get aboard."

The boy smiled at his mother as if she were a twelve-course meal. She was gracious and harbored no ill feelings toward him. She was truly an angel in his eyes. They began the trek to the dock area to find a sheltered corner for the night with mixed feelings of being destitute and fortunate at the same time. They would still board their ship tomorrow on the 30th of May and somehow felt lucky to be leaving even if they had rags for clothes and no money. Liverpool suddenly felt large and important as they insignificantly made their way down the street past crowds and buildings, past feral cats creeping through the alleys, and past the sullen faces sitting in corners, staring back with hands outstretched. They were still blessed to have the opportunity to leave for new lands that would finally give them a chance to begin a new life.

The following day, the bright sunlight shot through the window, waking Routh in his Liverpool accommodation. He rose and ate breakfast with Thomas, hearing about his son's cricket games, friends, and the new things he had learned in school. They would get the next coach to London so Routh could meet with Trevelyan and Thomas could return to school.

"Father," Thomas began, "why can't the Irish help themselves? Why do we always have to step in and help them?"

"Generations have put the unfortunate Irish in their current position, and it will take generations of assistance to help them be self-sufficient. Our government first needs to educate them. To be a truly great and respected country, there must be truly great and respected leaders. They will need to govern the country befitting to all, and I believe to do this accurately they will need to understand the common man and what affects his life. It is not completely their fault that this potato blight has caused thousands of deaths; the blame also lies on our government and our systems. You are a very lucky boy, son; it is by the grace of God that we were not born into the Irish peasant class. Do not take your own class for granted or your superior education."

"I won't," Thomas gulped, looking down. After a moment, he asked, "When we go home, can we go fishing before I return to school?"

"Splended idea," Routh said.

Thomas stirred in his seat, and Routh looked at him questionably.

"Do you think Brenton and his mother have left for America already?"

"I don't know, son, maybe."

"Well … I must confess something to you … I didn't mean to make matters worse for them … that's not true either, I did really. But somehow now I am very sorry."

"What have you done?" Routh asked.

Thomas reached into his trouser pocket, pulled out a red pouch, and handed it to his father. Dubiously, Routh opened the pouch and saw the money, brooch, and paper. Instantly, he knew and shot a glance at his son.

"This is theirs?" he asked.

"Yes, Father."

Routh jumped up, saying, "Let's go!"

Father and son ran through the streets trying to flag down a coach, but all in sight were loaded with passengers. They ran and ran past crowds of people, dodging this way and that until they reached the docks. Gasping for breath, Routh could see the billowing sails in the far-off distance, and he made his way to a passage broker.

Panting, he asked, "That ship ... for America ... are there any more ... leaving today?" he asked.

"No, master, 'twas the last ship, but that one's headed fer Canada."

"Canada ... are you sure?" Routh questioned.

"Aye, master," the broker said, walking away.

Routh walked back and saw Thomas staring out into the sea, watching the clipper ship slowly disappear over the horizon. He was extremely disappointed in his son for stealing such a precious item of someone's and could not understand why he would commit such an act. They both stood side by side until a spec was all that could be seen.

"What is going to happen to them, Father?"

"I wish I knew," he answered. "Now explain to me why you would do such a thing?"

The boy faced him.

"I didn't like Brenton because he was poor. He is not of our class ... and something just came over me ... I said despicable things to him ... and I stole the pouch when I pushed him over in the chair."

"*You* pushed him over?"

"Yes, I know ... you have every right to be angry with me. I know it is not right to be unkind, and I admit to saying terrible things to him. Sometimes the boys and I just get carried away, and now they were not even present ... I'm truely ashamed of myself, Father. Can we send them the pouch?"

"I have no way to contact them," Routh said stoically. "Perhaps Kathryn will write to me someday. And perhaps you should choose your friends more wisely. Rather, you should have enough common sense to not follow the crowd. The contents of this pouch are all those people have, don't you understand? To some degree, you do not need to know the appalling details of the famine, but maybe it's best you are exposed to some of it. I am trying very hard to get these people some help, and actions such as yours are so extremely detrimental. I want you personally to raise as much money as possible for this famine, and the next time you visit me in Dublin, you will hand over that money to help 'those people' that you have stolen from. And when you're there, we will also visit some places that I think you need to see. You have brutishly played with people's lives, and I'm certain your actions will hurt Kathryn and Brenton in ways we will never truly fathom. Don't ever let me see you be unkind to the poor again."

"Yes, Father."

"Now let's go home."

The two boarded a coach to London and spoke little on the long ride home, believing that Routh's lecture was all that needed to be said. Routh tried to concentrate on his meeting with Trevelyan the following day and how best to approach the man, but thoughts of what his son did crept into his mind and wriggled about like a determined worm through the soft, moist ground.

When they finally reached their home, each went to bed without speaking another word. After breakfast, Routh told Thomas that he would return shortly after his meeting with Trevelyan. The boy simply nodded. Routh boarded a coach and sat back. Truthfully, he was happy to be back in England and feel the normalcy of life in the air after his time in Ireland. It felt good to set eyes on familiar buildings and healthy people.

He had a bold walk as he strode into the office and shook Trevelyan's hand.

"Good day, Randolph," Trevelyan said, and getting right down to business, he added, "I am happy to see that private enterprise is finally functioning well in Ireland."

Routh cleared his throat as he reclined in the soft leather chair.

"Well, the people who require food the most are unable to purchase the goods due to the rising prices," Routh explained.

"Ahh … a mere technicality!" Trevelyan stated. "If they desire the food, they must indeed work harder."

"The Public Works pays 40*d*. per week. A man cannot adequately sustain his own life on that salary, let alone a family."

"You are here to rally for more food, is that correct?" Trevelyan sat back.

"Yes, sir, I am," Routh boldly stated.

"My dear Randolph, you are wasting valuable time. I have informed you countless times that under no circumstances shall I provide more provisions for a country that continues to selfishly consume all the food that is given and persists in asking for more!"

"I understand, although—"

"The Irish simply must help themselves; they cannot rely on England forever!" Trevelyan leaned forward as his voice began to rise.

Routh perisisted, "I believe you fail to fully comprehend—"

"I *fully* comprehend all aspects of this famine," Trevelyan snapped.

"Please let me finish, sir."

"We have given more than enough to the Irish," Trevelyan criticized. "We give; they take and keep asking for more!"

"That is a farrago of twisted facts!" Routh provoked.

"It is your duty to *obey* my commands, not demand your own!" Trevelyan banged the table.

Routh abruptly stood up.

"Please, sir!" he yelled. "I must complete my thoughts on this subject! I believe it is also my duty to perform my mission to the highest degree, and to do this, I must relay to you my conscientious judgment on this matter!"

The two men stared at each other for a moment, letting the sound of the loud words fall to the ground. Then Trevelyan gave one nod but did not speak. He thought it best to hear what his comrade had to say.

"Thank you, sir." Routh sat back down collecting his emotions. "As I stated in my last letter, I have witnessed with my own eyes the destruction of a country and its people within a few years. I fully agree that to simply hand out free food is not wise and does not benefit England or Ireland. However, I propose that exports remain in their own country to assist those that are the neediest and that a more aggressive plan is set in operation to change the governing system that is scarcely functioning at this point. The people need to be educated to wean themselves off the potato and make better lives for themselves. We must demand that the landowners give money to those that want to immigrate to Canada or America, and those that wish to stay will be the ones to begin a new administration. If we do not educate them to provide for themselves, Ireland will forever be dependent on England."

Routh looked at Trevelyan, mulling over how many years this transition would take and more importantly how much money it would eventually cost England.

"I would also propose," Routh continued, "that the landowners should be fully aware of the circumstances and that they should without question be required to subscribe to the belief of a new Ireland."

"Do you realize what you are asking?" Trevelyan asked.

"Yes, sir, I do." Routh stood and slowly walked about the room. "Unfortunately, I see no other way to mend this continuing famine problem. Every time a new blight contaminates the potato, England will have to step in to provide and countless people will indeed suffer. And the suffering, sir, is the worst part. I have witnessed such misery and anguish that it is beyond imagination. If you could only see as I have the numerous corpses walking aimlessly about, the moans and groans of death, and the torn pieces of rags the peasants wear as they have absolutely nothing left in the world, not even a spoon. I wish I could show you the families lying in the cold darkness next to dead relatives because they had not enough strength to remove or bury the bodies. The starving cats and dogs gnawing on limbs here and there due to the tragic fact that there are so many corpses they cannot be picked up fast enough. But I must say the little children presented the most piteous and heart-wrenching spectacle. Their faces were not of children, but of the famine itself. The infantile expressions were non-existent, and they lied next to one another, perhaps for warmth or some kind of mere comfort. Many were swollen from continuing starvation, but the arms remained thin, almost transparent. There was no flesh on the tiny limbs, only weak bone and sallow skin. If it was pulled slightly, the skin did not retract to its normal position; rather, it hung pinched and wrinkled as if it were 150 years old. But in all that I have seen these past years, I have heard only a few of them utter a modest complaint. They tend to one another as much as possible and have only resorted to violence out of sheer necessity."

Routh leaned in close to Trevelyan's desk and spoke with the deepest fervor and passion that consumed his heart, "Sir, I have looked deeply into the eyes of starvation and death. It is so hollow, alone, and more revolting than I can ever describe. These people are just like us. They treasure their wives, and on the birth of each child, they marvel at the tiny hand created out of love. And each day they watch in horror as that tiny hand grows weaker and weaker until it ceases to move at all. They have the same emotions and basic needs as any of us, and should they choose to work hard and prosper, they can marry, have children, and bask in the glow of their families. They have the exact same red blood flowing through their veins and an equal right to live as we do. They are our fellow citizens with purposes and goals in life; they worship the same Almighty God, and in the end ... identical to us ... they will stand before Him and receive the same exact judgment as we will. For God's sake ... we *must* help them."

Trevelyan sat motionless. It was rare indeed that someone or something could render him speechless, and Routh had painted a picture that he did not want to see.

After a moment or two, he spoke, "I understand what you have said, and I will consider your proposals. I cannot promise you anything further at this time. I am fully aware of the dire situation in Ireland and will do everything necessary to assist the present needy and the country as a whole. Now if you will excuse me, I have quite a lot of work to complete. I wish you a speedy trip back to Dublin and I will be in touch."

"Thank you, sir." Routh stood up. "I have one more thing." He laid the booklet on the desk that had belonged to the man he had buried in Clare.

"This was written by a dying man," he said. Then he walked out of his office and the Treasury building without uttering another word or looking back. If he had said any more, it would counteract his previous statements and irritate the man; and surely nothing would be gained from that. As he made his way back down the street, he heard someone calling out his name.

"Mr. Routh! Mr. Routh!"

He turned to see Trevelyan's secretary, Margaret, waving her hand in the air. He stopped for her to catch up with him.

"Mr. Routh," she panted, "I cannot let you leave without letting you know that I am so grateful to you for standing up to Mr. Trevelyan. I ... I suppose I heard all you had to say. It is just that everyone is so afraid of him. I heard what you said about the poor starving Irish and it's just dreadful; the papers don't print such terrible stories, and personally I think they have a slanted view. Please, if there is any information you need or anything I can do to help the Irish people, I would be glad to be of assistance."

Routh took both her hands in his and smiled at her. "Thank you, Margaret. I have tried my best, and now it is out of my hands. More than anything, the Irish need food and clothing. I know there are quite a few organizations here in England; contribute generously to those charities and you will be doing your part. Thank you for your concern."

He made his way down the street, wishing to walk instead of taking another coach and feeling uncertain about his meeting with Trevelyan. Perhaps he came on too strong? Trevelyan liked intelligent people with shrewd, inventive ideas, and perchance he might have ruined any possibility of crucial help for the Irish poor. He should not have interrupted the man—his healthy ego was surely bruised. He put them on the same level as the upper class, which was most likely a fatal mistake. Social rank and position is of utmost importance—how could he have been so reckless? Trevelyan ended the meeting rather abruptly; that must be a sign that he was offended, and now Routh had no one to blame but himself.

His feet felt heavy as he walked up the steps to his home, letting his conscience do battle in his head. Defeat rounded his shoulders as he entered and walked straight into his study. Placing his briefcase on the floor, he glanced at the red pouch atop some books. He held his hand over it and sighed, imagining what hardships Kathryn must now endure. His entire plan was to come to England and help the Irish, and now it was all backfiring—first Thomas's shameful actions against Kathryn, and now the meeting with Trevelyan that did not seem to go well. It all appeared to be going in exactly the wrong direction. Routh was not leaving for Dublin until the next day, and now that his son was home, he wanted to spend the remainder of the day with him. He found Thomas in the kitchen and announced, "I would like you to set an itinerary for the Irish fundraising and send it to me by early next week. But since we have one free day together … let us go fishing."

"Thank you, Father," Thomas said. "I have learned my lesson and I am truly, truly sorry."

"I know, and you should be."

"When my brothers and sisters are older, I will tell them about this instance." "Alright ... now get your tackle and let's get something for cook tonight."

The boy ran off and was back with two rods, a tackle box, and a fishing krill. They went to their favorite secret spot and cast their poles into the glassy stream. For a while, Routh forgot about Ireland's troubles and enjoyed the afternoon with his son. He tied a piece of bread onto his hook and flung it out toward a spot in the stream that looked promising. The reel whirred with the pull, and the bait plopped into the clear water, sending out ripples of circles. The sun's rays reached down and softly touched the clear water, leaving a sparkle that looked like a glimmer of the spirit. Routh sat on a large rock, soaking in the moment and relishing the feeling of being alive.

"Father," Thomas interrupted the quiet, "if the poor people are hungry, why don't they go fishing for food?"

"Good question, son," Routh answered, "but not as easy as it might sound. To begin with, fishing is not popular in Ireland as it is in England. Timber is almost non-existent, so the boats are small and not seaworthy. They use something called a curragh, which consists of hides and canvas stretched over wickerwork. This vessel is quite fast with four oarsmen, and it can go long distances, but Ireland's fish are many miles out and the curragh cannot handle spending days out at sea with nets. The mighty Atlantic swell gets its force from far away and has capsized many boats, leaving men dead. There are no fisheries in Ireland due to unseaworthy vessels, but, son, I have heard that in those waters swims the finest fish in all the world. I once learned of a man venturing out in his curragh on one treacherous morning when no other fisherman would dare. He caught a few with the tides and winds blowing so fierce that he ended up in Nova Scotia, barely alive. So the poor Irishman can only venture out in his curragh when weather permits, which could only be once or twice a month. He relies on the potato for his main foodsource, and by now he has pawned all his fishing gear anyway for food.

Nonetheless, these days, being employed on the Board of Works is more profitable and reliable than fishing."

Thomas's line pulled forward suddenly and then went back to its original position. He checked his line and found the bait had been eaten. He attached another piece of bread to the hook and cast out with one swift motion, watching the bread soar high above his head and plop into the water.

"Now I have heard the best fishing in county Mayo is found in Erris," Routh continued, "a small village where the only access is over a high swampy mountain. The ground there is so spongy and wet, it is tough to climb even in the summer. And if you do make it over the mountain, the weather is unpredictable; it could be sunny and clear in the morning as you set out with your curragh, and within the hour, fierce rain and winds can put your life in danger. This coastline is lined with cliffs reaching five hundred feet in height, and if I were a fish, I would live there too because I would be safe from any fisherman."

"Why doesn't England help with the fishing?" Thomas asked.

"As a matter of fact, they have, son. Quite a bit of money is needed, but Lord Russell only advanced £5,000 for this entire year. It has also been suggested that loans be offered to the fishermen, but strangely enough, Trevelyan thought it would mar the men's morale, and besides, experience has shown their repayment habits to be untrustworthy. The Society of Friends and the British government have tried to help, and even the Scottsmen visited to pass on their fishing knowledge. Alas, all these measures came to a close last year for the same reasons Ireland has not had fisheries in the past. The poverty, the improper boats, the remoteness from any market, and the treacherous coast all factored in. Furthermore, bringing in a boatload of fish in foul weather was almost impossible. The fish-curing stations had to close because there were not reliable boatloads of fish arriving on a consistent basis, and also getting it to other areas of Ireland was unachievable because the catch would not keep. It all sounds easy, Thomas, but as you can see, it is not."

"I had no idea all that effort went into trying to fish," Thomas said. "Maybe we could give the fish we catch today to some poor people."

"That sounds like a fine idea," Routh nodded. He was proud that his son was contemplating thoughtful and compassionate thoughts and wanted him to keep those character hallmarks. Thomas was handsome and showed leadership traits beyond his years, and Routh secretly dreamed that his son would grow to be a great political figure, changing rules and regulations to benefit all of Britain. He looked at his healthy, robust son and imagined that nothing in the world could be so horrific than watching your child die and being unable to help. It sickened him to think of children dying of starvation, the poor innocent souls that depended on adults to regulate the world until they reached an age of self-management. He felt so blessed that all his children would not know any kind of poverty.

During the beginning of the famine, Routh's position in Irish Relief weighed heavily upon his head when he received the number of death tolls in neighboring towns. He would go to Thomas and the other children and hug them with all his might. Clutching their small frames, he would secretly thank God for letting his children be spared. He wanted to give them the moon and the stars and ground them with the wisdom of humility and a kind-hearted sovereignty. He knew they would all be successful in life due to the financial and emotional backing he and Marie Louise would provide, but for the children in Ireland, it was a much different story. Was it honestly asking too much for the government to grant more aid to the peasant, educate them to grow their own food source, and help them to be more self-sufficient? Perhaps it was. But Routh knew it was too late for this generation, the lost souls that were destined to melt into the soggy ground of Ireland.

Routh's thoughts were interrupted by a familiar sound, and he asked Thomas, "Did you hear that?"

"Here what?"

"That bird in the hedge over there, do you see him?" Routh pointed.

"Oh yes, I see him now."

"That particular bird is called a yellowhammer, and he is so smart that if you listen real hard, you can hear him order lunch."

"Ahh, Father."

"Look at him, Thomas," Routh persisted, and the boy fixated on the attractive, little bird with the yellow head and chestnut wings flitting about the hedgerow. He darted about so swiftly and quickly as if putting on a show.

"Okay, now close your eyes," Routh suggested, and Thomas closed his eyes. "Now focus in your mind's eye on that bird, and when he chirps next, you can hear him say, 'Little bit of bread and no cheese.'"

Thomas sat motionless, concentrating and listening until the bird chirped its cadence. He peeked open one eye and looked at Routh who smiled at him.

"Ahh, come on, Father," Thomas laughed, opening both eyes.

"No, really," Routh snickered. "Maybe you're not listening hard enough,"

Routh's line abruptly jerked forward, and father and son instinctively stood up.

"Can I bring him in, Father?" Thomas asked as Routh handed him the pole.

The taut fishing line stretched steadily to the left and then to the right while a concentrating Thomas reeled him slowly in. A few splashes could be heard as the fish came to the surface and waved his head to and fro in a *no* gesture.

"He's a beauty!" Routh smiled.

"Look at the size of him, Father!"

"Yes, looks great!" Routh smiled again as Thomas lifted the fish from his comfortable liquid home and placed him on the hard bank.

"Just look at him!" Thomas beamed. "This will make a nice dinner for some family."

"Yes, he will." Routh watched proudly as the boy extracted the hook and placed him into his basket. The boy was excited and eager to show Cook, so they raced home and Thomas went searching into the kitchen for her.

"Cook will know who to give this to," the boy said.

Routh retired to his study and spent the remainder of the day going over paperwork.

The next morning, father and son had breakfast together and then strolled through the garden and talked until the valet announced that Thomas's carriage had arrived to take him back to school. Routh hugged his son tightly and told him how much he loved him. Then the boy ran off, looking back once to wave and smile at his beaming father. He knew how much he was loved and truly wanted his family to be proud of him. *They will be some day,* he thought.

During Routh's own return voyage to his temporary home in Dublin, he had many hours to think and ponder the happenings of his time in England. He was looking forward to being reunited with his wife and young children, but not to greeting the piles of work that must be waiting for him. He thought about Kathryn and Brenton quite a bit during the next few days and hoped that he could somehow return their red pouch.

Chapter VIII

Kathryn's mind awoke as she lay in her bunk experiencing the gentle sway from side to side as if she were an infant being rocked by her loving mother. They had boarded early and fell asleep as soon as they reached their bunks. All at once, the realization of her dire situation and the noise from the other passengers about smacked her into reality; she instinctively reached her right hand out to find Brenton. He slept silently beside her, huddled in his usual fetal position to keep warm. She swallowed hard, knowing their journey to America would be brutal with no food or water of their own, only the day's rations offered by the captain. The money was gone, the lovely brooch was gone, and with them any expectation for a bright, prosperous future. Their only hope left was finding Joseph.

"Mam?" Brenton awoke.

"Aye, I'm right 'ere."

"Ugh." The boy sat up upon his elbows and looked at the ceiling a few inches from his head. "I've gotta 'member not to sit up too fast," he smiled.

They looked around at the other passengers and summoned a courteous smile of camaraderie, the closed-mouthed quick grin given freely to strangers, evoking civilized politeness and absolutely nothing more. For every space available, there was a body, and with every body more noise and less privacy. Kathryn was told earlier that each day's rations were to be distributed in the morning and were meant to be an addition to the food each passenger brought on board with them. She wondered if she was the only disgraceful mother who had no other preparations for her family.

She swung her legs round and rose stiffly, hanging on to the bed for added support. By now, she was used to pain traveling through different parts of her body, as if it were an entity and had a mind of its own. Today the pain was gnawing at the lower parts of her legs, and she tried different positions to shift the entity to another location. She needed her legs most of all if she were to make it across the grandiose Atlantic Ocean; she needed every bit of strength left.

"I don't feel so good—kin we go on deck nar?" Brenton asked.

"Aye, we'll git food soon," she answered. "Git up nar, son, and stand in front 'ere so I kin ..." She stopped short, waving the bucket she held in her hand.

"At least this is included," she stated.

With each moment that passed, the clatter and pandemonium rose as more and more passengers awoke to begin their day. Kathryn and Brenton made their way down the smelly narrow aisle, past yawning, scratching people with filthy hair and bodies in all directions. Everywhere they looked, someone was sneezing, stretching, or using their bucket to vomit or relieve themselves, and it felt like a disgusting bleak dungeon in which they were rudely thrown together like cattle to be exported for immediate slaughter. Rows of wooden platforms held the unfortunate beasts that society loathed and the refined, sophisticated individual would gladly have removed from the world; this area was known to all the other passengers on the ship as steerage.

When mother and son reached the end, they climbed a ladder toward the bright sunlight upon deck. To Kathryn, it felt like she was crawling out from the dark depths of hell to the crystalline edge of life everlasting. What a glorious sight they beheld as the thick, shiny masts reached up toward the sky, holding the brilliant white sails that billowed in the breeze. They gazed about the vast sea and smelled the aroma of its water. The deck was vacant as they walked about, taking in every facet of the experience. As they turned one corner, they came face-to-face with a tall, respectable gentleman in his early thirties.

"Ahh ... beg yer pardon, Yer Honor." Kathryn cast her eyes down. "I didn't know anyone was 'bout. I hope we caused no offense."

"No offense taken, ma'am." The gentleman tipped his hat. "It is a beautiful morning."

Kathryn did not know how to respond to small talk with someone clearly out of her class. At least they were somewhat clean and Mr. Routh had given her some much-needed confidence to speak with the respectable.

"Aye, master," she responded. "Ameriky is jist as beautiful, I bin tould."

"America? Yes, I have heard it is quite picturesque," the gentleman nodded, "although I am looking forward to seeing Canada."

Kathryn knew she should not ask such a bold question, but could not refrain herself. "I beg Yer Honor's pardon agin fer bein' so free, but why are ye not on a ship to Canada thin?"

"This ship *is* going to Canada," he said, staring directly into her eyes. They were clear as the sea and reeked of distinguished seasoning.

Kathryn mulled the situation over in her mind, wanting to believe that the 10£ she paid for passage was taking her to America and to Joseph. She looked at Brenton and instinctively knew that she had been taken again, swindled by her own countrymen by artful selfishness and pure dogmatic greed.

"I am sorry, miss, you thought this ship was going to America?"

"Aye."

Kathryn walked away from the gentleman, and Brenton followed. He knew his mam was trying to keep positive and failing at every turn. She stopped at the bow, staring out into the sea.

"I wish Da was 'ere," Brenton said softly, "he'd know whit to say to you."

A few loud voices could be heard from the port as the captain came on deck mumbling and shouting orders to a few crew members. Standing not quite six feet, he had weathered, dark skin upon his face and round spectacles that rested halfway down his nose. His eyes were quick, his nose and mouth were straight, and his cleft chin made him somewhat distinguished. His eyebrows danced up and down as he spoke, making deep, definite lines across his wide forehead. His hairline began at the crest of his head, and for this reason, he let it grow and grow until it cascaded reddish-brown upon his shoulders. His usual stance was hands on hips or crossed in front, and his lips were either pursed in fury or shouting orders at some merciful soul. Solid legs with a wide gait from years at sea held up his thick, well-constructed body. He was the slow-moving king of his ship and demanded respect from all who sailed upon her.

In another moment, a woman appeared who was clearly his wife. Her long, sleek black hair flew freely in the breeze, and she delicately touched her husband's shoulders and back every time she passed him. It was as if she were trying to reach past them and grasp her husband's heart, to gently caress and soften it for the benefit of all. Willowy and swift, she moved sprightly in every direction to appease matters and soothe the mood of the ship. She was of German descent, although lived the last half of her life in France. Each word spoken was carefully delivered by her throaty, sultry voice, and everyone called her Demoiselle. Attractive and charming, her allure was apparent to all except the captain, who did not contain himself from shouting at her also. Fortunately, his somber mood did not seep into his crew as they whistled and worked, chanting in unison throughout the day.

Kathryn soon noticed the gentleman speaking to the captain, and before long, the two went down into the brig, probably for their morning meal.

"Alright all you people!" shouted a young man about fifteen years old. "Please listen over here! Listen please! Me name is Slater and I'm the cabin-boy apprentice here to pass out the daily rations. Step up here please."

He began passing out plates of food and water to bony outstretched hands. "This food is to last all day, so don't eat it all at one sitting!"

Slater was jovial and handsome, with a huge mischievous grin that stretched for miles in each direction. His tall, slight frame came and returned before you even knew he had gone, and his mind was even quicker than his feet. Born in Andover, England, as a child he came to Liverpool with his great uncle who raised him from an infant. Whenever Slater would ask about his mum and dad, the man quickly changed the subject, offering no information. He was barely a young man when his uncle hurt his leg and gangrene festered and sent poisonous toxins throughout his bloodstream. Both knew the end was near as the man lay on his deathbed, every breath a struggle. Slater pressed him one last time for information about his mum and dad, but the man simply moaned and turned his head. As he died, so did all the answers Slater would never hear, which left him wondering if the man before him was even a relative. With no direction, the boy walked the streets until he stumbled upon the Demoiselle at the docks one foggy afternoon. She loved children although was barren herself, believing that God wanted her to treat all others as her own.

With food to eat, Kathryn and Brenton lapped up half the meal and drank every last drop of water. Their stomachs grumbled for more, and it took great control to return below deck and store it for the evening meal. The two lay on their bunks with squabbling and bickering about and fell into a deep, dreamy sleep. With the continued rocking of the ship, they as well as all the passengers were sick now and again until the constant motion became normal.

The other passengers who brought food made their way to the three fireplaces the crew had assembled. They were made of large wooden planks that held up two layers of bricks and a boatload of coals. Three thick iron bars ran across the tops, making a griddle, and a wall of brick in the back protected it all from the wind. The shape itself resembled a boat, and as soon as the coals burned, scores of people horded around to cook their meals. From the second they were lit in the morning, the fireplaces were surrounded by people cooking. And when Slater doused the coals with seawater at 7:00 in the evening, the people never complained, even if their meal was drenched with water and barely cooked. They simply retrieved it from the bars, choking and half-blinded from the steam and smoke ... and ate it.

The next day, Brenton awoke and went on deck, leaving his sleeping mother to her dreams. Crowds of people still huddled about the fireplaces, elbowing one another as they tried to cook their meals. How lucky they were, he thought, to have brought some food on board. He got closer to smell something, anything, being cooked and peered through a few bent elbows. One arm was stirring some watery oatmeal in a pot; another was baking a cake of some sort on a makeshift griddle. Brenton noticed lots of these cakes being made and marveled at their existence, curious about the taste. About two inches thick around, they were poured onto the griddle and flipped over swiftly when one side was unintentionally burnt to a crisp. After the charring of the other side, it was abruptly eaten. Brenton followed one such cake as it was given to a young girl. She bit it in two and the raw inside oozed down her cheeks and hands, completely uncooked. It did not matter to Brenton; he was mesmerized by the image of someone eating, and he licked his lips as if he himself were chewing the ashes mixed with the raw batter. The girl left her spot for another cake, and Brenton and a few other kids immediately rushed to where she had been standing to eat a few burnt crumbs on the ground.

"Pardon me!" a rotten-toothed woman growled as she walked up and stood in front of the children on their hands and knees. "Outta me way nar!"

"Sorry." Brenton retreated and went looking for companionship.

He found it in Slater; healthy and rosy-cheeked, he watched him laughing and chanting a tune. Brenton longed for those days when smiles came easily. Slater noticed the boy staring and came over to him.

"Hello, young fellow," he grinned.

"Hello," Brenton smiled.

And the two became shipmates climbing and scouting the dock. Brenton assisted him with his work, and Slater gave him some food in return. On most days, they played with a few of the little children, half-naked and skinny enough to be almost transparent. The Demoiselle upon seeing these poor souls found some old sails and roughly sewed clothes for them. She knitted for pleasure and one day brought out an impressive light blue dress for one little girl. She had been making a blanket, she informed her, but it looked so much better as a dress on her. The little girl cried with gratitude, and the mate had to retrieve the Demoiselle lest she break down herself with weeping.

One day, Slater said he needed to get some food for the first mate and asked Brenton if he wanted to see the provision supply in the storage cargo. He didn't need to ask twice. The boys descended by ladder to a large room segregated from the rest of the ship. Slater lit the room's lantern, and Brenton's eyes beheld more food than he ever dreamed was available; he stood motionless with his eyes drinking in all they could. Sack upon sack of rice, meal, beans, tea, flour, sugar, potatoes, and coffee with beef and pork in the cooler. This was the ultimate buried sea treasure that taunted the palate and teased the mind.

"I niver seen so much food!" Brenton gasped. "We could last a yar out 'ere!"

"It's still an amazing sight for me as well." Slater sat on a sack patting it. He began getting the provisions he needed whilst Brenton looked about, feeling each bag for its contents. He went to the far back and sat on a white sack filled with rice.

"Ugh," came a moan from beneath.

The boys looked at one another, and before Brenton could speak, Slater was beside him rolling the bags over to find the source of the sound. Through the flicker of the lantern, a man could be seen sitting crouched on the floor.

"Don't you move!" Slater pointed a finger at the man. Then he looked at Brenton and said, "Stay here, I'll be back."

He left the lantern and was up the ladder and out of sight. Brenton stood and looked at the pitiful soul hovering between piles of sacks. He could see rather clearly that he had torn rags on for clothes, was void of shoes, and extremely gaunt with tousled hair and dirt caked all over his body. He looked about twenty-five years of age and was obviously destitute. Without speaking or moving, he shifted his deep-set eyes toward the corner of the room and awaited his fate. He was the sneaky mouse found in the cupboard, and the deadly mousetrap was swiftly coming to snap off his head. The clomping of thick, heavy boots descending the ladder did not affect the dour expression on the intruder's face. A thin, dowdy man of about twenty-one years of age came face-to-face with Brenton and demanded to know who he was, but before he could answer, Slater explained the situation and pointed the incriminating finger at the wispy, concealed man.

"Who are you?" the dowdy man asked without really wanting or waiting for an answer. He told the intruder to rise and shoved his rag-torn body up the ladder and onto the deck. Slater grabbed the lantern and motioned for Brenton to follow.

"That's Leonard the cabin-boy," Slater explained.

The frowzy cabin boy had a sickly, yellow complexion and immense, dark eyes. Each movement was oddly strained and

270

rather slow, especially next to Slater. His hair was thick, black, and wiry, amassed atop a rather massive ill-developed head, and his feet were unusually colossal for his height. Large, ball-shaped shoes and a duck-like stance made him look like a barbell standing on its end. His mind seemed to move in unison with his sluggish movements, which made it questionable whether he was dimwitted or merely slothful. Slater was clearly the better choice for the cabin-boy title, were it not for his young age.

Atop the deck, the intruder, Leonard, Slater, and Brenton walked across the planks until they reached the stern where another man was working. Leonard began explaining to the man about the intruder, and Slater whispered to Brenton, "That's the first mate."

The mate was short and stout with strong seasoned legs and tough skin from years at sea. He was ordinary in his looks and personality and relished everything about the sea. His knowledge about fishing and sailing was vast and he never married, referring to the sea as "my beloved." Fiercely loyal to the captain and Demoiselle, he once choked a crewmember into unconsciousness for planning a mutiny to throw the captain overboard and take his wife as his own.

The mate nodded his head at Leonard and went below deck only to return moments later with the captain and Demoiselle.

"A stowaway!" the captain yelled for the entire crew to hear. "What in God's name are you doing on my ship? How did you get on board? You have no right stealing food and water, why I should have you thrown overboard!"

"Please, Captain—" the stowaway spoke for the first time.

"You have no right to speak or call me captain! Only those that have paid to be on my ship have the right to address me, you dirty, sticky-fingered scoundrel!"

The stowaway stood shivering in the wind as the captain circled him, shouting and cursing at what an outrage such an act was and how never in his thirty years at sea had anyone sunken to such sly, dishonest thievery. On and on the captain wailed whilst the intruder's shoulders slumped over farther and farther until the swaying and wobbling almost tipped him over.

"Vat are ve going to do?" Demoiselle asked.

The captain ceased badgering at being interrupted and thought earnestly for a moment.

"Everyone on deck! I want the entire ship searched for more stowaways!"

The mate and crew members ran amuck searching every room. With all passengers on deck—the respectable, the feeble, the old, and the young—it gave everyone a good look at one another. Brenton found Kathryn and explained what had happened. She stood patiently with the sun shining down on her like the rest of the passengers until a familiar sound made her search out its origin.

"Whit a joke this is! The likes of us won't be keepin' no stowaway in ar beds."

The person with the familiar voice caught sight of Kathryn and squeezed between two people to get to her.

"Lord above, I didn't know you're on this ship," Gordis Flynn said.

"Aye," Kathryn nodded. "Me and Brenton, me son."

"Och! Thar's the lad … does he drink poiti yet?" she asked.

"*No!*"

"Hmm … not matter, there'll be plenty of customers in Ameriky."

"This ships goin' to Canada, don't ya know?" Kathryn stated flatly.

"Aye, I only had 'nough money fer this ship. Ameriky is £12 fer one ticket. Is not yer husband thar?"

"Aye," Kathryn replied, "we'll make ar way down to him layter."

"Thin maybe we kin travel together?"

Kathryn shot her a glance that spoke volumes and uttered, "Maybe."

"Did ya har 'bout the ship in Westport?" Gordis continued unphased.

"No."

"Sailed out a bit with a full load of people an' sunk with all the family members still wavin' good-bye," she explained.

Before Kathryn could respond, the mate returned from below deck and announced to the captain that the only one below was a sick boy, too ill to be moved.

"Vat shall ve do vith heem?" Demoiselle asked, motioning to the intruder.

"There is only one thing to do. We will have a trial for Paddy here to decide his fate," the captain announced. He ordered the mate to send all passengers back to their quarters and to arrange a council at once.

"Ahh … me name's not Paddy," the intruder whispered.

"By God, your name will be Paddy on my ship, and that's all I have to say!" the captain flung the words at the man and stormed below, leaving the crew to prepare the trial.

In ten minutes, the council was seated below deck in the lounge area on one side. Adjacent to them were Leonard, Slater, and Brenton, and Paddy the stowaway sat slumped by himself on the sidelines. There were a few crew members and respectable passengers as witnesses.

The mate stood in the middle ready to conduct the trial and wrinkled his brow when he looked at the council of three. He whispered something to Slater who left and returned with an unknown Irish passenger who sat next to the other council members.

"Alright," the mate began, "on this date of the 5th of June 1847, I hereby open this trial of Paddy here to decide his future. For the record, the council members are the captain of our ship, the *Sir William*, Demoiselle, the captain's wife, Mr. Montegue, a respectable passenger, and … and … what is your name?" he asked the Irishman.

"Patrick."

"Ugh, another one; whatever else." The mate shook his head. "And Patrick here, another passenger."

Brenton noticed that Mr. Montegue was the gentleman Kathryn was speaking to about America and knew that he would be partial since he spoke freely with someone of a lower class. For the next hour and a half, each step was reviewed and considered until it was time for Paddy himself to speak on his behalf. He rose awkwardly as the room grew silent. Every eye was focused on him.

"Captain ... and the rist of the council ..." he muttered, "I know whit I did was wrong. I truly beg yer pardon and meant no offense to anyone. I ain't got much larnin', but I ain't stupid. I know har to fish and farm. Me family's all ded and I've no money nor food and I don't know how else to git to Canada. I jist knowed that if I stayed in Ireland, I would have died. "

"Who let you on board?" the captain demanded.

"The passage broker, master," he explained.

"He let you board for nothing? You must have paid him something."

"Aye, the only thin I had left, me shoes," Paddy said.

"I say we throw him overboard," the captain suddenly said.

Paddy threw himself on the mercy of the council, weeping and begging with hands clasped together in prayer whilst kneeling.

"Please ... please ... Yer Honors, fer God's sake I ask to beg yer fergiveness. I'll be no trouble. I'll work day an' night ... don't lit me die like a rotten fish. I'm jist a poor man that be needin' food." He lay his head down to the floor.

The sorrowful display was too much for Demoiselle and Mr. Montegue, and both of them grabbed an arm to help the crying man to his feet.

"Don vorry, Paddy," Demoiselle said. "Now I have a suggesjon." She turned to her husband. "I propose ve let heem stay on board, but vithout provijons. It vill be up to the other passengers if he gets fed and up to God if he lives."

"That's a splendid idea," Mr. Montegue nodded.

"Aye, fair enough," Patrick the councilman added.

All present turned to the captain for the final approval.

"Very well then," he waved in reply, knowing he was outnumbered. "But if I catch this thievish scallywag anywhere near my provisions, I will personally send him overboard."

"I won't go nar it, master," Paddy promised. "I'm really not a thief, jist poor at the moment. Thank ye kindly all of you, thank you ... much obleeged ... much obleeged."

Brenton and Slater breathed a sigh of relief for the man as the crowd dispersed and everyone went their separate ways. Brenton went to find Kathryn who was sitting on her bunk. He relayed in detail the events of the trial as they ate the remainder of their rations.

The following morning, not a breeze could be felt from any direction. The hot sun sizzled and reflected sharp rays of light within the movement of the sea. Kathryn and Brenton went on deck and looked out onto the vivid blue ocean, lost in thought. Each was thinking of Joseph, the lost treasure, and of their homeland they left behind.

Back in his Dublin offices, Routh once again sat shuffling papers and reading memos. He had continued to work as many hours as possible, trying to save dwindling Ireland from the catastrophe hurled upon her. He could only administer relief that was approved by Trevelyan, and that approval, he knew, was not forthcoming. His strong sense of character and military background inconceivably forbade him from breaking the rules to suit his own conscience, however strong it may be. Gone was the gay mood around the offices as the staff performed their jobs with dismal energy and talk of the famine grew worse with every passing day. Everyone was well aware there were thousands perishing daily and thousands more withering on the coffin ships as they were woefully referred. Ireland was dying, and Routh could feel the weight of the ax upon his shoulders as it slipped further and further onto the throat of the entire country.

"Here is the mail, sir," Stuffy said, handing Routh a wad of papers.

"Thank you, Stuffy," he replied.

Opening each piece of mail, Routh heard from Trevelyan almost daily, although no new advancements were made in the Relief Scheme. All the suggestions and demands from all sides did not persuade him to vary from his plan. Amongst the correspondence was an invitation to a masquerade in London, and he scoffed at the idea. He further read the letter stating that it was given by Trevelyan's wife, and with that information he knew there was no avoiding it, he must attend. Routh walked out of his office to where his staff sat at their desks.

"Stuffy," Routh began.

"Yes, sir."

"Gather the necessary garments for a masquerade for myself by the end of the week. And ..." looking at O'Riley, "make arrangements for the wife and I to sail out next Thursday to arrive in London by Friday."

"Right away, sir," O'Riley replied.

Routh returned to his office, and Stuffy grinned wickedly at O'Riley.

"That's exactly what's wrong with these countries," Stuffy said. "Imagine all the festivities, drinking and feeding their faces whilst people are starving and dying. That's a great message to send to all of us ... that they really care about the unfortunate."

He looked at O'Riley who was busy making notes.

"And I suppose you would love to be invited," Stuffy challenged him, "walking around with all those made-up faces and trying to guess who's who. What fun that would be!"

"You don't know the specifics," O'Riley snapped. "Maybe it's to raise money for Irish Relief."

"Ha!" Stuffy scoffed. "You are more fool than I thought you were. These people are just tired of hearing about the famine, weary of the whole scheme and want to have a good time ... at whatever cost."

Stuffy looked hard at his workmate and then added, "You can believe what you wish, and those lords and ladies can merrymake all night, but they can't hide the truth from me as much as they want to hide it from themselves."

Out of nowhere, the black clouds slithered in with pelting rain and lightning jabs, angering the sea enough that it spit white foam and spray from the curled tips of its many mouths. The storm seemed to enjoy playing with the ship like a cat with a mouse as it tossed the *Sir William* about the ocean. A gigantic swell of blue water crashed down on one side of the deck, scattering about a few crew members making their way below deck.

The vessel was carrying four hundred passengers, far beyond the capacity of the small ship. It suitably had room to transport half that quantity, but greedy passage brokers and the captain thought otherwise.

Ironically, this July morning had begun quite clear and without much of a breeze. The captain spent most of his time in the brig and every so often would step on deck and look about giving orders here and there. On this particular mid-morning, he eyed the hills in the distance and sniffed the air.

Casually he called to the mate, "Double reef top-sail and make all snug."

Soon after, the storm hit and all passengers and crew were ordered below. The frightened Irish clung to one another all afternoon, mumbling prayers and looking about as if at any moment a gush of water might surge through the walls. The rough swaying was making many passengers ill, and panic overtook a few. Kathryn and Brenton sat on their bunks waiting for the rocking to subside when an old woman next to them began to cry out to anyone who would listen.

"I'm a fith generation fortune-tiller an' I'm tellin' you all not to worry, this is the devil hisself still tryin' to git us. No matter, these storms ar fierce an' short like a wee child that's had its sweet plucked away."

The mate suddenly appeared at the entrance, completely drenched, panting, and hanging onto the threshold for support.

"Everybody alright down here?"

"Har long's this goin' to last?" someone asked.

"I wish I knew," he puffed. "Captain's even a bit worried; this one's a right beast!"

"Aye," the old fortune-teller spoke up. "But we know somethin' 'bout bad weather, an' yer not usin' us to ar full potential."

"What do you mean?" the mate panted.

"Don't you know the Irish know 'bout them storms," she explained. "We know jist the right words to make it come to an end, an' God stands squarely behind us intirely."

"Are you telling me you're a witch and you know how to make this storm stop?" The mate wiped water from his brow.

"Not me," she looked about. "Jist mighty certain people know har to make it stop, an' thar not witches, jist bringin' the luck o' the Irish."

"I have never heard such a tale," he scoffed, turning to leave.

"I beg yer pardon, but wouldn't the captain be grateful?" she asked. "Ain't no harm done neither to try."

The mate contemplated the situation, still hanging on to the sides of the jam as the ship creaked and groaned.

"I might be daft and the captain would certainly not approve, but you give me someone that can make this stop and I'll believe you," the mate challenged.

"This boy 'ere, he knows har," the fortune-teller pointed a long wrinkled finger straight at Brenton, "for he is a boy without sin—a powerful talisman."

"Well come on then, boy," the mate said, then turned and began climbing up the ladder.

Brenton looked at the fortune-teller in amazement, whispering, "I don't know har to make it stop."

While placing a thick hand-held cross in the front of his shirt, she whispered, "'Tis nothin' quare, jist say anythin'."

"And what if it don't stop?" he asked.

"It will."

"But what am I—"

"You'll git fed, boy, to be sure," she interrupted.

And that sentence changed everything. Kathryn patted the cross in assurance, and he made his way up the ladder. He peeked his head out and was struck by water splashing in his face and the loud sound of the waves rising to and fro. He saw the mate waving him on, and he stepped on deck, grabbing any part of the ship to steady himself. He looked out into the sea and was punctured with fear at seeing the huge waves as large as mountains rising and falling before him. They ascended like gigantic, maniacal monsters, climbing and soaring until they loomed overhead, white foaming mouths grinning in malicious, tantalizing pandemonium and pounding down on whatever lay beneath them. Then the monsters swam to another location of the sea where they mounted again and again and again. Soon monsters were rising and falling everywhere, beating every timber of the ship until it groaned for mercy.

Jasus, Brenton thought, *whit am I doin'?*

The mate shouted something, pointing his finger at the boy's skinny frame.

"You're all talk ... I should have known ... all the same ... lousy Irish ... go back to yer mummy!"

Brenton let go with his right hand and raised it into the air. He saw it shaking with fear and weakness but knew he must conjure up some words.

"By the powers that be, I make bould an' obleege you to stop this storm!" he shouted as water splashed completely over him. "I say you mustn't throw the sea 'bout no more, an' I won't ask you again!"

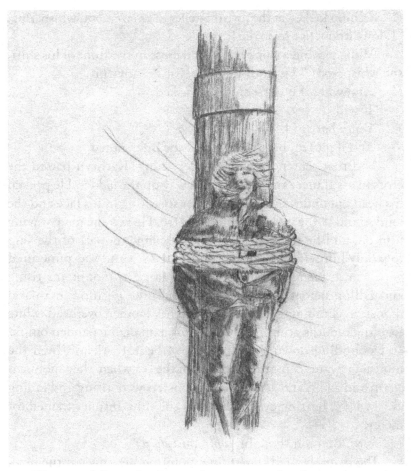

He waited for a change in the storm as the ship continued to rock back and forth.

Please, God, he thought, *please stop.*

A few more minutes passed until the mate pointed to the ladder for him to climb down. Defeated and shamed, the boy went below deck drenched and dripping with water. The phony sorcerer stumbled to his bed and lay down. The deceptive prank bluffed no one, and just as he was thinking himself the fool of wizardry, the boat abruptly ceased rocking. Brenton sat up and looked at Kathryn, then at the fortune-teller who winked at him.

Could it possibly be? Could the fierce storm have passed? Could he really have done it? A few more minutes passed.

"Where is that boy?" the mate shouted, descending the ladder.

"Right 'ere, Yer Honor!" Brenton stood up.

"Come here, my boy!" The mate hugged him. "The captain wants to see you."

Upon deck, the sun shone through a few light gray clouds, and the sea had returned to a steady mass of tame water. The monsters were nowhere in sight, and the gay chant of the crew chimed across the deck as they hoisted full sails.

"By God, son, the mate told me what happened, and you *are* good luck!" the captain bellowed from the depths of his gut. He placed his right hand upon Brenton's head and yelled to a crowd of crew members and passengers on deck, "If this ship is going to dock in Canada, it is because God himself wants this boy to survive! He's our lucky mascot that will lead the way!"

The young man knew exactly what the captain wanted and ran across the deck with several ropes tied around his shoulder. His face was eager as he pulled himself up on one side of the main mast. In one swift motion, the captain hoisted Brenton upon Slater's back and instructed him to hold on. Slater shot up the mast like a squirrel climbing a tree, with hands and feet popping in and out of the pegholes for merely a moment. When they reached near the top, Slater stopped and steadied himself as he reached for Brenton and brought him in front. He positioned the boy with his back to the mast and faced him outwards toward the vast, wide-open sea. Slater began to firmly tie the ropes around and around Brenton's body so that he and the thick mast became one and before making his way down again, Slater positioned the cross in front and squeezed Brenton's cheeks together as if he were an adorable wee child.

The crowd cheered in unison, clapping and patting the boy on his back.

"Slater!" the captain yelled over his shoulder. "Bring the ropes!"

Suddenly all hands were on deck cheering and yelling with fists in the air and fire in their bellies as the spectacle of the boy brought new hope and vigor. Brenton yelled, "Onward, ho!" swaying from the top of the mast. The spirit of the young lad pledging himself so the entire ship may advance through the sea and toward their ultimate destination was a sight to behold indeed.

The pipers and fiddlers appeared and struck up a tune, and a few women began to dance with one another. Joyous energy instantly filled the air, and everyone could feel it.

From Brenton's position, he felt as if he alone were driving the ship and willing it to go forth through the deep, dark waters of the ocean. He was not frightened to be up so high, nor uncomfortable with the ropes; he simply felt important as the guide, knowing all the people clapping and dancing below were in his care as scout. In the distance, he could see several porpoise jumping in and out of the water as the late afternoon sun turned orange. He sang a jovial tune and let the light spray of the sea douse his face and arms, laughing with glee as he had never felt so alive. He was taller than any man, riding the waves and slicing through the water like he himself were the legitimate ship.

The only thing missing from this festive occasion was food. No one offered although the continuous stream of people cooking around the fire pits continued. It was still evident that starvation continued as Kathryn noticed one wee girl sitting by herself and chewing on a portion of the rags she wore out of the dire need to be chewing *something*. The sight of her reminded Kathryn of her own girls, and the hollow space inside her soul ached. To ease the pain, she looked up at Brenton and thanked God for him.

She heard the captain ordering Slater about, and in a moment, he was climbing the mast with some water and food for her son;

she smiled inside. It was as if she herself tasted the nourishment, knowing that Brenton was being fed.

As the sun set, the music played and many danced, pounding the wooden planks with their bare feet. Even Demoiselle lured the captain out to dance a song or two, and being the only respectable female, she was gracious enough to dance with Mr. Montegue, the mate, and even Slater. The heartbeat of the ship thumped for one merry evening, and the entire ship became unified until the twilight indicated the close of the day. The last song played was "The Cliffs of Doneen," and all sang the haunting song whilst staring into the fire and missing their beloved ould Ireland.

You may travel far far from your own native land
Far away o'er the mountains, far away o'er the foam
But of all the fine places that I've ever been
Sure there's none can compare with the cliffs of
Doneen.

Take a view o'er the mountains, fine sights you'll see
there
You'll see the high rocky mountains o'er the west coast
of Clare
Oh the town of Kilkee and Kilrush can be seen
From the high rocky slopes round the cliffs of Doneen.

It's a nice place to be on a fine summer's day
Watching all the wild flowers that ne'er do decay
Oh the hares and lofty pheasants are plain to be seen
Making homes for their young round the cliffs of
Doneen.

Fare thee well to Doneen, fare thee well for a while
And to all the kind people I'm leaving behind
To the streams and the meadows where late I have been
And the high rocky slopes round the cliffs of Doneen.

"I'll get him down now, ma'am," Slater said to Kathryn. He disappeared up the mast and returned in a moment with a sleepy, groggy Brenton.

"Why can't I stay up thar?" the boy yawned.

Kathryn knew the adventurous spirit was still lit inside her son, but she merely smiled and said, "Lit's git some sleep."

"He's very sick," Kathryn overheard the woman say to Patrick, the man who participated as part of the council. The captain had dubbed him with the title "head committee" of all the Irish passengers, which meant any news or requests needed to be made through him, and he in turn would relay the information to the mate or captain.

"I'll speak to Demoiselle," Patrick said and disappeared up the ladder. Kathryn stood on an overturned bucket to peek over several rows of heads. She saw the woman tending to a young boy as he lay tossing and turning with the fever.

"If we stay in these close quarters, we're all goin' to git it," the fortune-teller predicted to anyone who would listen. She rose and climbed up the ladder with Kathryn and a few others following close behind. They reached the deck and sat about the floor in a circle. Kathryn saw Brenton working with Slater and knew he enjoyed the companionship and diversion from the sickness, death, and misery they left behind. He also thoroughly enjoyed the food that was given to him by his friend, much of which he passed on to Kathryn. They were quite fortunate to have that extra food, lest they be near starvation most of the time.

"He look like a regular swashbuckler, don't he?" The fortune-teller smiled at Kathryn, revealing her four rotten teeth.

"Aye," Kathryn replied. She looked around at the crew and respectable passengers and noticed a change in demeanor and attire. Knowing the day was the Sabbath, all the Irish passengers tried to look their best and brought out rosary beads and crucifixes for prayer.

"I don't have other clothes," Kathryn confessed to the fortune-teller.

"God don't car," the old woman replied.

Most of the morning and early afternoon was spent in prayer until a squabble broke out over a herring. Eventually several people sat down next to the two women and began discussing tragic stories and dreams for the future.

"Kin you really tell the future?" someone asked the old woman.

"Ever since 'twas a wee child," she said matter-of-factly.

"Kin you tell me mine?" the woman asked.

The fortune-teller looked at her, and everyone ceased talking to listen. The old woman took two long deep breaths and began speaking.

"I kin tell that you'll be fine in the new world. You might git sick or yer family might, but you'll be fine in the end."

"What about me?" a young girl asked as more and more people gathered.

"I see a handsome young man waitin' fer you in Canada."

"And me?"

"You'll go back to ould Ireland someday an' meet up with yer uncles."

"And fer you, well, the place you'll settle is Americky."

The fortune-teller predicted each person as they asked until she got to a man sitting with his wife at the edge of the crowd. She looked at him quietly for a moment, gathering information from around him, and the crowd parted as they all turned to look at him. He did not ask to be read, but sat looking pale and thin, enjoying the company.

"Thar's a specialness 'bout you to be sure," the fortune-teller began. "Yer a good man an' yer a farmer. Thar are many good larnin' yars ahead o' you. By the powers given to me, I kin see that you'll be havin' children … an' they'll be havin' children … an' one of 'em'll be a special boy. An' this boy'll grow up an' change the world by makin' things. God Almighty'll make him a very important man, an' Lord above, they'll all remember you this day, travelin' on this ship to the new world."

The crowd sat quiet for a moment, not moving their eyes from the man. It was hard to imagine such a great person would be a descendant of this penniless commoner, frail from hunger and completely powerless in his dire situation.

"What do ya think, Paddy?" someone asked.

"Me name's not Paddy."

"No ... 'tis not," the fortune-teller said, still staring at him. "'Tis Ford."

"Aye," the man grinned, "'tis. Me name's John Ford an' all this talk seems mighty quare intirely."

"Haa! Ha! Ha!" could be heard in all directions as the masquerade party was in full swing. Annoyed, Routh walked with his wife as white faces doused in makeup hid behind black feathered masks. White wigs bobbed about, and huge glorious dresses sewn of several layers swayed to and fro. The manor home of Lord Brynley was exquisite in every detail. Gigantic chandeliers spread sparkling light throughout every room filled with food and party favors.

"We have to find Trevelyan," Routh said to his wife behind his own disguise.

"And *how* are we going to do that?" she asked, looking about the room of several hundred behind her own feathered mask.

"Well ... I know he'll make a speech shortly. Let's get some food."

They walked over to one of the large tables heaping with meats, breads, sauces, salads, candies, and chocolate. The orchestra began playing, and the ballroom floor became filled with dancers lined beside one another in traditional, proper English fashion.

"Randolph!" someone said. "It must be you under that mask!"

"Yes, it is I," Routh tried to make light of the moment. "How did you ever guess."

"I hear that Ireland is reeking with fever. How do you ever stay in such a retched place?" the cloaked man asked with a laugh.

"Because it's my job," Routh replied.

"How dreadful for you!"

"Not as dreadful as being here," Routh said dryly, walking away with his wife.

"Who was that?" Routh's wife asked.

"I have no idea," Routh answered as they walked to a clearing. They watched the dancers in straight lines holding one another's hands high in the air. A nod this way, a nod that way, and a courteous bow to complete the dance.

"Ohhh, let me guess," another man said, coming up to Routh with his arms flailing wildly. Then after a moment, he exploded with, "Jack Peterson!"

"No." Routh tried to look in another direction.

"Hmmmm." The man looked intently at Routh, trying to sort out his bodily features. "James Harrison!" he said, pointing in a feminine fashion.

"Sorry," he said and gently lifted his wife's hand to escort her to the dance floor before another name was hurled at him. He knew it was the only way to get away from the irritating guessing game.

Routh did not feel like dancing, and his mind kept flashing back to images of the horrific conditions of Skibbereen. He failed those people, he thought, nodding. They needed someone to relay their despicable conditions, and he was not able to do that accurately. If he had, perhaps Trevelyan would have helped in some way. *Here I am healthy with a full stomach and dancing,* he thought. *How can I be attending this ridiculous extravaganza when so much work in Ireland still needs to be done? What am I doing here? Why don't these people realize the conditions of the Irish?* And at last the final chords of the pleasing song melded with the final ... slow ... bow.

"I know!" The annoying man was waiting for Routh when he exited the floor. "Alex Sheffield!"

"Robin Hood," Routh said to the man as he walked away.

"Ladies and gentlemen!" a man with outstretched arms said, standing in the middle of the dance floor. "May I please have your attention! I would like to introduce to you the head of the British Treasury and the Irish Relief Scheme. A man of unmatched taste and refinement who is single-handedly saving Ireland from herself and who has taken precious time off of his laboring work schedule to be here this evening. I am pleased to give you ... Charles Edward Trevelyan."

Routh and his wife clapped with the other merrymakers as Trevelyan took center stage.

"Thank you," he said, speaking to the crowd. "I am glad you're all having a wonderful time. Tonight is special for many reasons. It is the tenth anniversary of my lovely wife and I and also the day before her birthday. As many of you know, I am working steadfastly to assist the Irish in their peril, and I appreciate all the contributions England and her people have given to this cause—"

Then he locked eyes with Routh, realizing his presence as his mask had been removed.

"—although there is much more we need to accomplish. Many families are still in need of clothing, medicine, and of course ... food. With this thought, I would like to draw your attention to the bin at the exit and ask for any monetary contribution you may wish to give."

"I didn't know this was a charity ball!" one woman sarcastically spewed.

"And it is not, ma'am," Trevelyan answered. "Please understand it is completely optional. The two main reasons for tonight are to help us celebrate our anniversary and Hannah's birthday and of course to enjoy yourselves whilst finding out if you can truly distinguish people without facial features. And with that I thank you all for attending and I would like to call my wife up here. Hannah!"

Trevelyan's wife in a glorious dress made her way to her husband's side. He gingerly took her hand in his and held it.

"I am not one for ghastly public displays of affection, but since this is a momentous evening, I have a small gift for you."

He brought out an exquisite diamond ring and held it up as the crowd gasped.

"Happy anniversary and birthday, sweetheart," Trevelyan said as he placed it on her finger and kissed her cheek.

Hannah blushed with amazement and awe, uttering breathlessly, "Ohh! Thank you, Charles."

Trevelyan shouted, "Music, please!" and walked straight toward Routh as a mob of women engulfed Hannah.

"Pretty extravagant," Routh said as Trevelyan neared him.

"I knew you would not agree, but I'm glad to see you nevertheless," Trevelyan responded.

"I wonder how many will donate to your bin tonight?"

"I do not know, but it should come to the aid of some," Trevelyan said matter-of-factly. "Now, Randolph, let us not dwell on the unpleasant for *one* night. The duties of tomorrow will be awaiting us with the earliest rays of sunlight."

Routh wanted to share the same attitude as his comrade, but dancing merrily, conversing in small talk, and consuming rich decadent food was too much for this emotionally affected man. After what he experienced in Skibbereen and witnessing firsthand the crumbling of Ireland, he simply could not play the blithe part.

"Good evening, Charles," Routh said, cocking his head. "Splendid affair. I will be in touch."

And with that he turned to seek out his wife amongst the throng of white faces and masks.

"One! Two! Three!" someone yelled, and all the partygoers lifted off their masks to reveal themselves. Laughter, squeals, shrieks, and howls filled the great room as a grinning man stepped in front of Routh.

"Randolph, you scoundrel! Wherever have you been hiding?"

"Hmm ..." Routh searched for the right words.

"Are your grand talents still being wasted on those poor wretched Irish?"

"Aye," Routh said condescendingly, not wanting to argue.

"Oh, you are a card!" he half laughed, unsure if he was being made fun of. Truly he wanted more facts and to snicker unmercifully at Ireland.

"Well ... then ... how ever do you manage?" the man smirked. "The entire country must certainly reek of filth and ... and ... vile impurity!"

Routh signaled for the cold-blooded man to come closer until he leaned forward enough for a whisper.

"My good man," Routh whispered into the man's ear, "there is more vile impurity in your heart than in all of Ireland. Visit me in Dublin and I will show you."

At that moment, Routh's wife approached and placed her gloved hand inside his arm.

The confused man stood surprised and offended as Routh grinned and placed a hand on his shoulder.

"Good evening," Routh said and led his wife through the crowd and out the main doors.

Chapter IX

As the days passed, the *Sir William* endured windless days, beautiful days, bright days, and blustery days. She sailed through the Atlantic passing other ships grand and small. More and more passengers in the brig succumbed to the fever, lying on their bunks, shivering and sweating with sickness as water soon became short in supply. The captain ordered rationing for all passengers, and it was hardest on the sick as they lay begging for a single drop. Demoiselle took it upon herself to tend to the ill with the assistance of the mate and Patrick, the head committee. She scoured the ship's medical books and cabinets for any possible remedy that might soothe the sick despite the captain's comments that she was nurturing them like babies.

"Yer mollycoddlin' 'em," he told her. "An' you might get the fever yourself. It'd be enough fer you to give the medicine to the mate an' stay far away from the sick."

"I vill not," she uncharacteristically stated. "Za passengurs need my help, and I vill be there for them. Vee cannot abandon such sickness. I vill be alright, don vorry."

One night, Kathryn was abruptly awakened by someone pounding on a door. It was a low thud, but loud enough to bring her upright. She looked at Brenton fast asleep as well as the others on the bunks. Fortunately, the moon shone brightly and lit her way up the ladder and onto the deck. It seemed almost daylight as she looked up into the sky beholding an amazing sight. Kathryn's jaw dropped in incredible disbelief and awe. The entire sky was alive and moving with slashes and blasts of color and activity. There was a grand ball taking place in heaven with rhythm and radiant splendor, as if God graciously peeled back one transparent curtain to show the mere mortals a speck of life everlasting.

"Beautiful, ain't it?" a voice said.

Standing next to her was Gordis Flynn, and she immediately felt uneasy.

"Aye," she agreed.

"Don't know whit's happenin' up thar, mighty quare," Gordis said. "But down 'ere I heard the captain yellin' fer Mr. Montague to come out."

"'Twas him knockin'?" Kathryn asked, noticing the two men standing on the other side of the deck.

"Aye."

"It woke me too," Kathryn replied, "but 'tis not matter, this is ever so grand."

Suddenly Gordis noticed a flash of light flickering on the other side of the deck. It caught her eye immediately as it seemed to spread. Her staring invited Kathryn to turn around as a glimmer of brightness revealed that it was a flame.

"Jasus, Mary, an' Joseph!" Gordis shouted, running toward the light and to a sleeping Leonard. "Wake up, ya idiot!" she shouted, and Leonard bolted to a standing position surrounded by fire.

At once, Mr. Montague and the captain were on the scene, dousing the fire with pails of seawater until it was completely saturated. Immediately, the captain spewed his own verbal fire at Leonard who hung his large head in faulty inadequacy. The domineering wrath sent the three others creeping to their own bunks, and it was not until the following morning through the gossip channels that they understood the reason it began. Leonard had lit a candle, and it fell beside him as he dozed off watching the sky. As usual, Demoiselle soothed her husband well enough for him to speak to the others without raising his voice, although she knew quite well that Leonard would not work for them again after this journey.

Days ran into one another as sickness overtook poor souls, leaving Kathryn and Brenton once again praying that their lives would be spared. They lay on their bunks listening to the terrible coughing and wheezing, spending as much time on deck as possible to get some fresh air. One woman had died, and three others were undoubtedly going to follow her into the depths of the ice-cold, bleak ocean.

The ship was rounding freezing waters, and without proper attire, it was treacherous to be outside for more than a few minutes. It seemed the black cloud that began with the blight was hovering over the ship, wickedly laughing as poor souls fell sick with the fever one by one. And one by one their bodies were cast overboard, leaving weeping relatives behind. Many crew members were ill, which left more work for the others and the captain's temper in constant embroilment.

As Patrick wore the title of head committee, he strongly felt that all the actions of the Irish passengers would reflect on him, so he assigned three men to watch all the others and report to him any unacceptable behavior. No reports were made of any consequence except a quarrel or two regarding food. Upon eyeing a mob of rambunctious little boys acting silly, he made his way toward them. There were about twenty-five ragamuffin wee boys that scampered on deck, causing havoc and roaring with gibberish and senseless babble that Patrick could not accept. The tempestuous and boisterous bedlam seeped into his head until he disappeared and returned with a long, thick stick referred to as "the cat." He stormed on the boys, seething with fury as he thrashed about, hitting anyone in his path. True to the times, none of the other passengers even raised an eyebrow, and some bloodthirsty heathens even laughed in amusement. Anytime thereafter, Patrick just had to mention "the cat," and it would usually calm the boys.

Secretly, a few husbands of several sick women were seen whispering in the corners, nodding to one another with creased brows and clenched fists slamming into open palms. So it was a surprise to no one when the men stormed the rations, demanding water for their wives. Unbeknownst to them, the captain was no easy victim. He raged toward the men, puffed out like a fighting male lion, and ordered the men to their bunks at once—although not before informing them that due to their uncivilized misconduct, they as well as their wives would not receive a drop of food or water for three days. Then he shouted to everyone on deck that any more rebellions would meet the same fate. As expected, no matter how undernourished or thirsty a person became, the captain was not challenged again. Any cries of "Water, please, water" were either soothed or answered by some gracious saint.

One early evening, Kathryn was at the stern gazing over the railings, mesmerized by the continual motion of the water, the myriad of ripples that were created and the sparks of light that flashed intermittently from the setting sun. She ached for Joseph, remaining optimistic that he was still alive.

Me darlin', she thought, *whar are you? Do you ache fer me as well? I long fer yer arms about, tellin' me all will be alright. 'Tis so hard bein' without you ...* And her mind wandered freely, almost disconnected from her body as she thought of his laugh, his walk, the way he moved his hands when he spoke, and the scent of his clothes. Her brain concentrated so fully on remembering that it seemed her soul became detached on another plane of existence, the plane of pure memory that so transfixes the mind that no worldly noises or images are remotely noticed—however bold or loud they may be. It was only the rhythmic lapping of the water against the ship that brought her mind back into this world.

She felt her neckline, remembering the beautiful brooch and the money that would have saved them from the penniless situation they now faced and how happy Joseph would have reacted when she gave him the money. It would almost have been easier never to have had such fine things in her grasp than to have them one day and not the next.

A clamor erupted from the fireplaces as Slater doused the fires, and soon it grew quiet as all passengers headed below to their bunks. The sun was gone and abruptly snatching its light from all premises as Kathryn pulled away from the railings and walked across the deck, knowing Brenton would be wondering where she was. She climbed down the ladder and turned around when she heard a loud bump. The only light available was a small lantern on the side of the ladder as she made her way down the dark aisle. She heard nothing and decided to disregard the noise and headed in the other direction for steerage. Then she heard the sound again.

Thinking something was amiss, she changed direction again and pinpointed the sound to a small door. She opened it impulsively, and although the space was extremely small, there was just enough light to see the grotesque spectacle offensively revealed. Gordis Flynn with her four rotting teeth was hanging onto the side of the wall as a sweating Leonard was having intercourse with her from behind. He saw Kathryn plainly, but was not disturbed and did not stop his repulsive movement. Gordis simply shrugged her shoulders and raised her eyebrows as if to say, "At least we can't see each other." Kathryn slammed the door shut, went straight to her bunk, and lay down aspiring to escape the lewd picture swirling in her head. She hoped never to set eyes on Gordis Flynn again, but she was not so lucky. The following afternoon, Gordis approached her, snickering that it wasn't all that it looked like.

"Jasus, Mary, an' Joseph! Whit kind of talk is that thin?" Kathryn asked.

"Do you know that I didn't bring no food on board?" she explained. "Me poiti money got me aboard this ship an' that's it."

"We didn't bring any food either," Kathryn snipped.

"'Cept ya have a young chap that's gittin' ya food an' water nar, ain't he?" she shot smugly back. "To be sure."

"'Tis not matter what you do, none of me business." Kathryn began to walk off.

"Lit me jist say that I'm doin' it fer food, not pleasure!" Gordis roared.

And with that final comment, both women went their separate ways and avoided each other throughout the remainder of the voyage.

Demoiselle grew increasingly alarmed as many more passengers began to succumb to the fever. One wee child was playing with her friends upon deck when she suddenly dropped flat on her back, motionless. Her mother went to her, begging the child to awaken, and when she eventually did, it was not what her mother had expected. The child flopped about violently, shrieking blood-curdling screams. She was taken below and then died the following day. Another woman was at a fireplace cooking some sludge in a pot when her legs gave way and she collapsed onto the deck. Her husband was now caring for her and another brother as well. The atmosphere was now tense and reserved, not knowing who would be well one minute and miserably afflicted the next. As back in ould Ireland, some relatives abandoned their sick family members whilst others tended to those they did not even know. Along with many others, the stowaway fell ill and was being nursed by a gracious woman who had no family of her own.

Throughout the voyage, several crew members fished when the wind was inactive and at times distributed some to the poor passengers without any provisions. On average, the bounty was not impressive, but the captain was well seasoned on the voyage to and from the continents, almost carving the same deliberate line in the waves each time. And he knew the spot exactly where the swimming schools were abundant, where they gathered hungry and alert.

On one particular mid-morning July, the sea was like glass, and the warm sun made the temperature pleasant. Without speaking a word to anyone, the captain tossed his reel overboard and in seconds brought up a large mackerel. Again and again throughout the afternoon, he and Mr. Montague fished. The mate, several crew members, and Slater joined in using any gear they could find. Having witnessed their success, the Irish passengers rigged together rudimentary pieces of twine or string and weighed them down with anything, then lowered them into the ocean. And they too were rewarded with great gasping mackerel large enough to feed three people. Cheers erupted each time a catch tumbled onto the deck, flopping and laboring for breath, giving up its life so that others may live. Kathryn and Brenton obtained twine and weights from Slater and caught a few themselves. Everyone was in tune, fishing the entire afternoon, chanting, whistling, and cooking until a young man collapsed in the midst of a huddle as they counted their pile. He resembled one of the fish convulsing on the deck, and after he was taken below, no more outbursts of cheers were vocalized. God had presented some food but reminded them that tough times were still ahead and that death is inevitable.

Sickness now consumed the *Sir William* as it became one large afflicted vessel. There was no escape as the passengers fell one by one to their doom, and about half were wrapped and sent on their way into the ocean. Some that were ailing early on were recovering and coming on deck, paler and thinner than a delicate piece of rice paper. The highly irritable captain did not sympathize until the mate fell ill. Demoiselle ran to and fro trying to comfort and contain the infirm, then realized one hectic day that there was no more she could do. The fever and dysentery was obviously out of control, and no one could stop it from spreading. Some recovering were thrust back into deeper sickness simply due to being surrounded by the germs as it cloaked the steerage compartments.

One afternoon, Kathryn felt herself swirling down into the dark hole of affliction, and Brenton was fortunately able to care for her. Her body shook with fever, and sweat poured down her cheeks, and Brenton knew only one person could or would be willing to help them.

"I don't know har to thank you," Brenton said as he stood there holding food and water in his arms. He had secretly obtained it from Demoiselle with a strict promise not to tell the captain.

The woman brushed back her tousled hair that was usually kept neat and said, "You are velcome, my boy. Now, you being our lucky star, ve cannot let you down, no?"

"Ahh ..." he didn't know how to respond. "I'm mighty obleeged, Mrs. Demoiselle, mighty obleeged."

She lovingly cupped his chin in her hand and said, "You come to me if you need more."

"Aye," Brenton forcibly grinned though his heart was pounding with uncertainty.

He tucked the provisions as best he could under his shirt and hurried to Kathryn's bedside.

"Mam, Mam," he whispered, "eat some meat an' biscuit."

Kathryn opened her bloodshot eyes slowly, as if it took great strength, and turned her head toward her son. She looked at the food in his hands and licked her lips. Two days ago, she was looking overboard watching the waves and felt a severe pain on the lateral portion of her head, as if someone had hit her broadside. The piercing throbbing forced her to her knees, and she knelt there screaming. Brenton and Slater carried her to the bunk where she laid in agony amongst the hundreds of insipid others. In and out of consciousness, she sweated and coughed, feeling miserably weak and wretched. The hard plank beneath her instantly felt cruel and cold, and with every movement, her sharp bones penetrated the boards with razor-sharp, biting intensity. Her wrecked body was virtually void of muscle and fat and at the gross mercy of any evil-minded, foul virus that cursed every living soul in its path.

Brenton broke bite-sized pieces of the food and hand-fed her as she lay panting with ashen lips and cold limbs. She did not ask or care where he got the provisions and instead closed her eyes so all energy could be reserved for chewing. Brenton stayed beside his mam and tended to her every need. He sang to her softly, as she did him when he was a wee lad, and he emptied her bucket with ease. This was his mother and the only person left in the world that loved him unconditionally. Without her, he would be emotionally lost.

As the waning days pushed forth, more and more fell sick. The dead were now disposed of without any fanfare or coverings as all extra sails and clothes had already been used. Three days ago, a large family tended to a dying patriarch, knowing that all hope was lost. When he finally died, the relatives old and young gathered on deck to pray and say good-bye. All wept and comforted one another, except the brother of the deceased. He stood by himself, alone in his grief as he watched the body descend into the sea. There he remained, staring out into the vast ocean and firmly securing his long black coat over his cloaked, weeping spirit.

That very night, the brother fell ill and in one week was catapulted into the sea to find his sibling. The brother's wife was heartbroken and grieving, but alas, her wee son of four years was completely unaffected. He marched about the deck in his father's black coat, smiling at the treasure that he inauspiciously inherited. And because the boy did not fully understand the circumstances, it made all who saw him pity him all the more.

A very young bride cared for her new husband until the fever consumed her as well. With no relatives on board, they died holding each other's hand, in love and together until the very end. No one was quite sure who died first, but rumors circulated that the husband passed on as the wife watched; then she closed her eyes and willed her soul to proceed in the wake of her husband's.

Brenton came upon deck one afternoon to breathe some fresh air and stood at the bow watching the waves behind the ship. He noticed a large fin off to the left in the distance and was transfixed.

Slater joined him. "How's your mum?"

"Not good," he replied.

Slater looked out into the sea as well and saw the fin following close behind.

"That's a shark!" he said, pointing.

"Whit?" asked Brenton.

"A shark, ole chap, and that's not a sign we need."

Brenton still did not understand.

Slater continued, "A shark followin' a ship is a bad omen ... a bad sign ... that death is upon us," he said. "Sharks kill and eat anything and would eat us as well if we let them."

Brenton stared at the lone fin, strong and determined to be noticed but not intrusive. "That fin needs to go away," he said.

"Right," Slater laughed, "you will it to go away then."

Down in steerage, a father of six had no strength to carry on. His eldest son of approximately six years nodded through tears that it was acceptable to die, and the father did. With no mother or relatives, the children were now at the mercy of the other passengers for provisions. Demoiselle cared for them as best she could, but so many others were just as needy. They were thrown mercilessly into the brutal, savage world of a starving people, and only through sheer luck would they even manage to survive. As the oldest, the six-year-old took it upon himself to care for the others and tried his best to find them food and shelter. He did not run and play freely like the others; rather he walked around deck with a troubled head full of burden and hardship. The fortune-teller motioned to him one day as he walked by half-naked carrying his sleeping baby sister. His skinny, dirty legs carried him over to her side.

"By the powers that tould me, I want you to know that you'll be makin' it, me wee boy," she said to him. "To be sure. You'll make it an' grow into a big, fine man."

"An' me brothers an' sisters?" he asked.

Megan Blight

"I don't know," she lied, "but the love you have fer them, an' they fer you, will be with ya always an' guide you intirely along with the blessin' of Almighty God."

The boy stared at her hard and did not reply, and after a few moments walked away expressionless.

The days passed one after the other, and the cycle of sickness continued. Each day, many new cases were reported, and by this time, more than half of the crew was taken ill. This left a large working void that could not be filled, and the *Sir William* sailed on with the captain accompanying the crew. Slater and Leonard soon fell sick with the fever, and Mr. Montague was asked by the captain to assist in any way possible; the respectable man obliged. The ship came closer each day to Canada, and by this time, bits of land could be seen in the far-off distance.

"Water, water!" were the constant cries from within the steerage compartment. Over and over again, it was the same never-ending wailing of, "Fer God's sake, some water!" that ceased only with a person's last breath.

But alas, water was the one commodity that needed to be severely rationed. Unfortunately, two casks had small leaks that drained them of their precious liquid before it was discovered. Another vessel was spotted a short distance away, and the captain signaled that he wished to converse. They came alongside, and as the crew member and the captain shouted to each other, it was distressing to hear that they were worse off than the *Sir William*. The third in command was steering the ship as illness almost capsized the entire crew, and their water was almost depleted due to unsanitary casks. They bid each other adieu, wondering who would make it to the shore alive.

A young woman cried out from labor pains as her husband kissed her forehead and held her hand. No one was available to assist in this birth except the few kind souls that happened to be lying next to her. The woman's moans and groans sounded exactly like the sounds of the ill, so no one took notice that anything extraordinary was occurring. And then a faint infant cry came

302

from their area, and many people turned to see the father cradling his baby wrapped in an old, dirty cloth. He looked around at all the heads craning this way and that and smiled so wide that it reflected off the walls and bounced around the large compartment like a blazing torch. The head committee informed Demoiselle, and she brought a new blanket and took the infant to show the captain. She walked inside their compartment as he was growling like a lion that no baby should be brought into this area when a tiny arm sprung up from the blanket revealing a slight, fragile hand no larger than a doll's. The captain stopped mid-roar and peeked over the blanket into the newborn's pure, sweet face. Instantly he smiled and began cooing and speaking in a pleasant voice as soft as velvet.

He retrieved an egg from a dish and placed it in the blanket, clasping the fragile hand around it. Then he positioned two shiny silver coins next to the egg and rested his hand on the child's covering, as if in blessing. It was amazing to gaze on such beauty and perfection amongst all the wrath of sickness bestowing their ship, and it was lovely to see his beaming wife cradling a child as if it were her own.

"Is the mother alright?" the captain asked.

"Yes," answered Demoiselle, gazing lovingly at the child, "she is fine."

"Thank God." The captain sat down. "I hope this child will grow into a fine young person." He looked away as if the tenderness of the moment had reached his eyes.

As time proceeded, more crew and passengers fell to their knees with the fever, among them Brenton, the head committee, and lastly Demoiselle. The captain and a few crew members were among the handful that currently dodged the illness as the ship crawled to the shores of its destination. A few Irish paupers were summoned to help in place of sick crew members, and the men were more than happy to oblige. It meant a morsel or two of rations for them, so all that could summon the strength volunteered willingly. It seemed most passengers and crew were below deck fighting for their lives, and the remaining healthy cared only for their own class, as none of the healthy crew members dared to venture below, lest he never return. This left the steerage compartment to rot into internal damnation. The Irish passengers that were able and compassionate nursed the masses that were ill, only being able to administer immediate aid without cleaning the messes that were made; there was just too much filth to clean. Steerage had now wasted away into a stinking mass of dead bodies, vomit, and excrement. The good Samaritans were glimpsed upon deck now and again as they came to get food, wash the filth from their feet, or simply breathe fresh air. And then down again into the depths of the underworld the poor souls would lower themselves, into the pit of misery and anguish to dribble a few drops of water or a few bits of food into the suffering, moaning, weeping mouths that no longer resembled humans. And still daily, more and more of these good Samaritans fell exhausted and sick on their own beds, and the tables were suddenly turned as they were now at the mercy of any kind soul that would pass by with some nourishment.

The world of the captain revolved only around his wife now, and he could not pull himself away from her bedside; he became almost delirious with panic as she sank downward into the sickness. He peeked on deck once a day to give commands and spent the remainder caring for his Demoiselle. Every once in a while, he would visit some crew members, the mate, and Slater but could not bring himself to call on the hundreds in steerage. Oh yes, he heard the wailing calls for water and food, the cries of woe, and the moans of the damned, but he knew he could not possibly comfort hundreds with a small ration of food and water and instead opted to pour his energy into his one reason for living ... his Demoiselle. He was a firm believer in God but not of superstition, although as his wife slipped deeper and deeper from his reach, he began to grasp at all opportunities, foolhardy or irrational.

"God, please do not let her die," he solemnly prayed. "I will do anything you ask, but please do not take her from me."

A hand clutched Kathryn's hand and held it. She opened her eyes and saw Brenton lying next to her, sick and shivering. It broke her heart to see him, and she felt completely helpless as a mother. Every once in a while, some kind soul would bring by some water or food, but the stench of the steerage compartment itself was suffocating and enough to make anyone ill if they were not already. Kathryn was so severely weak that she could not retrieve the bucket, although there was hardly anything to put into it anyway. Between moans every now and then, her mind slipped in and out of sleep, and upon waking one morning, she found that she had soiled herself. Turning her head in shame, she thought what a despicable human being she was, not fit to be on this earth. The only thing left in her life was her son.

"Brenton," Kathryn whispered.

The boy slowly turned his head toward his mother and coughed.

"I've to tell you that I'm intirely sorry fer this," she eked out. "I niver thought it'd end as such. Whin I was a young lass, I never dreamed ..."

"Tell me 'bout whin you were young," Brenton asked.

Kathryn knew he needed something to take his mind off the miserable circumstances, so she told herself to focus her mind and remember.

"Whin I was a wee child in England, the manor house me mam worked in 'twas grand as a castle—flowers everwhere ... bonny things. I played and played and niver bin so happy ... niver worrin' 'bout anything. The rich children larnin' me all sorts a things, and not once did I worry 'bout not eating ... ugh ... 'tis not rightly far you growed up worrin'. I wish I could show you all those fine things, but 'tis not matter nar."

"Whit were the things 'bout the house?" Brenton asked.

"Och, things you've niver seen, me darlin', fancy teacups, grand things on the walls, stairs that reach the sky, toys everwhar, books and so much larnin' to do. And I wore the most bonny dresses in all of England." She paused, completely lost in remembrance, until a jolt of the ship slapped her back into reality.

"The noble and respectable in England and Ireland ... in their grand homes right nar ... they've no idea of whit we're goin' through. But I've seen the other side and I know har beautiful 'tis."

"And the food?" Brenton asked.

"Aye, the food ..." Her mind went into overtime. "The smells from the kitchen and the glorious soups, breads, and meat all piled high on shiny, sparklin' plates fer everone to gaze at. The meat rich with juice, the soup filled with so many vegetables you can't see the broth, and the biscuit so soft you kin barely feel it in yer hand. And whin you take a bite, part of the heat comes out from it and rushes yer mouth, and the warmness fills you up. No matter har many people thar is, thar's always enough and everone takes thar pieces to have thar fill ... har 'bout that, to have as much as you want."

Brenton licked his lips, repeating, "As much as you want ..."

"Ohh ... I cannot describe the taste of it all ... 'tis more thin I kin say."

"Tell me, Mam! Tell me!"

"Well nar ... 'tis beyond jist taste ... 'tis like the mouth inside burstin' with glorious dancin', music an' merrymakin' all at once like you've niver felt before. 'Tis like the sun itself explodin' into all the stars in the sky, an' this feelin' in yer mouth spreads in yer head and down yer body to all the parts until every fingertip is jumpin' fer joy."

Brenton was completely without words trying to envision this extraordinary feeling. Then he intentionally swallowed the thought lest he be stuck in dreamland for hours.

"Thin why does God lit us die like this whin others have so much?" he finally asked.

Kathryn thought for a while before answering, wondering herself what the true answer might be.

"I don't know," she said simply, "I ... I don't know. Life's too precious fer this to happen ... ugh ... we've come so far and 'tis all me fault nar."

"No, Mam," Brenton wheezed. "'Tis me fault fer losin' the money and brooch."

Kathryn looked at her withering son and said, "The money and brooch wouldn't be helpin' us nar ... ugh ... listen, me darlin' ... whitever should happen to me, I don't car ... I jist want you to live ... ahh ... I'm close to the end of me rope, and I don't know if I kin hang on ... but I love thee with all me heart."

Tears saturated Brenton's eyes, and the tight grip on his throat rendered him speechless for a moment. Then he slowly repeated an old Irish blessing Kathryn taught him, stretching out each word.

> Thar's but one and only one,
> Whose love will fail you niver.
> One who lives from sun to sun.
> With constant fond endeavor.
> Thar's but one and only one.
> On earth thar is no other.
> In heaven a noble work was done,
> Whin God gave us a mother.

And mother and son lay looking at one another until one tear slowly made its way down the boy's cheek.

"Ahh ... save yer water, son," Kathryn grinned, trying to comfort him and meaning it at the same time.

"Brenton! Brenton! Is that you, boy?" The captain suddenly appeared in the aisle, his nose and mouth covered by a cloth.

"Aye?" The boy tried to lift his head.

"Don't worry, son ... oh God ... don't worry." The captain lifted him in his arms and carried him from his filthy bed.

"Me mam ... me mam ..." Kathryn could hear her son faintly disappear down the aisle until his voice was drowned out once again by the cries of the afflicted. She watched as he was completely carried away and merely whispered, "Brenton … Brenton …"

Without the feel of her son's hand and the gaze from his eyes, she did not need to push herself. Once again, she began to panic and for a moment wished that God would take her soul and relieve her from this misery. But from somewhere a calming feeling came over her, and she tried to focus again on the reasons for surviving. Perhaps the captain was going to harm Brenton? Or maybe he was going to sell him to a pirate for money? Why did he choose her son over all the others? She needed to get up and save him lest he be gone forever! Oh no, not another one of her children! Get up! Get up! How could she explain it to Joseph … Joseph! He didn't even know if they were alive, and maybe *he* was even dead. Or maybe if they all died, they could be reunited in heaven! Oh why couldn't she find the strength to save her poor wee son? Why must his life be sacrificed like her other children, and why must God let her suffer so? Obviously she wasn't fit to be entrusted with such precious lives, and where was God anyway? Did he not hear her desperate pleas? Kathryn's mind slowly fell into a sorrowful state of sleep.

The captain placed Brenton on a soft bed next to Demoiselle and covered him with a thick wool blanket. He gave him a bit of water, and immediately after, the boy snuggled down into the soft warmth and clean air and immersed himself in sleep. The captain sat on the bed beside his wife and clasped her right hand between his.

"My Demoiselle, I have brought you the good luck charm, the boy Brenton from steerage. He is with the fever as well, but I know God wishes him to survive and he will help you to recover too."

The Demoiselle's features were beginning to change as the sickness ravaged her body. Her legs and feet swelled with pain, and she was unconscious most of the time, mumbling inarticulate phrases in German. The discouraged captain bowed his head over the two and prayed and prayed.

Meanwhile, Kathryn lapsed in and out of sleep for the next two days, thinking of Brenton and wishing she had enough strength to find him. During the day, the hours passed steadily minute by minute, but in the dark of night, the drawn-out seconds tiptoed methodically one after the other, and the drudgery and strain of merely staying awake was almost too much to bear. The lanterns placed about the black room cast shadows swaying to and fro and created an atmosphere of dreary isolation resembling ghosts laughing heinously through the air. Moans and groans ran amok throughout the compartment and bounced around the inside of Kathryn's head until she almost panicked and screamed, "Shut up!" Although upon working up the energy to make the yell, she realized the constant wailing came from within her own mouth. She was becoming severely dehydrated, and the grim reaper was rapidly making his way down the aisle ... closer and closer ... His footsteps were getting louder and louder, and she felt her sanity being yanked from her weary soul and slightly dismembering itself from her frail mind.

Thomas stepped off the courier ship as it docked in Dublin and embraced Routh with strong arms, smiles, and news of school. They strolled through the streets until they reached Routh's rented home.

"This is kind of cramped," Thomas said, looking about the small rooms.

"It's only until the famine ends. I expect to be back home within the year," Routh explained.

"My boy! My boy!" a voice preceeded a lady who came into view with outstretched arms.

"Hi, Mother, you look well." The boy smiled.

"Ohh ... I missed you terribly," she said, embracing him. "It's so grand to see you. Is everything alright? Would you like to rest awhile? Are you hungry? Do you need anything?"

"I'm fine, Mother." He shot a glance to his father at being fussed over.

"Alright," she sighed. "I'll inform Cook to make all your favorite dishes this evening."

"That would be great, Mother, thank you."

And his mother exited in a ruffle of taffeta, lace, and silk flowing about in all directions. Thomas looked at Routh and his face grew somber.

"Father, have you had any contact with those Irish people that immigrated to America?"

"No I have not, nor do I expect I will," he answered.

Thomas thought a moment before responding.

"I think about them frequently," he said.

"As you should," Routh was quick to answer.

"And I have thought about my actions that day and how I must have shamed you. Later, when I returned to Eton, I gathered the boys together and told them what I had done and how we should not speak ill of the poor. At first they laughed, calling me an Irish-lover, but I remained calm and sincerely asked them for assistance in raising money for the famine. Most of them laughed even harder, and now they are not my friends anymore."

"All of them laughed at you?" Routh asked.

"No ... Nigel stood with me against the jeers, and he stands with me still. We walked around knocking on doors in the city requesting donations, asking everyone and anyone that would listen."

"And?" Routh questioned.

"And we have raised a little money," Thomas placed a pile on the desk, "but we plan to raise more by helping in the library."

Routh rested a hand on his son's shoulder. "The amount is not nearly as significant as the alteration of your heart, for that you will carry throughout your life."

The mate took it upon himself to drive the ship, knowing the captain was not in his right mind. He was still somewhat ill, but with good food and rest was able to be escorted on deck twice daily to give commands. Land could be seen clearly on both sides as the *Sir William* made its way up the St. Lawrence toward Quebec. They passed by many ships large and small, traveling with either passengers or cargo, and it was pleasing to view normal, daily activity. Grosse Isle, a small island nestled in the St. Lawrence, was the destination of all ships carrying passengers from Ireland. They were first checked for sickness, and those that were carrying ill people were quarantined before proceeding on to Montreal.

The captain came on deck as they neared their destination and viewed the multitude of ships in the distance resting and swaying with the tide. It was questionable why so many were waiting as they pulled up behind the last ship and dropped anchor. Grosse Isle could be seen in the far-off distance as the flag on *Sir William* was raised to announce to the authorities that they were ready to be checked. A crew member crawled up the mast and looked out toward land. He called down to the captain that there must be fifty ships waiting to dock, which was disheartening news to hear. Nevertheless, he instructed all crew to dress accordingly and be on notice to dock. It was high noon, and during the next few hours, the crew stood idle, dressed in their best Sunday clothes whilst waiting for orders. They watched a small boat paddle from boat to boat, and one man disembarked each time. As the last bit of sun dipped over Quebec, the boat paddled up to the *Sir William,* and a smug Canadian in his sixties climbed aboard.

"Hmm …" He looked over the captain who threw himself together to be presentable. "I am the doctor—is there sickness on board? … Ah yes, I believe I smell the foulness of it."

"My wife—"

The doctor held up one hand to silence the captain, and without another word, he descended below deck and in a few minutes returned holding his nose with his handkerchief and going straight to the side of the boat.

"There is much sickness on board," he said to no one in particular as he climbed down the ladder and into his own boat.

The captain ran to the side, throwing his hands up, and yelling overboard, "What are we to do now?"

And as the boat rowed away, the doctor yelled, "Someone will be by to see you tomorrow!"

The captain stormed away, mostly angry at himself for letting the doctor leave.

Another day passed and not one person came by. Vessels carrying only imports or without passengers sailed on by without stopping. A few ships were given the approval to dock, and still more came up behind the *Sir William* and hoisted their flags to be inspected ... although to no avail.

"I cannot believe we are being treated so!" the captain shouted to the mate who was bundled and sitting beside him. He was still recovering, although quite nicely.

"We might as well be a million miles away in the middle of the ocean!" the captain continued. "We cannot stand by idle, letting the sick die beneath us without so much as a drop of water! This is preposterous!"

The next day, the captain was preparing to proceed to shore without permission until he spotted another small boat heading their way. This time, two men in black clothing came aboard and introduced themselves as priests.

"May we proceed to dock?" the captain asked the men.

"We are not at liberty to say, Captain," one of them answered in a low voice. "We are just priests here to administer prayer and last rites if God so wishes."

The captain nodded through his frustration and led the men first down to Demoiselle and Brenton. The priests laid their hands across the two sweaty foreheads and prayed aloud. Demoiselle's head was swollen beyond recognition, and she lay motionless, wheezing through each breath. Brenton opened his eyes when he was touched and looked about in alarm.

"I'm not dyin', Father," he said when the prayer ended.

"I know, my son," one priest smiled. "The prayer is to help you recover."

"Aye ... aye ..." the boy trailed off and fell asleep once more.

All three men exited the compartment and followed the captain to Leonard, Slater, and some of the crew. Then they followed him up on deck.

"Do you not have other sick passengers?" one priest asked. "The Irish?"

A large sigh exited the captain's mouth before he tried to explain.

"Father, steerage is wrought with the sick. They are in desperate need of help, and we need to dock as quickly as possible. I cannot in my right mind assist you to them because it is not fit for anyone to—"

"I understand," one priest interrupted. "And if you will point us in the right direction, we will see them now."

As the two holy men descended below, the captain was embarrassed and ashamed at what the men must be discovering. Five minutes passed, and the priests returned to the captain's side. Their faces were ashen with alarm, and one swallowed hard before speaking.

"I ... I will see to it ... that the doctor knows of the conditions here," he stammered.

"He already knows," the captain said dryly. "And those Irish in steerage wouldn't be suffering in rotting filth if I could get them some help."

"I see." The priest tried to wipe the images from his eyes. "I will tell somebody in charge, Captain."

"Thank you, Father," the captain replied. "I appreciate your help."

Another day passed, and a few more ships were allowed to dock whilst the others rocked back and forth in the water waiting patiently. Then another small boat pulled up alongside the *Sir William* and another man presented himself in front of the fuming captain. The man handed the captain some papers, explaining that he was a government official, the papers needed to be filled out, and that he would be back in one or two days to collect them.

"By God, you people have nerve!" the captain exploded inches from his face. "My wife and hundreds of others are dying here, and we're filling out paperwork! We need to dock *now* and get these people some medical help!"

"How dare you speak to me in such a manner!" the man shot back. "Grosse Isle is overflowing with the fever, and our country is not equipped to handle such sickness. *You* are the ones bringing such pestilence into our country, and we are kind enough to try and help all of you!"

"So how long are we to sit and wait then?" the captain said sarcastically. "Four more days ... ten more days ... two weeks? I will just dock without permission!"

The man replied, "All of these ships you see here are full of the sick. There are thousands waiting, and I forbid you to dock at this time! Good day, Captain!"

The government official returned to his boat and disappeared. The captain tried to swallow his frustration and went below deck to check on his Demoiselle. The next morning, the captain stood with the filled out government papers in hand, looking out to see any boat coming his way. Every once in a while, he would go below to check on his wife and return to the deck and wait. Meanwhile, other boats passed by the *Sir William,* which fueled his fury. One last visit to Demoiselle in the early afternoon pushed him over the edge. She was worse than ever, and the captain could not stand by idle any further. He and a few crew members hoisted sails at once and began making their way for Quebec.

The dying in steerage were not informed of anything, so they did not know if they sailed or were docked. Kathryn heard voices now and then but was unaware of anything else. The air inside the compartment was so foul and putrid that it almost hung about like a thick fog, and most of the ill gasped simply to breathe. At this point, Kathryn remained motionless, unable to move and without the desire to do so. She lay on her back, skeleton arms at her sides, eyes closed. *There's no way I'm going to survive,* Kathryn thought; *we're now a compartment of the dead and the dying and nothing more. Everything has been taken from me and now I am left to die.* She was not afraid, rather content that the suffering would end and she would be happily reunited with her loved ones.

As she lay there in between life and death, she felt strangely that her body was in a state of a higher sense of being. All the sounds she heard were magnified tenfold to the point where she could clearly hear the thwank of a rope against a mast, the flapping of a seagull's wings as it flew overhead, and the slight sigh of a sick passenger in another bunk. The unmerciful cold pinched her skin as it incessantly came into contact with it, and the weight of her head seemed enormous; she was completely unable to lift it. Ever so slowly, she opened her eyes to gaze upon objects whose colors seemed to radiate from within. A blue rag spilled out its color from all sides; a black lantern echoed black all about; a red shirt created red upon red upon red. She knew it was daytime because several streams of light made their way through crevices and lit the compartment enough to see objects about the room.

Brenton is almost a man, she told herself, *he will be alright. I'm ready, God,* she thought, *please take me soul ...* Then she spotted a small, black bug crawling on the ceiling, moving fast like it was in a hurry. She looked ahead to its destination and noticed a large gap in the wood beam where sweet sunlight pushed through. *If that bug reaches the crack in the wood,* she thought, *I will be dead ... but if someone gives me water or any aid before it reaches the crack, I will live.* She then watched the bug crawl, undeviating from its course, and then abruptly stop, scuttle one way and the next, then proceed forward. The insect was just shy of the crevice when Kathryn heard a tremendous bang as if a door had been swung open, and a loud voice yelled through steerage, "What in God's name!"

She heard many footsteps and felt gusts of fresh air. Then someone grabbed Kathryn's frail body, lifted her up, and carried her from certain demise. She kept her eyes closed and wondered if perhaps the angel of death was raising her from the depths of steerage and onward toward heaven. Without any muscle or strength within her limbs, her head, arms, and legs simply drooped and dangled with each step the person took. A sudden burst of light from the sun hit her eyes like a sledgehammer, and Kathryn squinted, trying to shield them until they adjusted. A bit more walking, then she felt her body being thrown into the air and landing hard on wet sandy ground. She lay motionless, trying to catch her breath, and heard gasps and ghastly utterances coming from some people in front of her and she knew that the spectacle of her lying on the ground must look despicable.

"Can you believe the look of her?" a Canadian voice said.

"She looks half dead already," said another voice.

"How can anyone just leave her like that?"

"I've never seen a living skeleton."

"Poor miserable wretch, someone get a blanket to cover her. She should not be naked in public."

Naked? Kathryn thought. *Am I naked?* Her fingers gingerly touched the cloth covering her body for positive confirmation. She was so weak she could barely move her head, but she did, facing forward and resting her chin upon the sand. Then she lethargically opened her eyes halfway and beheld a small crowd of respectable women dressed in lavish clothes pointing and shaking their heads. Then she saw the back of a woman, bent and faltering, trying to walk forward and not making much progress ... and *she* was stark naked. She had seen this woman before down in steerage, but with everyone starving or ill, no one took much notice of her. They were too busy trying to survive one more day themselves and keeping the torn rags they had on their own bodies. An elegantly dressed woman rushed the naked one with a thick blanket outstretched and consumed her in it, wrapping her up from neck to ankles. As the woman was led away, Kathryn opened her eyes wider and now noticed everything before her—land, rocks, buildings, roads, horses, more people, and food, food, food!

A burst of energy shot through her emaciated body, and she began to slowly crawl toward civilization, toward the beauty of radiant vivacity and zeal and toward life everlasting. Then she noticed other crawling individuals beside her, each trying desperately to save themselves.

"Ahh God ... please ... please ..." was all Kathryn could utter as she grasped the sand and inched her body forward with the last bit of strength left in her tattered soul.

Please, please give me some food and water, she thought, *any scrap or morsel you might throw me way. Please give me a blanket. Help me to git well and please return to me the life I had before the blight mercilessly stole everthing.*

"Och, a little trick don't seem so bad after all nar do it?" Gordis Flynn mocked as she stood hands on her hips above Kathryn. Then once again, she felt herself being lifted up and carried, but this time she looked at who was holding her. It was Gordis Flynn. The same Gordis Flynn she scorned and thought to be unscrupulous and villainous. How she wanted to thank her now, except the words would not form in her mouth. Instead, she slipped peacefully into unconsciousness.

She awoke to the loud sounds of people moving about and objects clanging against one another.

"Wah? Wah?" Kathryn opened her eyes.

"Lord above, she's awake," a voice beside her said.

Kathryn turned her head and saw Gordis Flynn with a cup, and she almost lunged forward as it came to her lips.

"Easy ... easy ..." Gordis cautioned as Kathryn drank the sweet, pure juice of Mother Nature.

After her fill, Kathryn lay back, panting with the energy it took to move. She looked about and asked Gordis, "Whar is this?"

"War in Canada on Grosse Isle, an' this 'ere bein' a place to take care o' the sick. Won't call it no hospital, but I be tould 'tis the right place fer you," she explained. She held a small piece of bread at Kathryn's mouth and fed her like a baby. Kathryn closed her eyes as she chewed, relishing the taste of food.

Gordis leaned in close, saying, "I'm not suppose to be 'ere, this is quarantine area fer the sick, but I tould 'em I was a nurse an' they lit me in." She sat back with a wink, satisfied at her cleverness.

Then the realization of what happened came to Kathryn and she asked, "Whar's me boy? Whar's Brenton?"

"Mustn't worry 'bout him; he be intirely fine, I think," Gordis said. "The captain lookin' out fer him, the rotten bastard, 'cept not carin' 'bout any of you.

"Whar's me boy?" Kathryn persisted, chewing another mouthful.

"Don't rightly know," said Gordis. "I don't see none of ar shipmates round 'ere neither. Lord knows whar everone is."

"Kin you please find him?" Kathryn asked. "I'm ... I'm so tired ..." And off she trailed into sleep once again.

The next three days, Gordis stayed by Kathryn's side, giving her food and water as needed. They were lucky a cot was available in the shed when Gordis brought her in, as a corpse was just being lifted out of it. Even though she was shoulder to shoulder with another sick person, she was very fortunate. Hundreds of others lay on the ground, and hundreds more lay outside in the cold wind. There were many makeshift sheds placed about the island, housing the infirm and the dead as Canadian doctors and nurses cared for as many as possible round the clock, making their way up and down each aisle. Never before had such an epidemic hit Canadian soil, and it was plain to see that a wild catastrophe was running rampant. Once again, there were simply too many ill to be housed and tended to, and Kathryn lay fighting for her life.

"Am I dyin'?" Kathryn whispered to Gordis one day.

"Nooo ... you jist be needin' rist," Gordis assured her, giving her more water and bits of food. "Almighty God's lookin' after you."

"Almighty God's in you," Kathryn said. "Much obleeged."

Gordis smiled slightly for the first time, humbled by the admiration she rarely received.

"Have you found—"

"No, but I be lookin'," she said. "An' whin you git well, we kin look together."

Kathryn awoke one afternoon, and Gordis was not by her side. She glimpsed around but saw only sick bodies lying about moaning, and the one beside her was disgusting. Then she surveyed herself, and upon realizing she was just as repulsive, lay back down. Gordis had probably gone to get more food, Kathryn thought, or maybe she went to look for Brenton. The old man touching her left shoulder was wailing in agony and had been for the last full day. She wanted to tell him to stop but refrained and instead turned her back to him. The wailing continued, and after three more hours, Kathryn could take no more.

She turned around and softly touched the man's shoulder. When there was no response, she shook him and said, "Please can you stop moaning." And as she did this, his head rolled to one side, lifeless and inches from her own face. His eyes wide and mouth agape walloped her inner core. The woman lying next to him was the one groaning, probably because she had to look into this man's face all day. Kathryn turned the corpse on his side again so he was facing the other way and inched herself away from him. She did not want death touching her lest it seep into her soul and carry her off, never to return. She looked in the opposite direction, hoping someone would take the body away.

Gordis retuned without any news of Brenton but with more food and water. Kathryn steadily began to gain strength in her limbs and even lifted her torso off the pillow one day to look around. The view was not much better than aboard the *Sir William,* so instead she turned toward Gordis for companionship and information.

"You didn't git the fever?" Kathryn asked.

"No, was eatin' well, mind you," she grinned unabashedly. "But don't think the captain was starvin' nar, do you? 'Twas 'nough food fer him an' his mates—them dogs, all of 'em—och 'twas plenty fer them. Jist not be givin' any to the likes of us."

"Whin did we dock?" Kathryn asked. "And har long have I bin 'ere?"

"We docked 'bout a fortnight ago an' it seems things ain't much better 'ere than in ould Ireland. Ever one with the sickness. Nar lit me tell you 'bout what you missed bein' sick."

And for the next few hours, Gordis spoke in detail about the docking of the *Sir William*, painting a verbal picture for her to view.

She told Kathryn about the captain sailing into the shore waters of Quebec without consent and no one there to stop him. When the anchor dropped and the sails were all put away and snug, the first rowboat was lowered and steadfastly filled with the captain, Demoiselle, Brenton, and a few other ill crew. They rowed away with the captain's back to the *Sir William* as he paid full attention to his wife and never looked back. The second boat carried Slater, Leonard, and the mate. Back and forth, the two boats were rowed by various crew members carrying sick persons in class order, of course. It had been announced that the ill were to be taken into quarantine and that healthy family members could not accompany them.

And then to the amazement of all, the captain returned himself to assist with the rest of his passengers. Other boats rowed alongside, offering to take people ashore, and the captain readily accepted. These men climbed aboard and went below deck almost fainting from the repulsive odors. One of them opened a small window above deck and was aghast at the visual sight of the revolting stench that was so abhorrent; it actually seeped out like a thick grey fog. The men worked alongside the captain, taking large breaths before entering steerage and retrieving the first body they came to.

And then the most horrific thing of all happened. Above deck, wee children clung to their ill mothers and fathers, crying out as if they themselves were being tortured. Their emaciated

Megan Blight

limbs were torn away from clutching the only thing that mattered to them. A sister wailed as her brother was lowered into a boat, and a husband wept openly as he stood holding his infant child as the corpse of his wife passed by. As each boat rowed away, it left behind heartbroken family members unable to cope with one more tragedy and the dreadful uncertainty of not knowing if they would ever see their loved ones again.

One boy of about five years was looked upon throughout the entire voyage as a tyrant. He had been traveling with both parents until his father died early in the trip. Then he and his mother traveled alone as the remainder of their family was dead. Instead of growing closer, the boy's angry heart turned against his mother, taking all his frustrations and unhappiness out upon her. At any given time, he would verbally torment her, clearly taking after his father, as he had also done the same. For any reason and no reason, the father had verbally abused his wife, and now the boy was filling his place. The weak-spirited mother simply sighed and looked in another direction each time her son lashed out upon her. The only time she showed any life was if anyone intervened. Like the day the boy encircled his mother in a wild frenzy, shouting obscenities and growing angrier due to his mother's lack of emotion. At one point, he stopped abruptly, and as a last resort, lifted a dimpled fist to strike her. It was only then that she sprang to life, although not to stop her son, but to pry the foreign hand of another passenger off her son's wrist.

"Me poor defenseless child," she cooed, showering him with sympathy. It was dysfunction at its best.

Well, the will of God has strange ways of straightening out unhealthy circumstances. When the _Sir William_ docked and the crewmen were unloading the ill, the boy's mother was one of the last to be moved. She had contracted the fever toward the end of the voyage, but had not given it to her son. All observed upon deck this August day as the realization of his mam leaving consumed the boy within every crevice of his tiny frame. He watched her being carried, limp in a crewman's arms and possibly near death.

He clung to her now, flinging himself to touch any part of her that he could grab—an arm, a foot, or the top of her head. He cried for the first time, deeply and so sorrowfully that all who watched the spectacle welled up their own tears. No crew or passenger could hide their own pain for this lone boy, now fully aware of his dire predicament.

"Mam! Mam!" the child wailed. "Please, Mam!"

The man carrying her stopped for a moment before lowering her into the boat. He knelt down for the boy to say good-bye one last time as he himself fought his own tears. The boy was sobbing uncontrollably as he lay across her chest with his head buried, trying to engulf himself within the comforts of her, as if he wanted to climb back into the safe, warm confines of her womb.

"I'm so sorry," he wailed. "I don't mean any of it. Please, Mam, don't leave me too … please, Mam … please …"

Then the woman sluggishly opened her eyes and gave the boy a maternal, gentle, loving smile before she was whisked away into the awaiting boat. The boy ran to a spot where he could see his mother as each row of the oars took her farther and farther away from him. He let the tears stream down his face, his chin quiver with sorrow, and his body shake with despair. His head careened this way and that to see the last bit of her as she was carried by the same crewman to the shore. Then there was no sight of her. The boy let his body slump down into a heap and continued to grieve and mourn his loss with tears. He was alone in the world now. The sight of the broken child, forlorn and absorbed in devastation, was too much for the captain. He went below deck to ease his own pain, and a few moments later, Gordis followed him.

She went toward his quarters and found him drooped over with his head in his hands, weeping miserably. And she knew, he was heavy hearted for Demoiselle, the other ill passengers, the lone boy, and the ship itself. This one voyage had changed the entire course of his life forever, and he did not know what lay ahead.

"Seems I was takin' car of everbody to be sure," Gordis explained to Kathryn, "but I followed the captain 'cause I jist checkin' that he was alright ... guess thar was nothin' I could do fer him anyway."

Kathryn listened intently, understanding that the captain was not all that bad and that he might even be saving Brenton's life, wherever he might be. She concluded that the lone boy would probably be orphaned and eke out an existence somewhere, shivering in the frigid Canadian winter, begging for food, and she desperately wanted to hear a happier ending.

"Whit happened to the wee child?" Kathryn asked.

"Don't know." Gordis shrugged her shoulders.

Then she went on to tell of another scene that seemed somewhat surreal. Whilst the few crew members and volunteers were unloading the sick to take into quarantine, Gordis watched from the deck, waiting until she herself was to be taken. Back and forth the men carted the feverish, deathly sick people and literally flung them on the beach until someone from the hospital transported them to a tent. The captain had come upon deck again and spewed his horror at what the men were doing, but they threw it back at him.

"What do you suggest we do then?" one of them asked. "The men from quarantine will get to them soon, unless you want to leave them down in the steerage dungeon where they will surely die?"

"No ... no ..." the captain said, shaking his head. "But isn't there another way?"

"I'm sorry there is not. You must remove your ship from this area as soon as possible as others are waiting with more sick people. We'll try not to throw them so hard, but believe me, we're doing the best we can under the circumstances."

The captain did not want to aggravate the crew helping to carry the sick passengers, lest they abandon the *Sir William* and leave him to cart them to shore himself.

"This is terrible," the captain muttered.

"Aye," a crewman said, "but you were the one who decided to dock without permission and for that you may even lose your ticket."

And then something extraordinary happened. A grand ship larger than the *Sir William* pulled up alongside and dropped anchor. Upon the deck strolled a few hundred respectable, upper-class Germans waiting to immigrate. They were talking excitedly amongst themselves and pointing at the scenery and buildings on land. Each broad-shouldered man stood straight and tall with a fashionable hat and a great pleated jacket. The women, on the other hand, stepped lightly upon their graceful feet and swished their glorious, fair hair from shoulder to shoulder under their own wide-brimmed hats. Their cascading, bright colored dresses swayed in the light breeze and matched their rosy cheeks and bright eyes. And even from the *Sir William*, it was noticeable that all of them had sparkling white teeth.

A large, white ferry made its way to that ship and out climbed a doctor to inspect the passengers. It was visibly evident that each person was in perfect health, although the doctor made each passenger stick out their tongue for him to examine. As each person was cleared, they smiled and laughed cheerfully as they climbed onto the ferry. When it was full of passengers and beginning to pull away from the ship, the merry Germans began to sing a delightful, jovial song in which all partook, those leaving and those that remained on deck. As the ferry began to make its way to the shore, the beautiful song radiated in all directions as they chanted in perfect harmony and waved at their comrades that were to join them in a short while.

Gordis stopped relating the tale, unable to speak another word due to her throat being squeezed by emotion. The women sat a moment with the image of the happy Germans in their heads.

"'Twas a beautiful sight, but mighty quare," Gordis finally said. "Jist seemed so unfair that ould Ireland's people were sufferin' so. Thin I seen you bein' flung on the ground like the others whin

I finally git off the boat … an' Lord above, I couldn't walk away an' forgit … I mustn't leave …"

"I'm mighty obleeged, Gordis." Kathryn touched her hands. "Mighty obleeged."

The women talked some more as their bond and acceptance of each other deepened. Each day, Gordis walked about Grosse Isle searching for Brenton, finding only other ill passengers from the *Sir William*. She spoke with the mate, but he had no information on the boy's whereabouts. She returned each day to Kathryn with little hope. Each new day also brought more strength to Kathryn's frail body as she began to recover and gain weight. Gordis made sure to gather as much food and water as possible from the Grosse Isle provisions, and the women also gave some to the sick around them. Fortunately, no one questioned why Gordis spent so much time with Kathryn, and when a doctor or nurse was spotted, she would tend to some of those around her and quietly slip out of the tent.

It was now the end of September and Kathryn was making great progress, sitting up and taking a step or two. Those around her were continually either being taken away for burial or gaining strength over the fever. For Kathryn, surviving her illness was a miracle. She stayed in the quarantine tent until one morning in mid-October when one of the doctors came by and announced that she was free of typhus and could leave. Kathryn and Gordis smiled at each other and stepped out into the fresh Quebec air with a determination to find information about Brenton. They searched the various tents with filthy wretches still moaning with sickness and stopped when they met up with Patrick, the head committee, wielding a shovel and a scowl upon his face.

"Beg yer pardon," he nodded to the women, "I'm off to bury me wife."

"Yer wife?" Gordis asked.

"Aye, she died last night, an' God Almighty, I'm mad as the devil!" he yelled. "Come see fer yerselves."

He stocked away with the women in tow toward a low hill out in a field. The ground was soft, and the dirt was rich with nutrients, but Patrick kept his eye on the task at hand. He dug furiously, flinging the dark soil over his shoulder and mumbling to himself. Kathryn and Gordis found a few thick sticks and fastened them together with bits of pliable twigs. When Patrick was finished, he left without a word and returned carrying the dead body of his wife. He placed her inside the hole with the assistance of the women and they wrapped her head and face with a blanket. Patrick began to throw dirt upon her body, and Kathryn and Gordis helped with their hands. When they were finished, they handed him the cross and he placed it in the ground as a headstone.

"She could've died in Ireland!" Patrick yelled. "Instead of this foreign country! Whit use was it comin' 'ere jist to suffer an' die? By God, Mary," he said, looking down at her grave as he clutched the spade in the air, "I swar to you nar, I'm goin' back to ould Ireland an' kill that landlord that put you in this 'ere ground! He don't car 'bout us, jist gettin' rid of us fast as he kin! Yer life will be worth somethin', Mary, an' I'm goin' to make it right if it's the last thing I do!" He stared at the gravesite, collecting his thoughts, then turned to the women. "Mist return this shovel nar."

Kathryn and Gordis said a small prayer and walked away from death and despair for the last time. They wanted to find peace and life, where there was harmony and love. Instead they found Mr. Ford walking outside the tents.

"Me wife's dead," he said without emotion. "She's restin' in peace nar, God bless her soul. Wish I could've laid her to rist back home in County Cork but ... on me own nar. Guess the fortune-teller was wrong 'bout me havin' a great ancestor."

"Whit ya goin' to do?" Kathryn asked.

"Goin' to make me way down to Ameriky, whar I kin git a piece of land and farm 'cause that's whit I do," he said. "Plan on goin' through the Great Lakes to Michigan. I'll niver forgit me wife, but maybe thar's still a chance fer a better life ... and a family."

"Aye," the women said in unison, bidding him good day as he walked away.

Unable to find any information on Grosse Isle, the women caught a free ferry to Quebec. There they found a soup kitchen and relished the hot meal.

"'Tis the captain!" Gordis pointed toward the door of the building.

Kathryn nearly climbed over all the tables and chairs to reach the man speaking with someone at the entrance.

"Whar's Brenton?" Kathryn demanded, staring into his face.

"Well, I've been lookin' for you!" the captain said, startled. "Come with me."

"Why did you take him?" Kathryn kept up the inquiry. "Maybe the likes of us ain't intirely whit yer used to, an' I beg yer pardon, but you can't jist take me wee boy without tellin' me whar he is!

The captain did not respond and kept walking until they came to a small door of a cottage. He opened it and motioned for her to enter. Once inside, she almost gasped at the interior, which was full of warmth. It was not grand in scale or furnishings, but it was someone's home and had a fire in the hearth and the smell of food brewing on the stove. There were chairs and rugs and paintings and a table and—

"Mam!" she heard the voice of her son.

Kathryn entered a bedroom where Brenton sat smiling, clean, and happy. Her heart leapt, and she ran to him, engulfing him in hugs and kisses. He was alive and well and nothing else mattered.

"Har are ya thin?" she said, brushing the side of his hair.

"Very well, Mam, the captain's bin lookin' after me mighty fine like I 'twas his own son. He bringed me an' Demoiselle 'ere

so we could git well an' I almost am nar. He gave me food and ...
and look at this bed! It has a pillow and everthin'!"

Kathryn looked over at the captain who was standing at the
bedroom entrance.

"Mighty obleeged, Captain," she said with a nod. "I beg yer
pardon over everthin' I said, an' I hope it's no offense, but—"

"None taken, ma'am," he said and left.

"Whar's Demoiselle?" Kathryn asked Brenton.

"In the next room," he said, pointing. "She's still sick, but the
doctor says she'll be alright."

Brenton yawned and sunk down in the comfortable bed and
closed his eyes, mumbling, "Think I'll sleep a bit."

Kathryn covered him with the blankets and joined the captain
in the kitchen. He fixed a small meal for them both and placed
the plates of steaming food on the table. Kathryn sat down and
said, "You're most kind."

She relished the flavorful bites of food, fresh and crisp, tender
and juicy, tastes that she had never encountered before; she felt as
though she were a queen dining with a prince. She had as much
food and drink as she wanted, piled atop a clean white plate, and
there was even a napkin!

"It's amazing that both you and Brenton pulled through. So
many passengers on board died ... Slater and Leonard ... they
didn't make it."

"Sorry to har that." She lowered her eyes.

"I took your son because I had nothing else to give my wife,
and I thought your boy would bring her good luck. I think he
did, even though her struggle is not yet over. She's still fighting,
but thanks be to God, we have this home for a while to help her.
It belongs to dear friends of ours who holiday here in the summer.
You are most welcome to stay the night, but tomorrow you will
have to find accommodation. We have another ill friend who will
need Brenton's bed."

"So whit you goin' to do with me boy had I not found you thin?" she asked sternly as they finished their meal. "Throw him out in the streets?"

"I beg yer pardohn, Capteen," a woman said, coming out of Demoiselle's room and sparing him having to answer, "I'm going to get some more supplies."

"Very well, Monique," the captain replied as the woman left the cottage.

"She's the nurse and doing a fine job," he said, standing and walking toward the door. "I'm confident my wife will survive, and I confess that I was not prepared for such a voyage as the one we partook. It saddens me deeply to think of how many perished into the sea and how many more will wander the streets this cold winter with nothing more than hope."

"Aye, I'll bet you are," Kathryn replied in sarcasm, standing at the door.

Suddenly Kathryn thought of Gordis Flynn and how she abandoned her.

"Och, I forgit somethin'—I'll be back shortly!" She hurried out the door, down the street, and through the entrance to the soup kitchen.

Kathryn asked the first person she saw, "Pardon me, I'm lookin' fer me friend; have you seen her? She's an old woman with brown har."

"Lots of 'em here, miss," the old-timer said, sloppily chewing a wad of food on the side of his mouth.

"Jist arrived—makes potcheen," she said matter-of-factly.

The old-timer stopped mid-chew. "I might know 'er."

"Kin you tell me whar she is thin?" she asked.

"Maybe." The old-timer began chewing again, sizing her up.

"Please, sir."

The groutesque, seven-toothed heathen leaned in close, smacking his gums with bits of food falling out as he grinned, and said, "What'll I git in return?"

"Disgustin' pig," Kathryn sighed, turning.

"Lord above, alright!" He threw his arms up. "She left with Arogo. Go down this-a-way, turn right, go to the end o' the street an' 'tis the brick house."

Kathryn followed his instructions, turned the corner, and found rows and rows of brick houses on either side of the lane. Undeterred, she decided to knock on all the doors, wondering if perhaps he had not even seen Gordis. Each door that opened had no information, only the same shaking of the head. Halfway down the lane, she was greeted by a dark-skinned woman with a hand on one hip. She was clothed in a muumuu of bright swirling colors and a matching scarf wrapped tightly about her head.

"Yes?" she asked.

"Beg yer pardon, ma'am, I'm lookin' fer me friend … A man tould me she was with someone named Arogo."

A sneer erupted on the woman's face. "What's yer friend's name?"

"Uh … Gordis Flynn."

"Speak up, child, I can barely here ya!" the woman ordered.

"Gordis Flynn, her name is Gordis—"

"I heard ya now," she interrupted. "What is your name?"

"Kathryn O'Malley."

The woman turned, leaving the door ajar, and walked into another room. Low voices echoed through the walls, and then the door flew wide open and Kathryn was embraced by Gordis.

"Lord above, look who's at the door!" Gordis's voice rang out.

"I hope it's no offense I lift you," Kathryn began to explain.

"Naaa! I be doin' business already. Come on in."

Kathryn followed Gordis to the back garden where Arogo, who answered the door, sat at a low table. Another dark-skinned woman holding an infant sat quietly beside her. She did not don the bright colored clothing, but rather a dirty grey dress that looked like it had been worn continuously for a year.

"This is me friend Kathryn," Gordis introduced her to the women.

"Sit down," Arogo ordered them and pointed to the mother. "And this is my friend."

"Did ya find Brenton?" Gordis asked.

"Aye," Kathryn smiled. "Me son was missin' an' I jist found him," she explained to the other women.

"Missin'?" Arogo asked.

"Aye, mighty quare, the captain took him like a good luck charm so's his wife wouldn't die."

The three women stared at her as if she were speaking another language.

"Anyway," Arogo stated. "Now before the knock on my door, we were discussin' a right business transaction."

"Aye." Gordis winked at Kathryn. "Men know the differ between the good stuff an' the watered down kind to be sure, an' I know har to be makin' the bist potcheen in all ould Ireland. With each boatload that docks, I kin bring you right thirsty mouths that'll come awalkin' from miles around! Tell her, Kathryn."

"Aye, 'twasn't much fer larnin' 'bout potcheen meself, but everone in Ireland knows Gordis 'ere as the one to buy from."

"Humph," Arogo said, shifting in her seat. "I'll tell you what. Since you have no home and I have no husband, thanks be to God, you can stay here fer as long as you like with two conditions. You pay half the rent, and I want to be yer partner. You teach me how to make potcheen."

"Fine," Gordis nodded, "an' soon enough we'll be openin' ar own pub!"

All the women laughed until their eyes fixated on the sleeping infant cradled in his mother's arms. All four watched the beautiful newborn with skin of gleaming nightfall and soft ebony hair exactly the color of a wet raven pebble.

"Whit's his name?" Kathryn asked.

"I haven't named 'im yet," the mother apologetically answered. "Can't think a one."

"What?" Arogo asked, astonished. "Well I'm just goin' to have to name him myself. Now let me think." She looked at the mother's tattered clothes and her hair twisted in knots. Then she looked at the infant with lips like a brilliant red strawberry.

"When I was growin' up in Africa, everyone's name meant somethin'. Not like here—what does John mean? Toilet? Anyway, my name means 'mother nagged a lot during pregnancy' because my weak mother let my father name me. That lowdown, decrepit man … my mother called him Kombo, meaning he was impoverished and bent. He didn't want to work! He was unfit for anything, always without a job and runnin' 'round. Of course he called her Mundufiki, which means 'good fer nothin'.' I tell you who was good fer nothin'—that was him!" Arogo looked down at the infant and placed a hand upon him.

"With so much sickness and death about, this baby is a radiant star in the sky. His life will be different. I would call him Nwakaego. It means 'more important than money.' She looked at the mother who smiled at the sound.

"I like that name," the mother said, looking down at him. "Nwakaego."

Thomas had returned to Eton with a firm mindset to achieve the character goals that would make his father proud. He was growing up and finding the sarcastic remarks of a few schoolboys distasteful and appalling. He would not jeer at the unfortunate; he would instead nurture the compassionate heart of his father. He sent a bit of money here and there to Routh and thought of Brenton whenever someone mentioned the Irish.

Thousands had immigrated to Canada and the United States out of necessity, and the destruction of Ireland was catastrophic. Entire villages were abandoned, businesses were boarded up or left unattended, and instead of green fields of crops, mud and decaying debris were strewn about. A handmade cross in the middle of a field, a forgotten can on the roadside, or bits of rags blowing in the wind were all the remnants that life once existed on these plains. Thousands of people were wiped clean from the terrain, like wiping the dust from a piece of furniture. Ireland was gone except for the scarce landowner or the meager few with a bold resolution to survive. The prince of darkness had whipped across the land and left with a lewd snicker slapped across his face and taken with him the satisfaction that he alone had battled and prevailed.

Routh sat at his desk toward the end of the workday. He filed a few letters and memos and gathered together another pile of letters to be sent out. He knew his tenure as head of Irish Relief in Ireland was coming to an end and he would be returning to England within the coming weeks. The last letter received from his superior suggested that Trevelyan felt the entire Relief Scheme had virtually been a mistake.

The people under it have grown worse instead of better, and we must now try what independent exertion will do. Whatever the difficulties and dangers may be ... I am convinced that nothing but local self-government and self-support ... hold any hope of improvement for Ireland. This year is not merely a cessation but a transfer ... it will be a real and final close of our commissariat operation, and we must dispose of everything to the last pound of meal ... ship off all, close your depots, and come away.*

The worst of the famine was behind Ireland, and all of the depots closed one by one. No relief was to be given to the scant peasant. He survived within the large city, such as Dublin, or was subsidized by a landowner. Rebuilding Ireland was on the tongue of the optimist as the fog of the famine slowly dissipated.

"I've filed all the famine correspondence as requested, sir," O'Riley announced to Routh.

"Very well, your services will no longer be required," Routh replied. "Have you found other employment?"

"Not yet, sir, although I'm sure it won't be a problem."

"I appreciate all your tireless devotion here, O'Riley," Routh said. "I will highly recommend you for any position pursued."

"Thank you, sir." O'Riley shook his hand and walked out of the office. He began cleaning his desk when Stuffy appeared.

"*Thank you ... thank you ...*" Stuffy leered sarcastically. "Oh, go on your merry way without a thought to the suffering or dead."

O'Riley gathered his belongings and stood straight to face his comrade.

"Stuffy, if I were as smug, complacent, and self-righteous as you, I could be the prime minister!"

"There is no need to be ridiculous," Stuffy huffed.

"Good-bye." O'Riley shook his head and left.

Stuffy walked to Routh's office and stood in the doorway.

"Our ship sails in two days," Routh said to him, "so we should have all our boxes packed properly by today. We can load them tomorrow and be on our way back to London by the following morning. Are you looking forward to returning home?"

"Yes, sir," he replied. "But I feel our presence here offered no assistance whatsoever and was a complete waste of time."

Routh looked up, astonished at such a blatant, disobedient comment.

"Under regular conditions, I would terminate your job abruptly for such contemptible criticism," he snapped, "although these past few years have been anything but ordinary. I understand your frustration and, unbelievably, I agree with you. I strived to the highest degree and obeyed orders from my superiors, believing what they were doing was righteous. And now our work is presumed complete, although we leave Ireland in unjust ruins."

"Yes, sir," Stuffy said. "I will never forget my time here, nor do I ever hope to come back under these same circumstances."

"Neither do I, Stuffy," Routh agreed. "Neither do I."

Chapter X

The following morning, Kathryn bid farewell to the recovering Demoiselle and the captain as he packed a suitcase full of extra clothing, blankets, and foodstuffs. She thanked him profusely for all his assistance and helped Brenton out of bed.

"I'm alright, Mam," he bravely said, standing as his legs wobbled from weakness.

"Where will you be going?" the captain asked Kathryn as she and Brenton stood idle at the front door.

"We have to find Joseph, me husband," Kathryn replied. "We'll make ar way down to Ameriky and Virginia."

"Do you know the way? Do you have any money?" the captain questioned.

Kathryn shook her head. "I'll find work—"

He placed into her hand a crumpled wad of money.

"This is for saving my wife." He smiled at them both. "And the worry I put you through."

"Much obleeged," Kathryn said earnestly.

Down the path of accustomed uncertainty, mother and son rode trains, small boats, and walked their way toward Virginia, never losing sight of someday finding Joseph. The money given to them by the captain helped with food and accommodations.

They reached Albany and asked a fast-talking man in the streets if there were any boats headed south.

"Yes, ma'am," the American said. "Head down this road until you come to the docks.

Two steam ships could clearly be seen as they made their way down to the dock area. White, powerful, and spirited, they waited in the water for their passengers.

"Twenty dollars for the both of you to New York," another American man with an upturned nose scoffed at her.

"I ... I don't have it." Kathryn knew her appearance and attire spoke more words than her thick accent.

"Then I suggest you remove yourselves from the premises," the man said.

"Psst! Psst!"

Kathryn noticed another man motioning for them to approach. When they reached him, he spoke in whispers and looked about as if someone were going to pounce upon him at any moment.

"Mustn't worry 'bout him," the whispering Irishman reassured her. "Whar ya wanna go?"

"Virginia, but we don't have enough money fer even New York," she said.

"Virginia? You far away from that!" He thumped his head. "But I kin git you both to New York on a canal boat; see these 'ere tickets, this'll take you all the way in.

"Aye," Kathryn nodded, "har much?"

"Six dollars," he stated.

When Kathryn counted the money without a quarrel and held it out, he finished his sentence.

"*Each.*" He smiled with affliction.

She sighed handing him more money, and he placed the tickets gruffly in her hands.

Motioning to a crowd of people, he said impolitely, "Wait over thar."

Once again, Kathryn surveyed the crowd, noticing that almost all the passengers were poor Irish as the canal boat arrived in the distance.

"All aboard!" A strong American voice bellowed as the hoard of Irish puppets shuffled and inundated the boat in one swift motion. A single crack of the whip provoked the horses and sent the boat skimming forward across the water.

"Tickets! Tickets!" the American bellowed once again, walking through the crowd, picking outstretched vouchers from every angle.

Brenton was admiring their own tickets depicting a picture of horses pulling a canal boat with the sun shining and white lofty clouds on each side. The canal boat captain plucked the ticket from Brenton's hands and scrutinized it.

"Boy, this ticket is worthless!" he shouted.

"Whitdaya mean?" Kathryn nudged her way in. "We paid six dollars fer it an' six fer mine as well."

The captain surveyed her stub and shook his head. "Lady, you've been had. This ticket shows three horses pulling a canal boat, and as you can see, we only have two horses. You need to pay me now."

"Lord above, har kin that be?" Kathryn was stunned. "The tickets ar fake?"

"Yes."

"Har could he cheat us, a fellow Irishman?"

"People do it all the time."

"But har kin someone—you sure these tickets—"

"Lady, you'd better pay up now or I'll throw you and the boy overboard myself!"

"I didn't know the differ ... uh ... don't know har much I have lift," she said, shuffling through her rags.

"'Tis only two dollars." A woman's face emerged from the crowd.

"Two? I have two." She handed it to the captain.

"Money, ma'am," the captain goaded, "it's all about money," he said and continued through the herd of passengers.

Kathryn turned to Brenton, feeling miserably naïve and completely ignorant.

"Could've happened to anyone, Mam," he soothed.

"But it didn't," she said bitterly. "I paid that man twelve dollars! Har could I be so stupid!"

"Those men prey on unfortunates like arselves." The face emerged from the crowd again and added, "Happened to that woman over thar too—ain't yer fault."

"'Tis!" she corrected her. "No one else to blame! But if we kin make it all the way to Joseph in one piece, I don't car 'bout those twelve dollars!"

Deep in the heart of New York, Kathryn and Brenton crept into the majestic city like two ants into a picnic basket. Hordes of other peasants scrambled about the newly formed Irish slums, instigating fights and provoking havoc. They were a rowdy bunch with broken hearts, ill tempers, and tattered souls. Forced to leave their beloved Ireland to become a derelict, a statistic, a cliché, a frayed creature shredded from all decency. Mother and son passed by a gloomy Irish vagrant panhandling for food and employment, and Kathryn was almost thrown to her feet by a staggering drunkard, half crawling on all fours. They walked through the reeking slums and through the fuming cloud of smoke that permanently hung above it, warning all that walked into its path that this was the abyss, the bottomless pit of despair. There was one way in and no way out, and Kathryn was bringing her son into such a place.

"'Scuse me, ma'am," a scrawny man said, approaching her. "You two have a place to stay?"

"No."

"Thin I'm jist the man to be of assistance." He bowed. "I know of a cheap boardin' house right 'ere—the cheapest in town."

"Alright," she said.

"Jist step thisaway, ma'am," he smirked, holding open the door. "The boss is waitin'."

Once inside, a short, dark, muscular man smiled pleasingly and greeted them with the same thick accent of their homeland. He was the landlord of the boarding house and spoke in a soothing, quiet tone. The housing included meals "of our blessed homeland" he assured them. The fee for the shared room would be inexpensive, and they could rent until they had enough money to purchase two train tickets to Virginia.

"Everythin' straight, no surprises?" she asked cautiously.

"Aye," he assured her.

"'Tis comfortin' the way we help one another out, nar isn't it?" she told him, satisfied.

"Aye, we Irish offer assistance 'cause we know har quare an' tough a new country kin be," he grinned.

"Can't trust every Irishman," she said. "I've bin had before."

"A big city's no place fer a lad an' a lone bonny lass as yerself. Not to worry, ma'am," the scrawny man said, grabbing at the handle. "I'll take yer luggage."

"Kin I not keep it in the room?" Kathryn asked.

"Och, no," the landlord confessed. "Too much clutter 'bout. We'll keep it in the cellar, an' you kin lit us know whin you need somethin'."

"Alright," Kathryn said. "Lit me jist git some things nar." She retrieved only the food that the captain packed and handed the suitcase over to the outstretched greedy, scrawny hand.

The landlord told them to follow him. Kathryn and Brenton walked down a hallway lined with doors, up a few stairs, and down another hallway with the same barricade of doors, until they reached one door sandwiched between many others.

"Mighty quare, they all look the same?" she asked.

"Not to worry," he assured her. "This one has a right scratch 'ere in the upper corner." He opened the door into a tiny room the size of a large walk-in closet. Four beds were flopped on the floor in each corner, and a beaten wooden table was placed in the middle. One small upper window opened to the outside, letting the stale air escape.

"Two meals a day," the landlord said. And without another word, he exited quickly.

Kathryn chose a bed that had the covers pulled over and sat down. They looked about at the small piles next to each bed—a brush, a pencil, a cup. Brenton stretched out on the bed as the door opened and in walked an old man. He took one look inside and screamed.

"Git off! Git off! Git off!" he yelled with his fists flying in the air.

Kathryn and Brenton cowered in a corner of the floor trying to shield themselves from the blows.

"Lit us alone!" Kathryn fought back. "We're off yer bed!"

"Right you are! Don't lit me ketch even one finger touchin' me bed!" he shrieked. He lay down with a grunt, a ferocious cough, and his back facing them.

Shortly after, a younger man arrived and sat down on another bed without a word.

"'Scuse me," Kathryn said to him, "all the beds taken?"

"Not that one," he said, pointing to one without looking up.

They quickly claimed it as theirs as a young couple came through the door. All the voices were Irish and the tenants dirty and obviously destitute. No one conversed, and they faced anywhere but toward one another. The couple whispered about their day and what a thief the landlord turned out to be. They whispered about the food and the lack of it, the job situation, the population of the people interfering with the Americans, and the starving animals running amuck through the streets. They questioned what had happened to Peter. Where was he? Why was he not here? Maybe something happened to him since they *had* been gone two days.

"If'n you both shut up, Peter's dead," the young man that pointed said. "Meet the new neighbors." He now pointed to Kathryn and Brenton.

The couple sat with their mouths open and were ready to unload an array of questions before the young man continued, "He came back with a gash as big as me fist on his belly, tellin' me a rabid dog tried to eat 'im alive. He lay thar," once again pointing to Kathryn and Brenton's bed, "bleedin' 'til he died. Landlord drug 'em out this mornin'."

Kathryn gulped, and Brenton lied down, trying to forget what he had just heard. With his arms folded his lips pursed, and his head on a soiled pillow that still had the smell of death, he stared blankly at the wall.

"Git warm under the blanket, me son," Kathryn tried to comfort him a little. She lifted the sheet and dingy blue blanket to reveal a deep, dark bloodstain in the center of the mattress and fleas hopping everywhere.

"Jasus, Mary, and Joseph!" Kathryn jumped back. "That filthy landlord! Git off the mattress, Brenton. I'll be back in a moment."

She hurried downstairs to the main reception area where the landlord sat squat in his chair.

"You said no surprises, but you could've tould us 'bout that man dyin' in ar bed!" she said, approaching him. "And with that blood stain starin' at me right in the face!"

"Nar hold on!" The landlord cleared his throat. "You people die every day. Bist I kin do is git you 'nother blanket so's the old one kin cover the stain."

"That's all you kin offer?" Kathryn scoffed.

"If'n you don't like it, go somewhere else!" he yelled. "And I suggest you go find a job 'cause the rents increased as of today an' don't forgit the storage fee fer your luggage!"

"Storage fee! You didn't tell me thar was a fee. I kin keep it—"

"No!" He stomped off and returned with a blanket, throwing it at her. She knew arguing would be futile and no alternative was available. Another Irish swindler. She walked back to her room and spoke not a word as she helped Brenton onto the bed and covered him with the blanket under her arm. The other tenants had already known what the outcome would be and did not even look her way. As Brenton slept, rain began to fall outside and Kathryn told herself she would find a job the following day and move out of this place. She looked about the room and noticed one single frame amongst the four blank white walls. It was not a picture, rather a copy of the famous speech given by Robert Emmet, the celebrated Irish political figure who was executed years earlier for treason. Shouting out his beliefs on the docks with both fists in the air and from the depths of his soul, it was delivered before his death and remembered by all Irishmen.

> *I have but one request to ask at my departure from this world: it is the charity of its silence. Let no man write my epitaph, for as no man who knows my motives dare now vindicate them, let not prejudice or ignorance asperse them. Let them and me rest in obscurity and peace, and my tomb remain uninscribed, and my memory in oblivion, until other times and other men can do justice to my character. When my country takes her place among the nations of the earth, then, and not till then, let my epitaph be written. I have done. —Robert Emmet, 1803*

"That scoundrel landlord be thinkin' that frame will make the likes of us feel taken car of," the young man said, once again pointing. "Me name's Harry. I saw you lookin' at it."

"I'm Kathryn, an' this is me son Brenton."

"Nolan 'ere know the song that was written fer Robert Emmet's fiancée," Harry explained. "An' Lucas two doors down know it on the fiddle."

"Whit you two talkin' 'bout?" the couple asked.

"You don't know 'bout Robert Emmet?" Kathryn questioned.

"I know ' bout his speech," the woman said, creasing her brow.

"Well nar thin," Kathryn happily explained, "after his speech, Robert was hanged, quartered, an' beheaded. He lift behind a beloved fiancée, Sarah Curran, who was, God Almighty, abandoned by her family an' loathed by all Ireland. Layter she married an' moved to Sicily whar she died. Niver fully recoverin' from the loss of her beloved Robert, she mourned fer him daily."

Kathryn's own situation came to the forefront as the canned words spilled out of her mouth, and she paused a moment to let the images in her head of Joseph pass.

"Whar's Sicily?" the woman asked.

"Don't know, but a song was written 'bout Sarah, an' I suppose he know the song."

Kathryn pointed to Nolan who lay motionless the entire time—the one that screamed at them to get off his bed and every now and then would cough to let you know he was still alive. They all stared at the back of the old man, waiting for him to say something. A few moments passed before Harry asked if he had heard them.

"By the powers that be, I see it all nar!" the old man sat up yelling. "All ye want me fer is singin'!" He looked at the faces of his roommates staring back at him and coughed once more.

Harry jumped up and out of the room and was back in a flash with Lucas and his fiddle. Both of them sat down on Harry's bed and waited for Nolan's cue.

The old man steadied himself and nodded to Lucas. The deep strum of the fiddle rung out and saturated the room as other boarders faces filled up the threshold one by one like stars suddenly appearing in the sky. Then Nolan began to sing beautifully.

She is far from the land
Where her young hero sleeps,
And lovers are round her, sighing;
But coldly she turns
From their gaze, and weeps,
For her heart in his grave is lying.

She sings the wild songs
Of her dear native plains,
Ev'ry note which she loved awakening—
Ah! little they think
Who delight in her strains,
How the heart of the Minstrel
is breaking.

He had lived for his love,
For his country he died,
They were all that to life
Had entwined him—
Nor soon shall the tears
Of his country be dried,
Nor long will his love
Stay behind him.

Oh! make her a grave
Where the sunbeams rest,
When they promise a glorious morrow;
They'll shine o'er her sleep
Like a smile from the West,
From her own loved
Island of sorrow.

Kathryn felt her throat tense as if an executioner had tightened a rope around her own neck. The words of intense love inevitably brought longing thoughts of Joseph, and with them came feelings of comfort and sadness at the same time. For the next few hours until the call of dinner was shouted out, Lucas and Nolan entertained the boarders with songs of love and of their beloved Ireland.

The following day brought clamor about the boarding house as the tenants began their day and more unexpected fees. The untrustworthy landlord had not mentioned a mandatory fee for the meals being provided. Kathryn left Brenton in the room and took to the streets in search of employment, all the while feeling irresponsible and foolish. Time and again, hurdles and deceitful con men were at every turn, and the only things that kept her focused were Brenton and finding Joseph.

As Kathryn walked the streets looking for Help Wanted signs, she had not realized that thousands of other Irish peasants had the exact same idea. Never before had she solicited herself, and she felt stressed, inadequate, anxious, and fearful. The enormous high rises with their beautiful architecture seemed to bend inward when she looked up, as if they were to fall upon her at any moment. She had never seen such buildings and was dwarfed mentally by their construction.

The Irish native that immigrated had no formal training or skills, and the lucky few found manual labor jobs, backbreaking work that practically killed the weak. Women had no skills whatsoever, not even cleaning or cooking skills since they had lived in squalor and the only food eaten had previously been the potato. And if they were lucky enough to find employment, the shrewd employer knew their circumstances completely and lowered the wage significantly. This led to more wage decreases until the previous American employee could no longer exist on such a low salary. Grievances resulted from the Americans as complaints of the low wages, high unemployment, disease, and filthy circumstances befell their cities. New York was the hubbub of such disputes, as alleys and walkways were piled with garbage and decaying filth of every kind. The stench from the paupers themselves and the chaos in which they lived was abhorrent to the American.

No Irish Need Apply signs were on every street corner that Kathryn passed as she bumped shoulders with thousands of other wandering, penniless paupers. In every nook and cranny, it seemed she passed the same beggar, the same down and outer that filled every space and could be seen for miles around. She tried to approach a few stores and was verbally abused and hit with a broom as if she were a varmint. Homeless, starving dogs and cats could be seen everywhere, and Kathryn felt she mattered as much as them. Lost in a sea of massive buildings that touched the sky, she was once again the ant scrambling for a morsel of food.

She walked through mud and rubbish until she came to a building three stories high. Below the building was a stable where horses were kept, and the putrid odor of the place was horrendous. The building was barely kept together by a prayer, as it practically swayed to and fro with the slightest breeze and pieces chipped off from the sides. As she walked nearer, she noticed all the Irish tenants inside, as large gaps were so numerous she could almost see to the other side of the building. Thick mold and green mildew clung inside and out, and portions of the roof were completely blown away where the rain fell freely and flooded the floors.

Thanks be to God, at least we don't live thar, Kathryn thought to herself as she made her way down another street. She turned a corner into a brick alleyway. Twelve young boys wielding thick sticks were beating to death rabid dogs. It was like one pack of animals fighting against another, savagely biting, howling, yelling, and whacking until blood poured from the dogs' noses and they lie there broken in mind and body. The boys triumphed in yells and eagerly grabbed any tail, paw, or head that held a canine body. Off they ran up one street and down another with Kathryn and a few other children following behind. Around the back of a city building, the boys met up with two gentlemen who laughed at the sight of the boys with the dead dogs at their feet. The boys held out their hands, and the men paid each one fifty cents. The boys walked away with the carcasses, admiring their coins. Kathryn stopped one of them.

"Pardon me," she said. "Why did you git paid fer killin' them dogs?"

"Rabid mongrels, ma'am. Tons of 'em runnin' 'round, an' New York don't want 'em," he said, and off he walked. He turned around after a few steps and yelled, "But ya gotta be careful; they know whin ya comin' an' sometimes hide out 'til ya leave. Surprisin' 'em's the bist way."

Kathryn made her way down another street where a farmer walked yelling out for his ox, calling out to anyone that he was red and fat with a white face. Kathryn had never seen such chaotic traffic of horses, animals, and people. One American man stood on a box and yelled out for a gathering crowd to hear.

"These Irish have got to go! They bring nothing but disease, filth, and low wages to America! A pig ran loose today down 5th Avenue, scavenging around, and even took food from the hand of a child! Yesterday another swine knocked down an American woman as she walked down 3rd Street shopping for her family! They don't want to assimilate with Americans; they congregate with one another, and in a few days that area is a slum! Not fit for animals! No more Irish! No more Irish!" he bellowed.

Kathryn felt ashamed for being part of the problem. She wanted to work, live in a clean home, to have different kinds of food. Somehow she had to find work, she thought. Her money was running out, and she needed to save for the train ride to Virginia. The grey clouds loomed over Kathryn as she walked through the streets back to Brenton. The sick and penniless leaned against any building available, and Kathryn wondered if she had simply left one miserable country for another.

As she walked inside the boarding house, the stout, irritable landlord came panting out of the kitchen and shouted to Kathryn, "Find work yet?" He wielded a huge knife with blood covering every inch of it, and his hands, arms, and most of his face and body were drenched with blood and sweat.

Lord above! Kathryn thought. *He's killed someone that didn't pay the rent!* Soaked from the rain herself and dripping on the floor, she just stood there and did not answer.

"Better find work soon!" He pointed the knife at her as he turned and went back inside the kitchen.

"Aye," Kathryn gulped. She heard low voices emanating from the kitchen, as well as the sounds of cutting, chopping, and sawing. Fearful curiosity led her to the threshold, and she peered inside. Never in her life had she beheld such a scene as the one before her! An enormous pig lay in the middle of the floor as the landlord and two other men cut off parts of its body. Blood was absolutely everywhere, as if someone had thrown buckets on the floor, walls, and the men themselves. The pig was dead, and its lips were curled, revealing clenched teeth as if it had suffered immense pain before death. Its throat had been generously cut, leaving a huge gash, and with each sawing motion, the wide flaps of skin waved up and down as thick, black clots of blood seeped from the wound.

"Jasus, Mary, an' Joseph!" Kathryn cried out.

"Got the names wrong, lady. They ain't 'ere," an American voice came from one of the men. "But if you find 'um, we could use some help," he chuckled.

"She was a sick one," the landlord explained. "Got her cheap fer yer dinner; bet you don't complain whin yer gnashin' yer gums 'round 'er!"

Immediately Kathryn went to see if Brenton was all right; she found him sitting up and smiling on the bed. Her heart breathed a sigh of relief as she concentrated on the following day, believing it would be better.

"Mam, wake up! I har somebody yellin'." Brenton gently shook Kathryn's shoulders as the next morning appeared.

"Wah?" she sat up startled. "Yellin'?"

"Aye, somethin' goin' on downstairs," he said.

"The Lord finally kitch up with that landlord, to be sure," she offered, making her way out the door with Brenton following. The shouting was coming from the front of the building and consisted of three voices. Kathryn and Brenton kept one eye and one ear on the hollering while retrieving their food from the breakfast buffet platters set out.

"She can't even come out to eat!" a tenant shrieked.

"Not me problem!" the landlord fought back.

"'Tis! We're obleeged to pay you the money we don't even have!" the tenant yelled. "Har kin we buy anythin' else?"

"Not me problem!" the landlord said again.

The tenant lunged at the landlord as if to throw a punch, but another man, taller in height, squeezed between them.

"Now we can settle this peacefully," the tall American said. "Now why can't your wife find work?" he asked the tenant.

"I've already tould 'im, she ain't got the clothes right!" he explained.

"She doesn't need fancy clothes; anything will do," the American offered.

The tenant immediately stormed off down the hall and returned with a skeleton of a woman whose tousled brown hair fell over her face in shame. She stood in front of the men, completely naked.

"Do ya see nar? She ain't got the clothes!" the tenant screamed. "An' I can't git her any if I have ta keep payin' 'im ever time I turn 'round! I don't have nothin' lift!" He turned to his wife and spoke softly for the first time, "Okay, Fanny." The woman walked back to her room, and the husband put his hands over his face to conceal his emotion. "Lord above, doctor, kin you please help the likes of us?"

The American doctor cleared his throat. "Well, it's not that simple, Mr. Mitchell. I understand you are poor, but the landlord here is simply trying to run an establishment."

"Have you seen ar filthy beds? Have you tasted the vile food? Har kin you—" Mr. Mitchell yelled.

"It seems to me you should not be complaining!" the American doctor interrupted. "New York has become overrun with you Irish, and we're doing the best we can. Let me tell you something. Before you infested our fine city, there were lovely old mansions lining the harbor that have now been turned into tenement housing and an instant slum. Boston authorities have declared Massachusetts is being made 'the moral cess pool of the civilized world.' Every decent building, schoolhouse, or church that has been given to you now oozes with muck and is surrounded by garbage, and because of you Irish, we have loads of filth and rotting manure piled on the roadsides you can smell for miles! The New York City inspector is trying his best to clean up our community, but with heaps of sewage rotting around homes that you live in, it's almost impossible! And where is all this impurity and sludge deposited? There is no solution at the present time, so it's collected and dumped at the end of the pier where it reeks for miles and spreads out to the shoreline where my own children play! Excuse me, but most animals are cleaner than you people! In fact, the pigs you live with are not as vile! And we have free soup kitchens for all of you and talk of more help and more help swirling around the city … How many handouts do you need? Why just yesterday, I was summoned to a hastily constructed cellar on Pike Street crammed with so many people living there they could not lay down without their limbs on top of one other. And another cellar adjacent to a churchyard—" the doctor almost choked on his words. He regained his composure and continued.

"This cellar was damp and the floor wet. A woman had died of starvation and was lying on wet straw, and if that wasn't bad enough, we found her husband and five children huddled in the same room in a corner moaning. Many immigrants come to America—like the Germans who go west, get a piece of land, and spend many fine years farming. No one gave them any handouts! But you Irish stay here in New York and succumb to the degradation of the lowest kind." He shook his head.

"And now you have the audacity to grip about the fees? I have a feeling if we gave a few dresses to your wife, you would complain about something else! Perhaps you should spend a few nights in the street! You are as able bodied as any other Irish pauper, and I suggest you stop complaining and work more hours or at a better-paying job. As it is, you foreigners are bringing down our country entirely because you 'will work for what Americans cannot live on.' Dear sir, better yourself and you better our city and country as a whole. Good day, gentlemen." And he marched off through the door and into the New York skyline.

Mr. Mitchell stood forlorn, watching the man melt into the crowd and the vindicated landlord slump joyfully back into his chair near the door.

"I'm tryin' ..." he murmured and returned to his room dreary and depressed.

Unfortunately, the dismal truth about the Irish was that they were the most unprosperous, unfortunate, and poor of all the immigrants that assimilated into the United States. Planting and maintaining a row of potatoes was the only type of work experience they had. They arrived completely unsuited for any type of labor other than manual and had to be trained in every trade. Only about 10 percent were pioneers that headed west for uncultivated lands; most remained in New York and accepted the slum life, destined to work for the lowest wages and at the worst jobs.

As the autumn melded into the winter of 1848, news of the potato blight once again reared its ugly head and spread across England. The meager potatoes that had been planted were being uprooted with the same disease as the previous three years, and it struck Ireland as yet another devastating blow. Much of the Emerald Isle had already been evacuated or exterminated, although many peasants still remained and somehow endured.

The blazing fire roared in the fireplace, and Routh sat in his favorite chair sipping tea. Grateful to be home in England with vogue surroundings and healthy acquaintances, he had tried to laugh and entertain with normalcy, but churning about the inner core of his being was the provoking hum of the inconceivable blight and unremitting famine. How could it come back? When would it end? And how could Ireland's poor possibly survive another year without the depots or aid of any kind now that Trevelyan had ceased all relief? There was no easy answer since the numbers were still in the millions. Nevertheless, Trevelyan felt his duty to Ireland was complete after working nonstop for three years and to the point of near exhaustion.

Routh retrieved a letter from a side table and opened it.

Dear Randolph,

I would like to express my sincere gratitude for your tireless effort and superior supervision during the last three years. Regardless of the persisting somber outcome throughout Ireland, I personally feel our efforts to rectify and improve the state of the people has been advantageous given the bleak task at hand. The secluded nature of the regions, the ignorance of the inhabitants, and the perverseness of their ill-bred, savage conditions are truly to be pitied. Ever since the first barbaric Celtic villagers first set foot on their land, the people have remained the same without moving forward with the great significant progress of mankind. There are numerous fish swimming off their shores, stock, produce, factories, mines, and a thriving metropolis in Dublin. Unbelievably, they would rather seek charity and petition for food than establish and maintain their own personal livelihood. Unequivocally, Ireland will remain an infantile country and indeed will rely on England throughout our lifetime and beyond.

> *Despite the grim future for this country, our substantial*
> *efforts should be commended with adequate satisfaction.*
> *Perhaps in time to come, we may be called to perform other*
> *assignments whereas our paths will cross again. Until then,*
> *I wish you well for a prosperous future.*
>
> *Yours admirably,*
> *Charles Edward Trevelyan*

Trevelyan had left for southern France a week earlier to holiday with his wife and son. He wanted to relax, tour the countryside, and dine at quaint cafés, and he strongly suggested Routh do the same. Routh had mixed emotions regarding how Trevelyan handled the Relief Scheme, but he tried to put the past behind him, as it had recently been announced that Trevelyan was to be knighted for his superior performance and services concerning the Irish famine. At their last meeting, he disclosed to Routh, "Never before have I ever worked with such utter conviction."

Routh believed his sentiment, but still felt considerably troubled over the current distressed conditions. Currently, his services were no longer a part of whatever Ireland was experiencing, and even though images of County Clare and Skibbereen flashed through his mind, he pushed them aside and brought thoughts of his wife, Thomas, and the other children to the forefront.

"Are you feeling alright, dear?" Marie Louise walked in and sat down next to him.

"I tried my best," he said.

"I know, dear," she replied, knowing what he meant.

"Perhaps there was more I should have done ... written more letters ... demanded more earnestly, but I was not the prime minister or Trevelyan who had the power at their fingertips." He looked toward the fire. "Those deaths are not on my head. I must believe that in order to live justly." He patted his wife's knee. "I am quite alright, thank God ... quite alright now."

Weeks passed steadily one into the other as Kathryn searched for work every day in the wind and snow. No one was hiring an immigrant Irish woman without skills. Day after day, it grew colder and colder as the temperature dropped throughout the city.

Complete desperation and a grim eviction threat from the landlord had Kathryn's mind spinning. She had used up the rest of the money the captain gave her for rent and was broke again. Every day, she searched for some type of work, but no one considered her for employment. One morning, the landlord came in and ordered her out.

"No freeloaders in me establishment!" he shouted. "I won't have it! You're three days past the rents, so out you go!"

Kathryn knew there was no arguing. She and Brenton left for the frigid streets, the unsheltered existence, and the unsympathetic life. Forlorn and dejected, there was only one thing left to do. Their blue lips and outstretched hands made Kathryn and Brenton the equivalent of many of the other beggars on the street corners. Day by day, the thick black coats and furry hats steadily sauntered by one way and then the other without a glance or a donation. No one offered and no one cared except the soup kitchen that ladled out hot soup once a day so mother and son could return to the street and plead for a bit of change. Every thousandth person that passed dropped a coin or two into their palm, making it worthwhile to remain. Kathryn loathed the act, and it angered her further to subject her son to the same demeaning performance. This was not what she had thought the new world would be like; it was the same if not worse than Ireland, and even if she wanted to return to her homeland, she did not have the money. Her goal at the moment was simply to stay alive in the bone-chilling New York winter as every bit of money went for food.

"Why do we have to suffer so?" Brenton whispered one snowy afternoon.

"I don't know," Kathryn replied. "God only knows."

"Thin whar is he? Why's he not helpin' us?" he asked.

Of course, she did not have an answer. All the misery of the past three years trying to eke out another day seemed futile. She had to believe things would improve.

"This winter will be tough, me son, but come spring and the warmth, we kin walk to Virginia if we mist."

One December afternoon, a flurry of snowflakes fell gently upon the heads of mother and son as they stood huddled in a blanket a passerby had given them. Their frosted breath made the only movement, and their blue begging hands were all that were visible. They felt weak and wanted desperately to sit down, but everything was covered in snow.

"Sit down here, me son." Kathryn brushed away the snow with her foot and gave him the blanket. "Git some rist nar."

Brenton closed his eyes and fell asleep as a spiffy coach trotting down the snowy lane caught Kathryn's eye. She followed it for no particular reason, down one street, then another. As she got further and further away from the boarding house, the filth in the streets partially dissipated. Down one lane, she lost sight of the coach and found herself directly in front of a flower shop. Gazing upwards, she read the sign outloud, "Forget Me Not" and instantly thought of her girls and Joseph.

"I've not forgotten you," she said aloud again.

A customer exited the shop, looking dapper in lavish clothes and swaddled in an invisible cloak of wealth. Kathryn instantly outstretched her hand. The woman drew back at the sight and smell of a pauper and hurried down the street. Kathryn stood staring at her freezing, shaking hand and hated herself for succumbing to the lows of begging. Without hesitation, she thrust her hands into a pile of snow on the ground in front of the store and flung it onto the street. Upon her knees, she pushed the freezing ice aside clearing off all bits of white piles from view. She continued removing snow from the steps of the store, the ledge of the large windows, and the small sign directly in front.

An American woman opened the door from inside the shop and said, "What are you doing?"

"I ... I ... I wanted to clean—"

"I can see that." The woman stood tall, looming over her like one of the imposing buildings. "But I'm not going to pay you."

"Aye," Kathryn noted, relishing the waft of heat that came from inside.

The woman closed the door, and Kathryn finished swishing away the few bits of white from the sign.

The door opened again, and the same authoritative woman stood austere against the threshold.

"Alright!" burst from her mouth as she eyed the immigrant. "I'll pay you a dollar a day to keep my storefront snow-free, but don't bring any friends around wanting the same deal. Just you, no one else."

"Aye," Kathryn smiled.

"Here's a hand shovel to help you out," the woman smirked. "Can't keep using your hands; you'll freeze them off. And one more thing," she said, pointing a finger. "Don't be hanging around my storefront or customers won't come in; walk down the street a bit or something when there are people about."

"Aye, ma'am," Kathryn nodded.

"Here you go." The woman held out a dollar, and Kathryn retrieved it gently, looking at the picture, the color, and feeling the texture of it.

"Much obleeged, ma'am, much obleeged."

She walked back to Brenton, elated that she had earned her own money in the new land. It was not a handout or a loan; it was money she earned herself by working. She bought food and another used blanket and was in high spirits when she returned the following day.

For two weeks, Kathryn cleared the bits of snow from the woman's shop and received the promised dollar for her work. The woman was kind and gave her a thick used coat and once a beautiful red flower with payment. Kathryn was grateful for her compassion and generosity and smiled whenever she saw her.

"Please call me Glenda," the woman said, winking at her one day.

When it did not snow, Kathryn swept the dirt away and received the payment as usual.

After clearing the store walkway one afternoon, Kathryn used a bit of rag to scrub the windows, and after she'd finished, the woman once again appeared like a towering statue standing atop a high mountain.

"Come around the back," Glenda said, motioning to her.

And waiting "around the back" was a hot lunch and a steaming cup of tea. Although she was graciously thankful, she asked the woman if she could save half of her meal and bring back the bowl the following day.

"Oh no, that will not do," Glenda said, shaking her head. "If you need more—"

"Lord above, that's not whit I meant," Kathryn forgot her manners and interrupted her. "I want to save some fer me son, that's all."

And from that day on, kindhearted Glenda fed Kathryn and Brenton daily and gave them necessities such as used coats, hair brushes, and soap, all accompanied by a warm, genuine smile. In return for all Glenda had given them, Kathryn and Brenton scoured her shop from ceiling to floor, inside and out, from left to right and back to front.

"Still not enough money 'ere," a landlord at a nearby boarding house growled as Kathryn showed him her money one day. She had tried to find accommodation in several boarding houses, but all were about the same price. One greedy proprietor or another, it didn't really matter. Glenda overheard them discussing their money troubles one afternoon and questioned Kathryn about it.

"'Tis no problem fer you, ma'am," Kathryn told her matter-of-factly.

"Oh, but it is," she responded. "You have become a friend, and here in America we look after our friends too." Without a word

Glenda took her hand and led her to a storage building in a far corner of the back garden.

"If you clean this out, you can stay here, rent free," Glenda offered.

Kathryn was overcome with gratitude and hugged the woman dearly. She felt vindicated and free, holding her head high as if she was without worry of any kind. She and Brenton cleaned out the back shed and began to feel respectable and lively with each passing day. Mother and son worked from morning until evening and were grateful for the generosity of this American woman, meanwhile saving as much money as possible.

For two months, Kathryn worked hard and during downtimes tried to recruit other shopkeepers to hire her, but to no avail.

"Sorry, ma'am," they said. "We don't need any help."

And alas, her job was short lived. One morning, a new face appeared at the flower shop door, explaining that the owner had died suddenly and that the shop was closing.

"I want you to be out of the shed this afternoon," the woman said. "The For Sale sign goes up tomorrow."

"Har kin this be?" Kathryn asked, trying to digest the unexpected information. "Glenda was young an—"

"We all die sometime, miss," the woman said dryly. "I'm sorry."

By the late afternoon, mother and son were on the street again, homeless and unemployed with a small bag of food and a few belongings. It was hard to focus on their uncertain future, and the disturbing up and down cycle was hard to swallow as a cold mist fell from the sky. Leaning outside a building, trying to keep warm, they stood for a moment wondering what to do and where to go.

Kathryn literally shook the bewilderment from her head and tried to concentrate on what she should do. They walked to the train station and inquired about two tickets to Virginia.

Surprisingly, their meager savings purchased two tickets to Virginia for the following morning; they had two pennies left over. They could eat the bits they had in their bag tonight and possibly buy a few apples for the trip, although when they reached Virginia, they would once again step into the veil of uncertainty. They had no money for food and no assurance that Joseph would even be alive.

"Come, Brenton." Kathryn tenderly wrapped her son in her arms and walked him down the street. "We'll be layvin' in the mornin'. Fer tonight, I know of a dry alleyway. Things'll be better tomorrow, God willin'."

She spoke hollow words that she herself did not believe. The futile utterances were thrown out into the atmosphere for someone—anyone—to grab hold of and hang on to, but no one did. They hung there like a soppy wet rag, having a purpose only if someone had the resolute persistence to wring them out.

Instead, mother and son clung to each other and shuffled aimlessly. The light of day was quickly disappearing as they walked past fellow homeless Irish men and women trying to find their own piece of shelter for the night amongst the brick buildings, concrete walls, and piles of dirty snow. Each time they stumbled upon a hideaway, another person had already claimed it as their own. Roaming down no particular alleyway, Kathryn found a vacant spot under a light and moved a few garbage cans aside so the space beneath them would be free from snow. Scrunching down onto a piece of floor they knew would be dreadful, they even longed for that blood-soaked, flea-infested mattress at the boarding house. Small bits of flurry soared through the air as they feebly huddled together for comfort and warmth like one round mass of unstable humiliation. Their coats kept them from freezing, although their exposed heads and their meager shoes might as well have been nonexistent as the frozen air lacerated their skin like serrated daggers. They sank deeper into their coats, but the dank, desperate emptiness of the moment weighed on their heads like a boulder.

"I wish Da were 'ere." Brenton shivered, reaching into the bag for a piece of bread.

"Aye," Kathryn murmured, chewing on her own piece. "I'm sorry fer this night, me son, but at least we'll be in the same state as yer da soon, an' we'll find him somehar. Times like this will only make us strong in the end, Father Murphy used to say."

Brenton gave a scowl. "He says that with nice clothes on his back, a full stomach, an' lyin' in a warm bed."

Kathryn patted her son's head. "I don't think I believe him neither. Mighty quare some o' the things he says."

All at once, a garbage can next to them fell over, and four scraggy dogs swooped in, scrambling and sniffing loudly for anything edible. Finding nothing, they turned their beady eyes toward Kathryn and Brenton chewing and clutching their bag of food. Instinctively, the mongrels encircled them as if preparing for an attack. The lips of each dog parted in front to reveal pointed teeth, their ears folded back, and a low growl escaped from their mouths.

"Go away!" Kathryn shrieked.

"Grrrrr ... Yap! Yap!"

"Git outta 'ere!" Brenton yelled.

The growling continued.

"Yaa!"

"Haa!"

Mother and son stood up, kicking the trashcans and crying out for their lives until the alpha dog turned and the others followed him down another alley.

"Let's pray, son," Kathryn gulped, and they closed their eyes. "Dear God, keep them dogs away. An' please help us find Joseph whin we git to Virginia. Almighty God, please help us this night not to freeze ... please spar us once again."

"Amen."

The sounds of the night kept them alert and unable to sleep for more than a few minutes as the howls of the rabid dogs haunted them.

In the morning, they boarded the train and were numb with the cold as they sat defrosting in the cushioned seats. Instead of feeling uplifted and excited, they felt exhausted and casually looked out the window as the train launched great billows of steam that brushed the ground below. A few people stood on the platform waving to passengers.

"No matter whar we go," announced Brenton, "me heart will always be in Ireland."

"I know," Kathryn said, nodding. "I know."

The whistle blew, the conductor yelled "Alllllllll aboard!" and the train slowly jerked forward, away from New York and toward yet another unknown land. If they could not find Joseph or if he was dead, Brenton thought, what would become of them? Gazing out the window as things slowly went by, he began to softly sing an Irish ballad to ease his mind.

> I've met some folks who say that I'm a dreamer,
> And I've no doubt there's truth in what they say.
> But sure a body's bound to be a dreamer,
> Whin all the things he loves are far away.
>
> And precious things are dreams unto an exile,
> They take him o'er the land across the sea,
> Especi'lly when it happens he's an exile,
> From that dear lovely Isle of Innisfree.
>
> Hmmmm … hmmmm … hmmmm …
>
> But dreams don't last, tho' dreams are not forgotten,
> And soon I'm back to stern reality,
> But tho' they paved the footways here with gold dust,
> I still would choose the Isle of In—

On the platform, a figure in the distance caught Brenton's eye and ceased his singing. He tried to speak, but words failed him.

Routh had been frantically walking up and down, yelling, "Kathryn!" for any and all to hear. As the train accelerated and the panes of glass rushed by, Routh became fixated on one window and let out a deep sigh of relief. Kathryn and Brenton had seen him at the same time, and they struggled to open the window. Routh now followed beneath, walking at a hurried pace and then a slow sprint. Still they struggled to open the window with help from other passengers. Finally it sprung open, and they each began talking at once. Routh was running now as he held out a small package with one hand that quieted them both.

Since the thunder of the train was now too loud for them to converse, Kathryn's only focus was that he was trying to give her something. What that something was, she had no idea. She stretched to grasp it but could not reach far enough. Routh stumbled and regained his footing without losing speed and forced his legs to move faster and faster as the train steadily gained momentum. With Kathryn's arm extended to the maximum and Routh panting for air and running at top speed, the package sluggishly inched forward from Routh's fingers closer to Kathryn's. Routh knew he had to ask his fatigued body for a bit more energy, and he stretched as much as possible until the package was thrust into Kathryn's fingers and hand. She clasped it, smiled, and held it up. Routh stumbled to a slow jog, blowing her a kiss and a weary smile of his own. The train now raced past him as he stopped running, gasping for breath, while a white wave of steam buried him as it swelled and surged into the sky. He looked up once more as the consistent badger of the wind pushed him away from the roaring train, like a subtle reminder that his mission had come to a close.

Kathryn sat back in her seat holding the small package in her hands. She unwrapped the paper to miraculously reveal the same red pouch dug up from beneath Lord Somerhaven's lavender rose almost a year earlier. She and Brenton scrambled to open it further to see if the money was inside, and indeed it was, along with the stunning, shining brooch. Both of their mouths fell open at the sight of it all, unable to fully grasp what was before them. She unfolded a crisp piece of paper and read:

Dear Kathryn,

I am writing this in the event that I am unable to meet with you personally.

It is my pleasure to return this item and apologize on my son Thomas's behalf that, unbeknownst to me, he liberated it from you. The unnecessary hardship you must have weathered due to my son's actions is absolutely inexcusable, thus I have added to the sum inside as a minor compensation.
I must inform you that this pouch occupied an area on my study mantel and, gazing upon it daily, brought about

the knowledge of the inevitable affliction you must have been enduring. This generated an irritating sting to my soul. The extraordinary melancholy was only set free when I received your letter from the flower shop, as I had previously planned to visit family in Canada at this time.

My son Thomas sends his sincere apologies to Brenton. He allowed himself to let narrow-minded discrimination occupy his heart, although it has since been significantly altered. You are a fine young man, Brenton, with outstanding character, and it is my great pleasure to have known you.

My duty with the Irish Relief has expired and my services are no longer required. The people that remain will need God's commiseration in ascertaining food and shelter.

I am content knowing your future and prosperity is here in the new world. You shall eternally have friends in England, and perhaps in the distant future our paths will cross one another again.

May God be with you always,
Randolph Routh

The tears flowed freely now from her eyes as she refolded the paper, absorbing the vision of what the future would now hold. Kathryn and Brenton sat staring at each other, shocked at the confession and unable to comprehend their next move. The rags-to-riches moment was again extraordinary to grasp. Whatever the future held from this moment on would be monumental, because with this money, they could buy some land, a house, livestock, and most importantly, they would not starve.

Brenton noticed one last object nestled in the brown paper. It was a thin wrapper with writing on it. He held it up and tried to read the large print on the outside.

"Ch ... choc ... chock–o–late!" Brenton screamed.

A woman sitting next to him noticed the packaging and smiled, saying, "The new fondant chocolate made in England is much better tasting than the old confection."

"'Tis unbelievable," he mumbled, not understanding a word she said. He tore open the wrapper, gazed at the chocolate's immense beauty, and held it before his nose. Closing his eyes with gratification, he breathed in the rich chocolaty aroma. He carefully broke off a piece and laid it on his tongue, as if taking communion, then held out the precious confection to Kathryn, offering her some. She relished the smooth, creamy taste as well, closing her mouth to enhance her concentration as each piece slowly melted upon her tongue.

"Heaven," Brenton announced to himself. "Jist as I thought."

The train chugged into the Richmond, Virginia, train station right on time in the late afternoon. The passengers disembarked, looking about for family members or friends. Cheers of greeting and hugs abounded as loved ones found each other amongst the bustle of people and luggage. Kathryn and Brenton stepped off the train and inquired at the depot for accommodation. They were steered toward a hotel that abruptly came into view.

"Looks grand," Brenton stated, looking about the clean, rich interior of the lobby.

"Aye." Kathryn walked up to the attendant. "Kin we please git a room here? We have money to pay," Kathryn said. It was a simple and basic hotel, but to her it was exceptional.

"Certainly, ma'am," the attendant replied.

She paid for the room and inquired about clothing. The attendant directed her toward a clothing shop right next-door.

With the assistance of the shopkeeper, she bought a dress for herself and a suit for Brenton.

"With a few alterations," the tailor smiled, measuring here and there, "the clothes should fit perfectly. I will send them to your room first thing in the morning. Is that alright?"

"Aye," Kathryn said, paying the shopkeeper.

They walked back to the hotel and met up with the attendant once again.

"Your room is this way, ma'am." They followed the woman to a glorious, warm room and stood looking about with their mouths practically hanging open.

"Your baths have been drawn already, ma'am, and the towels and robes are for your use. Would you like your dinners to be sent up?" the attendant asked.

"Up whar?"

"To the room, ma'am, so you may dine in relative comfort."

"Uh ... aye," Kathryn said, still in shock.

The woman left, closing the door, and Kathryn and Brenton stood in the middle of the room, gazing about at the furniture and fine furnishings. There was a large plump bed spilling over with pillows and fine blankets, beautiful chairs, chiseled tables, exquisite rugs, glorious paintings, and a large window framed by marvelous drapery. They walked to the window and gazed out at the lovely gardens below. Never before had they seen such a beautiful place—and to think it was all for them! They hugged each other, jumping up and down and laughing. It seemed odd to smile and laugh; it had been years since such joy had come into their lives. Kathryn saw her reflection in a mirror on a wall and dared to look at the despairing savage she had become. Looking deep into the unrecognizable face, she was transfixed at the withdrawn, foul creature staring back from the depths of hell.

"Let's take a bath, Mam!" Brenton jovially said, interrupting her engrossment in her reflection.

"Aye ... let's ..." Kathryn gladly turned from the mirror and never wanted to look into it again.

They went to a corner of the room where two tubs were filled with hot, steaming water. Each tub was surrounded by its own drape that was attached at the ceiling, and they immediately enclosed themselves behind them. Peeling off the filthy rags that had been worn for over a year, they washed in the grand tubs, singing out loud and harmonizing. Simply laying in the warm water was wonderful, aside from scrubbing the smut embedded in their skin. They had not soaked in a hot bath in so long that the illustriousness of the moment was almost overwhelming. Kathryn dried off, wrapping herself in the clean white robe, and picked up a brush from the vanity. Pulling and yanking the knots from her hair seemed futile, so with the aid of some scissors, a becoming hairstyle appeared. Brenton dried off, and she cut his hair as well.

For the next few minutes, they walked about the room, sat in each chair, ran their fingers through the fine fabrics, and marveled at the fine furniture before them.

A knock at the door brought in the smell of steaming food as the smiling woman laid it on the table and left. They sat down and gasped at each sparkling dish.

"Lord above, Brenton, lit's pray fer this wonderful moment," Kathryn said.

"Aye."

"May the blessin' of the day be with us ferever, and we're much obleeged fer all the goodness he has sent us. Thanks be to God."

"Amen."

And then they feasted as they had never before. Afterwards, they sat on the bed, counted the money, gazed at the brooch, told stories of Joseph and the girls, and laughed and smiled at their memories. When it came time for sleep, they crawled underneath the soft warm blankets and drifted off.

Morning came too quickly, and they stretched and walked around the room, gazing out at the gardens still dusted with snow. Another knock at the door brought the same woman carrying the morning meal and two large boxes. She gathered the chamber pots and left. Brenton ate his breakfast and went over to the boxes.

One had his name written across it, so he lifted the lid and gasped. He pulled out a crisp white shirt, dark grey jacket and pants, black shoes, gloves, and a double-breasted black wool coat and matching hat. He smelled the fabric and engulfed his face in it. Although they had picked them out the day before, it was still truly unbelievable that these were now his.

"Open up yer box, Mam!"

Kathryn breathed deeply as she lifted the top to reveal a stunning blue and white dress. Long and feminine, certain areas were adorned in wispy slivers of lace, and although it was beautiful, it was the type of dress to be worn by respectable women every day about town. There were also underclothes, shoes, gloves, and an exquisite, red velvet coat, muff, and hat to match. She sat clutching it all like a child with her toys at Christmas, completely and utterly overwhelmed.

"'Tis all more beautiful thin whin I saw it yesterday at the clothes shop," she sighed.

"Lord above!" She stared at herself in the mirror after getting fully dressed. "'Tis me?" She looked upon the face of a woman she did not know. *Who is this radiant creature staring back at me now from the kingdom of heaven?*

"You look *beautiful,* Mam," Brenton beamed, getting himself dressed. He attached the brooch to his mother's dress, and they stared at each other, pointing out bits here and there.

"I niver thought I could look like this," she sighed. "Mighty quare intirely."

Then they checked out of the only accommodation they had ever been in as two civilized individuals. They walked the streets with their heads held high, clean, well rested, fed, and full of energy, like once-drooping flowers that had just been given life-saving water.

After inquiring at every government office they could find, a passerby overheard their conversation about Cousin Miles Burnett and pointed them in the right direction. Just a short walk outside town led them to a meadow and a small path lined with stones. As they walked, the air smelled clean, and the apprehension about the moments ahead created excitement in their bodies.

"Do you think Da will be thar?" Brenton asked.

"Don't know, son, but in me heart he will be."

"We come so far, Mam, I wish the girls could be here."

"Aye," was all Kathryn could muster. She was filled with so many emotions about finally finding Joseph or possibly finding his headstone that she found it almost impossible to speak.

They passed by several fields with farmers working and dogs running about, and every one they passed, Brenton waved to from afar, solely for the sheer enjoyment of waving. And in each field, if the farmer saw, he would wave back. One farmer even took off his hat and waved slowly back and forth from side to side. They turned a corner, and before them was another large field. Brenton spotted the farmer in his field and waved; the farmer saw and waved back. Then all three of them stopped abruptly.

"Brenton! Brenton … 'tis …"

"Daaaa!" Brenton yelled for the world to hear.

The farmer stood with his arms at his sides, his mind racing. He saw the two people running toward him, and upon hearing another yell, his mind snapped into reality. He dropped the tools in his hands and ran as fast as possible toward the images. They ran down the path, crying and yelling with arms outstretched and with exhausted legs, depleted through the long arduous months of any extra vitality. None of them could wrap their minds around the encounter, that this long-awaited moment had finally arrived. Brenton reached Joseph first, and they clung together and hung on as Joseph kissed his son's head over and over again as if branding him with love. Then Kathryn reached them, and all three tightly embraced one other, holding close and rejoicing for the happiness of survival and the brand-new chance for a joyful, prosperous life together. All three wept blissful tears whilst kissing and hugging each other as if they were quenching their thirst of satisfaction.

There would be no more questions or lonely nights pining for the loving touch of a husband or wife. After enduring the famine, disease, being separated, and all the while being homeless and completely destitute to the point of withering away like a spent flower, they had survived. They held on to one another for a long time, saying nothing as the tears flowed freely down their faces.

"Och! 'Tis so good to see you!" Joseph broke the silence as he lifted Kathryn up. "I kept sendin' letters and money to you, hopin'—"

Kathryn quieted him with a kiss.

"We had to move out, so we didn't get the letters," she said.

"I'm still stayin' with Cousin Miles; he'll be so happy to meet you," Joseph said.

Kathryn somberly informed him about the girls, saying, "I wish they could be here too. We bin through so much, but with God's help, we come 'ere an' found you. 'Tis not matter what's past. Ar home is 'ere nar to be sure. God almighty, thar's nothin' lift of ould Ireland."

"But look at ye nar!" Joseph gazed at them at arm's length. "Whit fine clothes! I didn't know you."

"We have lots to tell you." Kathryn smiled, clutching the pouch.

Joseph held on to Brenton on one side and Kathryn on the other as he walked them back to a farmhouse in the near distance. Kathryn informed him about the details of the girls' death and other friends in their village, and he sighed and gasped at the hearing of each one. Speaking of the girls' was especially hard to take, and the melding feelings of joy and sorrow were confusing and unsettling. They entered the cousin's cabin, and what a glorious sight it was. A table, chairs, fireplace, several beds, and a fully stocked kitchen—after their ordeal, Kathryn was astonished at the sight.

"'Tis a mighty fine house he has," Joseph announced. He turned to a man standing near the kitchen. "This is Cousin Miles."

"Good to meet you." They embraced one another.

"I don't have a wife or wee ones," Miles said to her. "Your family is like me own, and you kin stay as long as you'd like. I come in to make some tea; I'll make more nar.' "

Kathryn was speechless; she felt so grateful to have her family together and finally a home to stay in. Now they were together again, and the sparkling road ahead was healthy and clean of all debris. The blight had taken three family members and millions of other lives, but it had not dismembered the tender affection or pure, sweet sentiment of love. As she walked about the home, Kathryn recited an old Irish blessing:

God bless the corners of this house and all the lintels blessed.
And bless the hearth and bless the board and bless each place of rest,
And bless each door that opens wide to strangers as to kin,
And bless each crystal window pane that lets the starlight in,
And bless the rooftop overhead and every sturdy wall.
The peace of man.
The peace of God.
With peace and love for all.

Epilogue

No one knows exactly how many perished in the great potato famine, but it is estimated that around 4–5 million people either died or immigrated to another country. When reference to the famine is mentioned, it is mainly concerning the first few years, but it did not end as quickly as it had begun. It continued year, after year, after year, accompanied by suffering and countless deaths. There was no one year that it can be said it officially ended, and decades after 1845, the destitute Irish's children's children were continuously eking out some kind of existence on the potato—still, just enough to barely survive. The main thing the famine left behind and nurtured was hatred—hatred toward the English for what they did do, and moreover for what they didn't.

Charles Edward Trevelyan was knighted on April 27, 1848, for his superior services concerning Irish Famine Relief. Moving to India, he became governor of Madras from 1859 to 1860 and then finance minister of India from 1862 to 1865 promoting the public works. On March 2, 1874, he was made a baronet. He returned to England in 1865 and directed his energy toward army organization. Later, he was involved in social problems and charities. He died at 67 Eaton Square, London, on June 19, 1886. His son was historian George Otto Trevelyan.

Sir Randolph Routh became K.C.B. (Knight Commander of the Bath) and died November 29, 1858. Edward, his eldest son from his second marriage, became highly educated, earning numerous awards and honors for mathematics. Well respected by all who met him, he became a surpurb teacher, author, and a founding member of the London Mathematical Society and formulated "Routh's Rule." He is remembered as one of the greatest mathmeticians of his time. Thomas Alfred, another son, served for forty years in Somerset House.

Kathryn and Joseph O'Malley bought 180 acres and built a house, barn, and other outbuildings. They lived happy, prosperous lives in Virginia farming and raising horses. Kathryn had two more children and died at the age of eighty-nine. Joseph died two months after his wife. Brenton attended a local school, and with the help of his parents, attended New York University. He became a scholar, scientist, and chemist. He married into wealth, raised four children, and never returned to Ireland.

Gordis Flynn married and was widowed twice, raised five children, and established Flynn Distillery, one of the oldest in New England. It was bought out in 1901 for $700. Gordis died one month after the sale at age eighty-eight.

Glossary

ar — our
aye — yes
ars — hours
car — care
dar — dare
'ere — here
har — hair
lift — left
lit — let
och — an expression like "oh"
mist — must
nar — now
nowar — nowhere
obleeged — obliged
wist — west
yar — year

Bibliography

Whyte, Robert. *1847 Famine Ship Diary*. Ireland: Mercier Press, 1994.

* Woodham-Smith, Cecil. *The Great Hunger*. England: Clays Ltd., 1962.